the Ultimate Guide to

DARCY CARTER

BOOKS BY TERESA SLACK

A Tender Reed

The Ultimate Guide to Darcy Carter

The Jenna's Creek Novels:
Streams of Mercy
Redemption's Song
Evidence of Grace (coming soon)

the Ultimate Guide to
DARCY CARTER

TERESA SLACK

Tsaba House
Reedley, California

All scripture quotations, unless otherwise noted, are taken from the King James Version of the Bible.

Cover and text design by Bookwrights
Senior Editor, Jodie Nazaroff
Author Photo by Andrea Lundgren

Published by
Tsaba House
2252 12ᵗʰ Street, Reedley, California 93654
Visit our website at www.TsabaHouse.com

Printed in the United States of America

First Edition: 2006

Library of Congress Cataloging in Publication Data
Slack, Teresa D., 1964-
   The ultimate guide to Darcy Carter / by Teresa Slack.
      p. cm. — (Jenna's Creek novels ; 4th)
   ISBN-13: 978-1-933853-47-5 (pbk. : alk. paper)
   ISBN-10: 1-933853-47-6 (pbk. : alk. paper)
   1. Women authors—Fiction. 2. Self-perception—Fiction. 3. North Carolina—Fiction. I. Title.
   PS3619.L33U48 2006
   813'.6—dc22
                                                    2006018678

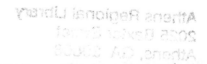

Dedication

This book is for all my sisters in Christ that I have known through the years and those I have yet to meet. Your influence on my life is a blessing I will always cherish.

"Who can find a virtuous woman? for her price is far above rubies."

~Proverbs 31:10 KJV

The call came after two agonizing weeks of waiting. Even though it turned out like it always did, the way she knew deep down it would, it didn't make the wait any easier. She'd been doing this a long time, more times than she cared to count—well, twenty times to be exact, counting this one—and she was all too familiar with the things that could go wrong from one project to the next. Just because they liked the last one didn't guarantee they'd like the next. The powers that be could always change their minds, the market could change, or competition could become too fierce to turn a profit. Then there were all the unforeseen factors that might play too big a role. She had been around long enough to know how the business worked. She couldn't rest on her laurels. Neither she nor her work was indispensable. If something happened to her tomorrow, someone just as qualified would step up to fill her shoes before they had time to take her name off the letterhead; not that her name was on anyone's letterhead.

Money had to be made. It always boiled down to money. In her line of work, she was the product, and when the product stopped making money, it was replaced with something else that would. Those were the cold hard facts, and they alone pushed her to work harder with each new project.

What if this manuscript didn't measure up to the last nineteen? She had never reached the celebrity status that left the reading public clamoring for her books even if she turned out drivel. After ten years and nineteen bestsellers, it was still possible they might reject her. The dreaded rejection hung over her head like a dark cloud. She tried not to think about it, but she did. Was it possible that her well of talent might someday run dry and her latest book not sell out of the first printing? Had it already happened?

She couldn't retire; she was only twenty-nine. Then again, she was too old to learn something new. At least she felt too old. And after the ride she'd been on for the last ten and a half years, what else would bring her such joy, such fulfillment, such terror?

No matter how many times over the past two weeks she reassured herself that this time was like every other time, she couldn't help thinking something had gone wrong. The manuscript, *The Ultimate Guide to Starting Your Own Home-Based Daycare*, had been sent Priority Mail, along with a CD, preceded by an email telling her editor to expect it, just like always. Ordinarily things went smoothly once a manuscript was in the mail. She would take a deep breath, sleep in the next morning, and begin tossing around ideas for the next book. There were always plenty of ideas swimming around in her head at any given time. It was simply a matter of choosing the one that felt right, grabbing onto it, and sinking her teeth in before it skittered away into oblivion. She studied markets, researched the topic to make sure it was worthy of a seventy-five-thousand word book, took notes, and even read some fiction curled up on a chaise lounge on the back porch in her bathrobe. By the time she heard from New York that the book had been accepted, she was ready to roll on the next one; just like clockwork.

She seldom took time off. She didn't waste time on a beach regrouping. She didn't sneak away to a mountain cabin to meditate. She hadn't written twenty books since dropping out of college at the age of nineteen to write her first book, *The Ultimate Guide to Writing Your College Thesis*, by lying around on a beach.

The knot she got in her stomach every time she sent a manuscript off was nothing new. Now that she had established a reputation in her publishing house, it only took a short time to receive an answer. Still, those two or three weeks of waiting were pure torture, though by this time she had quite a bit of confidence in knowing what the publisher and her readers expected. Instead of letting the knot in her stomach incapacitate her, she learned to occupy herself. Don't think about the book; get busy on the next one while putting the last one behind you—it was the only way to keep from losing your mind in this business.

Nearly eleven years had passed from the conception of that first book in her college dorm room until this moment. Twenty books in what now seemed like an incredibly short amount of time. Wow! It never ceased to amaze her when she thought of her career in terms of time. She knew writers who worked eleven years on one book. She ran into them all the time at writers' conferences where she was a sought after instructor; well-meaning people who desperately wanted to write the "great American novel", but spent more time discussing and plotting than pasting their backsides to their chairs and doing it. *Just do it* was her advice, though most of them didn't want to hear anything so simple. They wanted a twelve-step program that guaranteed success. There wasn't one. The serious ones listened to what she said and within a few years, showed up at a book signing or a conference with their own book in their hands.

"Look, Darcy," they'd proclaim proudly, "my baby! I couldn't have done it without you."

She lived for those moments. But the wannabe writers who didn't heed her advice far outnumbered those who did. They returned to the conferences year after year, enrolled in the same classes, and discussed the same book idea every time she met them in the elevator.

For two weeks Darcy told herself to relax. Everything would work out the way it always did. Her talent hadn't deserted her. Her writing skills were as sharp as ever. Carla, her editor would contact her any minute. Surely she was pleased. After Darcy's last book, *The Ultimate Guide to Online Investing* which had been released last month, a book outlining the steps to setting up a home daycare might seem a little on the lighter side to the editorial department. Was that it? Carla didn't like the topic—or worse—did Brad "the Barracuda" Yerian, the head of the department, think she was stepping down from the meatier subjects. It wasn't true. She had proven repeatedly over the years she knew her readers. She connected with everyone from thrill seekers to new parents to retirees.

But this time something wasn't right. She could feel it, and it scared her. For one thing, she still hadn't started book twenty-one. Instead of mulling over possible topics, drawing graphs, and researching, she hadn't written the first word since putting *The Ultimate Guide to Starting Your Own Home-Based Daycare* into the mail. She hadn't even settled on a solid idea. She hadn't gone this long without writing since the dreaded writer's block incident of 2001. That time she didn't write for two months. She got it into her head that she was ready for something else, something besides Ultimate Guide books. She'd written eleven at that point, and she was tired of them; tired of being the expert on everything, everything but her own life. She wanted something new. So she stopped writing and started thinking—big mistake. She didn't make the big bucks by thinking.

Finally after numerous pep talks from Carla, and a long hard look at her savings account passbook, she realized—like it or not—she *was* The Ultimate Guide Girl, a moniker given to her by a book reviewer after her fourth or fifth Ultimate Guide book was released. She could guide anyone into anything; she just couldn't guide herself out of a paper bag.

Maybe that was it. She was tired of being Darcy Carter, the Ultimate Guide Girl. She was no longer a college sophomore-turned-best-selling-author. She was just another writer who charged $16.95 to solve every conceivable problem known to man in plain simple English. Well, more than plain, simple English—she had since been translated into six languages.

Darcy was on a ladder in her kitchen, with a whiskbroom in one hand swiping at the grime on the crown molding along the ceiling just out of her reach, when the phone rang. The big Victorian was too much house for one person with its twelve foot ceilings and heating grates she could drop a cat through; common sense told her that when she bought it six years ago after receiving the largest royalty check of her career up to that point. But she had adored the house on the corner lot two blocks from where she was raised for as long as she could remember. She walked past it every day on her way to and from school. She and her best friend, Dee Woodmansee, loved to scare each other with tales that the old place was haunted. They convinced each other a curtain in the attic window fluttered whenever they walked past, and occasionally they claimed to catch a glimpse of a sad looking young woman gazing down on them. The young woman took on all types of personas over the years, depending on their mood of the day. Sometimes she was suffering from a broken heart. Other times, she was a captive of her evil grandmother who blamed her for the untimely death of her parents. And still other times, the girl was plain mad, totally out of her head, a danger to society, and held there for her own safety and the safety of those around her. That was Darcy's favorite version. It was no small wonder she chose a career in writing.

As it turned out, the house's history was far less colorful than Darcy and Dee's imaginings. Built in the early 1900's by a local merchant, he sold the house after losing his business during the Depression. The next owners had six kids and plans to remodel. They added a large back porch that was eventually converted to a family room, two bedrooms, and upgraded to modern plumbing. The next family did have a daughter, but she never spent time in the attic, according to what she told Darcy. The woman's parents died around the same time Darcy was quitting college and moving back home to write her first book. In the ensuing six years, the house stood empty. Darcy liked to think it had been waiting for her.

Her royalty checks continued to grow in size and she hoarded them away in the bank, cautious lest each one prove to be her last. Getting paid four times a year was a difficult thing to manage. So much could happen between paychecks. Consequently, she became downright miserly. She hated to spend money she didn't have in her hands.

Then one day a For Sale sign appeared in the front yard of the Victorian, which was looking quite forlorn by this time. Darcy immediately began doing calculations in her head. She had enough money in the bank for a sizable down payment, regardless of the asking price. She was confident she could earn enough money with conference appearances and book sales to pay the rest off in a reasonable amount of time even if she never wrote another book. Still it was a big step to take for someone with her cautious nature.

"Pray about it, honey," her mother said when she told her the house was for sale. "You don't want to leap into anything without looking, but you are twenty-three, you're making a good living. You aren't planning on living here with your father and me forever, are you?"

Her words were spoken lightly, but Darcy knew her parents were concerned that she might never leave the nest, even though she had the means to support herself.

Darcy mentioned it to God, but she didn't really seek His guidance with the fervor her mother had implied. He was busy, and she had been handling her life pretty well up to this point without much input from Him.

Two weeks later when she received her quarterly royalty check, she took it as a sign from above. After counting zeros to make sure she wasn't seeing things, she called the realtor and set the wheels in motion. She could afford to pay cash for her dream house, as long as they were willing to come down a tad on the asking price. Within days she had a mortgage free house and the means to furnish and maintain it. Even after moving into a house designed for upwards of six children, painting, redecorating, scouring estate sales and furniture stores to furnish the behemoth, she didn't miss a beat on her writing schedule. Two months to the day after moving in, book number eight, *The Ultimate Guide to Parenting Multiples*, was accepted for publication.

Darcy stopped worrying about money. She was still cautious, but she no longer fretted every time she spent a dime.

The house still took up more spare time than she had, even though she loved every minute she spent inside it. She paid a landscaper twice a year to prepare the lawn and flower beds for summer and winter. All major renovations were contracted out. But the rest of the upkeep, she did herself. She was proud of the work she had accomplished in the last five years, but conceded there was plenty more to do. This house would keep her busy for the rest of her life. Most of the time, she didn't mind. It was beautiful. It was full of personality. It was hers and hers alone.

Her heart leaped to her throat like it always did when the phone rang while she had a manuscript out. Then she took a deep breath and reminded herself it was probably her mother inviting her to dinner, the library letting her know the new Karen Kingsbury title she reserved was in, or a telemarketer wanting to sell her some kind of travel plan or magazine subscription she didn't want or need. The only thing she needed was for Carla to be on the other end of the line with a release date for *The Ultimate Guide to Starting Your Own Home-Based Daycare.*

As quickly as she was able, she scampered down the ladder and grabbed the cordless phone off the kitchen table. Her eyes stole to the caller ID and her heart skipped a beat. A New York City area code—Carla.

"What took you so long?" she wanted to blurt out as soon as she hit the talk button. She refrained. For all Carla knew, she was busy at work on her next book and totally unconcerned with what was going on in New York. "Hello?" she said, in a deliberately unaffected tone.

"Hello, yourself, Darcy. How are you?" Carla asked.

Better now that you finally called.

She could tell by Carla's voice the manuscript had been well received. Thank goodness.

Darcy smiled. "I'm fine. How's New York."

"The same, the same—I guess you know why I'm calling."

"You finished the book, and it's the greatest thing ever put to paper?"

"I don't know if I'd go that far. But, yes, I loved it. So does everyone else."

Darcy exhaled. What had she been worried about? There wasn't a subject created she couldn't write a book about in three weeks time if she took a notion. "I'm glad everyone's happy," she said benignly.

"So, what's next on the agenda?" Carla asked. Darcy heard

the inhalation of cigarette smoke. Carla worked in a nonsmoking building like all city dwellers these days, but it didn't stop her from enjoying a smoke. No one was going to tell her what to do.

"I thought you were using the patch," she said.

"Lighten up, Darcy, I already got a mother." Carla laughed good-naturedly. "Those crazy patches give me nightmares."

"You're not supposed to wear them while you're sleeping."

"I do if I don't want to wake up in the middle of the night craving a cigarette."

Darcy chuckled, "Okay, enough lecturing from me."

"Doesn't bother me, I hear it everywhere. That daughter of mine is the biggest nag you'd ever want to meet. Kids these days think they know everything." Carla inhaled deeply and then covered her mouth to muffle a cough. "So anyway, where was I? Oh yeah, the book. We're thrilled with it. I knew you could handle it, but more importantly, what are you working on now?"

Darcy ran her tongue across her top lip. She had some ideas; she always had ideas, but was she ready to tackle another Ultimate Guide to something. How would Carla react if she told her she was thinking maybe she didn't want to write anything at all?

At her hesitation, Carla jumped in. "You know what I want you to do?" She rushed on before Darcy could head her off. "It's long overdue; you should have done it years ago."

Darcy had a clear picture of the gears turning in Carla's head. Yes, she knew what Carla wanted; what she'd been trying to talk Darcy into for the last six books.

"I don't know, Carla—"

"Sure you do, honey. You know I'm right. You finally have the credibility for the topic if anyone bothers to look at your picture on the back cover. You don't look like an inexperienced kid anymore. This one would jump off the charts—a New York Times bestseller for sure."

"It's not that I don't think I'm ready…"

"Well good, because it's time. *The Ultimate Guide to Finding Mr. Right.* Maybe this book will even do me some good, Darcy. Heaven knows I'm batting a thousand at finding Mr. Not Even Close." Carla had been married and divorced three times, with a dozen or so serious relationships in between. Her last marriage lasted a mere eight months. With each one, she was sure she had finally found the real thing, only to realize —sometimes within hours—she had missed the mark again. At forty-six, she was able to laugh at her mistakes and move on, but Darcy knew it had taken its toll on her friend.

Darcy picked up a sponge and wiped out her already clean sink. "No one believes in finding Mr. Right anymore, Carla. The idea's too old fashioned."

"Nonsense, everyone believes in romance, even the diehards like me who don't have any luck at it."

Darcy put the sponge back into the little ceramic rooster one of her nieces had given her on her last birthday. "Well, I think you'd be better off finding someone else to write about Mr. Right," Darcy said, hoping she sounded firm. She moved to the baker's rack to straighten the cookbooks on the shelf. A title jumped out at her; *A Southerner's Guide to Down-Home Cooking.*

Inspiration struck.

"I'm already working on my next book," she lied. She flipped the cookbook over and saw a picture of a tiny café that looked like a renovated train depot. "*The Ultimate Guide to Disappearing Diners and Cafés of the South,*" she said quickly. "You know those little Mom and Pop operations that manage to survive even after the Interstate's passed them by."

"Title's too long," Carla said dismissively. "The research alone for a project like that could take years. While you're working on Mr. Right you can do some Internet research on your diners and cafés. Then after you're finished with him, you can move on to the diner idea if it still interests you."

Now that she had a solid idea, Darcy wasn't backing down. Carla had been pushing her to write the Mr. Right book for a long time. She told her time and again she didn't do dating guides. She could muddle her way through potty training, retirement accounts, or the NFL draft—but romance; she didn't have a clue.

"Carla, do you know the last time I wasn't writing a book?"

"What are you talking about, Darcy?"

"Yeah, that's what I thought. Well, neither do I. I need a

break. The cafés and diners book will be vacation and research at the same time. I need it. To be perfectly honest, I'm wiped on the whole Ultimate Guide thing."

Carla groaned louder than necessary.

"I'm serious," Darcy repeated. "I need to get away. Even if this one takes more time than it's actually worth, I want to do it." The more she thought about it, the better she liked the idea. She could feel the creative juices thawing inside her. "Everyone is into nostalgia these days. I think this book would be a big hit."

"You can stop writing any time you want, honey. None of us know how you keep up this pace anyway. But..."

Darcy saw the "but" coming a mile away.

"...those cafés have survived the onslaught of McDonald's and Wal-Mart. I think they'll be okay without you for another few months. I hate to see you tie yourself up in a project that will take way too much of your time, and then might not even be marketable. I agree that nostalgia sells books, but I don't have a lot of confidence in the idea myself."

Darcy couldn't believe her ears. "When did you stop trusting my judgment? I've written books before that you were hesitant about in the beginning, but you always supported me, and I always ended up being right."

She heard the snap of a lighter. "Darcy, honey, listen," Carla said, after a deep draw on a cigarette. "I never said I don't trust your judgment. I'm just saying the Mr. Right book is a sure thing. This cafés and diners idea may not fly with readers. It's a bigger risk. That's all I'm saying. By all means, take a break from writing. Haven't you been telling me for years you were going to take your brother's kids to Disney World? It's seventy-eight degrees in Florida today; not like here or that tundra where you live. Go ahead and enjoy yourself. Then when you get back, give some thought to Finding Mr. Right. If after some serious consideration, you still want to take your trip down south, go with my blessing, and sample all the deep-fried chicken parts and black eyed peas your arteries can stand."

Darcy knew there was no point in any further discussion with Carla, but she wasn't wasting a moment of her time on Finding Mr.

Right either. Maybe the diners and cafés had survived the last fifty years, but he obviously hadn't.

She hung up the phone and logged onto the Internet. She typed in diners and cafés of the South, hit the search button, and put the conversation with Carla out of her head. All that mattered right now was the publishing house loved *The Ultimate Guide to Starting Your Own Home-Based Daycare*. Another winner, so where was her usual excitement and enthusiasm?

"What's the word on the new book, Darcy?" her dad, Ben Carter, asked that night over pot roast. "Heard anything yet?" Always a first question when she had a manuscript out.

When she decided to quit school after only five quarters to write a book, it was back to her parents' home. They were stunned to say the least and a little dismayed at her announcement. Ultimately, they were supportive, even though Darcy suspected they didn't think the book thing would ever happen. But the Carters trusted their levelheaded daughter, even if her pronouncement had thrown them for a loop. The first book was written in record time, much to their delight. Unfortunately, finding a buyer took considerably longer. By the time Darcy found a house willing to publish *The Ultimate Guide to Writing a College Thesis*, she had written another book, *The Ultimate Guide to Caring for Your Aging Parent*. Her third book, *The Ultimate Guide to Planning Your Dream Wedding* was written, accepted, and awaiting the final editing process by the time *Writing a College Thesis* hit the bookstore shelves two years later. Her family knew all too well the frustration of waiting to hear from publishers and then further waiting and hand wringing for the book to become a reality. Sometimes Darcy thought the waiting was easier for her than those who cared so much for her.

She swallowed a mouthful of scalloped potatoes before answering. She was already envisioning the extra half-mile she would run in the morning to make up for this family dinner, a weekly ritual at her parents' house. Across the scarred oak table where she once did homework sat her older brother, Keith. The table had expanded to keep up with the growth of Keith's family, including his wife, Becky, their two preteen girls and five-year-old son.

"Carla called today," she said with a relieved smile. "Everyone loved the book. We didn't really discuss the particulars of a publishing calendar, but I'm assuming it will be released by Christmas."

Sharon Carter, Darcy's mother, reached past her youngest granddaughter to pat her hand. "I never had any doubts. I'm very proud of you, dear."

"I'm proud of you too, Aunt Darcy," twelve-year-old Samantha piped up.

"Thank you, Sam."

"She just wants to go to Disney World," Samantha's younger sister Bethany explained. "Remember, you said after the next book you'd take us."

Darcy arched her eyebrows. She wondered if Carla had called the girls after their conversation this morning to remind them of her promise. She did want to take the girls on a vacation when she ever found the time, presumably after finishing a book. Funny, she never finished one project without launching straight into another.

"Don't put Darcy on the spot," Becky, the girls' mother, admonished. "You know how busy she is."

"She's always busy," Samantha lamented.

"And you did say Disney World," Bethany reminded Darcy from the other side of the table with all the wisdom of her eleven years.

"Do I get to go?" Zachary wanted to know.

"You're too little to go without Mom," Samantha informed her brother.

Zachary gripped his fork in indignation. "No, I'm not." He looked at Becky. "You could go, too, Mom, couldn't you?"

Becky smiled and reached across the table to pull his glass of milk away from the edge. "I think we have plenty of time to discuss Disney World." She looked surreptitiously at Darcy. "I'm sure Darcy's busy on her next book already."

All three kids groaned and turned to look accusingly at Darcy.

She felt like a heel for disappointing them again. The first time she promised Disney World, little Zachary was not old enough to be considered for the trip. If she put it off much longer, she'd have to turn it into a honeymoon trip for Samantha.

"I have started researching my next book," she admitted. "I'm afraid I'll be out of town for awhile."

Everyone looked startled. "You're going out of town already?" Sharon exclaimed. "We haven't seen hardly anything of you in the last three months. I thought you'd at least take a little break to spend time with your family before heading out to who knows where."

"I know, Mom, but I've got a great idea and I really want to get on it." She paused, gathering her nerve. "I'm thinking maybe this will be my last Ultimate Guide book, and I kind of want to get it over with."

The girls cheered. Becky and Keith's mouths dropped open. Ben furrowed his brow. Sharon was the first to find her voice. "You know we'll support whatever decision you make, honey. What are you thinking of doing instead?"

"Maybe take a break from writing altogether." She could see the doubt on their faces. The girls cheered even louder. Little Zachary joined in. "Or I could try my hand at fiction. I'd like to write something fun for a change. I'm tired of telling people how to do everything."

"But you're so good at it, Sis," Keith quipped.

Everyone at the table laughed. "Ha-ha," Darcy said. She threw her napkin across the table at him. He caught it and threw it back.

Darcy refolded the napkin and put it in her lap. "It takes a lot more energy bullying people into doing things your way than you'd think."

Sharon, Keith, and Becky laughed and nodded. They knew better than most people what she was talking about. Sharon taught high school English. Keith taught math and coached junior high basketball and track while his wife taught seventh grade social studies.

"If that's what you want, honey," Dad said.

"Maybe I'll go to law school."

"I think fiction would be fun," Becky said, ignoring Darcy's attempt at a joke. "Your Ultimate Guide books are always conversational, with a little bit of humor. Not like those usual how-to books that drone on and on. You'd be a natural at fiction."

"You think so?" Darcy asked hopefully. She had often felt the same way about her work but was also her harshest critic. "I've got some ideas—"

"Mom," Samantha wailed, "why'd you get her going on fiction? Now we'll never get to Disney World."

Becky cocked one eyebrow. "Did you ever think maybe your dad and I will take you to Disney World?"

Samantha sniffed, "Yeah, right."

"It could happen."

Samantha exhaled, exasperated. "Mom, school teachers take their kids to the zoo or museums for vacation. You people can't afford Disney World."

Keith nudged her with his shoulder. "You people?"

Samantha sighed and shook her head in abject misery.

"We'll get to Disney World yet, Sam," Darcy assured her. "I'm kind of tired of working all the time too. It's only March. You've still got three months until summer vacation. I should have my research done by then."

"Three months?" Mom said startled. "Goodness, Darcy, where are you headed?"

"South. I'm thinking of focusing my research in the Carolinas or Georgia."

"What kind of book is this that you have to go all the way down there?"

"Something like, *The Ultimate Guide to Diners and Cafés of the Old South*. You know—the kind that has been converted from old railway stations and antebellum houses. I even found one on the Internet that used to be a grain silo."

Samantha wrinkled her nose. "Gross. Besides a pig, who'd want to eat out of a grain silo?"

"I think it's a great idea, Aunt Darcy," Bethany said. "Can I go with you?"

Samantha reconsidered. "I get to go, too; you could home school us."

Becky snorted. "Oh, that would comfort all those parents whose kids are enrolled in the public school system! Two of their teachers home schooling their own kids."

"Your Aunt Darcy is going south to work," Keith added. He arched his eyebrows at Darcy. "At least I presume that's what you're doing."

"Yes, work," Darcy assured him.

Samantha propped her elbow on the table and lowered her chin into her hand. "Work, that's all she ever does."

Darcy smiled but didn't say anything more. Samantha was right. She was twenty-nine years old, the author of nineteen, no, twenty books. She had educated the masses in everything from decorating a nursery for a new baby to summer camp for seniors. After telling everyone else what to do, when was she going to start doing a little living of her own?

Three weeks later Darcy's phone rang while she was adding another small southern town to her list of places worth visiting during her trip. "How's it going out in the 'burbs, Darcy?" Carla sounded her usual upbeat self, but Darcy knew she wanted something. She never called out of the blue to chat.

"Everything's fine," Darcy answered just as chipper. She lived in a small town, not the 'burbs, but it never did any good trying to explain the difference to Carla. To her, any place boasting less than a million people was uncivilized anyway. "How are things in the city?"

"Couldn't be better. Now, Darcy, the reason I called…"

Darcy braced herself for the lecture surely on its way.

"Have you given any thought to the next book?"

"That's all I've been thinking about. In fact, my research here at home base is finished, and I'm packing up to head south."

"South?" Carla sounded thoroughly confused. "You shouldn't have to go any farther than the soccer field, mini mall, or wherever you people congregate to find Mr. Right; or even, Mr. He'll-Do-In-A-Pinch."

"Carla. Hello! Did you hear a word I said the last time we talked? I'm not doing the Mr. Right book. I'm researching cafés in the South, remember? I've found all sorts of interesting places I want to check out; renovated gas stations and five and dimes lost in those little throw-away towns that most of us bypass on the freeway without thinking about the people who live there."

"Sounds great," Carla said with little enthusiasm. "Nostalgia. Still sells books. I love it. But I thought you wanted to take a break before starting Mr. Right."

"I am taking a break. That's why I'm going to North Carolina. I plan to relax and unwind and get some research done at the same time."

Carla chuckled, "Same old Darcy. You never change, do you? But see, the thing is, I mentioned the Mr. Right book to Brad and he went crazy. He loved it. Says it's just the kind of title we need, something edgy. He wants you to get started on it right away. The wheels are already turning on our end. Not necessarily the way I prefer, but he's the boss. You know how it is. So Darcy, it really means a lot to the company that you write this book…"

Darcy was no longer comfortable with the way the phone call was going. This wasn't just Carla giving some friendly helpful editor advice. "Carla, what are you saying? Does the publishing house have a problem with my books? Because last time I checked I'd sold over two million copies for the big happy family I thought we all were a part of." She heard her voice rising and felt her face getting hot. "Am I nothing more than a Jerry Springer guest now? Whatever happened to quality nonfiction that continues to sell books? According to my last quarterly report, my first one is still selling strong."

"It's all right, Darcy, calm down," Carla said a little too forcefully. "No one is saying you haven't done more than what was expected of you. But, well, we all know there is more in you than sweet little pieces about selling your home or landing the job of your dreams."

"So, you're siding with Brad, Brad the Barracuda?" She enunciated Carla's own nickname for the senior editor of their department.

"Darcy, you know I love you, girl. I'd gladly go to the mat for you. I have more than once." She took another drag off her cigarette, and her voice softened. "Listen, sweetie, I think you should know what's going on here. Yes, your books are still selling strong, but the company's changing. Old man Baxter is getting older. He's about to hand the reins over to George. Once that happens, George will be moving Brad up to V.P., and Brad wants a more contemporary backlist."

Darcy's heart sank. She remembered the two years of looking for a publishing house for her first book, and then getting it published. It had been a long frustrating journey. Once the first book was in print and the next two in production, things went much smoother. For the past eight and a half years she had been home pumping out books with no concerns about what was happening in New York. Each book she wrote was well received, smooth sailing, just the way she wanted it. *Now* they wanted edgy. Well, she didn't do edgy!

She imagined herself back on the frontlines looking for another publisher. Yes, she had credentials now; almost three million books in print and a twenty-book backlist. But would that be enough if the whole publishing world was looking for "edgy"?

"Darcy, are you still there?"

She blew out a puff of air. "Yeah, Carla, I'm still here."

Carla only had her best interests at heart, but she also had a job to do. Keep the writers writing, the books on the bestsellers' list, the money flowing in. Just how much going to the mat was she even capable of doing on Darcy's behalf?

Darcy decided to take a stand. "Listen, Carla, I'll think about everything you said. Tell Brad I'm headed to North Carolina next week. I'm already in love with this new book idea. I've got reservations at this little B&B in the heart of the Smoky Mountains that'll serve as my home base. It's called the Danbury Inn. Doesn't that sound gorgeous? It's been in the same family since the First World War. They're doing something right because they're known all over the South. They've been showcased in all kinds of magazines. Talk about nostalgic. Perfect location, you couldn't ask for a more picturesque town. There are also quite a few diners and cafés in the area where I can get a lot of work done."

"This sounds like it could take months," Carla said, her tone doubtful.

"It might," Darcy admitted.

"Just don't forget the clock's ticking. I need a finished manuscript on my desk by August if you want a book on the shelves next summer."

Darcy took a deep breath. "I'm not working against the clock this time, Carla. It won't be the end of the world if I don't release a book every six to ten months."

"All right, whoever you are," Carla shrieked in mock horror, "what have you done with Darcy?" She leveled her voice. "Listen, sweetie, you're the one who got us all used to your hectic pace. Don't blame us if we have a hard time accepting that you want to slow down now that your age is catching up with you."

Darcy chose to ignore the old age comment, although at this moment she felt very old indeed. "Regardless, I'm not changing my plans because Brad wants edgy. I'm still the creator here. I can't change what I write to please a glorified bean counter."

"Hold on now, Darcy," Carla cautioned, "that glorified bean counter helped turn you into a million-copy selling author."

"I realize that, Carla," Darcy said, fighting to keep her voice even, "and I appreciate the company taking a chance on me way back when. But I had a lot to do with selling those books, too. I'm not a puppet. Just let me write this book, okay? I won't be out of town more than a month or two. When I come back, I'll bring it to New York personally. Then I'll have a meeting with you and Brad, and we'll discuss my future."

"Oh, Darcy, honey, I hope you know what you're doing."

"I love you, Carla, but you have to trust me. I need this."

"Well, have a good time in Mayberry, then. Get this café book out of your system. I'll keep Brad out of your hair. As far as he's concerned, you're taking a break. This isn't a slave state, you know. He can't expect you to keep pumping out books at your pace indefinitely." Carla chuckled. "When you get home, we'll have our meeting with Brad. But trust me, Darcy, it isn't only him who wants more contemporary titles. This idea is past due. I'll agree to whatever you want, but I'm not giving up on Finding Mr. Right."

I already have, Darcy thought ruefully as she placed the phone on its base. She stared out the window. Finding Mr. Right was a useless pursuit. She knew it and Carla had been around long enough to know it, too.

She wouldn't be bullied into writing a book she didn't believe in. She shook her head in disbelief. How had her career come to this? Twenty books behind her and she could be without a publisher by summer. She sat down at the kitchen table and put her chin in her hands. What would she do then? Maybe that change in careers would come about sooner than she anticipated.

One thing she knew, she wasn't going to spend the next few months looking for someone who didn't exist. She might as well search for Sasquatch while she was in North Carolina for all the good looking for Mr. Right would do her.

$\mathcal{D}$arcy headed out of town at five a.m. the next morning. She wanted to be far away from the city before rush hour, which seemed to start earlier and earlier. As she turned onto the Interstate and headed south, she murmured a prayer of thanks that she didn't have to face a commute every day. Her entire life had been blessed. Her parents were the supportive kind whose kids didn't end up in therapy. Ben Carter was the fire chief of his station house. He was the kind of Dad they wrote Father's Day cards about. He was attentive and patient and possessed the greatest quality of a successful father; he loved his children's mother.

Sharon Carter honored her husband. She brought her children up in church, took their needs and concerns seriously, and was always compassionate with them and their friends. More than once during Darcy's teenage years, a friend would tell her; "I wish my mom was more like yours."

The only dreams the Carters had for their two children were that they be happy and fulfilled in whatever path they chose for their lives. Keith was six years older than Darcy and a wonderful brother. Without hovering or making a nuisance of himself, she knew her big brother was always there should she need him to be.

Keith excelled in school, athletics, and nearly everything else he put his hand to. Regardless of having a brain that made any career choice a possibility, he wanted to teach school and coach ball. Ben and Sharon didn't measure their children's success by the size of their paychecks, and were thrilled to see Keith enter a field based on a desire to give and earn a living doing something he loved.

Darcy's life was never as mapped out as Keith's.

By the time she entered college undeclared, Keith had earned his degree, married Becky, had a second baby on the way, and taught full time at the same school as their mother. Darcy didn't miss the nervous glances exchanged between her parents every time the topic of college or her future came up. But true to form, they never mentioned their concerns to her. They trusted her to act responsibly. She almost wished they didn't have so much faith in her.

The last thing she wanted to do was disappoint them, especially since they insisted she could never do so. By the end of her first year at Ohio State while all her undeclared classmates were making decisions, she was beginning to question her presence there.

Focusing on a major depressed her. *You're being lazy*, she told herself. *You don't want to grow up.* She settled on English Literature, because it came naturally and she knew it was something her mother would approve of, and started her second year of classes. But the voice inside her head wouldn't leave her alone. She had left the piles of notebooks of stories she'd written all through school at home when she went away to college, determined to find a job like her parents and brother where she could change the world. No selfish pursuits for her.

She almost volunteered for a mission trip to Guatemala with her church group over Christmas break, but remembered in the nick of time she despised mosquitoes, humidity, and eating bad food. She considered the possibility that she was a selfish person with no hope of redemption in spite of her parents' best efforts.

She maintained a decent grade point average, but dreaded getting out of bed every morning. Regardless of how hard she tried to squelch the impulse, all she wanted to do was write. She started researching subjects of interest to her, tossed around the idea of romance or mystery novels, and waited. After five quarters and more money spent than she cared to think about, she approached her parents.

No sense beating around the bush. "I want to come home," she said simply.

Of course they misunderstood. "You want to go to school in the city?"

"No, I don't want to go to school at all. I've been researching writing a college thesis…"

"Sweetheart, you've got a lot of time before you need to worry about that."

"No, I'm talking about writing a book that teaches people how to write a college thesis. I want to quit school and focus completely on it."

Ben Carter spoke up for the first time. "Wouldn't it make more sense to have actually written a thesis before you write a book about writing one?"

"You'd think that, wouldn't you? But seriously, I'm already halfway finished with the book, and it's pretty good." Darcy's eyes were shining by this point and her heart rate quickening. Every time she thought about her book, she experienced the same euphoria. Talking about it was even better. "I showed it to my English professor, and she thinks it's excellent. She says I have a knack for making an ordinarily boring, tedious subject interesting."

Sharon crossed her arms over her chest. "Was it her idea that you quit school?"

"Of course not. She doesn't know I'm thinking about that."

"I would hope not."

"But I'm going to do it," Darcy stated, her voice resolute. "There's no point in continuing my classes. I want to move back home and finish my book. I have tons of ideas for more books. All I can think about is getting this one done so I can move on to the next one."

She was so excited from talking about the book, it was all she could do to remain in the living room explaining this desire to her parents instead of running back upstairs to her computer so she could write some more.

Ben took her arm, steered her to the couch, and sat her down. He settled onto the ottoman in front of her, leaned forward, and cupped both her hands between his large calloused ones, "Darcy, what about your education? It has always been your mother's and my dream that you and Keith earn your degrees. I didn't get to go to college myself, and I always felt that I missed out on the greatest opportunity of my life."

Darcy had anticipated every argument they might throw at her. She had to make them understand why this was so important. "I know, Dad, and I appreciate everything you and Mom have done. But college isn't for me, at least not now. Writing is the only thing I've ever wanted to do. I'm really good at it and it makes me happy. And this book, it's just screaming to get out. It won't keep quiet. I don't see a point in wasting more of my life taking classes about things I don't even believe in and that aren't going to help me accomplish what I really want to do."

Sharon stayed next to the fireplace, determined not to put her daughter on the defensive. "What about all those English Lit classes you've been taking?" she asked hopefully. "Isn't that what writers major in—or Journalism? We're not saying you can't write a book. Just stay in school, get your degree, and write in your spare time. That way, if the book writing doesn't work out, you'll have something to fall back on."

Darcy's face fell. Sharon wished she hadn't spoken. "Darcy, I..."

Darcy couldn't contemplate that her book might not work out. She stared at her hands for a moment and tried to put her thoughts in order. She didn't want to fall back on something. She wanted to finish her book. She had to finish it, or she'd never have any peace with herself.

Finally she looked up, first at her father, seated in front of her on the ottoman, and then to her mother, motionless in front of the fireplace, her face etched in maternal concern. "I know college is supposed to teach you how to think for yourself, not accept everything at face value. Well, you two have already taught me that. I am thinking for myself. If things don't work out with the book, I promise I will go back to school in a year or two. I'll still qualify for most of my scholarships." She smiled at Ben and then stood up to face her mother. "But it will work out. It has to. I'm not going back to school. What I'm asking from both of you is that you not turn my bedroom into a sewing room or anything yet. I'm really hoping I can keep living here for as long as this writing thing takes?"

Ben and Sharon looked at each other. Ben shrugged and Sharon left the room. Darcy knew they didn't approve of the idea, but she had to do what was right for her. It might take a while, but she would show them this was not a mistake. She was not a failure.

For the next year, the failure possibility haunted her night and day. She finished *The Ultimate Guide to Writing a College Thesis* two months after returning home and sent it off into the great unknown. Three weeks later she received the first of many unkind and impersonal rejection letters. She shrugged off the disappointment and submitted elsewhere. She had done her homework. She didn't expect any part of the process to be easy. She had written a good book and was confident someone out there would appreciate her hard work. She set about writing her second book and refused to acknowledge the growing apprehension on her mother's face or the growing stack of rejection letters in the bottom drawer of her filing cabinet.

Finally she received a contract for *The Ultimate Guide to Writing a College Thesis*. The publisher immediately accepted the second book and proposals for two more. With four books sold, it was still two and a half years after quitting college before receiving her first royalty check. Thank goodness she had parents willing to support her during that time. With a sinking heart, she realized many of the people whom she had started classes with at the university had already graduated and found jobs that offered security and a steady paycheck. But this was the path she had chosen. She had no regrets. Thankfully, within another year she was making more money than she could have in an entry-level position for the average college graduate.

Two years later, with the release of her eighth book, she bought her Victorian and flew the nest for good. Her family stopped giving each other the look that translated into; "We'll be taking care of Darcy in our old age, won't we?"

Darcy grabbed a doughnut out of a glass case and an iced cappuccino for breakfast at a Quick Mart off I-77. She'd been traveling for three hours. She thought of calling her mother to let her know she was all right and quite enjoyed traveling alone until she realized it was eight thirty. Sharon would already be at school, teaching her first period ninth grade English class. That was the thing about traveling. You lost all track of time and how life was still going on as usual for the rest of the world.

She climbed into her red SUV and headed back onto the highway. A sense of euphoric freedom washed over her as she bit into the sugary, greasy, yet still tasty doughnut. She always felt fresh and alive at the beginning of a new project. This time was even better. No self-imposed deadline or written in stone plan of action. Other than having the next five days planned out as far as reservations and a map with red dots all over it marking towns that boasted of diners and cafés that fit into her agenda, she was free to do whatever she wanted—take detours, sleep late, chat with locals, whatever struck her fancy.

Carla would hate it. "You're taking too long, Darcy," she would fuss. "Check out a few diners and B & B's if you must, and then get back home and fake the rest of it. How different can they be, for pity's sake?"

Darcy accelerated and ducked into traffic. The best part about this book was it would be her last Ultimate Guide. She had definitely decided on that much. Twenty-one Ultimate Guide books were enough for anybody. This one would be the end of her legacy. She would have fun with the research, take as much time as she wanted, and not let anyone, especially Brad or Carla suck the fun out of it. No one was dictating this trip but her. There was no one to point out that she was wasting too much time on one project—no one to remind her of the bottom line. All that mattered was for her to enjoy the process of writing again. It had been too long since she had done that.

She wouldn't quit writing, she decided. The little voice in her head would never stand for that, but she was ready for something else no matter what Brad and Carla wanted. They didn't own her, regardless of what they thought.

A black Jetta swerved in front of her, and she mashed on the brakes to avoid rear- ending it. She checked her rearview mirror to make sure nothing was about to rear end her and caught her breath. She turned her thoughts back to her future. What would she do if the publishing house let her go? Was she ready for the whole search mission again? Surely she would find another house with no trouble. She had so many successful books behind her. They were all niche books with less than astronomical sales numbers, but she earned a good living. She had proven she could produce. She had a bulging portfolio of reviews that told the world her books were "witty…", "entertaining…", "fresh…" Wasn't that enough?

Two hours later she crossed the bridge in Marietta that spanned the Ohio River into West Virginia. It was only ten a.m. She should arrive at her first stop, a little diner in a tiny town south of Charleston, in time for the lunch rush. Between lunch and dinner, she planned to crisscross southern West Virginia and the western tip of Virginia before crossing into North Carolina for her last meal of the day.

After spouting off to Carla the first book idea that came to mind, she realized the potential harm this project could do to her waistline. She wasn't one of those women who counted carbs or ordered green salad and water at a steak house, but she was conscious of her figure. Her mother called her big-boned, which meant she was tall with a large frame like the rest of the women in her family, and could pack on the pounds if she let her guard down. She liked chocolate, honest-to-goodness ice cream, and homemade rolls too much to watch every morsel that went into her mouth. Instead, she jogged nearly every morning, took Tae-Bo classes at the Y, and exhibited a little control whenever she sat down at the table. A few months tooling around the South investigating what kept people coming back to the small town cafés and diners could be her undoing.

She rubbed a hand over her face. She was tired of driving, and the stale doughnut and flat cappuccino she'd had for breakfast two and a half hours ago were sitting ill on her stomach. She needed to find a place to pull over and stretch her legs. The SUV's OnStar reported a rest area twenty miles ahead. She rolled her shoulders, arched her back, and then dug in her tote bag on the seat beside her for her cell phone.

"Hey, Mom and Dad," she said when their machine picked up, "it's me. Everything's fine. I just crossed the river into West Virginia. It looks like it's going to be a gorgeous day. I passed through some rain clouds a while back and thought they might follow me, but it's cleared off. Everything's going good. If all goes as planned, I'll call you tonight from Statesville, North Carolina when I stop for the night. Love ya! Don't worry."

She closed the phone, slid it back into her tote, and accelerated to keep up with traffic. The rest area ahead beckoned.

The café she had chosen for lunch proved to be a treasure trove in character and small town charm, but a bust as far as the food was concerned. Nevertheless, she filled three pages in a spiral bound notebook with prices, daily specials, décor, and most importantly, character sketches. This was the part of her job she liked the most. Writing was a solitary existence, and she always enjoyed the opportunity to get out from in front of her computer and into the sunlight.

It was late and she was road weary by the time she pulled into the parking lot of the national chain hotel where she would spend her first night. She was too queasy from carsickness and overeating what her stomach wasn't used to for any more research. She dropped onto the stiff, disinfected mattress, too tired to even transfer her notes into her computer. Tomorrow would be soon enough for the real work to begin.

She was up and on the road early the following morning. In the next town was a café where she planned to have breakfast. In order to get a feel for the place and the regular customers, she needed to get there early. On her way out of Statesville, she passed a diner fashioned after an old railway dining car and found a place to turn around, forgetting about the café in the next town. This was exactly what she was looking for. Chloe's Express was written in neon and hanging on the inside of the front window. The parking lot was nearly full. When she walked in, she had to wait for a table. She was still full from last night so she ordered only toast and coffee. She could still learn a lot about Chloe's even without sampling the food.

"*Then why go all the way down there,*" Carla's voice rang in her ears. "*You could have stayed home and called Chloe on the phone.*"

She smiled and jotted notations in her notebook. Carla didn't understand. She never would.

Before nine she was back on the road. She should make her destination by lunchtime. Hopefully by then, she'd be hungry. She had perused the Internet for two weeks leading up to her trip, fine-tuning what she wanted her final Ultimate Guide book to accomplish. During her search, she found what she hoped was the perfect place. Winchester was a small college town in the hills of western North Carolina boasting a population of about eight thousand people. During the school year, the population swelled to around twelve thousand. Winchester was also the location of the Danbury Inn. It was the largest such establishment in the area, boasting twelve rooms for rent. It had been featured in several travel guides and national magazines. After twenty-four hours of driving and eating too much, Darcy was ready for a comfortable bed on which to rest her backside.

The Danbury Inn was everything she expected when she pulled into the driveway in the quaint historic district of Winchester, North Carolina. The tallest and grandest building on the quiet tree-lined street, the Danbury Inn rose out of the tall oaks and pines like a sentinel. The façade was a mixture of brown river rock and cream-colored siding with brick red roof shingles and coordinating wood shutters on every window. The most captivating feature was the turret that loomed three stories above Darcy's head as she exited the car. She tilted her head back and gasped audibly as she surveyed the magnificent structure. She fell instantly in love and wouldn't mind spending her entire spring here. She made her way up a brick sidewalk to the wide front porch. Two red rocking chairs shifted in the breeze. Someone had left a cozy looking, hand-stitched afghan hanging over the back of one. Intentionally, Darcy supposed. A small table between them made her thirst for lemonade and a good book while she looked out over the quaint neighborhood in spite of the distinct March nip in the air.

A petite smiling woman well acquainted with sixty answered the doorbell. "Hello," she sang out in the sweetest, most gentile voice Darcy had ever heard. "Welcome to the Danbury Inn." She stepped back and motioned Darcy into the two-story foyer. The smell of cinnamon hung in the air. Darcy's stomach growled in response in spite of the fact she still hadn't recovered from yesterday's overindulgence. She was going to gain ten pounds within the first week of this trip.

The woman closed the door behind Darcy and turned to face her. "I'm Marjorie Reed. My husband, John and I own the Danbury. We're so pleased to have you. And you are..."

Darcy extended her hand. She decided the thing she liked most about B & B's, besides being able to explore someone else's home, was the warm welcome and congenial atmosphere. She sighed heavily. "I'm so happy to finally be here. I feel like I've been on the road for a month. But it's only been a day and a half. Anyway, this place is even better than the brochures claimed. Have you lived here long?" she asked, even though she knew most of the answer from her research.

Marjorie Reed beamed under the praise. Her eyes swept the magnificent entryway. "The house has been in John's family since before the First World War. We moved here after his mother died. We always wanted to open a bed-and-breakfast. I see to most of the operations while John teaches Civil Engineering at the University. Fortunately his down time at the school is also the busiest time here, so it works out perfectly."

Everything Darcy needed to know in a matter of seconds. She loved her job.

She followed Marjorie through the foyer into an open sitting room to a Dresden table where a guest register sat open in front of a quill pen. Marjorie picked up the pen and looked down at the register. "Now, what did you say your name was?"

Darcy realized in all the excitement of her arrival, she hadn't introduced herself. She let her tote bag slide to the floor. "I'm Darcy Carter. I called a couple of weeks ago."

For the first time since opening the door, the smile on the proprietress's face slipped. The lines on her brow knitted into a tiny V as she studied the register. She grimaced. "Carter, you say. Oh, dear." She glanced down at the open book and then at Darcy. "Honey, you're not on here." She flushed all the way up to her perfectly coiffed white hair. "I don't know how this happened. When did you say you called?"

"Um…about two weeks ago, yes, it was the twelfth. I'm in the area researching a new book I'm working on. I plan to stay awhile. I haven't decided how long yet."

"Oh, yes, the writer." Marjorie's face darkened farther. "I do remember your call now. I can't imagine how I missed putting you into the book. I am so sorry about this."

Darcy shrugged. "Oh, that's no problem. All that matters is I'm here now."

"Well, not exactly."

Darcy's suddenly felt very tired. Her vision of relaxing on the front porch with a book and the breeze on her face vanished with the wind. This was the end of March, not exactly peak tourist season, but from the look on Marjorie's face, her presence had become a big problem.

"You see," Marjorie began apologetically, rolling the quill pen between her finger and thumb, "this is Parents' weekend at the university. I always get totally booked for all the big university weekends. You know, football games, student registration, that sort of thing. I'm so sorry, Miss Carter. I don't know how this could have happened. It's totally inexcusable on my part, I realize that, but I simply don't have room for you."

No room in the inn, Darcy thought ruefully. "But I don't see how this happened. I called a couple of weeks ago…" she repeated unnecessarily.

Marjorie was nodding sympathetically as she flipped pages in her register, presumably searching for Darcy's name. "Yes, dear, I remember speaking with you myself. You don't know how embarrassed I am. I know this looks terrible for someone in my position, and you writing a book of all things. I don't suppose I'll be shown in a very attractive light."

"Well, I hadn't planned to write that kind of book…" Darcy's voice trailed off. All she could think of was spending the night in another motel or moving onto another city. She already had her diners and cafés chosen. All she wanted was a nap and some time out of the car.

"This is so careless of me," Marjorie continued.

Darcy's irritation faded at the sight of the woman's obvious dismay.

"I am so sorry. There are a few other hotels in town and a smaller bed-and-breakfast, but I know everyone is booked. We usually fill up at least a month ahead on these big weekends. I don't know why I didn't tell you that when you called." Her finger slid down the page and came to a stop. "Oh, my, here you are. You said you called on the twelfth. Well, I must have had my head screwed on wrong that day. I have you written down for arriving on the twelfth of next month. Oh, I can't believe I made such a mistake. I am so sorry."

The last thing Darcy wanted to do was look for lodging in a town totally booked for the weekend, but there was no need to make Mrs. Reed feel worse than she already did. "Don't apologize. I can see how that could happen." She reached down and hefted her tote bag off the floor. "You doubt there's anywhere else in town to stay?" She would cry if only Mrs. Reed didn't look so pitiful.

"Not this weekend, I'm afraid. If there was anything I could do, I would. I feel terrible. I haven't made this big of a mistake for as long as I've been doing this. John will never let me live it down. I am usually very professional."

She was rambling, and Darcy found herself feeling even sorrier for the older woman than herself, even though Mrs. Reed had a bed to sleep in tonight while she did not.

"How far is the next town where I might find a room?" she asked, cutting off the woman's lament.

"Well, Talmedge is about ten miles east on Highway 16. They have a lot of overflow from the university, but you should be able to find a room there." She turned back to her register. "Tell you what, since you're going to be in the area researching your book awhile, you come back here at the first of the week, and I'll give you two nights stay free. I feel absolutely horrible for getting your reservation mixed up. But I have eight sets of parents and grandparents due to arrive this evening after the welcoming festivities on campus besides the four occupied rooms I already have." She pulled open a narrow drawer on the table and took out a phone book. "Let me make a phone call real quick."

She was already turning pages. Darcy slid her tote back to the floor. She really wanted to sit down, or fall down. She glanced at the overstuffed sofa and dreamed of sinking into the cushions and grabbing a quick snooze.

Marjorie gave her a heartening smile and started punching numbers. After a pause, she spoke; "Leanne, is that you, honey? This is Marjorie Reed at the Danbury Inn. Yes, dear, how are you? Well, I seem to have made a terrible error over here. I have a young woman who looks like she's about dead on her feet. I booked her for the weekend, but got my weekends mixed up, and I don't have anywhere to put her. Is there any possibility...Yes, I know, Parents' Weekend and all. I'm booked solid. Oh, thank goodness. Well, I'll send her right over. Thank you so much, Leanne. As always, you're an answer to prayer."

Marjorie replaced the phone and turned back to Darcy. "The Ravenswood Inn is the nicest one in the area. Next to the Danbury of course," she added with a chuckle. "It's owned by Vince and Leanne Ravenscraft, been in their family for years. A lovely bed-and-breakfast, though quite small. Only four guestrooms and all but one are reserved for the weekend. Leanne is a darling. She'll make sure you're very comfortable. And don't forget, I owe you two nights at the first of the week." She wrote out the directions on a sheet of vellum letterhead and handed it to Darcy. She was still apologizing as she walked Darcy to the door.

Darcy stuffed the sheet of paper into her tote and trudged back to her stale smelling SUV. She thought of finding a carwash but decided it was nothing that wouldn't wait until tomorrow. "So long, Danbury," she said aloud as she backed out of the driveway. She was disappointed that she wouldn't be staying tonight. She could only imagine the Ravenswood would be a grim disappointment compared to this place. Then again she doubted Mrs. Reed would send her somewhere substandard, especially since she was concerned with what Darcy might write about the Danbury Inn in her book.

She scanned the road signs for Highway 16, and then reached back into her bag for the directions to the Ravenswood Inn. She had already forgotten nearly everything Mrs. Reed had said. She put the paper on her thigh and smoothed out the wrinkles with one hand. Her adventure had begun. She was a firm believer that most things happened for a reason. Mrs. Reed claimed she never made mistakes on reservations, especially on big college weekends. Was the reservation mix up part of some big plan she couldn't see at this point in time? Was it more than a coincidence that she had chosen to begin writing her new book on Parents' weekend when every hotel in the area would be booked, thus forcing her to the Ravenswood Inn? The only time she went to church these days was when her mother shamed her into it. Maybe God was testing her. He wanted to see how determined she was to write this last book. Maybe this was His way of telling her to pack it in, her writing career was over, or maybe Mrs. Reed was a serial killer like those old ladies in Arsenic and Old Lace, and He was simply getting her out of harm's way.

She found Highway 16 and stopped listening to her inventive imagination. Surely Mr. and Mrs. Ravensbrook, or whatever the name, were as friendly as Mrs. Reed, and their inn as comfortable as the Danbury, if not as beautiful. The inconvenience had earned her something. She had two free nights at the lovely Danbury Inn coming to her at the first of the week. Everything was always better when it was free.

Leanne Ravenscraft hung up the phone and turned to face the sun porch she had been sweeping when Marjorie Reed called. She could always count on Marjorie for at least one referral during big weekends at the university. The Ravenswood Inn wasn't as conveniently located to the campus as the hotels in Winchester or the Danbury Inn. They always filled up first, the hotels because of price and location, and the Danbury because it was the most coveted place in the area to rest one's head.

The hotel and inn owners in the area looked out for each other and were always willing to refer people to the next bed-

and-breakfast once they filled their own rooms. Marjorie knew intuitively which overflow guests to send to Leanne and which ones to refer to one of the many area hotels. Her utmost concern was for the comfort of the guests, but she could also be trusted to never send Leanne a potentially troublesome guest.

Leanne set one hand on her hip, clutched the broom with the other, and surveyed the sun porch she had just finished cleaning. Neat and tidy, just the way she liked it. In fact it was how she liked everything in her life. Orderly, secure. She stuck a finger into the dirt around a potted ivy and pulled it back satisfied the plant had enough moisture for another day. She brushed the dirt off her finger onto her pant leg and gave the room a final once over to make sure she hadn't missed anything. Plant leaves free of dust and spider webs, rugs straight, sofa cushions properly fluffed, magazine rack straightened and up to date. Yes, just the way she liked things.

Vince had enclosed the porch three summers ago when she convinced him that converting the family home into a bed-and-breakfast was a worthy endeavor. He had balked when she first mentioned it like she knew he would. He always resisted when something new and potentially risky crossed his path. It took some patience and ingenuity to persuade him. She couldn't rush him or bully him. That never worked with Vince; it only made him dig his heels in that much deeper. He was a slow mover. It wasn't that he was lazy or un-ambitious, just cautious. So cautious that sometimes she wanted to smack him upside his head. But he seldom made mistakes, especially when money was involved.

What once had been a simple back porch was now enclosed by glass on three sides and half of the ceiling. The porch jutted out sixteen feet from the back of the house, offering a year round view of the pristine hills surrounding the inn. A door on each end of the porch opened onto expansive decks. One of the decks pointed in the direction of a creek that gurgled behind the house where a visitor could find two well-laid trails leading to a beautiful waterfall. One trail was wheelchair accessible and better suited for those not desirous of a strenuous climb. The other trail wound up, around, and through the woods and hills, while bringing the more advanced hiker to the same state owned waterfall. Leanne preferred the more difficult trail, making the two-hour round trip every day if time allowed.

The other deck led guests around the side of the house to a narrow secluded porch. It was a popular spot for relaxing in rocking chairs, reading, filling out postcards, listening to nature, or watching the quiet country lane leading up to the Inn, unobserved. The wisteria and hydrangea bushes had grown up around it, providing an adequate hedge for privacy and shade, making the porch practically invisible from the front of the house if you didn't know where to look. Every fall when it was time for pruning, Vince threatened to cut the bushes to the ground.

"You can't even see out the windows on this side of the house," he'd grumble, totally exaggerating the situation.

"The day you cut Mother's bushes down will be your last," Leanne would warn him. "The world's a small place, and I will hunt you down and punish you severely."

The hydrangea and wisteria bushes weren't the only things that reminded Leanne of her mother. The porch opened off of Mother's old sewing room. Even now, every time Leanne walked through the sewing room to get to the porch, she could feel Olivia's presence. She could even smell the fabrics and sewing machine oil and her mother's rose milk hand lotion she used to keep the material from drying out her fingers.

Leanne used to sneak out onto the side porch anytime she wanted to be alone when she was a kid. She would sit on one of the family's old white metal lounge chairs that were anything but comfortable, pull her knees up into the chair, and rest her chin on her knees. She'd look out over the property and wish she were anywhere but here.

In those days the university was a small college with no sports program or Parents' or Sibs' Days. Tourism wasn't the cash cow it was now, and no one was interested in the waterfall behind the house. No one but family drove down the lane at the end of Elm Street, and there wasn't much of them left these days. If not for the school bus that rescued her from eight until three five days a week, Leanne was sure she would never see anything other than the Blue

Ridge Mountains fencing her in, and the same three faces staring back at her from across the supper table.

"I'll die in this house," she'd lament to the overweight cat usually napping in the other chair. She would pick him up and hold him close to her face. "Oh, Pumpkin, can you imagine anything more depressing than this town? There's nothing here for us—no future, no jobs. Let's get out of this old house before it drains the life right out of us."

Leanne smiled at the memory of those words. Funny, her words to the cat had proven prophetic to a degree. She had never left, never lived under another roof, never attended classes at the college just ten miles from her home. Nothing in her life had changed except her attitude toward it. She no longer hated the house, resented the hills or her heritage, and for everything her life had become, boring was not a word she would use to describe it.

She knew the exact moment everything changed. The summer she turned seventeen, her parents came home from the city with the announcement that Daddy had cancer. There was an operation and a few months later, another one. The doctors were optimistic and so was Daddy. "We're lucky this time, Annie," he said, pulling Leanne into his once steely embrace. "It'll take a little more than cancer to get the better of me."

Leanne didn't miss the fear and anxiety on her mother's face.

He gained some of his weight back. By Christmas, he was looking like his old self. Then at the first of the year—Leanne's senior year in high school—the cancer came back. There was little optimism this time. Daddy got really bad really fast. He started talking about going home. He and Mother made "arrangements." The pastor of their church became a frequent visitor to the house. That spring was spent running to and from the hospital. In those days there was little to be done for terminal patients. No oncology centers, no talk of research and procedures that could make a difference.

Leanne often thought the whole ordeal was harder on Mother than Daddy. Daddy knew what his future held. He knew where he was headed. Mother was terrified. She had never been without

Daddy to take care of things. She didn't know where he kept the family's important papers and couldn't make sense of an insurance policy if she had to. But she learned. She slept on a cot next to the hospital bed they set up in the old sewing room. She argued with insurance agencies and hospitals. She made appointments and fielded phone calls from bill collectors. All the while, the terror and anxiety never left her face—except when she was talking to Daddy.

He died on Good Friday. The significance broke the family's heart.

Leanne had given up any notion of college as soon as he was diagnosed. Daddy's illness had taken too much out of her mother for her to think about her own future. Besides the emotional toll, the family needed to make ends meet. Daddy's pension and insurance settlement took care of most of the big expenses, but there was still day-to-day living, and Mother was a wreck. She never recovered from losing Daddy.

Leanne realized she had been a selfish young woman when she sat out on the porch and complained to the cat. She had to grow up. Mother needed to be taken care of, and she'd be the one to do it. Her social life dwindled away to nothing, and if it hadn't been for Vince, she would have become a total recluse. Upon graduating from high school, she got a job answering phones for a man in town who sold tires. As his business grew, so did her duties. About the same time her boss relocated to a new building in Winchester, Leanne realized Olivia's increasing needs would keep her from working full time. At least there was Vince, who was willing and able to provide for them financially.

She quit answering phones and keeping records for the tire seller and stayed home to take care of her mother. Vince went to work with Hank Haywood every day; roofing, hanging drywall, and whatever other jobs they could find, the whole time, keeping his own dreams safely tucked inside his head. Dreams neither Mother nor Leanne knew anything about.

Their lives in the big house at the end of the lane went on pretty much the same for another ten years. When Olivia caught pneumonia one winter, she had no desire to fight it. She died a relatively young woman at fifty-six.

Leanne found herself barely in her thirties with nothing to do. Besides selling tires for a few years and taking care of her parents her entire adult life, she lacked the necessary skills to enter the working world. Her friends from church suggested she go to nursing school. She politely told them nursing wasn't for her. She had taken care of her parents out of obligation, not because she was particularly good at it. Vince set her up on the Internet, and she started researching jobs she might find interesting. She soon realized all she was doing was answering email and playing Solitaire. So while waiting for her dream job to be revealed to her, she drove into Winchester and got a job answering phones for the county's Community Action Organization. If nothing else, she was good at that.

That was four and a half years ago. She enjoyed her job at Community Action. She met more people than she ever would have sitting at home, and she felt like what she was doing had a positive effect on the people around her. But she wasn't particularly fulfilled. Then the dream of converting the old family house into an inn took hold in her head.

She checked out every book on the subject from the county library and then requested more books from other libraries. She took personality profiles, investigated the costs of adding bathrooms, and searched the Sears and J.C. Penney ads in the Sunday paper for white sales.

All the while she secretly dreamed of opening her own bed-and-breakfast, Vince was doing some research of his own. When he told her he was going to buy the old abandoned café on Main Street in Talmedge, she thought he was kidding. She actually laughed and then stopped short when she saw the hurt on his face.

A café, what in the world did either of them know about running a café? Apparently plenty, or at least Vince did. The whole time he had been sub-contracting work with Hank, he had been coming home to research cafés and diners on the Internet. By the time he brought it up to Leanne or anyone else, he knew exactly what he was doing. That's how Vince did everything—slow and deliberate. If he said he was going to buy the old café, renovate it, add a few more tables, and open up at six a.m. to cook eggs, grits, and sausage gravy for everyone in the county, you could rest assured he had a well-laid plan to make it happen.

So when Leanne finally admitted her desire to convert the house into a bed-and-breakfast and showed him her own research for making it happen, her feelings were hurt that he was less than enthusiastic.

"We've got the café," he said. "If you're tired of working at Community Action, I can give you all the work you'll ever need."

"But the café's your dream, Vince. This one's mine. We'll be co-owners of course, since you own part of the house, and I'll need you to do a lot of the renovations for me. I can't afford to hire out everything I need done. We need a back deck on the house with a direct route to the walking trails. I'm thinking of enclosing the back porch so guests can have a way to get outside all year round. We can convert all of the bedrooms upstairs. That'll make four guestrooms. I know I can handle that many in the beginning. They really don't need that much work. Just some wallpaper and a few period pieces. I can find nearly everything I need at estate sales and auctions. The biggest challenge will be adding two bathrooms upstairs. There's no way that little one we've got now will be approved by the state…"

At this point, Vince had thrown up his hands in horror. "Whoa, whoa, whoa! There's no way we can do all this. You're talking major renovations. All I did to the café was buy a new oven and hang up some curtains. This is major, Leanne, and expensive. Have you thought about what all this is going to cost? I'll tell you how much. More than we're gonna have in a million years."

She let his arguments go in one ear and out the other. Her plans were out there, and Vince was talking about them. That meant he was thinking. When Vince wasn't talking was when the battle was lost and the case closed. At that point she let herself get excited. Her bed-and-breakfast was going to be a reality. It would take hard work on her part and patience with Vince. For all his grumbling and pessimistic predictions, he would help out when she needed him. She loved him. He was wonderful and supportive, albeit more hard headed than any person had a right to be. But he was all the family she had left.

According to Marjorie, the young woman on her way over from the Danbury would arrive in about fifteen minutes if she didn't get waylaid by a mountain vista or antique shop along the way, as was often the case. Leanne allowed whichever guests arrived first to choose their rooms from the ones that had not been spoken for. Latecomers got what was left. All her rooms were beautiful so she never worried that a guest would be stuck with substandard accommodations. Minnie's Room, which faced east, had already been requested by the Hudsons, a returning couple who loved to rise early in the morning and watch the dawn paint the side of the Inn a soft pink. The other three rooms were up for grabs.

Leanne was excited that, thanks to Marjorie, all her rooms were booked for the weekend. She seldom had an empty room on college weekends. That's the way she liked it. Breakfast was always a more spirited affair when the table was full of people from all over the country getting to know each other, even if she was wore to a frazzle by the time the table was cleared.

She made her way through the house, her trained eye perusing the furnishings for anything out of place, anything that might make a guest uncomfortable or enjoy their visit a fraction less. Preparing for guests was her favorite part about being an innkeeper. She loved receiving guests and making them feel like company instead of a source of income. She entered her mother's old sewing room and opened the door leading onto the side porch. A cool breeze rustled the gauze curtains. Anytime weather permitted, she left the door open when guests were arriving. They seemed to enjoy the unencumbered view of the outdoors through an authentic wooden screen door, she supposed because there were so few of them left. Her grandmother's old cabinet-style treadle sewing machine had been cleaned up and brought down from the attic to replace the Kenmore Mother used while Leanne was growing up. The bookcase had been cleared of the "made in China" bric-a-brac along with the circa 1970's dress patterns Olivia could never bring herself to throw away and replaced with her father's old hard back book collection, some of her own porcelain dolls, and a few period pieces to go with the overall theme of the house.

The curtains had been replaced, the Queen Anne sofa

reupholstered, and the carpet ripped up to reveal the long forgotten wood planks underneath. With a few rag rugs and large area rug, several strategically placed lamps, and ample flat surfaces for writing home or checking email, the room had been transformed into a comfortable retreat where the traveling businessman or harried family could retire in the cool of the evening.

Leanne continued her inspection through the remainder of the inn's first floor. Few rooms were off limits down here, only hers and Vince's private living quarters at the back of the house, and even those were kept shipshape in case a guest opened a wrong door. She cringed at the thought of someone finding mismatched towels, a crumpled piece of clothing on the floor, or a forgotten dirty dish in a windowsill. Yes, this was their home, but also her business.

She had already cracked all the guest rooms' windows so the fresh scent of pine would be the first thing each guest experienced. She could imagine the breeze ruffling the curtains upstairs, the sun dappling the hand stitched bedspreads she'd found in Olivia's trunks in the attic. She could already hear Sandy Hudson's squeals of delight and Dwayne's exhalation of relief that he'd survived the rush hour traffic from Raleigh. The Hudsons owned a window replacement company with offices throughout the tri-state area. Even though Dwayne threatened to retire every year and turn the reins over to his children and grandchildren, Sandy and Leanne knew he'd be an integral part of the company until they laid him in the ground. For the past two years though, their trips to the Ravenswood Inn had increased to six or seven weekends a year, especially now that both a nephew and a grandson were attending the University.

Leanne entered the room they would occupy and straightened the eyelet coverlet over the back of the rocking chair. Minnie's Room, named after Leanne's maternal grandmother who passed away while Leanne was in her teens, was generously decorated in shocking white lace. Not only did the décor remind Leanne of the room's namesake, it took full advantage of the four tall windows that sprinkled the room with sunlight. She took a pen out of the drawer of the marble-topped dresser and laid it atop a clean steno pad. Dwayne was never "not working", even though he no longer brought his laptop on their weekend getaways, per Sandy's insistence. He still liked to take notes when ideas crossed his mind and jot down reminders of what he needed to tell to whom as soon as he got back to the office on Monday.

Satisfied the room would meet with their satisfaction, Leanne crossed the hall to George's Room. George, her mother's father, had died when she was ten. She didn't remember much about him, save the smell of pipe tobacco and a deep, booming laugh that seemed to shake the rafters above her head. She remembered climbing into his lap and listening to him tell stories of when he was a boy. George was the youngest of six children, and if his stories were any indication, the orneriest of the bunch. Upon deciding to convert the house into a bed-and-breakfast, George's Room, in honor of her grandfather, was the first one she designed in her head. Now, except for the absence of the lingering scent of pipe tobacco, the large room made Leanne think he had just stepped out and would be back any minute. Two high backed rocking chairs faced the wide window that overlooked the shaded back yard and pine-covered hills in the distance. An old pipe she found among Grandma Minnie's things laid on the marble topped lamp stand situated between the two rockers even though the Inn was nonsmoking. The largest of the guest rooms, it contained two scroll sided, double beds with plenty of room left over for a rollaway bed to be brought out of the closet should the guests have need of it. A tall cherry armoire accented the high ceilings, and local handcrafts and calico curtains on the windows completed the room. Whether the room actually reminded her of Grandpa George or an illusion of him in her mind, Leanne was no longer sure. Time and nostalgia had blurred the lines of her childhood memories and reality. It didn't matter. She loved the peaceful, sweet feeling she got every time she entered George's Room.

She doubted the woman on her way from the Danbury would desire such a large room. Marjorie hadn't mentioned any traveling companions. She would probably feel more comfortable in one of the two remaining rooms. Olivia's Room, named for her mother, was usually the ladies' choice with its huge four-poster bed and

Dutch eyelet-lace canopy. Men always preferred the spaciousness of George's Room or Russell's Room, named for her father, which had the feel of an exclusive gentlemen's club with its bold red and paisley wall coverings, brass bed, and green leather wing chair.

Leaving the door to George's Room open, Leanne headed down the hall past one of the two shared bathrooms Vince installed once she convinced him she was opening a bed-and-breakfast with or without his blessing. For a brief moment, she wondered what this young woman Marjorie had sent her way was doing here in the middle of nowhere all alone. Was she applying for a position at the university? Was she some kind of inspector or computer programmer needed for a short time? There were always people of that sort flitting in and out of the area. She wondered what it would be like to have a job that took her all over the country, meeting new people, seeing new places, living out of suitcases. It might be interesting for a while, but she didn't have much of an urge to see anything new anymore. She was thirty-six years old and pretty much relegated to the state of her life.

Years ago, she wanted to leave here, wanted to see the world, but that chapter of her life was closed. Things hadn't worked out the way she thought she wanted at the time, and now she had no regrets. This was her life; she was content with it, like the Apostle Paul advised her to be.

Occasionally she let herself think of what her life would have been had she gotten away from the mountains. If things had been different, maybe she would have children by now. She was only too aware of her biological clock ticking away. Before long it would start winding down. She didn't watch the calendar or dread each birthday, but she knew she had enough love in her heart for a child. Still, women all around the world went to their graves without feeling a baby of their own at their breast, and they were satisfied and fulfilled and found a way to contribute to the world. Babies obviously weren't meant to be a part of her life. She had accepted that long ago, too.

She trusted that God had fashioned her life to suit His purpose, and she was willing to live accordingly. Some friends at church were privy to her thoughts on such matters and lifted her up in prayer that she would know peace in her situation. God was gracious and kind and He would give her the strength and wisdom to face whatever situation He saw fit to place her in.

She opened the door of Olivia's Room, certain it would be the one the young woman chose. She fluffed the pillows and straightened the cloth-bodied, bisque doll that nestled against the headboard. She had no regrets that this was all her life would ever be, preparing for other people who sought time away from their daily grind. This was her daily grind, and she wouldn't trade it with anyone.

𝒜𝓈 𝐿𝑒𝑎𝑛𝑛𝑒 𝓈𝓊𝓈𝓅𝑒𝒸𝓉𝑒𝒹, Darcy didn't make the ten-mile drive from the Danbury Inn to the Ravenswood in the tiny dot on the map known as Talmedge without making a stop. Trees just beginning to bud grew up against the highway on either side. She drove slowly, her gaze traveling up every lane, gravel road, and towpath she passed. She let the driver's side window down a little and breathed in the crisp, mountain air. Getting off the Interstate and onto the small secondary highway with hardly any other traffic had served to refresh her almost as much as a shower and break from the confines of her vehicle would have.

She almost missed the Talmedge city limits sign half hidden among the trees. She looked to either side and saw nothing resembling a town. She was beginning to imagine a rundown ramshackle inn like those in scary movies in some backwater town where all the inhabitants looked like the walking dead—the kind of place where conversation came to an abrupt halt every time an outsider entered the general store. She could see them now, staring at her, unflinching, uncomprehending as she tried to explain how she'd witnessed two good old boys burying what looked like a body bag containing a family of four behind the high school.

Then her SUV topped the next rise. The highway narrowed and the trees took a demure step back to give way to yards, split rail fences, sidewalks, and houses.

Whew! No walking dead. No body bags. She had to stop ordering movies off pay-per-view.

As she drove farther into what she imagined they still referred to as a village in this part of the country, the houses grew larger and closer together. Apparently even tiny dots on a North Carolina roadmap had suburbs.

A quick-stop gas station and a tastefully discreet sign for a local funeral home pointing down a side street alerted Darcy that she had reached the town's business district. Beyond the quick-stop were several closed down storefronts. Across the front of several of the old buildings were the faded, but still legible business names; Miller's Mercantile, Kennedy Farm Supplies-Since 1925, Talmedge Water Works. Painted on the windows of a few of the buildings were the business names of current occupants who had updated their services to appeal to the residents of the small community. Inside the Mercantile building that now housed Tricia's Tangles, Darcy saw a stylist, presumably Tricia, chatting amiably with her only customer as she circled the raised chair with a pair of long-nosed scissors. The old Water Works office advertised homemade pizza and subs. A video rental store, whose sign had misspelled one of Hollywood's latest blockbusters, occupied a building whose former use was unapparent to Darcy. An Ace Hardware and a tiny shop boasting the grand title of Arts and Crafts Mall occupied the buildings on either side of Ermaline's General Store across the street. Posters advertising weekly specials, national brand ads, and the latest lottery jackpot made it impossible to see inside Ermaline's. A post office and what used to be a traditional filling station with a sliding, eight-panel glass door and concrete pad that once contained gas tanks before the EPA swept through the countryside removing all the tanks that didn't meet new environmental codes made up the end of the town. The Marathon emblem had been removed from the sign by the road, but you could still make out the faded letters on the side of the building. The glass doors were open, revealing a foreign sedan sitting on the risers. The artful scrollwork lettering across the glass doors that read, *Chuck's Body Shop and Auto Repair,* stood out in contrast to the paint chipped, block building and broken pavement.

What remained of an old feed mill, including a dismantled grain elevator and bin that pointed to nowhere, was located on the other side of the street. Next to it and the other city limit sign, was a café. If not for the full parking lot and surprisingly legible hand lettering on the window that read, *The Raven Café*, Darcy never would have suspected the old dilapidated building served anything one might want to eat.

Darcy looked down at the clock on the dashboard, 12:20. Her stomach rumbled at the thought of lunch. Yesterday's overindulgence and this morning's coffee and toast had worn off. She eyed the café, not entirely sure of what to do. Under any other circumstances she wouldn't dream of going inside the rundown cement block building with the intention of procuring a meal, but the number of cars and pickup trucks equipped with gun racks and tow winches parked fender to fender in the parking lot assured her this place must have something going for it besides the ambience. She reminded herself this type of establishment was precisely what she'd driven five hundred miles to find.

She flipped on her turn signal and came to a stop in the middle of the street to wait for an approaching vehicle to pass. At the last second, the other car whipped into the parking lot without signaling and parked in the last available spot. Darcy growled under her breath as she turned the SUV into the gravel lot. She squeezed into a spot between the end of the building and the grain elevator. Surely no one would object to her parking illegally. It didn't look like anyone would be having their corn ground anytime soon, and she doubted this town had cops who would issue her a ticket if she had indeed parked illegally.

She climbed out of the car and headed toward The Raven Café. Suddenly the significance of the name dawned on her, another reference to a raven. The Inn where she would be spending the night was also named after the ominous bird. Just a tad bit strange that two businesses in the same tiny town had the same bird in their names. She thought of the walking dead and the family buried behind the high school. Was it possible she had landed in the middle of a bad Twilight Zone episode?

Consider if you will, Darcy Carter, a young woman discontented with life. She heads south to research her latest book, a book she doesn't even want to write. The picturesque, mountainside hamlet of Talmedge, North Carolina seems the perfect backdrop for her book…or is it? Everywhere she turns she sees references to the mysterious black birds famed by Edgar Allen Poe. Darcy finds no churches, no upstanding citizens, no one who even speaks her language. What Darcy doesn't know is all the people of Talmedge are reincarnations of the infamous poet, bent on re-enacting Mr. Poe's work. How can she find peace within the boundaries of Talmedge when she has taken a wrong turn into…The Twilight Zone?

Darcy glanced over her shoulder half expecting Rod Serling himself to step out from behind the feed mill.

Her sister-in-law was right. She had missed her calling when she decided to spend the last ten years writing Ultimate Guides. She could have been another Ray Bradbury.

She shrugged and opened the door of the restaurant. A bell tinkled over her head. The conversation in the small building came to an immediate halt for a half breath as everyone looked up to see who had entered. Inside Darcy's head, she heard the distinct sound of the Twilight Zone's theme. Satisfied that she was just another harmless diner, the noise and clatter of a busy café during lunch rush resumed in an instant.

No hostess was on duty, or if she was, she couldn't fit in the tight quarters between the front door, cash register, the first of six booths, and the stools that lined the gleaming counter. Darcy wasted no time in claiming the last empty booth in the rear corner of the room. She sat down facing into the restaurant and congratulated herself on finding the perfect spot in which to spy on the hungry patrons of the Raven Café. From where she sat, she also had a bird's eye view of the swinging double doors that led into the kitchen and a narrow hallway with two signs above the door. The first was a red, lighted EXIT sign and below it, one that read Restrooms. She plucked the menu from its position between the napkin holder and the windowsill. She hoped the two signs did not indicate the same door, thus forcing patrons to use the alley between the café and the feed and grain whenever nature called.

She scanned the menu, looking for the most authentic

sounding item to order. All the usual fare one would expect to find on a café menu in the South was listed. Red beans and rice, grits, pecan pie, fried chicken, beef and noodles, chicken and dumplings, cornbread.

Her stomach rumbled again. She could almost feel the waistband of her jeans tightening.

With her head still bent over the menu, an eerie, prickly sensation telling her she was being watched raised the hair on the back of her neck. She looked up from her menu and saw two elderly men in faded bib overalls standing over her. Gray hair stuck out from under their John Deere caps in wild disarray. Their faces and hands bore the scars of years of labor under an unrelenting sun. Surely they weren't here to take her order.

"Hello," she said uncertainly as they continued to stare down at her.

The one on the right crossed his arms over his chest. Not taking his eyes off her, he said to his companion, "Lookie 'ere, Jim, that tourist from up north with that fancy little rice burner outside's done got our table."

The man Darcy presumed was Jim nodded, "Yup."

Darcy wasn't sure what to do. It was true she had taken the last empty table in the place, but no one told her it was reserved for anyone else. She was about to apologize and get up, when the first man cracked a smile.

"I guess ya don't mind ta share, do ya, little lady, seein's how ya got this whole big table all to yerself."

"Um, well, sure." Darcy dropped the menu on the table and made a sweeping gesture to the opposite side of the booth. It did seem unreasonable that she take an entire booth when there were other people waiting to be seated, especially since they claimed this was their usual table. "Be my guest."

The two men were already sliding in across from her as if their request had only been a formality.

"I'm R.T. Cavanaugh," the spokesman of the two said. "And this here's my brother, Jim. We been comin' here fer lunch every weekday since Alberta said she warn't cooking us lunch no more. What's that been, Jim, three years now?"

Jim wasn't answering. It was just as well since R.T. didn't give him time to speak before continuing. "We usually git here afore noon, and ever'body 'round these parts knows this here's our table." He smacked the table top for emphasis. "We knowed we might be outta luck t'day since we was late, but since it ain't tourist season, we was a hopin' nobody'd be sittin' here. Then when we seen that little vehicle a ye'rs out front, well, I turned ta Jim and I said, 'Uh, oh, Jim, I bet somebody done got our table.' Didn't I, Jim?"

Jim was staring straight at Darcy, his big hands folded on top of the table. He made no effort to speak.

Darcy cleared her throat. "I didn't realize this was anyone's table. When I came in it was the only empty place, and there was no hostess to show me where I should sit."

R.T. barked out a one-syllable laugh. Jim actually grinned. "Hostess," R.T. chortled. "Ain't no hostess in this whole county. Leastways, if there was, the old man wouldn't see no need a hirin' one." He jerked his thumb over his shoulder toward the kitchen door without turning around. Darcy assumed he was referring to the owner of the café. "Ever'body jest sits wherever they please— 'cept here. This here booth is mine and Jim's. Ain't that right, Jim?"

Darcy opened her mouth to apologize again, but this time it was Jim who interrupted her. "T'was our fault for bein' late. Ain't no need for ya ta concern yerself." He clasped his hands in front of him again and sealed up his mouth.

R.T. nodded solemnly. "Yup, Jim here's right. Durin' tourist season, we often share our table with 'em what don't know better'n ta sit here. In fact, we kinda purfer it." He leaned in toward Darcy and lowered his voice. "Truth be told, gits a mite dull in here, talkin' ta the same ole folks year round. Ain't that right, Jim? We don't never leave this holler so it's mighty convenient when folks like you come ta us."

Darcy was beginning to enjoy the fact that she'd sat down in Jim and R.T.'s booth. Not only was she starving by this point and anxious to get some research done before moving on to the Ravenswood Inn, these two characters were proving to be quite entertaining in their own right.

A harried waitress approached their table. "Afternoon, fellas, what kept you? Look's like you lost your table." She smiled warmly at Darcy, her round face erupting into a map of wrinkles. Darcy liked her immediately. Her name badge read June. Her graying hair was pulled into a neat bun on the back of her head. She stood a little over five feet tall, but managed to look like she was in charge of the place.

"Afternoon, June," R.T. said. "We was late t'day on account a Bertha went ta calvin' early this mornin'. Had a rough time of it, but we finally got everything taken care of though. I thought there a time er two, we was gonna have ta call Doc Sharpe. But she did fine, delivered her a fine little heifer."

From the concern and interest on the waitress's face, Darcy assumed a calf's birth was acceptable dinner conversation in Talmedge.

"That's good to hear." June sounded genuinely relieved that calf and mother were doing well. "This calls for a celebration. Coffee and pecan pie all around."

R.T.'s eye's widened. He put his finger to his lips and made a shushing noise. "Don't be lettin' the old man know yer're givin' away his food. He'll have yer head on the choppin' block."

June swatted at him before pulling a pad and pencil from the pocket of her apron. "I ain't afraid of that old bear. Don't ya know his growl is worse than his bite? Now, before the coffee and pie, which I'm beholden to tell you right away," she directed her comment to Darcy, "is the best in these parts, you'll probably be wantin' your lunch."

Darcy nodded and smiled hungrily.

"Well, I worked up a mighty big appetite this mornin'…" R.T. began.

June smacked the back of his hand with her pencil, "Ladies first."

"Oh, yeah, sorry there, little lady, fergot ya was even sittin' there. You go on ahead."

Darcy eyed her menu. "Everything looks good. What do you recommend?"

She immediately received two different recommendations from June and R.T. She listened and then turned to Jim who was watching the exchange with polite detachment. "I'm mighty partial ta the catfish platter myself," he said without pause. "Take the coleslaw instead a the salad. It's the old man's specialty."

She turned to June. "I'll have the catfish with the slaw, and water with lemon."

"That sounds good," R.T. said. "Make it catfish all 'round. Only gimme an iced tea."

Darcy couldn't imagine drinking iced tea this time of year, but apparently his request was not out of the ordinary. Jim nodded his agreement over the tea, and June disappeared behind the counter five paces away.

"Ya won't be sorry 'bout the coleslaw," R.T. assured Darcy. "Ain't nobody can whip up a kettle a slaw like the old man."

Jim nodded solemnly in agreement.

"I am so glad I sat at your table," Darcy said sincerely. "My name is Darcy Carter." She reached across the table and shook both men's hands. "I'm a writer. I'm from northern Ohio, and I came to North Carolina to work on a new book."

Jim snapped his fingers and pointed at her. "That's where I know ya from. It's been wearin' on me ever since we sat down. You're the Ultimate Guide Girl."

Darcy's jaw dropped.

Jim placed his hands palms side down on the table and leaned back. "I jus' finished The Ultimate Guide to Online Trading. Saw yer picture on the back cover, fine work. I been doin' some investin' fer 'bout twenty years. Been interested in online tradin' for some spell now."

"Thank you, Jim," she said after recovering from the unexpected compliment. She had a hard time picturing someone like Jim who spent his mornings delivering calves and tooling around the countryside with his brother, reading her guide to online trading. "That means a lot to me. Online Trading was one of the more difficult topics I've covered in my books."

"I could tell," he replied frankly. "But yer writin' style's improved from yer earlier work."

Darcy tried to mask the surprise on her face. Jim looked even less like a typical book critic than he did an online trader.

"Jim here reads a lot," R.T. offered by way of apology. "Been doin' it ever since we was kids. Pop was always hollerin' at him ta knock it off. Said he'd never 'mount ta nothin', wastin' all his time on 'em books. Ma said ta leave him be, he'd quit on his own someday." R.T. shook his head dismally. "But he never did."

Darcy smiled at the image of Jim and R.T. as boys; Jim quiet and studious, with R.T. badgering him to come outside and torture frogs or some other wildlife. She wondered about the Alberta they mentioned who refused to cook lunch. Was she the wife of one of them, a sister, or a housekeeper? She was afraid to ask.

"What kinda book ya workin' on down here?" R.T. asked. "Jim really liked that'un ya wrote 'bout changin' careers. Was a waste a time readin' it though, I told him, seein's how him changin' careers is 'bout as likely as me winnin' a beauty contest."

Darcy smiled at Jim. "I'm glad you liked it. It was one of my earlier books."

Jim nodded gravely. "Yup, I could tell."

Again, Darcy didn't know if she should be insulted, or relieved that readers could see how her writing had improved over the years. She chose the latter.

She turned to R.T. "I'm here researching an idea I have about diners and cafés. Something like, The Ultimate Guide to Dining on America's Back Roads."

He sniffed. "Don't see why anybody'd wanna read a book like that. Only folks eat in these here places is folks like us who ain't got no other choice."

Darcy chuckled. Maybe he had a point. "I'm sure that's why some people eat here, but I like to think there's more to it than that." She motioned at the crowded restaurant over R.T. and Jim's shoulders. "You said yourself you often have to share your table with tourists. Why do you think that is?"

The two men turned in their seat to look behind them as if realizing for the first time they weren't the café's only patrons. When they turned to look back at her, Darcy continued, "There has to be a reason why some cafés succeed and last for generations while others fail. Is it the food, the management, location?"

Before either of them could further ponder her point, June

appeared with a tray of plates and glasses perched on one shoulder. She expertly deposited each item onto the table in front of them. "These two old geezers ain't giving you a bad impression of our neck of the woods, are they?" she asked Darcy as she worked.

"Oh, no, they're making me feel right at home."

"That's good. Well, you just let me know when ya'll are ready for that pie."

They assured her they would as they savored the sight and smell of the catfish platters. Darcy doubted she would have enough room left over for pie and coffee after only sampling everything on her plate. The menu had listed the price of the platter at $6.95. She would never get this much food at home for anywhere close to ten dollars.

While enjoying the food, which Darcy had to force herself to sample sparingly not only to save room for dessert but to avoid gaining twenty pounds in one meal, R.T. talked nearly nonstop and she and Jim listened. Darcy nodded and chewed and took notes in her notebook about the food and café's atmosphere. By the time they finished eating, the crowd had thinned out. As some of the diners were leaving, R.T. called them over to meet Darcy. She answered as many questions as she could while savoring the best catfish dinner she'd ever had. She thanked Jim more than once for his recommendation.

"What about the man who owns the café?" she asked after allowing herself only three bites of the delectable pecan pie. She hoped June would come soon and clear the table, thus removing the temptation. "Do you think there's a chance I could talk to him?"

Jim immediately shook his head.

"Not durin' workin' hours," R.T. said. "All business, that'un. If yer lucky, he might give ya a minute er two when the café's closed, but even that ain't likely."

"Oh. I'd really like to talk to him. If nothing else, I at least want to compliment him on the food. Everything was delicious. I can see why he has no shortage of customers."

"Yup, yer right about that. Folks keep comin' back here, even the tourists. If they stop once, they're hooked fer life."

"What time does the café close? I'm staying here in Talmedge. I can come back then."

"Place closes at three. They're only open fer breakfast and lunch. But I still don't think the old man'll talk ta ya. Don't cotton much ta folks askin' questions."

Darcy sighed, exasperated. She couldn't imagine a business owner who wouldn't appreciate the nationwide publicity a book could offer. "If I could talk to him, I can explain that if my book is well received, an interview with him wouldn't benefit only me."

"It ain't you, Miss Carter," Jim spoke up for the first time since the food arrived. "The old man don't talk much ta nobody."

Darcy would not be dissuaded. The Raven Café was too perfect an example of what her book was about. She couldn't exclude it simply because the owner was a tad on the crotchety side. She had picked up a little charm and finesse in her years of interviewing reluctant sources. She could certainly handle a backwoods café owner. "I can't leave until I tell him how much I enjoyed my lunch. Is he in the kitchen right now?"

"I'd be surprised ta find him anywhere else this time a day," R.T. said. "But be warned, he ain't too friendly, 'specially when he's busy."

Darcy slid out of the booth. She was only going to compliment the man on the food, especially the cole slaw he was known for, not subject him to a two-hour interview. Only two booths still held customers and the stools along the counter were nearly empty as well. "Looks like the lunch rush is over, I'll just pop back there and introduce myself. Maybe after he finds out my purpose for being in the area, he won't mind setting up an appointment with me when he has time."

R.T. shrugged. "Suit yerself. Jest don't expect much gratitude— or manners, fer that matter. He can be an ornery ole cuss."

Darcy smiled one of her winning smiles and pulled her tote bag over her shoulder. "Thanks for everything," she said to the brothers. She leaned forward and pumped first R.T.'s hand and then Jim's. "It was so nice meeting both of you. I appreciate all your help, and I hope we can share lunch again sometime soon. I'll tell June to let me take care of your bill."

"No, no, ya can't do that," they blustered together.

"Oh, please," she said, still smiling. "It would mean so much to me."

They hesitated some more. Jim seemed to be taking the idea of a young woman paying for lunch harder than his brother. Finally R.T. grinned and tipped an imaginary hat at her. "Thank ya kindly, little lady. Hope ta see ya 'round agin."

"Oh, I hope so, too."

Darcy stopped at the cash register and paid for the three lunches before stepping behind the counter. A swinging door led back to the kitchen. A large window framed by a ledge for exchanging orders for food looked onto a huge grill. Through the window she could see a young man loading an industrial size dishwasher, and a younger waitress scurrying around to prepare another plate for a late eater. She eased through the door, mindful that someone could be exiting as she was entering.

The waitress looked up as she entered. "Hi," Darcy said, "I'm looking for the owner."

"Out back," the woman said as she hurried past Darcy. Even though Darcy's belly was full, the hamburger and fries in her hands managed to look appetizing. She'd have to come back another time before she left Talmedge to sample more of the Raven's cuisine.

The young man at the steaming dishwasher barely looked up as Darcy made her way through the crowded workspace to the back door. Darcy smiled anyway before opening the door and stepping outside. Beside the back door was a metal bin with a tiny trapdoor she assumed was used to deposit grease. A narrow gravel driveway for deliveries, circled the building. She set her hands on her hips, mildly irritated at the waitress for telling her the owner was outside when he obviously wasn't—unless he had sneaked over to the feed and grain for a smoke. She turned to go back inside. When she did, she saw movement at the left corner of the building. A figure was crouched in front of her SUV.

Her first impulse was to go back inside to let someone know a strange man was fooling around with her car. Then she remembered where she was. She was definitely overreacting. Wouldn't a car thief typically try the door first or at least pop the hood instead of kneeling at the front end? She wasn't exactly certain how one went about stealing cars, but she was pretty sure it couldn't be done from the grill. Maybe she'd write that book someday. The Ultimate Guide to Hotwiring a Car—nah, not only would the authorities frown on the idea, this was going to be her last Ultimate Guide book.

This man, whoever he was, had probably noticed she had an oil leak or something and was acting the part of the Good Samaritan. And here she was, ready to call the police, the sheriff, or even R.T. and Jim Cavanaugh.

She hiked her tote bag up on her shoulder and started toward him. "Hello? Can I help you?"

The man straightened up and shoved a lock of thick chestnut brown hair away from his face. He was at least six feet tall, with broad shoulders and narrow hips. His chiseled jaw line already showed the faint sandy colored line of a five o'clock shadow, even though it wasn't yet two in the afternoon. He was handsome in a rugged, outdoorsy kind of way she didn't often run into in her small circle of friends and associates. She imagined he would be more at home hip deep in the middle of a trout stream than a boardroom. Her appraisal of his appearance halted abruptly when she noticed the fierce expression in his hazel eyes.

"This your car?" he demanded.

She rethought her decision not to go back into the café for help. "Um, yes it is. Is there a problem?"

"You're blockin' the dumpster," he announced. "Trash man should be here any time and your fancy little car here's in his way. How do you suppose he do his job?"

She saw it now, a dumpster on the other side of the gravel drive. "I'm sorry—I didn't realize…" Darcy stammered. She hated it that the man with the snapping green eyes, or were they blue, no, gray…had her so rattled. "When I got here for lunch, the parking lot was full and there was nowhere else to park. Had I noticed the dumpster, I certainly wouldn't have parked in front of it."

The man pivoted around and pointed at the dumpster with the scrap of paper he held in his hand. "Don't see how you could have missed it. It's sitting here plain as day. I was about to take down your license number and give it to the town cop. Yes, he's been to the police academy and everything."

Darcy wanted to tell him the sarcasm was uncalled for, but her mouth wouldn't cooperate.

"Here in Talmedge," he continued, "we don't take kindly to folks coming down here thinking since we're not much more than a dot on a map, our laws don't need to be obeyed." He looked again at her license plate. "Cuyahoga County," he snorted derisively, "city girl—that's what I figured. We get a lot of your type down here. We can't keep you from comin', but we sure can keep you from disrupting things while you're here."

His tirade finally loosened Darcy's tongue, "My type! What's that supposed to mean? Like I already told you, I did not realize I was blocking the dumpster. Probably because it's fifty feet away and any moderately competent driver could get around me. If you have a problem with that, go ahead and call the authorities. I will be happy to clear it up with the town cop."

The man snorted again. He stuffed the scrap of paper into his pocket. "Snotty city girl," he mumbled under his breath, "think the whole world owes 'em a living." He started past Darcy, headed toward the back door of the café. "All cut from the same cloth, aren't ya?" he growled as he drew abreast of her.

Darcy spun around and glared at his retreating back. She wanted to tell him he didn't know a thing about her. Living south of Cleveland didn't make her a city girl nor had she ever expected anything from anyone. She was too angry. She only wanted his head on a platter. "Well, you'll be happy to hear I can't say the same," she shouted to make sure he heard every word. "You're the first rude person I've met since I crossed the Ohio River."

The man didn't stop or acknowledge her comment. He opened the back door of the café and stepped inside.

Darcy stared at the closed door for a moment, her nostrils still flaring and fists clenched. The back up signal of a truck slowly penetrated the pounding of blood in her ears. The trash man had arrived. She climbed into her SUV and prepared to move, but the truck had already maneuvered around her. The truck driver looked down at her, smiled, and nodded his head in greeting. Darcy put her car into gear and backed out of the parking lot. She was about to turn onto the highway when she realized she never did find the owner of the café. She was probably better off. If he was half as cordial as the beast working for him, she wasn't up to an interview. She'd take R.T. and Jim's advice and find another café for her research.

$\mathscr{D}$ · $\mathscr{D}$ · $\mathscr{D}$ · $\mathscr{D}$ **4**

$\mathcal{D}arcy$ checked the directions $\mathcal{M}arjorie$ Reed had written out for her and turned right onto the highway. She clicked off the radio and drove on in silence. She was still seething from her encounter with the man in the parking lot. She couldn't believe anyone would have the nerve to throw such a fit over blocking a dumpster, an infraction she hadn't even committed. He obviously had a problem with out-of-towners. R.T. and Jim said Talmedge saw its share of them, but they didn't seem to mind. They even enjoyed sharing their table with tourists when the need arose. Darcy smiled at the memory of the two brothers. Marjorie Reed had been equally charming and friendly. Even June, the waitress was nice as could be. She hadn't exaggerated when she told the man in the parking lot he was the first rude person she'd met since heading south. She would forget about him and concentrate on all the friendly and colorful people instead. There was one bad apple in every barrel; she was thankful she'd gotten her encounter with Talmedge's out of the way.

She breathed a sigh of relief when she found Elm Street on the edge of town like Mrs. Reed said she would, and a sign with an arrow pointing out the Ravenswood Inn at the end of the street. Darcy turned onto Elm and drove past quaint cottages and a few newer brick ranch houses until she spotted another sign at the end of a lane that disappeared into some trees. The trees were not yet in full bloom so she caught glimpses of a sweeping front yard and a grand old Edwardian house as she started down the lane. The house was beautiful, not as elegant or spacious as the Danbury Inn, but just as charming. A fleeting thought of selling her own house, moving south, and opening a bed-and- breakfast crossed her mind. She was made for a job like this; she loved meeting people. She already had experience making them feel comfortable in her presence. An image of the man from the parking lot of the café flashed through her mind, but she pushed it aside. Some people you just couldn't please. She was a decent cook and she loved to bake. She was a natural with landscaping and outside maintenance.

Then she remembered the never-ending housework such a business would require, the complicated accounting system, keeping a place up to code with all the zoning committees and insurance companies, the possibility of obnoxious guests and crying kids who inconvenienced everyone else. She was much better off living down the street from her parents working alone day after day with no one to please but herself—and Carla—and Brad—and her readers.

She was definitely better suited for the solitary life of a writer.

She pulled into the circular driveway and came to a stop just short of the steps leading onto a wide front porch. The porch ran halfway across the front of the house and down one side. Two three-sided bay windows flanked the wide front door. The second floor boasted another bay, flanked by six conventional windows, four on the right and two on the left. From her vantage point, they didn't look like the newer tilt in windows that could be washed from the inside. Yet, she could see no dirt. She shuddered at the thought of climbing a ladder in the dead of winter to keep those windows sparkling clean. Let the Marjorie Reeds of the world take care of such matters.

A tiny sign on the front door instructed visitors to enter and make themselves welcome. Darcy tried the knob. Sure enough it turned in her hand. Maybe the guy from the café was right and she was more of a city girl than she realized. Even in her quiet neighborhood, she couldn't imagine leaving her front door unlocked with a sign on the door inviting anyone to come in and make themselves at home.

Inside the front door was a tiny writing desk with an open guest register like the one at the Danbury. A tiny bell sat on the table next to the register. She picked it up and gave a gentle shake. She wondered how anyone could hear the tiny sound in such a big house, but didn't want to risk ringing it again in case the innkeeper was on her way through the door at this very moment.

While she waited, she read the names of the previous guests. The last guest, a Mr. James Bennett from Poughkeepsie, New York had signed out on Wednesday. Before him, no one had stayed at the inn since the weekend before last. She wondered how a person could stay in business with only a few guests a month. Quick calculations determined that the Ravenswood would need to accommodate at least ten paying weekly guests during a fifty-two week period in order to make the operation profitable. According to the guest register, that wasn't happening.

How did the owners manage? Was he retired from something else? Did she write children's books from a desk overlooking one of the many vistas the house provided? Did they make bootleg moonshine in a mountain hideaway that their guests and the revenuers were unaware of?

A wooden display mounted behind the writing table caught her eye. She leaned over the table to read the titles of the pamphlets advertising various tourist attractions in the area. Cherokee artisans, underground caverns, waterfalls, hand blown glass makers, apparently millions of miles of hiking trails crisscrossing the area; there was more here than she could ever see and do on one getaway. She plucked out an area map highlighting some of the area's waterfalls just as she heard feminine footsteps coming her way. A tall blonde stepped through the rounded foyer doorway. The woman was already smiling and extending her hand.

"Hello, I'm Leanne Ravenscraft. You must be the one Marjorie Reed called about."

Darcy tucked the map into her tote bag and shook her offered hand. She estimated the woman to be in her mid thirties. She had a wide, genuine, Julia Roberts smile that was pretty and interesting without being intimidatingly beautiful. Her shoulder length blonde hair had probably come out of a bottle but still managed to look naturally sun-kissed. She wore it parted slightly off center and flipped out on the ends. It looked windblown and carefree like the woman wearing it. She didn't seem like the type who spent half the morning in front of the mirror fooling with it. Her face was all angles with a straight nose, pronounced jaw line, and high cheekbones. But the woman's most redeeming quality was her eyes. They were gunmetal grey, a perfect fit to her face, and sparkling with life and vitality. Darcy immediately liked her in spite of the fact that she could tuck her shirt into her jeans if she wanted and still look great.

"Hi, I'm Darcy Carter. I can't tell you how glad I am you have room for me. While I was planning my trip I had no idea this was also a family weekend at the university."

Leanne's smile broadened if that was at all possible, and she stepped behind the writing table. "A lot of people don't realize we have a school so close. I'm afraid housing always gets scarce during these weekends. But it's good for people like me. Generally this time of year is slow for the bed-and-breakfast industry. Having the university close by helps fill the rooms." She turned the guest registry toward Darcy and offered a pen. "Marjorie didn't say how long you were planning to stay."

Darcy dug into her tote bag for her wallet and identification as she answered. "I'm in the area researching a book I'm writing. So I'll stay here through the weekend if it's not a problem. Marjorie promised me two days at the Danbury for my inconvenience, but after seeing this place, believe me, it's no inconvenience."

"Oh, that's sweet of you to say. Can I ask what type of book you're writing?"

Darcy's fingers closed around her wallet inside the recesses of her tote. She pulled it out and laid it open on the desk. "It's about cafés and diners. You know, the little out of the way places that the highways have bypassed, yet they still manage to thrive. I hope to interview the owners and people who work there, along with the locals who frequent them. You know, find out what makes them succeed when so many such places have been bulldozed under to make room for the golden arches and strip malls."

Leanne copied Darcy driver's license information into a

second ledger she kept in the desk's locked drawer. She looked up from her work. "We have a place like that right here in Talmedge," she said with a smile.

"The Raven, right? I stopped there on my way over. The food was great. I couldn't believe what I got for under ten dollars. Is it always so busy?" She didn't bother to mention she had already decided not to include it in her book.

"Yes, but it's only open for breakfast and lunch. Everybody around here knows if they want a good, cheap, home-cooked meal, they have to get there early. You must have got there right in the middle of the lunch rush. I'm surprised you got a seat."

"I got the last table. Then two farmers actually came over and asked if they could sit with me."

Leanne threw back her head and laughed. "R.T. and Jim Cavanaugh, right?" She laughed again when Darcy nodded. "Those two are absolute sweethearts. In the summertime when the café really gets busy, I've seen customers take their plates outside and eat off the tailgates of their pickups."

"Now that's a story."

"You need to come back later in the year and see for yourself. It's great. Great for business, too, people passing through have actually pulled in to see what was going on and then stayed to get something to eat."

Darcy's curiosity was piqued. Maybe she'd give the Raven Café another chance. "I'll have to do that," she said.

Leanne replaced the ledger into the drawer and locked it. "Are you ready for a tour of the house, or would you rather go right upstairs?"

"The tour is definitely tempting. I can't wait to see the rest of your beautiful home, but I am wiped out. I've been on the road for two days, and I'd like nothing more than a shower and a ten or twelve hour nap."

"Well, then, by all means, let's find you a room."

Leanne took one of Darcy's suitcases and led the way upstairs. "Minnie's Room is already reserved for a couple who'll be arriving this evening," she explained as she turned left at the top of the stairs. "But you can have your choice of the other three. The one across the hall from it is our largest room, probably more than what you'll need, but you're welcome to have a look." She stepped inside the nearest room. "This is Olivia's Room. It's named after my mother. It's always a popular choice among the ladies."

"Oh, it's gorgeous." Darcy stopped next to Leanne and set her suitcase and tote on the floor. She would be more than happy in this room until the first of the week when she returned to the Danbury. "Did you do all the decorating yourself?"

"Yes," Leanne said, coloring slightly at the praise, "with a lot of help from Martha Stewart and HGTV."

"Well, it's lovely." Darcy crossed the room to the window. "Oh, what a view, does all this property belong to the Inn? Where does that trail lead?"

Leanne stepped up beside her. "Back to that stand of trees is where our property meets up with the State's. About a quarter mile through the trees, the trail Y's off into two trails. They both lead to a gorgeous waterfall. Most of the waterfalls in the area are only accessible via the property of a hotel, Inn, or private individual who keeps the information to themselves. One of our trails is a little over a mile of relatively easy travel before you get to the waterfall. It's wide and wheelchair accessible with several benches along the way to sit and relax. The other one is a strenuous two-hour trip for me, and I'm used to it. It isn't as cleared off as the other trail, so you spend a lot of time going around rock slides and trees that decided to sprout right in the middle of everything."

"That explains why you look so fit," Darcy said.

Leanne shrugged. "You'll never find that view inside a health club. I noticed you took one of the hiking maps downstairs. If you have the time and you'd like to see the waterfall from the best vantage point, I'd love the company."

"That'd be great. I'd go anywhere to see a waterfall."

"Great. Well, if you're okay with this room, I'll leave you alone. The bathroom is next door on your right. You'll have to share it with the room on the other side. I hope that's not a problem. The other guests aren't due for a couple of hours so you have plenty of time to yourself."

"Sounds good."

Leanne went to the door and turned back to face Darcy. "If you need anything, I'll be downstairs in the kitchen or out back in the gardens. Just give me a holler."

"Thanks, Mrs. Ravenscraft."

"It's Leanne, just Leanne."

"Oh, okay, Leanne. Then would you mind if I ask a really stupid question that's been bugging me since I left the Danbury? If your name is Ravenscraft, why is the Inn called the Ravenswood?"

Leanne smiled. "It's not a stupid question. Everybody asks sooner or later. It's really quite simple. Wouldn't you rather rent a room at a place called the Ravenswood Inn than the Ravenscraft?"

Darcy considered it a moment. "I suppose I would."

"Me, too." Leanne smiled again and turned to leave the room.

"Just another sec," Darcy called after her, stopping her in mid-stride. "The Raven Café? Any connection there?"

"You picked up on that one too, huh? Sure, that's Vince. You'll meet him later."

She wiggled her fingers good-bye and backed out of the room, pulling the door shut behind her before Darcy could question her further. Darcy turned back toward the window. She looked past the flower gardens and trees to the trail snaking through the mighty pines. A contented smile crossed her face. One bad encounter with a rude local couldn't squelch the peace she knew this trip would bring.

Darcy seldom felt inclined to soak in a tub but she couldn't resist the cavernous claw-footed bathtub she found next door to her room. She helped herself to the peach scented bubbles in a wicker basket next to the tub and luxuriated until the water started to cool. Emerging from the water, she felt better than she had in weeks. Her desire for a nap gone after the soak in the tub, she headed back to her room to unpack. She was amazed to see by the clock on the nightstand that it was almost four o'clock. She wondered when her fellow guests were due to arrive. She was anxious to talk to them, and see if she could find any insight on what kind of people spent their weekends at a bed-and-breakfast, when it was easier and cheaper to check into an impersonal hotel and never have to meet or smile at anyone.

She finished unpacking her things into the freestanding wardrobe and armoire. She looked out the window to the back yard. The trail into the trees beckoned her. It was getting late. There was no way she could make the long hike to the waterfall before she lost the light. It would be completely dark in a couple of hours. Under the canopy of thick pines, darkness would fall even sooner.

Deciding against a hike, she realized she wasn't in the mood to write anything either. She picked up a fresh spiral bound notebook, in case inspiration should strike unexpectedly, and left the room. Treading softly down the stairs, she felt a little like an intruder in Leanne's home even though she was a paying guest at the Inn. A bed-and-breakfast definitely took some getting used to. It was completely different from the anonymity a frequent traveler such as herself found in motels.

At the bottom of the staircase she stopped and looked around. Across the hall to her right was another parlor as large as the one where she now stood. High ceilings, what looked like original crown molding and woodwork, and a beautiful antique chandelier reminded her of the houses in those old Noel Coward movies her dad used to watch. To her left was an open doorway leading to a much smaller room. On the opposite end of the room was an open door leading onto a small covered porch. Darcy glanced around. Leanne was nowhere to be seen and the house was quiet; empty but not lonesome. She headed in the direction of the small porch. She moved slowly through what looked like had once been a sewing room, taking in the beautiful refinished furnishings. This was how she imagined her house if she ever found the time to decorate it properly. Maybe she'd snap some pictures while she was here and take them to a professional decorator when she got home. She knew what she liked when she saw it but wasn't any good at designing the desired effect in her head.

She pushed open the wooden screen door. It squeaked loudly and banged shut behind her. She smiled, thinking of the episodes of The Waltons she used to watch on TV when she was a kid. All she remembered about the show, besides the never ending parade of redheaded children, was that the family lived in the mountains in an area that reminded her of this place, and the screen door squeaked whenever anyone came or went. She wondered why the father, who always seemed to be out of work, never got around to oiling the hinges. Probably the same reason Leanne didn't. There was something strangely comforting about a squeaky screen door.

Nostalgia; people paid big money for it, or at least she hoped they still did.

Three high-backed rockers sat in a row on the narrow porch. A small table stood between two of them. A few pottery urns had been placed here and there, though nothing was yet in bloom. Still the porch looked restful and inviting. Darcy lowered herself into the nearest rocker and set her notebook on her lap. Her sleepiness was completely gone, but she was bone weary. She loved seeing new places; it was the getting there that wore her out. Even airline travel was daunting these days and seldom worth the effort.

She pulled the ink pen from the spiral binding, flipped to the first page and clicked open the pen. She smoothed her left hand over the clean page. She loved the feel of a brand new notebook; the clean, empty lines, the smell, the possibilities. She gazed out at the trees and hills around her and set the rocker in motion with her foot. She clicked the pen open and closed a few more times then put the end of it in her mouth.

She couldn't think of a word to write. All the way here in the car from Ohio, she had thought about the new book, or she thought she had. Maybe it was the act of writing she had pondered rather than what she would actually write. A long car trip was usually the best way to get her creative juices flowing. If nothing else, these mountains should spark something. She focused on a bird in a tree, then a leaf, and finally the sound of rushing water in the distance. Nothing—she clicked the pen a few more times and chewed furiously on the end.

She thought of the two brothers she had eaten lunch with. Those two were a book all by themselves. She put the point of the pen against the paper and wrote their names, R.T. and Jim

Cavanaugh. She furrowed her brow and concentrated. Her mind was a total blank.

She was thinking too hard. *Forget what your mind is saying and let the words flow.* That's the advice she poured out to her students at various writers' conferences. *The words are already in your head. It's your job to give them voice.*

She couldn't believe people actually paid her for such poppycock!

She clicked the pen closed a final time and stuck it back into the binder. She needed to relax, a vacation. Hadn't she told Carla that very thing? Wasn't it possible her mind was refusing to produce the words because it knew better than she that her writing career was already headed in a new direction?

Well, if she wanted to relax, she had come to the right spot. This place—not only the Inn, but the mountains around it and the little town of Talmedge—was so tranquil and restful. Surely it was what her tired mind needed.

She heard a car slow down on Elm Street, followed by the crunch of tires on gravel. Through the trees she saw a newer model pickup truck coming down the lane. Guests. Again she felt like an intruder. She leaned back in the rocker so she could watch the truck's progress without its occupants seeing her.

The pickup truck moved past her parked SUV and pulled in front of the garage. The driver probably wasn't a guest. It must be the Vince Leanne referred to, the apparent owner of the Raven Café. R.T. and Jim had called him 'the old man'. Darcy wondered if he was Leanne's father. No, she wouldn't call her father Vince. Maybe he was her father-in-law. If she had a father-in-law, that meant there was a husband around here someplace and possibly children, although Darcy hadn't seen any evidence of little people yet, no bicycles in the yard, worn patches in the grass, or toys in the hallways. Either Leanne had incredibly well behaved children or none at all.

The truck's engine shut off. Darcy dipped her head to see past a tree limb growing across her field of vision. A long, denim clad leg immerged from the driver's side door. The limb blocked the top half of the body disengaging itself from the truck, but it was definitely male. Leanne's father-in-law appeared to be a fine example of the upper-middle-aged male. No paunch, stooped posture, or shortened strides. She leaned forward in the rocking chair and craned her neck to catch a glimpse of the rest of him above the tree limb. A powder blue team cap with white trim she immediately recognized from the University of North Carolina came into view. She didn't spend all those winter weekends watching NCAA sports with her dad without picking up a thing or two.

She couldn't see anything more than the ball cap, but it appeared Vince had a full head of hair underneath his Tarheels ball cap. Around the corner of the house not more than forty feet from where she sat, she heard the front door open, and someone step onto the front porch. Darcy ducked back into the chair. No doubt about it, she had become a snoop. Inappropriate behavior, even if she had paid for a room. Still she strained her ears to hear the exchange. It wasn't hard. Sound traveled easily among the hills and bare trees surrounding the house.

By the light tread, she guessed the person on the porch was Leanne. Her guess was confirmed when Leanne called out to the person coming toward the house. "There you are. Did you have a nice day?"

Darcy knew she should mind her own business. She should go back to her writing, or whatever it was she had come out onto the side porch to do, and stop concerning herself with Leanne's life. In spite of herself, she stopped the rocking chair in its forward position and dipped her head again to see under the tree limb. Long legs advanced to the front porch. She leaned farther still until she had a clear view of narrow hips and a flat stomach. She wished she knew what genius had planted a tree directly across her field of vision.

Leanne's father-in-law said something that sounded like a grunt.

"You be nice," Leanne chided in reply. "We have guests for the weekend."

This time Darcy could hear the man clearly. "Perfect. I guess you got a list of chores for me to do."

The voice sounded vaguely familiar.

Leanne stepped off the porch and into Darcy's field of vision. "No," she said, "everything's squared away. Just stay out of trouble and out of everyone's way."

"Ha—ha. Very funny."

Darcy furrowed her brow and leaned even further forward in her seat to get a look at the man whose voice she was sure she had heard before.

Leanne came to a stop. She put her hands on her hips. Her face softened. The long legs stopped a few feet in front of her. Darcy considered moving over to the next rocking chair where her view would be unobstructed. She marveled at how being in a small town for one afternoon had turned her into such a busybody.

Leanne reached out and touched the man's arm. "Come on inside. Your dinner'll be ready in a little bit. I'm expecting more guests later, and I want to have the kitchen cleaned up before they arrive."

The man mumbled a reply and followed Leanne to the house. Two steps further and he stepped completely into view. Darcy's breath caught in her throat. No wonder he sounded so familiar. It was the horrible man from the diner. What was he doing here? Then the pieces fell into place. Vince wasn't Leanne's father-in-law, he was her husband! R.T. and Jim had called him 'the old man' because of his cantankerous attitude, not because of his age. She should have realized Jim and R.T. wouldn't think anyone under the age of seventy was old. Well, they hadn't been kidding when they warned her Vince was an ornery old bird, even if he did look to be a few years younger than Leanne.

Darcy groaned and rested her head against the back of the rocking chair. How could she spend the entire weekend in the house of such a nasty creature? If not for the mix-up with her reservation at the Danbury, she'd be enjoying a nice leisurely evening right now with people who treated her decently. She had already decided to steer clear of the Raven Café because of this man, and now it looked like she would have to find another bed-and-breakfast.

The front door slammed as Leanne and Vince went inside. She pulled her pen out of the notebook and wrote a few notes from what she could remember about her lunch, even though she was determined not to give the Raven Café one inch of promotion inside the covers of any book she'd ever write. She jotted down physical descriptions of Talmedge's main street, Jim and R.T., and June, her waitress. She would probably never use any of what she wrote, but hoped the simple act of putting words to paper would spark her creativity. It was an old trick that usually worked. Not this time. All she could ponder was what a sweet woman like Leanne could possibly see in such a loud mouth jerk, regardless of how handsome and long-legged he was.

Just as she was closing her notebook in disgust at herself for not being able to form a coherent, if not at least interesting sentence, a Park Avenue drove down the lane and pulled between Vince's pickup truck and a stand of trees. More relatives or repeat visitors. Once again Darcy leaned forward in her chair and craned her neck to watch a mature couple climb out of the large car. She wondered again if it was the small town atmosphere or the fact that her writing was going nowhere, leaving her nothing else to do, that had turned her to voyeurism. These people were probably the couple who had reserved the room at the front of the house. The woman was dressed in a plum pantsuit designed to make her plump, petite frame appear longer and leaner. Her hair and nails were professionally done. Her shoes were a stylish wedge heel without a mark on them. When Darcy traveled she opted for sweats, her hair pulled back in a scrunchie, and her face free of makeup. Now she could see what a difference some effort on one's appearance made.

The man was a head taller than his wife. He did nothing to disguise the fact that his silver hair had receded past the halfway point on the top of his head. Other than a slight paunch over the top of his leather belt, he looked to be in great shape for a man in his sixties. Dressed like he'd just left the clubhouse, he moved to the back of the car and took a small overnight bag out of the trunk and handed it to his wife. He took out two large suitcases, shut the trunk lid with his elbow, and followed the woman to the house. She hadn't stopped talking the entire time. He wore the resigned look of a man who hadn't finished a sentence in thirty years.

They moved onto the porch and out of Darcy's line of vision. These were the first people she had seen since Leanne and her awful husband. By now she was sure the Ravenscrafts had no children. She would have seen or heard some evidence of little ones by now. *Hmm, no kids, no dogs or cats—how does Leanne stand living out here at the end of this long lane with only Vince for company between guests?*

Darcy shuddered. From what she had seen of Leanne and what she deduced it would take to run an operation like an inn, she didn't seem the kind of woman who would be attracted to a prickly pear like Vince. Oh, well, who was she to judge? The last serious man in her life had been in college. She winced. Had it been that long? What was wrong with her? She wasn't horrible looking. She made good money. She was well traveled and had lots of friends in the writing circuit. So why couldn't she find anyone whose company she wanted to be in for more than five minutes?

She remembered the last literary fundraiser she attended at the Cleveland Society for the Arts. She spent the entire evening listening to people drop names and discuss grants and awards until she thought she would gag. She had left as soon as she could get away. She remembered hanging her dress back in the closet and thinking of all the money she'd wasted earlier that day on her hair and nails. She decided then and there that she didn't care how important it was to the publishing house that she make an appearance, she was through with that pretentious crowd.

But, what other crowd did she have? Working alone greatly reduced the number of people with whom she came into contact. She didn't participate in the club scene. She stopped attending church regularly when she moved out of her parents' house. The organizations and groups that had once been important to her had been pushed down on her priority list as her writing took up more and more of her time. All her friends from school were either married with children or had moved on to other things. She had lost touch with the young women in Bible study group that used to mean so much to her. With a start she realized most of the people she now considered friends, she knew only through online writers' groups. It was almost pathetic.

She listened for activity inside the house, and when she had given Leanne ample time to check in the new arrivals and show them to their room, she headed inside. She stopped in the doorway of the little sewing room and looked both ways. The last thing she wanted to do was run into Vince. When she was sure no one was between her and the stairwell, she hurried across the hall, through the formal parlor, and up the stairs. Just as she reached the landing she heard the front door open, followed by a male voice and feminine laughter—more guests. She dashed into her room and shut the door behind her.

She sat down on the bed, breathless. Then she realized how silly it all was. She burst out laughing. Did she plan on spending the entire weekend ducking from pillar to post until there was room for her at the Danbury Inn? She was a grown woman. She really liked Leanne and the Ravenswood Inn. There was no reason why she couldn't enjoy her stay here even if she did run into Leanne's husband on occasion.

She replayed their exchange in her head. Maybe Vince had a perfectly good reason for being upset over what she considered a minor infraction. Maybe he had been vandalized recently and distrusted everyone he didn't know. Maybe people were always blocking the dumpster and the trash man asked him to keep an eye on out of town visitors who wouldn't know where they could or couldn't park. Maybe he had a rough day and the sight of her SUV was the straw that broke the camel's back.

She needed to cut the guy some slack. Generally when people flew off the handle over a seemingly small matter, there was more to the tale than met the eye. At this moment, she couldn't exactly remember what he'd said that made her so mad. She had surely blown the whole episode out of proportion, too.

She checked the clock on her nightstand. Food was the last thing on her mind after the lunch she'd had at the Raven Café, but she didn't want to sit in her room all night either. She thought of the wall display of pamphlets downstairs that advertised things to do in the area. It was too late for hiking and she imagined most of the craft malls would be closing soon, but surely there was something she could find to do that didn't involve eating or writing. She pulled on a heavy sweater over her blouse and grabbed her leather coat. She already detected a marked drop in temperature now that the sun had set.

She pulled open the door of her room and almost ran into Leanne's fist.

She gasped, startled.

Leanne put her hand over her heart. "Oh, Darcy, you scared me." She chuckled and caught her breath. "I was just coming to see if you had any plans for the evening."

"Well, no, actually, I was on my way downstairs to see what I might find to get into."

"Well, it's a good thing we ran into each other, then. We're starting a game of Trivial Pursuit, and we need another warm body. As usual, Vince isn't interested, so we're a man short."

Darcy hoped her relief didn't show on her face. Trivial Pursuit sounded fun, but not if it meant she had to sit across the table from Mr. Personality. "Sure, that'd be great. Let me hang my coat up." Instead of hanging the jacket up, she tossed it on the bed. She'd keep the sweater on for now.

Leanne waited in the doorway, and then led the way down the stairs. "We do this sometimes on winter evenings when there's not a whole lot else to do after dark. I'm afraid the shopping malls close early this time of year and unless you've got family or something to do in the area, it gets kind of boring. Not that I would ever print that in the brochures."

Darcy laughed. She so enjoyed Leanne's company; she again marveled at how two opposite natured people such as Leanne and Vince could have ever gotten together. Then she realized she was being unfair to Vince. It was wrong of her to base her entire opinion on only one encounter with the man.

Whatever the reason for Vince's behavior at the café, she would give him another chance. It was worth it to nurture this budding friendship with his wife. The man had to have some redeeming quality to make Leanne fall in love with him. Besides she liked the Ravenswood Inn; the location and setup was perfect for her research. She didn't want to find a new place to stay after two days. She especially loved Trivial Pursuit.

Leanne led Darcy past the formal parlor and sitting room, past the dining room with an impressive table that could comfortably seat at least twelve, past the industrial sized kitchen, and into a family room.

The elderly couple she'd seen earlier was seated side by side on a suede camel-colored couch. The man was reclining back into the cushions like he'd been here more than once. His wife was perched on the edge of the sofa, leaning toward a woman sitting cross-legged on the floor on the other side of a low coffee table. The other woman looked to be in her mid to late forties. She looked equally comfortable on the floor despite a haircut and sweater that looked high end. Another man sat on an ottoman next to the woman on the floor. He was setting up the Trivial Pursuit game with one hand and holding a Diet Coke in the other. He wore a long sleeve knit pullover and his feet were bare under his chinos. A pair of loafers lay under the coffee table as if they'd been kicked off with no regard to where they ended up. Darcy immediately fell in love with the friendly casualness of the evening. If only she had a group like this of her own back home.

The older man spotted Leanne and Darcy and jumped to his feet. "There you are. I see you found our even player."

The other man put down his Diet Coke and stood up. He leaned forward to shake Darcy's hand as Leanne made introductions all around. The older couple was Dwayne and Sandy Hudson from Raleigh. The woman on the floor was Kimberly Wright and her husband Brian was the one who had set up the game. Both couples were regular guests at the Ravenswood. The couple occupying the Inn's last room was on their way from a church somewhere in Virginia where they had just gotten married. For obvious reasons, no one expected them to join the others for Trivial Pursuit, and it would be a surprise if they made an appearance downstairs at all.

Sandy Hudson pushed a menu and sheet of paper into Darcy's hands. "We're ordering Chinese. Write down what you want and Leanne will call it in."

"Wow, you get Chinese out here?"

"If you tip big enough," Dwayne answered with a loud laugh. "This is their lean time of year, too."

"You didn't have any other plans for dinner tonight, did you, Darcy?" Leanne asked.

Darcy shook her head and read what everyone else had ordered for reference. She noticed the address on the menu—Sylva, nearly fifteen miles of winding mountain roads away from the inn. It was either an accommodating restaurant or a mighty big tip.

After adding a few items to the already long order, Leanne motioned for Darcy to follow her into the kitchen. "Get yourself something to drink while I place the order," she said motioning to a refrigerator large enough for Darcy to climb inside.

Darcy took a soda from the fridge and waited for Leanne to finish her call. "I appreciate the invitation to join you and the others," she said after Leanne hung up the phone. "I didn't really have anything to do tonight. I was getting ready to go out and see the town."

"If you took Highway 16 from the Danbury, you've seen all there is of this town," Leanne quipped with a laugh. "Besides, we love new blood. I gotta warn you, it can get pretty competitive in there. We always play couples, and sometimes I worry Sandy is a hair away from belting Dwayne when he blows an answer."

"Does Vince usually play with you?" Darcy thought she already knew the answer, but wanted to hear it from Leanne in case she was the reason Vince was making himself scarce.

"He's not much for games, or socializing for that matter." The fact didn't seem to bother Leanne. "I always play with whoever else is unattached, or whose spouse doesn't feel like joining in. You know that condition they talk about on TV, social anxiety disorder? I always tell Vince I'm going to order those pills for him. For a man who chose to work in a public field like food service, he doesn't have much to do with people."

She turned and headed into the living room carrying her own can of soda and a glass of ice. Darcy followed, amazed at Leanne's flippant attitude about her husband's personality quirks. Most wives would be at least a little irritated that they always had to find a partner for games or sit them out. She reminded herself it was none of her business. Even if Leanne did get irritated at Vince, she wouldn't let on to Darcy, who was a paying guest, not a girlfriend.

Darcy only hoped the bride who would soon be arriving at the Ravenswood with her new husband had come into her marriage with her eyes wide open.

By the time the delivery boy rapped on the back door with the food an hour later, the game was just getting warmed up. As Leanne had predicted, the competition was fast and furious, but Darcy held her own. She was used to playing with her dad and brother who were always out for blood no matter what the stakes.

Even paying for the food turned into a competition. Dwayne and Brian were instantly on their feet digging for wallets, telling the other his money was no good here. Darcy reached into her back pocket for her share of the damage but was waved aside by Sandy and Kimberly.

"Let them take care of it, honey," Kimberly said. "Some kind of male ritual thing, since they didn't go out and kill the food and drag it back to the cave, it makes them feel better if they can at least pay for it."

Finally the delivery boy made his exit with an extra thirty-five dollars for his effort, and the game resumed in earnest. No stopping for dinner. Darcy popped egg rolls and wontons off a soggy paper plate in between conferring with Leanne on answers. Leanne was a more than adequate partner, but it was soon apparent the game belonged to Kimberly. Darcy was proud of herself at the end of the evening that she and Leanne were beaten less and less by the time Brian and Kimberly won the third game. At least they had made progress.

Leanne disappeared once to see in the new arrivals who had gone straight upstairs. That was two hours ago. Darcy was amazed to see it was ten-thirty. Where had the evening gone? She had meant to be in bed early so she could head out in time for breakfast at a diner ten miles away. The small crowd thanked her profusely for joining in and being such a good sport, then broke up and went their separate ways. Vince didn't make an appearance. Darcy was relieved. Even though she hadn't done anything wrong in the café's parking lot, she didn't want Leanne to know they had exchanged barbs with each other.

$\mathcal{O}$. $\mathcal{O}$. $\mathcal{O}$. $\mathcal{O}$ 5

$\mathcal{D}arcy$ $awoke$ $before$ the $alarm$ went off at six a.m. in spite of the two day drive and her late night game of Trivial Pursuit. As she showered and dressed, she listened to the area weather report and dressed accordingly. The trees may be budding, but it was still cold outside. Rain was on its way for later in the day with no promise of sunshine. She went downstairs with every intention of going straight to her car. At the sound of activity in the kitchen and a delicious aroma drifting her way, she found herself heading there to bid Leanne a good morning. Just as she reached the kitchen door, she realized Vince could be the one making breakfast. She thought of backing up and leaving without saying hello, but decided she was being ridiculous. Normally when someone insulted her or behaved rudely, she attributed it to stress, a poor upbringing, or plain insensitivity and went about her merry way. Why this man's behavior had so disconcerted her, she didn't know. Nor did she want to give it much thought. Vince was married to Leanne and any personality faults or phobias were Leanne's problem, not hers.

She squared her shoulders and marched into the kitchen. If there was any discomfort to be had, it would be him when he discovered the woman he yelled at was a guest in his inn.

All her worrying and personal examination was for nothing. Leanne stood over a butcher block island with her back to the door, chopping vegetables for omelets. "Good morning," Darcy sang out.

Leanne whirled around. "Darcy." She glanced at the clock above the stove. "You're up early. Did you sleep well?"

"Divinely," Darcy assured her. "I'm an early riser. I guess I should have told you."

"No need. Around here we come and go as we please. Vince is already up and gone for the day. As long as I know you're not having breakfast, it doesn't bother me if you're up with the sun or sleep all day. Care for any coffee, juice?"

Darcy advanced into the kitchen and peered at the large quantity of breakfast ingredients in various stages of preparedness. "No, thanks, I have a feeling I'm going to be filled to the gills in a little while. I almost regret not having breakfast here, but I need to get out and sample what the locals are eating."

"Where are you headed?"

"Winchester."

"The Emmitt Junction Diner? You won't be disappointed."

"That's what I'm afraid of." Darcy put her hands on her hips. "I think I might have been better off working on the book my editor wanted me to write, or at least my waistline would have."

Leanne smiled and went back to her chopping. "What did he want you to write?"

"She," Darcy corrected. "My editor, Carla Daniels, has been bugging me for years to write a totally useless book, *The Ultimate Guide to Finding Mr. Right*."

Leanne looked at her over her shoulder. "Now that research could be a lot of fun and you could do it right here while you're researching this book."

"No, thanks, my life's complicated enough." Darcy turned toward the kitchen door. It was already a little after seven. She wanted to get to the Emmitt Junction Diner for the breakfast rush.

"Well, when you get it done," Leanne was saying, "let me know,"

Darcy stopped and turned around. "When I get what done?"

"*The Ultimate Guide to Finding Mr. Right.*"

Darcy was thoroughly confused. "Why do you want to know that?"

"So I can get a copy." She scooped her vegetables into a bowl and headed for the refrigerator. "A book like that might come in handy."

Darcy stared. She couldn't think of a thing to say.

Leanne laughed at the expression on her face. "I'm just kidding, Darcy. Heaven knows it's too late for me." She shook her head as if in defeat, and set a block of cheese on the counter.

Darcy was now totally off balance by Leanne's remarks. Talk about first impressions. She never dreamed Leanne was the kind of married woman who would make jokes about finding another man. But that's all it was, a joke. Not the best one Darcy had ever heard, but a joke nonetheless.

"Have a good morning, Darcy. Be careful if Gigi's your waitress. She means well, but the poor thing's as graceful as a linebacker. If she wasn't the owner's sister, she'd owe him her whole paycheck in broken crockery."

"Okay, thanks. I'll see you in a couple of hours."

Darcy left the kitchen. She fastened her jacket around her before opening the front door. It sure looked like a northern Ohio March morning out there to her.

She made it out of the Emmitt Junction Diner in much better shape than the day before, but she still ate five times more than her usual morning toast or bagel and coffee. By carefully measuring her portions, she was able to sample nearly everything on the menu and still get a good feel of what the Emmitt Junction Diner was like. As she suspected, it wasn't the need for sustenance that brought people out so early on a Saturday morning, much like the ambiance at the Raven Café in Talmedge wasn't responsible for its success. Some towns supported places where people could gather to swap gossip and news while they broke bread. People here remembered what the important things were—knowing your neighbor, supporting the local economy. It made Darcy dream of small town life; gathering on a ball field to root your team to victory even when you didn't have kids competing; listening to Christmas carolers on the bandstand in the village green; ice cream socials and chili cook-offs.

She was probably romanticizing all of it, but her full belly, the sound of clinking dinnerware, friendly jibes, and laughter were playing tricks on her mind.

She turned up the radio and sang along with a country music song, *when in Rome...* She couldn't wait to get back to the Ravenswood and change into a light pair of sweatpants. The earlier threat of rain had proven to be a mistake on the part of area meteorologists. As the sun's rays had descended into the valley, the temperature soared to a beautiful day, one she planned to enjoy. If Leanne was free, she'd see if she was interested in serving as guide up the mountain to the waterfall. If not, she'd manage on her own. She had a few thousand calories to burn off.

She lowered her window enough to fill the car with fresh air without letting in so much that her hair whipped out of control around her face. She thought of her nieces, Bethany and Samantha. They would love it down here. Of course, they loved going anywhere with their aunt, not that they had much experience. The Disney World trip had been waved under their noses and withdrawn so many times Darcy didn't know how they believed a word she said. This time she would make it happen so long as she didn't give in to Carla about the Finding Mr. Right book and write it just to please Brad and the suits at the publishing house.

Regardless of her writing success, she didn't know how much of an impact being without a publisher would have on her eleven-year career. If possible, times were harder on a writer these days. She knew of writers with more titles under their belts than she had, and with better track records, who had been released from their contracts for a variety of reasons and they had a difficult time getting back on track. She liked to think her reputation would stand on its own, maybe even secure a better deal this time, but she wasn't a risk taker. She proved that when she didn't move out of her parents' house until the release of her eighth book.

Then again, she had to stand up for herself sometime. All the books she had written were because she felt strongly about the subject matter. Sure, she was willing to listen to suggestions and had researched a few titles based on someone's input. But she wrote what she wanted. She had no desire to write the Mr. Right book. It was Brad's way of lining his pocket at the expense of lonely women who would buy anything that eluded to a chance at happiness. In good conscious, she could not write a book on a subject she did not wholeheartedly believe in.

When she finished this book, she was going straight to New York to talk to him in person. *You can't force me to produce a book I don't believe in,* she'd say. *That's not how I work. This isn't about the money, you know. It's more than that. It's about...*

What exactly was it about? Why was she fighting this project so hard? Maybe it wasn't her values, but her own realization that looking for Mr. Right was futile. He wasn't out there. She'd been wandering around for almost thirty years and seen a lot of the world. If he was out there, surely she would have tripped over him by now.

Sandy and Dwayne were sitting on the front porch when she pulled into the drive a little after ten. A pickup truck equipped with toolboxes on the sides and a ladder across a rail on top was parked in the driveway. Darcy parked behind it and climbed out of her car.

"There's the early bird," Sandy called out. "Don't tell me you've put in a day's work already. You're as bad as Dwayne."

Darcy patted her stomach as she climbed the steps. "It's good work if you can get it."

"Leanne told us you were writing a book about diners in the South," Dwayne said. "I've got a place or two you might want to check out if you feel like coming east. Not too far from where we live—"

"Now, Dwayne, she's not interested in that greasy spoon you eat at all the time." Sandy looked to Darcy. "Don't go within a hundred miles of that place, honey. The food'll kill you."

"Don't go influencing the girl, Sandy. She might have a different opinion than you. She's supposed to be doing research.

Why don't you let her come and see for herself? Leroy's been in business for forty years. He must be doing something right."

"Would you trust somebody named Leroy to cook your food?" Sandy asked and then went on without waiting for an answer. "Well, neither would I. Take my word for it, honey, you'll find all the good food a body can hold right here. Have you been to Vince's place yet?"

"The Raven? Yes, I had lunch there yesterday."

"Now that's some good grub we can agree on," Dwayne said.

Darcy smiled. It was the most conversation she'd heard out of his mouth. The front door opened, and Leanne stepped out onto the porch. "How is everybody doing out here? Can I get anybody anything? Darcy, how was breakfast?"

"It was very good. Too good, in fact, I'm on my way upstairs to change so I can go for a walk. I thought I'd try out your trails."

"Leanne, I think I found your water leak." A stocky fellow about Leanne's height with a mustache and severely receding hairline stepped out onto the porch. "I'm sorry. I didn't know you were with guests."

"That's all right." Leanne took his arm and pulled him up beside her. "Hank, this is Darcy Carter. She's the writer I told you about. Darcy, this is a dear friend of Vince's and mine. He spends a lot of time here doing odd jobs or remodeling something. You already know Dwayne and Sandy Hudson don't you, Hank? They're sort of in your line of work. They own a window replacement company."

"Five locations throughout the Raleigh-Durham area," Dwayne said, his chest swelling with pride. He gave Hank a hearty handshake. "Nice to see you again. I don't get out to the job sites anymore, I hate to say. I sure do miss getting my hands dirty."

Sandy stiffened. "Dwayne, don't you dare."

Dwayne went on talking as if he hadn't heard. "Got a water leak, has she?"

"Yeah, same spot I found last fall. I'm afraid a patch job isn't going to work this time. Some pipes are going to need to be replaced." Hank turned apologetically to Leanne. "Old houses like these you don't know how long the pipes have been there till you get down in the ground."

Dwayne crossed his arms over his chest. "Yeah, I know what you mean. I see a lot of the old buildings. Some of them have been allowed to go to rot. I could give you a hand if you're going to be working on it today."

Hank looked at Leanne. "Well, it's a pretty big job to get into on a Saturday—"

"This is supposed to be our vacation, Dwayne," Sandy cried, plaintively. "And the man doesn't want to start a job like that on the weekend. You'd just be in the way."

Dwayne gave her a withering look before turning hopefully back to Hank.

"I don't mind taking care of it today, Leanne," Hank said. "Wouldn't be more than a four-hour job. I'd charge you the regular rate."

From Darcy's position on the edge of the porch, she thought she detected something in Hank's expression as he studied Leanne. But no, she must be mistaken. Hank knew Leanne was a married woman. He wouldn't be hitting on his friend's wife at his friend's house, and in front of strangers. She didn't know Hank at all, but he didn't seem like an absolute letch. Then as quickly as the look he gave Leanne appeared in his eyes, it disappeared. He addressed Mr. Hudson. "I wouldn't want to keep you from whatever plans you have."

Darcy relaxed. Her imagination was working overtime on this trip.

Dwayne brushed aside his comment, "No plans—no plans at all."

Hank eyed Dwayne's attire. "Might have a pair of coveralls in the truck you could wear. They'd probably be a little short."

Dwayne brightened like a little boy with a chance to help Dad. "I'm sure that'd be fine."

Sandy heaved a sigh. "Dwayne, I thought we were going to the antique mall."

"You heard the man, won't take but a few hours. We can go later, or you can go yourself. You've been there often enough."

"I might just do that," Sandy said, looking hurt.

Hank swallowed uncomfortably. He hadn't meant to cause a

rift in the Hudsons' marital bliss. "Okay, then." He stepped off the porch and headed toward his truck. Dwayne bounded down the steps after him.

Leanne put her hand on Sandy's arm. "Are you all right, Sandy?"

The older woman shrugged. "I don't mind. In fact, I prefer it. Dwayne is tired to death of that antique mall. He'd go if I insisted, but he'd pout the whole afternoon. This way, he thinks I'm upset, so he'll go out of his way to make it up to me. Now he gets to crawl around in the dirt, and I can spend the day shopping in peace. We both win."

"I was on my way to the waterfall," Darcy told her. "Would you like to join me?"

Sandy shook her head, "No, thanks. You're probably interested in the long trail and I couldn't keep up. Dwayne and I will do the short trip later today." Her smile broadened. "Another thing he hates to do, but he owes me big now."

"If you don't mind the company, I'll go with you," Leanne said to Darcy. "I have a few hours before I need to start dinner."

"I was hoping you'd say that. I'll go upstairs and change."

"I'll meet you on the back deck. Wear a sturdy pair of shoes. Sandy, there's sandwich fixings in the refrigerator if you want something for lunch. Are you sure you'll be all right..."

Darcy headed inside without waiting to hear Sandy's answer. She was anxious to see the waterfall and start working off some of the extra calories she'd consumed since leaving Ohio.

Darcy and Leanne chatted easily on their way to where the two trails divided, one going straight ahead into the forest, and the other angling up a steep incline. Darcy was in good physical shape, she jogged four to five miles nearly every morning, but she was soon out of breath. Leanne moved over the rocks and ruts in the path like someone who made the trip often.

"I have a personal best," she said when Darcy tripped over an exposed tree root and nearly pitched off the side of the mountain.

"Sometimes I like to see how fast I can make it. Other times, I relax and enjoy the experience. There is a clearing in the tree line not much farther up the hill before we get into the woods. The view is amazing. Sometimes I bring my Bible and have devotions there."

"Sounds lovely," Darcy said noncommittally.

Leanne smiled at her over her shoulder. "Are you born again, Darcy?"

Darcy concentrated on the path in front of her, suddenly uncomfortable. "I go to the same church I was brought up in. That is, when I go," she admitted. "To tell you the truth, my church attendance hasn't been the same since I moved away from home."

Darcy was glad Leanne was still walking ahead of her so she couldn't see her face. She had always considered herself a Christian, even though she never gave much thought to whether she was born again or not. She was raised in church, she'd been baptized when she was ten, and she didn't break any commandments on a regular basis. As far as she was concerned, that was above and beyond what God expected from people nowadays.

Leanne didn't say anything until they reached a point where the ascent leveled off. She slowed her pace and waited for Darcy to catch up. "I didn't ask how often you went to church."

"Oh." Darcy felt silly and a little confused. Wasn't that one in the same?

"What I meant was do you have a personal relationship with Jesus Christ?"

"Oh, well sure. I was raised in church."

"Mm," Leanne gave her a look that said she still wasn't giving her the information she wanted, but she turned and resumed walking without asking for more clarification.

The slope descended slightly for about fifty feet. Darcy used the opportunity to catch her breath. She didn't know why, but it was important that Leanne not think of her as a heathen. "I admit the last few years I haven't been as faithful in my Bible study, church attendance, or anything as I once was; I've been really busy. My writing has taken up most of my time. I release two or three books a year. I travel a lot and teach at conferences and things like that. I figure as soon as my schedule lightens up some, I'll get back into the church routine."

"And I imagine Satan will never allow your schedule to lighten up," Leanne said without breaking stride or turning around.

Darcy wasn't sure she appreciated someone she didn't even know discussing Satan with her. Nor did she agree that since her relationship with God wasn't what she once enjoyed, Satan was now pulling her strings. She liked to think she was stronger than that. Her own parents didn't even hassle her about it anymore. Her mother called every couple of weeks whenever something special was going on at church, like a performance by a visiting music group or a revival, to invite her. Every time Darcy turned her down, she would say something like, "You know, Darcy, you should really get back into church."

She would answer, "Yes, I know, Mom."

And that would be the end of it. That's how Darcy liked it. No real pressure.

She didn't even know Leanne, and here she was preaching at her. She wondered if Marjorie at the Danbury knew how to mind her own business, or if every innkeeper in the South berated their guests about their spiritual wellbeing.

"I don't think Satan's any too concerned with me or my schedule," she said, ending with a little chuckle she hoped would let Leanne know she wasn't interested in continuing the conversation.

To her surprise, Leanne chuckled back. "He's more concerned than you think. We don't realize what a threat we can be to him when we're walking with Jesus. Most of us don't even believe he exists anymore."

The ground under their feet sloped sharply upward. Leanne jumped over a fallen log with an energy Darcy didn't possess and took a few running strides up the hill. "Here we are. Wait till you see this vista."

Darcy picked up her pace the best she could. The climb deprived her of the ability to respond, which was just as well since she was still considering Leanne's remark about being a threat to Satan. She'd never heard that before. She still believed in the

Satan she had learned about in Sunday school, although he had become an almost Hollywood type, boogieman caricature in her mind.

Leanne reached the crest of the hill and stepped out onto a rock outcropping. When Darcy reached the level ground, she gasped audibly. Below them and on three sides, the ground gave way to empty air, offering an unencumbered view of the Smoky Mountains. She stepped gingerly onto the outcropping and peered over the edge. She stomped her foot and then jumped up and down.

Leanne laughed easily. "Don't worry this has been here far longer than you or me."

Darcy chuckled, her initial anxiety disappearing. "Good to know."

Leanne put her hands on her hips and turned her face to the wind. She closed her eyes and inhaled deeply.

Darcy did the same, but opened her eyes immediately when she swooned and imagined she was falling. "I can see why you love to come up here," she told Leanne.

Leanne sat cross-legged like a child on the outcropping. Darcy dropped down beside her, thankful for a chance to rest. The two women sat in silence and surveyed the mountains. Below them a road was barely visible through the trees. Darcy wondered how far up they were but didn't want to spoil the beauty of the moment by speaking.

It was Leanne who finally broke the silence. "My dad used to bring me up here when I was little. Sometimes I'd pretend I couldn't make it so he'd carry me on his shoulders for a while." She sat quietly for a few moments before speaking again. "We'd come up to this very spot and sit and listen to nature. He'd test me to see how many species of birds I could identify."

"I never noticed they sounded different," Darcy said.

"Oh, yeah, it's amazing what we don't hear because we don't know how to be still anymore. Dad would have me close my eyes and listen to the water, the birds, and the wind. He always said creation was having church. He'd point to the tops of the trees and say, 'Look, Annie, see how the trees are lifting holy hands.' He said the river provided the music while the birds sang the chorus. He always told me if we would pay closer attention to nature, we'd see how to worship God the way He intended."

Darcy wasn't sure of an appropriate response so she kept quiet. She kind of liked the picture his words conjured up in her imagination, but at the same time, she wondered if the man wasn't a little too fanciful for her tastes.

"Lots of times we'd sit up here and not say a word," Leanne continued, "but other times we'd be the ones having church. Dad had the best baritone singing voice in our church and he wasn't ashamed to belt it out. You could hear him singing from anywhere in the building." Her voice cracked with emotion. "Vince is the same way. Such a powerful voice, but he doesn't use it for the Lord anymore. Not since Amber. I still catch him singing once in a blue moon when he thinks I'm not listening."

Darcy wrapped her arms around her knees and rocked back. "Who's Amber?"

As soon as the question was out of her mouth, she wished she could take it back. Wasn't it apparent? Leanne and Vince had lost a child. How could she be so insensitive!

Leanne's answer was the last thing she expected to hear. "She was Vince's wife."

Darcy blinked. "His wife?"

Leanne nodded and looked back over the vista. "Look there between those trees," she said, pointing. "That's Talmedge's business district." She laughed at her own joke. "See? It's right there. Can you see that church steeple? That's our church. It's just a little country church. Only about sixty or seventy people on any given Sunday, but we all love the Lord. I'd love it if you would go with me tomorrow."

Darcy followed Leanne's pointing finger. It took quite some searching to spot the speck of civilization through the trees, especially since all she could think about was Vince *and his wife.* A nasty divorce would certainly explain his personality, or rather his lack thereof, but what about Leanne? She sure seemed to take his behavior in stride. Darcy thought of Hank Haywood and the look he gave Leanne back at the house. She wondered if Leanne knew how Hank felt about her. Maybe she even shared his feelings, and that was how she could put up with a husband who still held a candle for his late wife.

"Well, what do you think?" Leanne asked.

"It's beautiful."

"No," Leanne said. "I mean it is beautiful, but what I meant to ask was, do you want to go to church with me in the morning? I promise not to preach at you. If you're worried about not having anything to wear, don't be. We're used to visitors. Or you could borrow something of mine."

"Oh, no, I brought a skirt and jacket with me."

"Is that a yes?"

Darcy smiled in spite of herself. She could see Leanne was hard to refuse. "I don't know. I'll think about it, okay?"

Leanne stood up and brushed her hands across the seat of her pants. "Fair enough. Breakfast is at eight on Sunday mornings, and then I hide everything in the dishwasher so I have plenty of time to get ready for church. We need to get moving if we're going to see that waterfall."

Darcy nodded and followed her along the trail. It leveled off as it led into the dark pines. "We go uphill a little farther on, and then it's all downhill to the waterfall. You're in for a treat. Oh, I should have reminded you to bring your camera."

"I'll come back before I leave to take pictures," Darcy promised.

"Almost there," Leanne encouraged when they had traveled on for quite some distance. Even she was beginning to sound breathless.

Darcy became aware of the sound of rushing water. Leanne heard it too and quickened her pace. Darcy lengthened her strides to keep up.

"There!" Leanne shouted over the roar of the water. "Do you see it?"

Darcy stepped around her and gasped in delight. "Wow, it jumps right out of nowhere, doesn't it?"

"Only this time of year, when the trees are mostly bare, you should see it when there's snow on them."

The two women practically ran down the hill to the base of the waterfall where the other trail joined theirs. The parks' department had put a railing around the water's edge, a plank walkway, and several benches at intervals for resting and admiring.

"It's gorgeous," Darcy exclaimed.

"It's one of many in the area," Leanne told her, "but my personal favorite. If you have time before you go back home, maybe we can drive around and check out some others."

"I'd love it."

They walked back and forth across the walkway several times to enjoy the waterfall from all angles before sitting down on one of the benches.

"I love coming here," Leanne said, a look of joy on her face. "It's the closest place to heaven I can imagine. I was a kid when the state built up the trails and everything. Before that, it was really a hike. Mom used to freak out whenever I came here by myself. She was sure I'd fall to my death. I guess if I had kids, I'd worry too, even with the hand railings and all the improvements that have been made."

"Did you ever want kids?" Darcy asked, and then mentally kicked herself again. She came here to write a book, not get so personal with her host. Leanne just made it easy to talk, not that Darcy generally needed encouragement.

Leanne shrugged. "I used to think about it. But when I was younger, I was so busy taking care of my parents. Then I guess time got away from me."

"What about Vince?"

She shrugged again. "Oh, I don't know. Men don't talk about stuff like that."

"It isn't too late, Leanne. You're both still young enough for kids."

Leanne smiled. "Vince is, but not me. I mean I'm not physically too old." At Darcy's questioning look, she smiled. "I'm thirty-six if you must know, but sometimes I feel like that stage of my life is past. Besides, we'd have to get married first."

"Married?" So she and Vince were living together. Another first impression missed by a mile. But didn't they have the same last name?

"Yeah, around here that's what people do before they go having kids," Leanne said with a smile. "Well, most of the time. Since neither one of us is seeing anyone, I don't see kids in either of our futures."

Darcy put her foot up on the bench in front of her and propped her forearm on her knee. "Hold on a minute, Leanne. You lost me. Are you married to Vince or not?"

Leanne threw back her head and laughed. "Married—to Vince? What gave you that idea? That big doofus is my brother."

Darcy laughed along with her. "Oh, my goodness, no wonder I've been so confused. Last night you said he never plays games with the crowd, and I haven't seen him around the house at all. I thought the two of you had some kind of distant relationship. Then when I saw the way the handyman looked at you on the porch, well, I just thought…oh, never mind."

"The handyman? You mean Hank?" Leanne shook her head. "He doesn't look at me any way. I've known Hank all my life. He used to be Vince's boss before he bought the café."

"That doesn't mean he can't fall in love with you."

Leanne stood up and fastened her attention on the rushing water at the bottom of the ravine. "Darcy, you are way off. Hank's a sweet guy, but he doesn't think anymore about me than he would a sister. He was married before, a long time ago, and it was pretty bad. He got divorced and his ex remarried, like the next day. Hank was devastated. I don't think he's ever gotten over it."

Darcy held up her hands in front of her. "Okay, if you say so. You know him a lot better than I do. I'm just telling you what it looked like to me." She stood up.

"I'm sure it's your writer's imagination playing tricks on you," Leanne said, although her assurance sounded a little weak to Darcy's ears. "You people see romance where none exist."

"I write nonfiction, remember? I don't have a romantic notion in my head."

"Sure you do. Now, come on. I'm cooking dinner for the guests tonight, and I need to start. Let's take the short way back."

Darcy's leg muscles had tightened while she was sitting on the bench, and Leanne didn't have to work hard to convince her.

"I always cook on Fridays and Saturdays when I have company," Leanne explained as she led Darcy down the path to the easier trail. "Last night we all decided on ordering in, but usually I cook. I expect you to have dinner with us. I like for my guests to think of themselves as part of the family."

"Sure, sounds great."

Leanne looked at Darcy over her shoulder as she kept walking. "I guess that's one of the reasons I loved the idea of running a bed-and-breakfast. I always wanted a big family, and after it became just Vince and me, this really appealed to me."

Darcy had to ask the question that had been weighing on her since she found out Vince had been married before but not to Leanne.

"What happened to Vince's wife?"

Leanne didn't answer right away. Darcy was beginning to think she should have left her curious nature unsatisfied this time when Leanne finally spoke, "The poor thing." Darcy wasn't sure if she was talking about Vince or Amber. "They'd been married four years, high school sweethearts, voted best couple and all that. You know how small towns are. Then one night Amber lost control of her car and was killed. Vince fell apart. It wasn't long after Mom died, so I think that made it even harder on him. But anyway, he moved back home with me, sold his and Amber's house and bought the café. That's where he's been ever since."

Darcy felt like a jerk for being so hard on the guy. Of course he was a grouch. How could he not be? She was determined not to form any more opinions of people she didn't know anything about. Her mother was right. She mustn't judge someone until she'd walked a mile in his shoes.

$\mathcal{I}$ · $\mathcal{I}$ · $\mathcal{I}$ · $\mathcal{I}$ **6**

$\mathcal{B}$ack at the $\mathcal{I}$nn, $\mathcal{D}$arcy and Leanne found Hank and Mr. Hudson up to their knees in a muddy hole near the back deck. "How's it going, fellas?" Leanne asked, eyeing the thick black mud on the bottom half of Dwayne's borrowed coveralls. Sandy was going to throw a fit.

Hank looked up and grinned. "We're getting her taken care of."

Darcy couldn't help but wonder if there was more in Hank's grin than plain old good-naturedness. Leanne had assured her they were just old friends. There had to be more to it than that, especially since Leanne was suddenly going out of her way to avoid eye contact with Hank.

"Do you need anything? Dwayne, are you all right?" Leanne asked.

"Finer'n frog hair," he laughed. At least he was having a grand time.

"Okay, well, you two stay out of trouble. Hank, would you like to stay for dinner? It's on me."

Hank took off his cap and wiped the back of his forearm across his forehead. "Nah, that's not necessary."

"I insist," Leanne stated amicably. "Consider it my down payment on your bill."

Hank replaced his cap and climbed out of the hole to stand beside her. He pulled a bandana out of his back pocket and wiped his hands clean. "You don't owe me anything, Leanne."

She put her hand on his arm. "Watch what you say in front of witnesses, Hank. I may hold you to that someday. I'm fixing veal parmesan. If you ask nice, I might whip up a batch of my Mississippi mud fudge you like so well."

"Well, since you put it that way…"

Darcy watched the exchange, her eyes whipping from Hank to Leanne and back again. Hank didn't take his eyes off Leanne as she headed for the door and went inside. Darcy followed her. She caught up with her in the hallway and grabbed her arm, forcing her to turn around.

Darcy let go of Leanne's arm and set her hands on her hips. "Okay, tell me you didn't notice that." She couldn't keep from grinning. It was like being in junior high again.

Leanne shrugged out of her sweater and started toward the kitchen. "Darcy, I honestly don't know what you're talking about."

Darcy stayed abreast of her. "Give me a break, Leanne. Don't tell me you don't know the hold you've got on that man." She wasn't sure if Leanne's pink cheeks should be attributed to the cold outside or her comment about Hank.

"Oh, Darcy, that's just Hank. He likes everybody."

"He may like everybody, but he's got it bad for you. Like my grandma used to say; 'A blind man could feel it with his cane. '"

Leanne laughed. "At least now I know where your overactive imagination came from. I've known Hank Haywood forever. His sister, Iris, was my best friend in school."

"That may well be, but I think you underestimate him. Remember, I'm the one the world thinks is qualified to write Finding Mr. Right. Your Mr. Right could be right under your nose."

Leanne hung her sweater on a hook by the door and led Darcy into the kitchen. "Like I told you before, Hank's family and ours have known each other for generations. There has never been anything romantic between us. Good grief, Darcy, he's ten years older than me."

Darcy sniffed. "Ten years. That's nothing unless you're in kindergarten, and he's in high school."

"I guess you got a point, but still, Hank…"

Darcy pulled off her coat and folded it across her arms. "Okay, however you want it is fine with me. If there's no chemistry between you, far be it from me to push you two together or anything. I'm just pointing out as someone watching from the sidelines that Hank is crazy about you."

Leanne headed to the utility sink and turned on the water full blast. Darcy didn't miss the blush creeping up her cheeks. Maybe Leanne didn't want to admit it, or she had never thought of Hank in that way, but she was obviously flattered now that the idea was planted in her mind. She squirted some soap onto her hands and scrubbed them together. She kept her eyes on her hands as she spoke.

"Vince started working for Hank as soon as he got out of high school…"

Darcy smiled to herself. She knew what Leanne was doing. She wanted to change the subject and get Darcy's mind off matchmaking. If Hank were nothing more than a friend like she claimed, she wouldn't bother.

"I thought Vince loved doing contract work with Hank. He was good at it. But after Amber was killed, he up and quit and said he was buying the café." She shook her head. "I never saw that coming." She turned off the water and ripped a length of paper towel from the roll hanging at her elbow. She turned around and leaned her hips against the countertop as she wiped her hands. "But he loves that café, and he's happy. Well, maybe happy is too strong a word. I know he's lonely."

She suddenly stopped talking and looked at Darcy.

"What?" Darcy asked. "What are you staring at?"

"Nothing," Leanne said around a sly smile.

"Leanne, I can see the gears turning in your head."

"You're not the only one who can do a little matchmaking."

Darcy hooked her finger in the collar of her jacket and tossed it over her shoulder. "Okay, I'm outta here. I think I'll go upstairs and take a shower and maybe a little nap. All this running around has caught up with me."

"I didn't mean to run you off."

Darcy looked back to see her grinning from ear to ear. "I think that's exactly what you meant to do. Just remember, I'm here to work on my southern dining book, not Mr. Right. If he's out there, he's too good at hiding for me to find him."

Leanne shook her head. "You're the one who said he might be right under your nose."

"Under your nose, not mine."

Leanne put her hands up in front of her. "Okay, truce. I won't try to set you up with my brother, and you won't get anymore ideas about me and Hank."

Darcy nodded. "Truce."

"Do you want a wake up call?"

"No, a little power nap is all I need."

Darcy dashed upstairs before Leanne could forget that they'd agreed to stay out of each other's love lives. She had time to check out another local diner during its lunch hour, but at the moment she couldn't stand the thought of one more morsel of food. And she wanted to save room for Leanne's veal parmesan. This was supposed to be a combination research trip and vacation anyway. That's what she told her family and Carla. She needed a break.

She grabbed a comfy tee and pair of sweats out of the drawer of the highboy and went next door to the bathroom. She'd relax, get comfortable, read a little, and allow herself a short nap. She might even get around to transcribing her notes into her laptop.

She took a quick shower before Hank had a chance to turn the water off again and dashed back to her room. She sat at the antique dresser and combed out her long wet hair. Her cheeks were still flushed from the hot shower. She leaned forward and examined her face. At twenty-nine, her skin was firm and wrinkle free. She hoped it was a sign of things to come. Her mother still had youthful skin and a nice figure. Darcy had inherited her thick mahogany hair and olive skin tone from her side of the family, as well as her long legs and statuesque frame. Her upturned nose and wide eyes had come from Dad, but fortunately all her features worked together. She wasn't vain; she seldom looked in the mirror longer than necessary to whip on a quick layer of foundation and mascara and comb her hair back from her face. Maybe it was all Carla's talk about the Mr. Right book and Leanne's talk about Vince.

She laughed at the notion of finding Mr. Right here in this backwoods town in western North Carolina. She got up and moved to the bed. She turned back the bedspread and sheet and lay down. Her Mr. Right wasn't here. He wasn't in Middleburg Heights, Ohio. If he existed at all—which she seriously doubted—he had already been snagged by a Ms. Right.

Either she was more tired than she realized, the large amount of food had induced a sugar coma, or the mountain air had cleared her head, because she fell asleep almost instantly. Instead of waking refreshed quite some time later, she felt like she'd been horse whipped. She sat up and groaned and put her hand over one eye. She was reminded of why she didn't usually nap in the afternoon even when she was sitting at her computer and could barely keep her eyes open.

The room was cast in shadows. Through her open eye, she looked at the clock on the nightstand and saw she had been asleep for three hours. No wonder she felt so crummy. She swung her legs over the side of the bed and put her hands on the sides of her head. She could feel her pulse pounding through her fingers.

She stood up and her leg muscles cramped in protest from the long hike. She leaned forward at the waist and let her hands hang loose near her feet. Then she squatted and slowly straightened back up. Her legs felt better, but now her head was pounding. She stumbled to the wardrobe for her purse. It was buried under a pair of jeans she'd stepped out of and hadn't bothered to fold. Without turning the light on, she rummaged through the purse and then the drawer on her night table, but couldn't find anything to relieve a headache.

The bathroom medicine cabinet also came up empty. She splashed cool water on her face and grimaced at her reflection. Her eyes were puffy, her usually rosy complexion pale and splotchy, and her hair was a fright. She went back to her room and got her brush and makeup kit. After brushing the tangles out of her long tresses, she put some foundation and blush on her face and a little mascara on her lashes. She looked better, except for the squint of her brow against the pain that continued to throb against her skull. No question about it, she was going to have to go downstairs and beg some aspirin off someone. She stepped out of her room and pulled the door shut behind her. All the other doors on the second floor were closed. She heard whispered voices behind the honeymooners' door. No headache, no matter how severe, was worth interrupting them. She hadn't laid eyes on the pair yet, and she was willing to put money down that she was the last person they wanted knocking on their door.

She hurried past the honeymooners' room and padded downstairs in her stocking feet. Amazing how comfortable she had become at the Ravenswood Inn in only twenty-four hours. She headed to the kitchen to find Leanne. She kept one hand over the left side of her face from where the pain originated. Even in her discomfort, she couldn't help noticing how gorgeous the house was. She still hadn't received her tour, but now wasn't the time. Later, she'd get her camera and take pictures of the woodwork and heavy antique furniture. When she got home, it would be fun to shop a few estate sales for some pieces for her own house.

The kitchen was empty save for what looked like the beginning of a delicious dinner. There was even a batch of what she assumed was Mississippi mud fudge on the gleaming countertop. She wondered if the rush of caffeine from a piece of the fudge would banish her headache, but decided an aspirin would work better at this point in time. The fudge would destine her to another hike up the mountain to the waterfall, and she wasn't feeling that motivated at the moment. She went through the kitchen to the back door and stepped out onto the deck. She breathed in the crisp mountain air. Some of the tension slipped from the back of her neck. She hugged her arms around her and walked the length of the deck. She looked around the corner of the house. No Leanne or other signs of life.

She closed her eyes against the sun and massaged her forehead. She was getting desperate. If she didn't get rid of this headache soon, she wouldn't feel like doing anything the rest of the day.

She stepped off the deck and walked around the house, past the mound of fresh dirt that marked the spot where Hank and Mr. Hudson had found the water leak. The Hudson's car was gone from the driveway, evidence that Dwayne was making it up to Sandy for the four hours of their vacation he spent playing in the dirt with his new friend.

She came to the back end of the wraparound front porch. She went up a narrow set of steps and stopped in front of a side entrance she hadn't noticed before. The door was unlocked. She pushed it open and found herself inside a dark-paneled den. A stone fireplace and library shelves dominated one wall. A mounted bear's head glared down at her from above the fireplace. Darcy shuddered and turned to face an oversized walnut desk on the opposite wall. A computer monitor sat to the left of an ink blotter. A keyboard, mouse pad, silver penholder, stress reliever, and a tiny silver picture frame were the only other items on the desk. On the wall behind the desk, two mounted deer heads watched her with the same eerie malice as the bear. She turned from the gaze of the glass eyes and turned the frame with the tip of her finger just enough to see who was in the picture. A lovely young woman stared dreamily up at her.

Amber. It had to be.

This was Vince's office. His thumbprint was everywhere, from the dark jacquard curtains and stone fireplace to the menacing animal trophies. This was definitely not a part of the house where she had been given free rein. She turned to leave the same way she had come in. At that moment the pocket door that led to the rest of the house slid open. She whirled around. A pair of flashing eyes with about as much warmth as the bear over the fireplace glared at her.

Vince's eyes fell to the silver frame. "What are you doing in here?" he growled, sounding like the bear he resembled.

"I—I came..." She pointed lamely toward the door off the porch.

He moved to the desk with two long strides. He reached around her and repositioned the picture frame the way it had been before her invasion into his private sanctum. "I don't know what would make you think you could come into my office and go through my things."

"I wasn't going through your things." Even as she defended herself, she had to admit it must look that way to him. "I was looking for Leanne, and I came in this door from the porch," she finished weakly.

Eyes narrowed, recognition dawned on Vince's face. "You. I thought I recognized your car outside."

Darcy straightened her shoulders. She had about enough of his rudeness and accusations. She explained why she was in here. If that wasn't good enough for him, well, too bad. Certainly looking at a woman in a picture wasn't a crime in any part of the country. "I didn't realize it was your office," she said, her temerity replaced with indignation. "The door was unlocked. I had no reason to think I couldn't use this entrance. I have a headache, and I was going to see if Leanne had something for it."

His face softened but only by a degree. "The door shouldn't have been unlocked."

Darcy stepped around him. Her head was pounding. She had neither the patience nor the desire to apologize again for a simple mistake.

"Hey, city girl."

She whirled around, ready for battle despite her aching head. This guy had more nerve than anyone she'd come across in a long time. She opened her mouth to give him a piece of her mind.

"Sorry I jumped to conclusions," he said, looking sincere for the first time since she'd met him.

An apology was the last thing she'd been expecting. "Um, okay."

"You startled me, that's all. This room is off limits to guests, but doors do get left unlocked sometimes."

Darcy couldn't think of a word to say. She should tell him she understood, that she'd been known to fly off the handle herself, but the words wouldn't come. She looked into his hazel eyes and couldn't remember how she'd ended up in his office in the first place.

Wordlessly, she headed for the door.

"Did you say you have a headache?"

Without waiting for a reply, he opened the top drawer of his desk. He pushed a few things around before extracting a tall bottle of Tylenol. He flicked off the childproof lid and held the bottle out to her. "A peace offering."

Darcy couldn't help but smile in return. She held out her hand, and he dumped two pills into her palm. "Thanks," she mumbled.

He recapped the bottle, set it back in the drawer, and slid it shut. Then he sat down in his office chair and turned his attention to the computer. Darcy waited for a half second before realizing she had been dismissed. She exited the office, sliding the door gently closed behind her. Just when she thought she had Vince Ravenscraft figured out, he went and did something out of character that made her think there was a real heart beating inside that broad chest. Then he did another complete one-eighty and went back to being his usual frustrating self. She didn't know if he was sorely lacking basic social graces or was just plain rude. Surely his parents had tried to teach him manners since Leanne was friendly enough.

She headed for the kitchen to find a glass of water, making sure she didn't make any other wrong turns and end up in another part of the house that was 'off limits'. For sanity's sake, she would put Vince Ravenscraft out of her mind. She had enough to do over the next few weeks without fretting over what made the man tick.

Vince didn't dare look up from the computer screen as it booted up until he heard the door close behind her. He stared at the polished panel door, almost willing the young woman to come back in. He assumed she was the writer Leanne had mentioned last night, Tracy or Kasey something-or-other. He hadn't been paying attention when she told him about their new guest. He seldom listened when she talked about the inn unless it included a job he needed to do. He'd learned over the last few years to tune out whatever didn't affect him. He had gotten very good at it.

He had not realized until finding Leanne's latest guest in his office that she was the same woman he'd yelled at outside the Raven Café for blocking the dumpster— something everybody did, but it still irritated him to no end. When he saw the candy apple red SUV parked beside the café yesterday he went over as a matter of curiosity to see where the malefactor was from, a habit of someone with too much time on his hands. He liked to guess from the type of vehicle where the driver was from, what he looked like, and what he did for a living. Strange cars pulled into the café parking lot everyday, and he'd gotten pretty accurate at pegging its driver and occupants. He immediately surmised that the sporty little SUV belonged to a single person. Probably a college kid living it up on Daddy's money or a group of young Republicans getting a head start on spring break. When he recognized the Ohio license plate, he suspected Cleveland, and he had been right. He was still in the middle of giving the annoying hothead an occupation when the young woman approached. She looked like he knew she would from the appearance of the vehicle—tall and willowy, leather tote, and designer shoes he could almost bet hadn't come from J. C. Penney's.

So he let her have it with both barrels, not that she particularly deserved it for a minor infraction such as inconveniencing Stu who would have to maneuver the garbage truck around her car, but because she and countless others like her thought they could drive into Talmedge and do whatever they pleased with no regard to the locals. As soon as he started railing on her, he realized he was out of line, but he was already good and mad by this point. It was too late to stop. The shock in her innocent brown eyes, the color of semisweet chocolate morsels—since opening the café, Vince associated everything with food—the hurt, followed by indignation and anger made him consider apologizing; something he hadn't done in four years. Instead he turned and stomped into the café never looking back, sure he'd never see her sweet little injured face again.

It wasn't as though he went out of his way to hurt people. On the contrary, he ignored or avoided them as often as possible. His restaurant was his life. He ran it with a firm hand; his employees respected him, his customers made jokes about his hard exterior, but they kept coming back day after day, meal after meal, scarfing down his grub and loving every bite.

It was the only pleasure Vince Ravenscraft found these days. He liked to watch a customer's expression when he sampled a new recipe. He enjoyed the compliments he overheard to June or Missy about his pecan pie. He liked seeing diners push themselves away from the table and dab the corners of their mouths or pat their stomachs in satisfaction. He just never let them know he watched them. They thought he had no feelings; that nothing matters one way or another to the "old man" as long as the receipts were straight at the end of the day. He liked that image of himself so he perpetuated it. He stayed cool and distant. No one, not even Leanne, knew how much certain things did matter to him. He had a habit of losing things that mattered to him—his parents, his marriage, Amber...

Amber, the thought of her still sliced through him, opening the old wound. He hadn't spoken her name aloud since the funeral, and it was seldom spoken in his presence. *The grieving widower*, everyone thought when they saw him. What they didn't see was her killer.

Oh, he hadn't put a gun to her head. He hadn't driven her car into that tractor trailer truck, but he may as well have. They'd been fighting that night, again. The same old argument they'd had since a year into their marriage. Amber wanted out of Talmedge, out of the mountains they both called home. She wanted no part of any of it, while Vince was satisfied growing old looking out onto the same two-lane road that snaked past their small house. Her desire to leave strengthened at the same pace that his resolute determination to stay put grew.

An old girlfriend of hers lived in Philadelphia. She called on a regular basis and told Amber about the jobs and opportunities that were theirs for the taking. Amber could taste it. Vince had no desire to live anywhere but Talmedge, and Philadelphia was barely one step up from Hell itself in his book.

He wanted Rob Dooley's old café. The building had been for sale for five years, empty for ten. It had such potential. Every morning he drove through the tiny cross in the road that made up Talmedge on his way to whatever job Hank and he were doing at the time. His eyes were drawn to the empty and decaying café, and he'd dream of what he could do with it. It took eight months of stewing, debating, and going over figures in his head before he got the nerve to broach the subject with Amber. She reacted the way he knew she would.

"Who in their right mind would sink good money into that dump," she had shrieked, "into this town? You're crazy, Vince. No way! Absolutely no way."

That had ended the conversation—that night.

Amber's lack of enthusiasm didn't kill his dream of running his own café. He talked to the woman at the real estate office in Waynesville in charge of the property. She gave him copies of the fiscal reports of Dooley's last three years in business. He instantly spotted ten things Rob had done wrong; things he knew he could do right. He kept the papers hidden in the bottom of the chest of drawers and studied them every chance he got. On rainy days or when he and Hank were between jobs, he used Leanne's computer to research the business of running a café. The more he learned, the more he fell in love with the idea.

He wanted it bad. As badly as Amber wanted out of Talmedge, he wanted to make a go of Rob Dooley's café. Six months went by while Vince nursed his dream. The real estate agent called the house to tell him Rob had lowered the price five thousand dollars. If Vince was truly interested, Rob was willing to make it happen.

Amber took the message. When Vince got home from work, she lit into him like an angry she-bear.

"I already told you, Vince, this ain't happening. We aren't buying that café. We can't afford it for one thing. I'd like to know where you think the money'd come from, but more than that, I don't want it. Don't you see what happens to people who run cafés in broken down towns? They get broken down. I've got better things to do than spend my days in a greasy café slinging hash and getting slapped on the rear by farmers. Forget it, Vince! Not in this lifetime."

"It won't be a greasy café," he countered. His eyes brightened as he tried to convey to his reluctant wife the image that kept him awake at night. "I've been studying. With the right management and good food, that restaurant can be a cute little place. I'm going to tear out a wall and expand seating. The kitchen is perfect, lots of space. You know the location is good. This place is teeming with tourists six months out of the year. It won't be some little dive where anybody but locals are afraid to stop. If you'd just sit down with me and listen to what I'm thinking..."

Amber was shaking her head, her heavy blonde mane swirling across her face. She crossed her arms. "Vince, you're talking like it's a done deal. Well, it's not! How many times do I have to tell you that? I've lived in this little nothing of a town my whole life. I can't take it anymore. I want out. I've been doing some thinking of my own. Let's sell the house. After we relocate, if you still have this crazy dream of yours, we can look into investing in a coffee house or something. You could manage one for a while and see if it's something you really want to do."

Vince didn't try to disguise his surprise. "Sell the house? Where did that come from? We picked this place out together. You never said a word about hating it around here three years ago. Remember our first night here?"

He reached for her hand, but she jerked away from him.

Tears glistened in the corners of her eyes. "I don't want to remember anything about it. This house, this town, this life," she said gesturing wildly with her arms, "is your dream, not mine. It always has been." She sank onto the sofa, and her voice softened. "I loved you, Vince. I loved the idea of being married to you. I couldn't bring myself to stand up to you. I wanted you to be happy. But I can't live your dream anymore."

He sank to his knees on the floor in front of her. "You *loved* me?"

She reached out and touched his face. "I didn't mean that. I still love you."

Even as he listened to the words he saw something in her eyes, something he didn't want to acknowledge—doubt; a worm of uncertainty. He wasn't sure if even she believed what she was saying.

"I can't keep living here, Sweetheart. I just can't." She put both hands on either side of his face and smoothed them back through his hair. His resolve weakened. She knew the power her touch had over him. A smile played across her lips. Her hands continued to knead his neck and shoulders. "What if we buy the restaurant and end up hating it? It's a fulltime job. You said yourself the busiest time of the year would be tourist season. That means every summer for the rest of our lives we'd be stuck here. No summer vacation like normal people. What happens when we have kids? What about them?" Her hands traveled down his back, her fingernails sharp through the fabric of his shirt.

He tried to focus on making his point. "I don't have all the answers, Amber. I know this has to be something we both want. But I do know I don't want to move to the city and manage a coffee house. I couldn't stand those city people with their café lattes looking down their noses at this country bumpkin. I already get that here in Talmedge from the tourists. I am who I am, Darlin', and I can't change for any man. I won't."

"Vince." Her voice was low and throaty. She scooted to the edge of the couch and leaned into his chest. "No one's asking you to change. I just expect the same courtesy from you. I have no intention of waiting tables when I'm fifty, barely scraping by on tips, and washing grease outta your clothes every night. It may be your dream, but it's not mine."

"It wouldn't be that way," he insisted.

She put her finger against his lips. "Hush, now. Let's talk about it later."

The next week Vince withdrew his offer on the café. He drove the long way to work, bypassing Talmedge's main street that took him past the little block building. He tried to let it go. He tried to concentrate on the contracting jobs that kept him and Hank busy and the bills paid, but he grew more dissatisfied all the time; dissatisfied with his job, dissatisfied with his marriage, dissatisfied with Amber's ploys to distract him whenever she saw the way his mind was leaning.

A few weeks later, she broached the subject of moving. "I talked to Dianne today."

Vince braced himself. He knew what talking to Dianne meant. "There's a deli in her neighborhood for sale. It will probably by bought by a local chain, but it'll need management. The pay won't be great starting out, but there'll be decent benefits."

Vince cut her off before she could get going. "I'm not working for somebody else. I do that already. That's what I want to get away from."

Amber realized the sweet act wasn't working so she went after his ego. "Then why don't you work for yourself? You don't need Hank Haywood. You know as much about drywall and plumbing as he does. Go into business for yourself."

The same old argument Vince had heard a hundred times before.

He wanted to tell her that he wasn't the only one in their marriage who didn't know how to listen. He wanted to tell her he wasn't happy working for Hank, and he wouldn't be happy living down the street from Dianne in her upscale Philadelphia neighborhood, making sandwiches for yuppies. Instead he kept quiet. There were plenty of people in the world who weren't happy with what they did for a living, but they got up every Monday morning and went to a place they dreaded all weekend. Most of them never saw their dreams fulfilled. They dreamed of living on a tropical island painting sunsets, climbing mountains, or saying goodbye to the rat race of daily living—but they didn't. They acted responsibly. The sooner he did the same, the better.

When the real estate agent called and said Rob Dooley was willing to talk with Vince about the café, he politely explained he was no longer interested. He didn't mean a word of it, but he said it anyway.

After giving up on the idea of the café, Vince thought everything was fine at home, but things between he and Amber continued to spiral downward. Apparently it wasn't just Talmedge, North Carolina she was dissatisfied with. Dianne broke up with her boyfriend so Amber spent a weekend with her in the city. Two months later Dianne was having trouble at work so Amber stayed a week. Vince tried not to think about what was happening. When Amber came home she was always loving and attentive. He enjoyed at least a week of honeymoon bliss before she started in on him again about something. He closed his eyes and tried not to notice that his wife became more of a stranger after every visit to Philadelphia.

Then Dianne's sister was getting married so Amber needed to make more frequent trips to the city to shop with Dianne for bridesmaids' dresses, flowers, and caterers. The list went on and on. "Dianne has to be there for her sister," Amber explained whenever Vince complained. "And I have to be there for Dianne. Getting married is a very stressful time for everyone involved."

Vince didn't remember a lot of stress and brouhaha surrounding his wedding, but in all fairness to her argument, men remembered little about getting married other than the expenses and the wedding night.

Wedding preparations drew on for several months. Vince, like a turtle with his head in his shell, slowly started to get suspicious. Reasoning that he wanted to surprise Amber with a romantic weekend in the city, he got off work Friday evening, showered, gassed up the truck, and drove to Philadelphia. He arrived at Dianne's building at three o'clock the next morning. Someone at the party rang him upstairs where he found Amber barely dressed in a red bustier Vince had never seen, dozing in Dianne's bed in the arms of a young attorney.

Vince drove home alone. After some time, he accepted Amber's apology and assurance that she had too much to drink at a party and couldn't even remember how she ended up in Troy's arms. He had to believe her. She was his wife. What choice did he have?

He wished he had someone to talk to. His dear mother had passed away a few months earlier. Leanne was busy trying to figure out her place in a world where she suddenly had no apparent purpose for being. He had never been one to discuss his problems anyway; like all men, he watched football and waited for them to resolve themselves. But in this instance, the problem wasn't going away.

Even with all their troubles and differences staring him in the face, Vince was blindsided when Amber told him she wanted a divorce. He didn't want to let her go. In his family, people were either happily married or pretended to be. Divorce wasn't an option. Their fights increased in occurrence and severity.

One night she packed her things and announced she was moving in with her sister in Raleigh. She hadn't been back to Philadelphia since she found out Troy had moved in with Dianne.

When begging didn't convince Amber to stay, Vince tried guilt. He reminded her of the vows she'd made in church.

"That was before I knew what a close-minded horse's behind you are," she defended herself.

Around midnight, Vince got tired of fighting and started working on a six-pack of beer he had in the fridge. A few parting barbs on both sides and the sound of Amber's tires on asphalt screeched through the neighborhood. A half hour later, Vince didn't even look up from the television when sirens pierced the night air. He sent the last empty beer can in an arc toward the garbage can in the kitchen, missing by a good ten feet, reclined back in his chair and closed his eyes on an old Seinfeld episode.

The telephone woke him up. He sobered instantly when Brendan Slater, a county deputy, said he needed to meet the sheriff on the new highway. Amber had been involved in an accident. It looked serious.

Amber was gone by the time Vince got there. From the severity of the accident, he suspected she was gone by the time anyone got there, but he never asked for details. He was never asked why three packed suitcases were in the back of her little car or why he reeked of alcohol when he arrived on the scene. His wife was gone. Nothing could be gained by placing blame.

After Amber's death, Vince couldn't bring himself to go home. Instead Leanne met him at the hospital and took him home with her. In a dazed stupor he made funeral arrangements and answered the same questions to Amber's family. He moved his things into his old room in the house where he grew up and put his and Amber's house on the market. It sold in a record twenty-four days to an elderly couple retiring from Charlotte. A month later a check arrived from an insurance company from whom Vince didn't remember ever buying a policy.

He sat on both checks, torn over the possibility of spending Amber's death benefits on the one thing she hated more than him—the café. He didn't speak to anyone about it. He continued working for Hank. Leanne did her best to make him comfortable, but he could see she was preoccupied with her own thoughts; thoughts he didn't know at the time involved converting their parents' home into a bed-and-breakfast. He began to feel guilty for taking advantage of Leanne's and Hank's patience and compassion. He needed to act. He called the real estate agent in Waynesville and asked if Rob Dooley's café was still on the market. He knew it was; the For Sale sign had never left the window.

Swallowing his guilt, shame and grief, he signed on the dotted line. Rob Dooley and his wife burned asphalt on their way out of town headed for Florida. Vince sunk all his time and energy into the café. In return, it flourished.

In what should have been the happiest time of his life, Vince agonized that none of his dreams could have been realized if he hadn't driven his young wife to her grave.

"Vince?" The door to his office slid open and Leanne stuck her head inside. "There you are. What are you doing in here? You haven't had a shower yet and dinner's almost ready."

So much for stating the obvious—he cocked one eyebrow in response. He understood her surprise. A creature of habit, he always went straight to their private quarters upon arriving home from the café where he showered and changed out of his smelly work clothes. He hated to get the café smell anywhere else in the Inn. It turned out Amber had been right; he did always smell like greasy food.

"You *are* joining the rest of us for dinner, aren't you? Veal parmesan."

He considered her offer. The writer would be there with her deep brown eyes and thick tangle of hair. It had been some time since a woman's presence stirred him like hers did. He'd be better off with a ham sandwich in his room watching Sports Center.

"I invited Hank," Leanne added at his hesitation.

Vince gave a thoughtful nod and a shrug as if Hank's presence was the deciding factor. "Yeah, I'll be there."

Leanne smiled, satisfied, "Seven o'clock, then."

"Seven o'clock."

He watched her back out of the room and close the door behind her. His dear sister, where would he be without her? She had been there when he needed somewhere to run after Amber's death. He was here for her when she needed confirmation that she was doing the right thing by turning their family home into a country inn. They depended on each other, probably too much. Vince had a disturbing image of he and Leanne, gray haired and arthritic, rattling around the Ravenswood Inn, waiting to see which one would outlive the other.

Dinner was sometimes offered at the Ravenswood Inn on Friday and Saturday evenings at 7:00 depending on the season, the mood of the guests, and the hostess. After last night's Chinese take-out and Trivial Pursuit, Leanne was determined to have a sit-down dinner in the formal dining room on her fine china on Saturday. Sandy, Kimberly, and Darcy insisted she join them at the table and she acquiesced, but continually jumped up and down to fetch something for someone even though they assured her they could live without it or get it themselves. Darcy had a wonderful time in spite of the fact that Vince spent the evening glowering at her from his end of the table. It wasn't her fault she was the center of attention.

As almost always happens when a group discovers a writer in its midst, everyone wanted to know everything there was to know about the mysterious world of publishing, and bombarded her with ideas for the great American novel. During her career, Darcy had been on the receiving end of more novel ideas than she could write in ten lifetimes, but she enjoyed the conversations. They always told her so much about the people she was getting to know.

"I always thought about writing a book," Dwayne announced to the room.

"This is the first I ever heard about it," Sandy exclaimed with a snort.

"Do I have to tell you everything?" he asked before addressing the rest of the table. "I spent twelve years in the Army, in Korea, you know. I had a chance to meet General Douglas MacArthur, but his plans changed at the last minute."

"No one would want to read a book about some old soldier who almost met Douglas MacArthur," Sandy pointed out.

"That's not the only thing that happened to me while I was over there."

"If you have a story to tell, you need to get it down on paper," Darcy advised quickly before husband and wife could start their own war. "The years have a habit of getting away from you, and you'll never get your book written."

Dwayne laughed. "I'm afraid that's already happened, little lady. I'm too old and tired now."

"It's never too late."

Others contributed advice, even Jeremy Washington, the groom who'd made his first appearance with his bride, Julie.

"What about you, Vince?" Hank asked his old friend who had contributed nothing to the evening's conversation. "You gotta have hundreds of stories to tell from working in that café every day."

Vince shrugged and speared a broccoli floret. "I don't pay attention to much."

"Don't give me that, nothing gets past you. You're so quiet, folks forget you're around, and they tell their secrets right in front of you."

"You should try that, Sandy," Dwayne said elbowing his wife. "See if it's true."

Sandy laughed along with everyone else at the table. Darcy couldn't help but wonder if their ribbing one another was all part of their relationship or if one of them occasionally went too far and hurt the other's feelings. She didn't have to wonder what the newlyweds thought of each other; they couldn't keep their eyes or their hands off each other. Kimberly and Brian seemed like they were made for each other; both intelligent, cultured, but maybe it was all an act and they fought like cats and dogs when no one was around to hear.

Despite her promise not to meddle in Leanne's love life, she couldn't help watching Hank watch Leanne. Leanne seemed to be oblivious to the attention. Neither did she seem mindful of her own inadvertent attention to Hank. She blobbed sour cream on his baked potato without asking and refilled his ice tea before it was empty. Of course she paid attention to all her guests. It was probably that she simply knew Hank so well she didn't realize what she was doing, but Darcy realized and by Hank's love struck expression, he noticed it, too.

The evening reinforced Darcy's perception that Carla had made a poor choice when she and Brad decided Darcy was the person to write *The Ultimate Guide to Finding Mr. Right.* She was utterly clueless when it came to recognizing what drew people together. What made the honeymooners crazy about each other, or the Hudson's marriage survive through the ages, or her own parents' marriage grow over the years when so many of their acquaintances'—even those who occupied the pews in the same church—withered and died? She was unqualified to write a book about snagging Mr. Right. When she finished the research on this book, she was going to New York to tell Carla and Brad she wasn't writing it. There were plenty of qualified writers at the publishing house. Let one of them do it. There was no question that the book would be a success. It would make someone a ton of money, but not her.

Darcy turned her attention to Vince. He was on the top of her list of those she couldn't figure out. He contributed nothing to the conversation except the occasional distracted smile when Hank or Leanne made an attempt to include him. For all intents and purposes she should despise him, but after what Leanne told her about losing his wife, she felt sorry for the guy. There was something deep and mysterious about him. More than likely, she would never have the opportunity to find out anymore than she knew right now, but she couldn't quiet her curiosity. Who was Vince Ravenscraft? Was he as hard and impenetrable as he seemed? Once or twice she caught his eye, but she looked quickly away before he could notice she had been studying him.

Leanne invited everyone to church for the following morning.

"I appreciate the invite," Hank said, "but this is the Sunday I drive Mom and Dad to Ashville to take Grandmother Haywood to church."

Brian and Kimberly also declined. They planned to sleep in before heading home late morning. Darcy didn't think they looked much like churchgoers anyway. The newlyweds said they were checking out early to take advantage of their last day of sightseeing before heading home. Dwayne and Sandy were also checking out first thing and had plans to attend chapel with their nephew and grandson at the University. Vince simply shook his head. Leanne didn't pry for details. She didn't even look surprised. Darcy assumed she'd been down this road before.

Leanne turned expectant eyes on Darcy. She hated to add to her disappointment, but there were a hundred things she'd rather do than waste a beautiful Sunday morning sitting in some country church with Leanne. It was probably one of those snake-handling, mountain churches anyway, where everyone would whoop and holler and drag her up front to expose her sins and convince her of the error of her ways.

"Wish I could," she said, shaking her head, "but I've got more places on my list."

"Everybody's closed tomorrow," Vince spoke up from his end of the table. The sound of his voice surprised everyone. Darcy wasn't the only one who turned and stared at him. "Least they are this time of year," he continued. "You won't get any research done tomorrow unless you plan to include McDonald's in your book."

Darcy was so surprised to hear that many words out of his mouth at one time she had to force a reply. "Well, then, I can get started on my writing."

Vince went back to his dessert like he couldn't care less. "If you're sure then," Leanne said clearly disappointed. "If anyone changes their mind I leave the house at nine-fifteen."

It didn't look like anyone would.

7

Sunday morning Darcy resisted Leanne's big breakfast and helped herself to a bagel and a glass of grapefruit juice from the refrigerator instead. She took her breakfast upstairs to her room to get an early start while the remaining guests enjoyed their last country breakfast before going back to their normal routines. Darcy carried her laptop to the rocking chair by the window and sat down. She set her breakfast on the small table next to her, put her feet up on a wooden ottoman, pushed back in the rocking chair, and opened the computer in her lap. Instead of turning it on, she reached for the bagel. She dug out a huge raisin with her fingernail and popped it into her mouth. She leaned back in the chair and gazed out over the smoky hills.

She sighed. Sunday morning used to be her favorite part of the week. But she couldn't remember the last one she'd really enjoyed. Down deep where she could most easily ignore it, was a nugget of guilt over where she knew she ought to be. It wasn't that she had anything against church. It just didn't fit into her schedule anymore. The fellowship, the sense of belonging, the nostalgia, wasn't enough to forego a peaceful day in the yard or on her porch swing, unwinding from a week in front of her computer.

Maybe that was where the problem lay, the unwinding of something that never came unwound. The conversation between her and Leanne on the mountaintop had replayed over and over in her head last night while she waited for sleep to come. She hadn't thought about her relationship with God, or God himself for that matter, in a long time. She was too busy. It had slowly gotten pushed to the back burner until she forgot it was even there, dried out and turning to ashes.

Back in college when she first got interested in writing her first book, she prayed fervently. She was on the verge of making the biggest decision of her life, and she needed God's guidance. During the months upon months of submitting her finished manuscript to publishers and waiting for the inevitable rejections, she prayed even harder. She prayed for God to open doors, to give the publisher a burden for her book, for a kind hearted editor in some publishing house somewhere to miraculously come across her manuscript in a mountainous slush pile, take a peek inside, and fall in love with her prose.

"*I know it's a good book, Lord,*" she prayed more than once. "*Let someone take a chance on me. Let me prove myself.*"

Then suddenly it happened. She received a contract. She was going to be a published author.

She had rejoiced. Her brothers and sisters in Christ rejoiced with her.

More months of waiting followed. Darcy wrote another book and kept praying. The first book was published. The second book was accepted, and the publishing house accepted two more proposals.

She rejoiced some more. But somewhere between seeing her second or third book on a store shelf, her hundredth or so book signing, and receiving royalty checks that had become her due instead of her delight, she stopped rejoicing.

She hadn't meant for it to happen. She didn't wake up one morning and decide to stop praying, going to church, reading her Bible, and considering God's ways. It just happened. She couldn't remember how or when, just that it had.

Her successes became everyday, mundane. She had earned her accolades. She deserved the good reviews she found in newspapers and journals. She was a good writer. Writers' groups and conference coordinators began calling the house. *Could she come and bestow her wisdom and knowledge on others?* She became a frequent guest on panels and local morning television programs. Her book signings became events to which people arrived early and waited in line to have their pictures taken with her.

She no longer needed her Heavenly Father who gave all good gifts liberally. She had arrived—and she soon forgot the journey.

But that didn't mean she was no longer a Christian, did it? She hadn't stopped believing in God; she simply didn't bother Him with every little concern the way she did back when she was immature and lacking in self-confidence. Wasn't that the way it was supposed to happen? She had grown and learned to stand on her own two feet. Much in the same way she no longer turned to her parents to satisfy her needs; she was now responsible for herself.

But you still honor your parents. You reverence them. You have dinner at their house, talk to them on the phone, and spend time with them.

Darcy pushed the uncomfortable thought aside. It wasn't the same. She didn't know anyone who communed with God in the same way as they did their natural parents. God was the ruler of the universe; surely He had better things to do than seek fellowship with her. Yes, her relationship with Him was lacking; it didn't mean anything. She hadn't experienced peace or contentment in any capacity in a long time. It wasn't that she didn't have a great life. She was making a living doing something she loved, which was more than she could say for most people. She was healthy, and her family relationships were strong.

Maybe she was expecting too much. Was it possible to have everything; a wonderful career, a loving family, *and* peace and contentment?

She shook her head to break her chain of thought. What was wrong with her? She was supposed to be on vacation. A break from writing and worrying about what Brad and Carla wanted. So why couldn't she relax? More importantly, why wasn't she writing? Writing used to be a passion. She couldn't wait to get out of bed each morning and begin; she hated to stop at night; she wrote everywhere she went; when she was riding in the car or working in the yard, she was drafting something in her head; her mind was constantly teeming with ideas; it was all she could do to finish whatever task she was involved in so she could get to her computer and put everything down.

Where had that passion gone? When had writing become a source of a paycheck instead of something she needed as desperately as her next breath? She tried to remember the last book she'd actually enjoyed writing; the last time she sat down and wrote something for the sheer joy of the craft, not because a self-imposed deadline loomed on the calendar.

She drained the last of the grapefruit juice and dropped the Styrofoam cup into the wastepaper basket. She'd loved writing at the time she bought her house, but that was twelve books ago. Surely it hadn't been that long since she truly enjoyed what she was doing. She pursed her lips and stared out the window trying to remember the last time she sat curled up in her house, intent on nothing more than letting the words pore through her fingertips onto her keyboard. She thought of the winter a few years ago when Northern Ohio received fifty-nine inches of snow in February alone. She had written like crazy the entire month as fresh snow blanketed the state twenty four out of twenty eight days. She had sat at the kitchen table and watched through her wraparound windows as the snow fell and her laptop hummed with new thoughts and ideas. Had that been two, no three years ago?

No more recent episodes came to mind. At least three years had passed since she wrote for the sheer joy of creating. What did it mean? Was this her big wakeup call? Was she supposed to quit? What else did she know how to do? She was a writer—she'd never been anything else. She didn't know how to be anything else.

If she wasn't a writer, what was she? If not Darcy Carter, the Ultimate Guide Girl, who was she? She'd never had any doubts of what she would do with her life. She went to college with women who still didn't know what they wanted to do with their lives even after years of working in their chosen field. She used to feel so sorry for them. Now she realized she was one of them.

She needed to talk to someone. She thought of calling her mother, but she couldn't do that. Her parents would be at church. Besides her mother, she had no one who could possibly understand what she was feeling right now. She didn't even know what she was feeling. Her old friends from her young adults group at church weren't such young adults anymore. Many of them had husbands and children and concerns she couldn't identify with. They certainly wouldn't identify with her petty problems.

She could hear them now.

"Pray, Darcy. Seek the Lord while He may be found. He created you. He knows what you need better than you know yourself."

She stared out at the mountains and tried to quiet the fear rising up inside her. She wasn't used to uncertainty and doubt. She didn't like it.

Leanne leaned into the small TV room where Vince was sitting in his recliner watching a chipper young woman give the weather report. She didn't think he was paying attention. She figured he came in here where he thought she wouldn't disturb him. He had set up this room after she announced the family room was now a common area for the Inn's guests. She never watched TV or did anything else in here, preferring instead to be available for her guests should they need her. "I don't want them to think I'm inaccessible," she had explained. "I want our guests to think of us as one big happy family."

Vince had snorted. "Even big happy families need to get away from each other now and then."

Leanne had smiled and shook her head. She couldn't fault Vince for wanting his own space in a home that she had suddenly turned into Grand Central Station. But she loved the constant flow of guests in and out of the house. She had been so lonely while taking care of first Pop, and then Mom, as they withered away. She couldn't bear to go back to the silent rooms and oppressive atmosphere. Vince was the opposite. He didn't need people in and out of his life. No one but Amber, and she'd been gone four years now. When would he move on?

When would she?

Vince sat on the sagging loveseat that once occupied the

family room back in the days when he and Dad watched NCAA football every Saturday. Her heart swelled in her chest at the sight of him. If things had been different in both their lives, he could be sitting on the same loveseat explaining the nuances of the game to his own son. Instead he sat in the stale, darkened room alone and watched as the weather announcer was replaced by scores and highlights from yesterday's basketball games. March Madness, his reason for ushering in Spring.

"You wanna go to church with me this morning?" she asked brightly.

He didn't look up. "No, I'm fine right here."

"It's a gorgeous day out there. Everybody'd love to see you."

He clicked the remote, bored with the station. "They can see me any day of the week at the café."

Leanne ground her teeth in frustration. "Come on, Vince, this is the only day you don't go to the restaurant. Don't waste it in this little cave you've made for yourself. You haven't been to church since..."

Since Amber's funeral, she almost said.

Vince hit the mute button and gave her his full attention. "Don't worry, Sis. I don't plan to waste this gorgeous day. Your flowerbeds need some work if you're going to be planting any annuals in a couple weeks. I thought I'd get a jump start on it before you start riding me about them." The barb was spoken lightly and with a twinkle in his eye.

Leanne went to the couch and put her hand on his shoulder. "I won't give you a hard time about them if you go to church with me this morning."

Vince reached up and patted her hand where it rested on his shoulder. "Not today. Maybe some other time."

You always say that, she thought to herself. At least he didn't flat out refuse. That left a hope that some Sunday he would say yes.

"All right then. I'm going to get ready. Can you take care of Brian and Kimberly when they're ready to check out? The Hudsons and our newlyweds are already gone. By lunchtime it'll just be us again and Darcy."

Vince nodded and hit the volume on the TV. Another weatherman spouting the same forecast blared in the little room. Leanne listened long enough to decide if she should wear short sleeves or long and left the room.

She missed her brother. Vince was always quiet and introverted, but he once knew how to laugh. He had known how to make her laugh, but not anymore. He was never the same after moving back home. Leanne knew it was more than Amber's death that had changed him. She was aware of their marital problems long before the accident. Naturally Vince never said a word, but Leanne could see it in both their faces. She saw it in the way they didn't hold hands or touch during Mom's last days and her funeral. She felt the distance widening between them when they came to the house for dinner on the odd Sunday. When Hank told her about the three packed suitcases in the backseat of Amber's car the night of the accident, she knew their marriage had been over for a long time.

Leanne knew her brother well enough to know he was blaming himself for Amber's death. His young wife was leaving him when she was killed on the highway. Oh, the guilt that must plague him! Where was Amber going that night? Had there been another man involved? Had she planned to leave for a long time, or had one last fight pushed her over the edge? If Vince had any of the answers to her questions, he would never admit them.

She did what she could and let him know she was here when he needed to talk. But he didn't talk. She would've been shocked if he had. Vince wasn't one for airing his grievances. He had hung a sign in the café that read: *This establishment charges a five dollar fine for whining.* Vince was fond of pointing it out to employees and patrons alike when they complained a little too long about something.

For four years now it was just the two of them, besides the guests who regularly filled the rooms upstairs. Leanne didn't know what she'd do without the company. She surely didn't want to go back to answering phones for the Tire Man. She didn't want to work at the Community Action Center. Sometimes she got lonely, even with all the things she now had to do since opening the Inn, but loneliness she could handle. She never let it last long.

A smile turned up the corners of her mouth when she thought of Darcy's comments about Hank Haywood. Hank, her Mr. Right? Was he part of God's plan for her life? Her smile grew wider. Well, Hank had been under her nose all along where Mr. Rights liked to hide, according to Darcy.

Hank was the oldest of five kids. His youngest sister, Iris, was Leanne's best friend, or she had been until she went away to college, got her teaching degree, married a young business student, and moved with him to Columbia, South Carolina. Now the friends' communication was limited to Christmas cards in which Iris sent pictures of her kids, four and counting, and Leanne sent her color swatches and photos of whatever current renovating project she was working on at the Inn. It was funny how she still thought of Iris as her best friend even though they hadn't seen each other in nearly three years when Iris brought her family home to visit the last time.

Most of her growing up years, Leanne hadn't been aware of Hank at all. He was simply Iris's older brother. Her first memory of him was when she and Iris were fourteen and they attended Hank and Sue Ellen Fyte's wedding. Iris was too young to be a bridesmaid and much too old to be considered for flower girl. Sue Ellen had plenty of female relatives on her side of the family so Iris was left with no role to fill. She felt terribly left out and snubbed by Sue Ellen's family. Nearly every night she called Leanne to complain about whatever mistreatment she had endured that day. The wedding was a huge production. Iris and Leanne discussed different ways to sabotage the entire affair, from giving the limousine driver directions to the wrong church, to setting mice loose in the reception hall. Of course they didn't have the nerve to act on any of their schemes. They sat in the fourth row back in the packed sanctuary and elbowed each other and made mocking faces as Sue Ellen traipsed down the aisle in all her bridal splendor.

Hank was only the groom, an accessory in black to showcase Sue Ellen, and Leanne barely noticed he was there. The highlight of the evening was when Hank and the best man, whose name Leanne couldn't remember but who she and Iris thought bore a striking resemblance to John Cougar, pulled the two girls out on the dance floor. Hank danced with Iris first, and Leanne was thrilled to find herself in the arms of John Cougar, who sometime later added Mellencamp to his name. Then the two young men switched partners and Leanne danced a moment with Hank before Sue Ellen reclaimed her groom for more pictures with a visiting aunt who was rumored to have money.

Leanne and Iris relived that dance for years to come when they—dressed in new clothes and wearing heels and make up for the first time in their lives—were the focus of everyone's attention, especially that of the handsome best man.

Leanne thought no more of Hank Haywood, and when she did, he was simply Iris's older, married brother. Then Vince grew up and went to work for Hank, and he became a regular fixture around the Ravenscraft home. Sue Ellen was already gone by this time; she had divorced Hank to marry the owner of the real estate company where she worked, and the two of them moved to Georgia. Leanne thought a lot of Hank, but romance never entered her mind. He was still Vince's old boss and Iris's big brother.

No wonder Darcy didn't feel qualified to write the Mr. Right book, she had missed this one by a mile.

Leanne dated a few men she met through her previous job with the Tire Man, but for some reason, none of them seemed anymore interested in her than she was in them.

By the time both her parents were gone, she figured that chapter in her life was closed. Sometimes she thought, *I'm only thirty-six, it isn't too late for romance. I'm still young enough to become someone's mother.* Other times she scolded herself, *You're thirty-six, Leanne, way too old to be swept off your feet or dream of holding your own baby in your arms.*

She probably had another thirty or forty years to look forward to if the Lord tarried. Her life was a good one, even if it didn't offer everything most women felt entitled to. She had a beautiful house with not a dime against it. At any window she could look out onto God's beautiful creation and feel His presence all around her. She had a brother whom she loved and who loved her back. What more could she want? She had learned long ago to be content with where she was at any given moment and let the next thirty years take care of themselves.

$\mathscr{F}$. $\mathscr{F}$. $\mathscr{F}$. $\mathscr{F}$ 8

$\mathscr{D}$arcy kept busy the next two weeks. She traveled throughout the area, venturing into South Carolina, Georgia, and Tennessee for her research. A few nights she spent at motels on the road, but most of the time she was back at the Ravenswood by bedtime. She didn't bother with uprooting herself and moving back to the Danbury even though Marjorie Reed called her on Sunday night to remind her she had two nights' free lodging coming. She was perfectly satisfied with the situation at the Ravenswood. Vince Ravenscraft no longer intimidated her. He was gone every morning by the time she came downstairs and seldom came out of the back of the house in the evenings. It was easy to forget that anyone occupied the inn besides her and Leanne.

She started thinking of her book more on the terms of the people she met and less on the food she was eating. Her notebooks were now loaded with anecdotes and character sketches to pepper her book with authenticity. She and Leanne hiked a few of the hundreds of walking trails that crisscrossed over and through the mountains to keep the pounds from creeping on, with limited success. She chatted with people of every race, age, and occupation.

The only problem was she wasn't writing.

Most evenings upon returning to the Ravenswood, she would carry her laptop out to the back deck and sit down to write. She felt creative and inspired until she booted up her laptop. Without fail, the ideas promptly flew out of her head. She listened to the wind rustling through the pines, the birds chattering overhead, the distant screech of a blue heron, and she couldn't think of a thing to write. So she'd close the computer, get up, and take a walk, have a chat with Leanne about growing up in the Ravenswood when it was her family home and not an Inn, or drive into Talmedge to find R.T. and Jim or someone else to talk to. Her notes continued to grow, while her manuscript remained a sketchy outline.

The only time she saw Vince was at dinnertime when she would join him and Leanne in the kitchen for a simple meal of leftovers from the day's special at the café. She and Leanne always monopolized the conversation while Vince's contributions were limited to, "Pass the salt".

At the beginning of the second week, she called home to let the family know she was alive and well.

"Darcy, you should call Carla," Sharon said after the usual greetings. "She's called here looking for you a couple of times. She sounds like it's really important."

"No need for concern, Mom, Carla always sounds like that."

"No, I'm serious. Are things all right at the publishing house? I'm concerned about you."

This would be the perfect time to share her own concerns about where her career was headed. If she didn't write the book Brad wanted there was a good chance she'd be out of a contract, but maybe that was exactly the kick in the pants she needed. Then she'd be forced to do something, to move on to something else that might not even include writing. If the rate in which her current project was slogging along was any indication, it was looking more and more likely she'd reached her limit with Ultimate Guide books. But what else did she know? She hadn't lived enough to write fiction well. Law school was out of the question, regardless of how interesting John Grisham and prime time TV made the profession look. She certainly wasn't qualified to go out and get some kind of nine-to-five job. The prospect of that sent a shiver down her spine.

But she couldn't say any of that to her mother. If she confided in her, Sharon would worry herself sick. She'd tell Dad as soon as she got off the phone, and the two of them would call Keith and Becky and ask if they knew what could be going on inside Darcy's head. Then the whole family would get together to discuss the matter and plan some sort of intervention until she got back home where she could assure them she wasn't about to become a ward of the state. The Carters were into goals, lists, and achievements. They couldn't stand the thought of one of their own floating aimlessly adrift on life's ocean without a clear view of a destination on the horizon.

"Mom, you needn't worry," she said soothingly. "Carla doesn't know my exact location, and it's frustrating her. She likes controlling me from afar. When I don't tell her where I am or when I'm coming back, she freaks out. That's just Carla, the ultimate drama queen. She can always email me if something's that important."

"I suppose, if you're sure that's all there is to it…"

"I'm sure, Mom. How was class today? Are the kids anxious for Easter break?" She knew the later it got in the school year, the more difficult it was to control a classroom of restless teenagers who would rather be anywhere than in the classroom.

She chatted a little longer to her mother, sent hugs and kisses to Dad and the rest of the family, and hung up. She had done the right thing by not saying anything about her doubts surrounding her writing. At least, not until she decided for herself what those doubts were. She had a lucrative career, something that would take her to the end of her life, with or without Brad and his company. She was still young enough to do anything she wanted to do.

If only she could figure out what that was.

After the Hudsons, the Wrights, and the honeymooners from Virginia left the Ravenswood, Darcy was the only guest left at the inn. Leanne had explained she used the slow period from January first to April first for spring cleaning, general repairs, and helping Vince out at the café. Darcy didn't mind the solitude and quietness of the inn. It was exactly what she was hoping for in her attempt to relax. Many days when she wasn't writing and Leanne was too busy for sightseeing, she would hike the trail to the waterfall to work off breakfast and lunch and clear her head. She had spotted a few off shoots of the trail that tourists usually missed—especially in

summer when vegetation made everything difficult to navigate—
and explored them until the threat of walking off the mountain
became too great. She came across a gate or two with warnings
posted that someone had lost their life after venturing off the trail.
Darcy had no desire to go back north in a body bag so she stayed
in the designated hiking areas.

Friday afternoon, her two-week anniversary as a Ravenswood
guest, Darcy found herself on the back deck with her laptop perched
across her knees. She had spent the last hour catching up on email
and other time-consuming and often pointless pursuits. She logged
off and opened her research files. She had already added what she'd
gathered today. She scrolled to the beginning of her file and reread
her last two weeks work. There was plenty to start her book. She
opened a blank document and titled it "Outline for Country Inns
and Country Dining". Then she stared pensively at the blinking
cursor.

The book wasn't going the way she had envisioned it last
month when she'd discussed it with Carla. The book wasn't going
at all. She pinched her nose with her thumb and forefinger, typed
a few words into the computer and immediately deleted them. A
bird flew under the roof eaves and out again, mocking her. It was
ready to build a nest, and she was in the way. She looked over
her shoulder and studied the space between the siding and the
downspout the bird had abandoned. She closed the laptop and
set in on a small table next to her chair. She went over to where
the bird had been working. Up close she could see a small hole in
the siding smeared with dried mud. She'd have to point it out to
Leanne before the creature could finish the nest and lay her eggs.

She turned away from the wall to stare at the surrounding
mountains. She set her hands on her hips. She had already been
to the waterfall this afternoon. She'd found no inspiration there,
just gorgeous scenery and time for reflecting on how much she
should be writing but wasn't. A glance at her watch showed she
had at least an hour before dinner. An hour to spend writing, not
daydreaming. With a sigh of frustration at herself for not being able
to focus, she realized writing today was futile. She'd stared at her
computer long enough with nothing happening to see that. For

some reason this project wasn't getting out of her head and onto her hard drive. Was it just the project she had lost interest in? She was one of those fortunate few who had never started a project she couldn't finish or couldn't sell.

What was wrong with her? Had she lost interest in this project, or writing altogether?

Rather than face the possibility that she might cease to be a productive member of society, she'd take a shower and relax until dinnertime. Maybe all she needed was a clear head. She was thinking too much, fretting over her lack of productivity. Well, not tonight. Tonight she'd relax, and the words would come when she least expected them. She sure hoped so. She stuck her pens into her tablet, picked up her laptop, tucked everything under one arm, and reached out to open the back door.

Movement near her feet caught her eye and she looked down. The longest, widest snake she'd ever seen stretched lazily across the door's threshold. If it hadn't moved when it did, she wouldn't have seen it, and probably stepped right on it on her way through the door.

Darcy leaped backward and let out a scream that sent the birds in the trees scattering.

The blacksnake tensed at the sound and smell of her. Its small head turned in her direction. A tiny black tongue flicked out of its mouth and wiggled mockingly. Darcy leaped back another step. She was suddenly lightheaded. She wondered if this is what happened to a person right before they fainted. But she mustn't faint. If she did, she'd fall right on top of the horrible thing. She shrieked again and did an involuntary dance near something akin to panic.

She had always been more tomboy than not. She baited her own fishing hooks and didn't shriek over spiders and mice, but this was different. She had never been this up close and personal with such a loathsome creature. It was huge. She didn't notice the intricate pattern on its back or the taut muscles beneath its skin, only that it was longer than the doorframe it guarded by at least four feet.

Over the pounding of blood in her ears, she heard running

feet behind her. A pair of hands took hold of her arms and spun her around. She screamed again, unable to do much of anything else. The hands belonged to Vince. It took every ounce of resolve she possessed not to leap into his arms.

"What's going on?" he demanded breathlessly. Even as the words left his lips, he saw the answer at Darcy's feet, and the color returned to his face. "Well, what d'ya know?" he commented lightly. With his hands still holding her, he moved her to one side and stepped around her. He leaned over the snake, opened the back door, and brought out the broom Leanne kept leaning in the corner for the purpose of keeping the mountains' dirt from getting tracked inside.

Keeping himself between the snake and Darcy, Vince pushed against the snake's heavy body with the business end of the broom. The snake whipped around in protest, and wrapped its long body around the broom and his legs.

Darcy screamed again. Her eyes filled with tears. This was awful. The snake was about to kill Vince. It would crawl up his body, wind itself around him, and squeeze the life right out of him. That would leave her trapped again on the back porch. Oh, why had she come to this wretched place? She should have stayed home and written the book Brad and Carla wanted. At least while researching a book about Mr. Right the snakes were always in plain sight and easily recognizable.

The tip of the snake's tail brushed against her sandal and made contact with her bare toes. She'd seen enough. Vince was on his own. With another whoop of terror, she leaped onto the chair she'd recently vacated, and from there, climbed onto the deck railing. She clutched her laptop and notebooks in front of her like a shield. The railing shook beneath her trembling legs. If she didn't do something, she would fall off on top of Vince and the snake. She tried to lock her knees to better maintain her balance, but she couldn't even do that.

The ink pens slid out of her notebook and clattered to the deck. What was she going to do? After the snake killed Vince, she'd be trapped. Snakes could climb, couldn't they? Didn't they live in trees? She looked to the end of the porch railing and calculated the distance. If she ran to the corner and jumped, she could get around the side of the house and to the front door to get help, or when she got to her vehicle, she could just drive away, leaving Vince and Leanne to deal with the snake. But then again, it was a five-foot drop to the ground from the porch railing on that end of the house. What if she landed badly and broke her ankle? She could already feel the snake's disgusting body tightening around her.

Vince didn't seem perturbed in the least by the snake's resistance. He was either very brave or crazy. His knuckles whitened around the broom handle from the effort as he gave the snake another shove. It untangled itself from his legs and scooted begrudgingly off the side of the deck. Even after its tail had disappeared from view, Darcy could hear its progress through the dried bushes and leaves at the side of the house. Another shudder ran through her and she almost lost her precarious balance on the deck railing.

Vince leaned the broom against the deck railing and exhaled from the exertion. He looked surprised when he turned around and spotted her perched three feet above his head. She tightened her grip on her laptop. If he laughed or made one wisecrack, she was going to bash him over the head.

"Sorry about that," he said, genuinely concerned. "Are you all right?"

Darcy decided it might be easier if he did laugh. Then she could channel her fear of the snake onto him in the form of unreasonable anger. She shook her head. Words wouldn't come. Her legs were aching by now, and she wanted nothing more than to give into the hysterical sobs ready to erupt.

Vince stepped closer and held out his hand. "Do you want to come down?"

Darcy craned her neck in the direction the snake had disappeared. She very much wanted to get down. "Is—is it gone?"

For her benefit, Vince followed her gaze. "Oh, yeah, she's gone."

"Sh—she?"

"Yeah, that's Maude. We see her every year about this time. Waking up from her winter siesta, I guess. But now that she knows she's not wanted on the porch, she'll most likely stay out of your way. She'll remember the broom. It's a surefire way to get rid of snakes."

"What about a shotgun?"

Vince laughed for the first time. He reached out and took the laptop and notebooks out of her hands and set them on the table. "You don't mean that. She's just a harmless ole blacksnake."

"Yes, I do mean that. I almost stepped on her." She could still feel the spot on her toe where the snake had touched her skin.

Vince held out his hands. "Come on, let's get down from there."

Darcy cast another nervous glance toward the side of the house.

"It's all right," he coaxed again.

Darcy knew she had to get down. Her legs were about to collapse. If Vince was familiar enough with the creature to give it a name, he must be confident their lives were not in danger. She leaned forward and rested both hands on his shoulders. He deftly swung her down onto the wood boards. Her knees buckled under her when her feet hit the deck, and she stumbled into his arms.

"Easy there," he said, tightening his grip around her waist.

"I—I'm sorry." She shuddered again, partly from the image of the big snake's body around Vince's legs, and partly from the touch of his wide hands on her waist. With her hands still on his shoulders, Darcy found herself staring into his striking hazel eyes. They stared back at her, unflinching. He seemed powerful and rugged, almost dangerous. His arms felt good around her body, safe. She imagined him tightening his arms around her and lowering his mouth to hers.

Vince dropped his hands from around her waist, and Darcy took a self-conscious step backwards.

Suddenly she felt very silly. "You must think I'm a big baby to overreact like that over a snake."

"No, I don't think you're a big baby," he said gently.

Darcy could still feel where his hands had held her. "Thanks." She wiped her sweaty palms across the seat of her pants and took a steadying breath. "Is she the only one?"

His look told her what a silly question that was. "I found a snake skin last summer. It was eight-feet long. I assume it belonged to Maude."

She gasped and turned to look at the mountains behind them. "You mean there could be another one out there even bigger?"

One corner of his mouth turned up in a wry smile. Darcy imagined he could get about anything he wanted from most of the women she knew if he smiled like that in their presence. She could already hear Carla. "Honey, I could eat him with a spoon."

"Would you prefer the truth, or should I tell you what you want to hear?" he was saying.

She pursed her lips as if giving the matter serious consideration. "Forget it," she said with a dismissive wave of her hand. "I don't want you to lie."

"Good. I'm a terrible liar." He picked up her laptop and notebooks and bent over to retrieve the two pens. He moved to the back door. Darcy stayed close, nearly walking on his heels as her eyes scanned the porch for signs of Maude or any of her errant relatives. She practically leaped over the threshold into the house, her nerves still crawling.

Safe inside, Vince handed over her things. "Sorry, I got all girlie on you," she said.

He broke into another of those gorgeous smiles she was so unaccustomed to seeing on his face. "Think nothing of it. I never get a chance to rescue a damsel in distress when it's just Leanne and me. She's not afraid of anything."

Darcy felt her cheeks warming. Did he mean he enjoyed the thought of rescuing her or that she should be like Leanne and sweep the snake off the porch herself the next time?

She couldn't believe she hadn't realized until this moment how handsome he was. Maybe because he'd never smiled so widely before or maybe she was experiencing some mild form of hero worship over his rescuing her from Maude.

"Besides," he continued, unaware of the thoughts going through her head, "I'd expect it from a city girl."

Before she could get angry all over again about his reference to their altercation in the parking lot of the café, she saw the lopsided twitch of his mouth.

Was he teasing her? Why now after all this time? He hadn't spoken two words to her since the day he found her in his office. Every time they crossed paths, he seemed nothing more than annoyed by her existence. "You need to reevaluate the way you look at city girls, Mr. Ravenscraft," she advised, deciding she could tease right back. "We're not nearly as helpless as we look. We can usually handle a snake as soon as we recognize it's a snake."

"If you insist, Ms. Carter, because I sure thought that was your voice I heard screaming like a banshee when I got out of my truck." He grinned and a dimple appeared in his left cheek.

Darcy had to force herself not to stare. "I told you, it's all a matter of recognizing the snake for what it is."

Suddenly the grin dropped from his mouth. "You've got to remember you're in the mountains now. There's bound to be snakes. It's either them, or mice and vermin everywhere."

What did she say wrong? Had he not realized she was only teasing? She wasn't implying he was a snake. Maybe she was the one who misunderstood his playfulness. Was he even capable of such a thing?

"Um, sure," she stammered. "We wouldn't want that." She thought about apologizing or at least trying to explain she didn't mean anything by her comments, but she couldn't think of a thing to say without sounding like she was making more of the situation than he obviously was.

"Don't worry about Maude. You shouldn't see anymore of her this spring." He brushed past her and disappeared through a door that opened off the kitchen.

Darcy stared at the closed door and tried to figure out what had just happened. Apparently Vince was better at dishing it out than he was at taking it. Oh well, she had come here to work anyway, not flirt with a tall mountain man whose easy southern drawl had her imagining kissing his crooked mouth.

Vince rolled over in bed and punched the pillow, then lowered his head into the dent. He had to be at the café in six hours. He was usually asleep by ten and up at four. He didn't know what was wrong with him. He'd been lying in bed for nearly an hour and still wasn't drowsy. He kicked at the covers and resituated himself. This was ridiculous. Like most men, he usually shut off his mind like a valve as soon as he hit the sheets and fell asleep as effortlessly as a cocker spaniel. Insomnia was for people too eaten up with themselves and their dumb problems, like women.

He closed his eyes, only to be visited again by the visage that kept him tossing on his bed at eleven o'clock. Darcy Carter, her face mere inches from his own, her wide chocolate eyes still moist with emotion from seeing Maude sprawled across the porch. He could feel her narrow waist under his fingers, so small his thumbs nearly met at the front of her stomach. He sat up and swung his feet over the edge of the bed. He groaned and ran a hand through his shock of reddish brown hair.

A woman—the last thing in the world he needed to be thinking about when he should be sleeping. He got out of bed and strode to the window. He pushed aside the curtain and stared up at the clear night sky. The moon was waxing and the yard was illuminated all the way to where the hiking trail met the forest. He had seen Darcy emerge from the trees several times after a hike, her face sweaty and flushed. The first time he saw her coming off the trail, he thought she was Leanne. Leanne walked the trail nearly every day regardless of the weather. It wasn't often that someone else immerged alone onto their property this time of year.

Almost immediately he realized it wasn't his sister. A cap pulled low over her ears couldn't hold her curly tresses in check. Her cheeks were red from exertion and her wild hair windswept. She wore loose fitting sweats and tan hiking boots, a combination chosen by someone more concerned with comfort and serviceability than fashion; someone very different from his late wife.

Vince had thought about Amber more often in the past two weeks than he had in the entire past year. He was finally able to admit, if only to himself, that he had stopped loving her long before her accident. He wasn't in love with her the night he found her in bed with the lawyer from Philly. Had he been, he would have folded the little weasel up and put him in his pocket and worried about the lawsuit later. He hadn't loved her all the times she ridiculed his dreams of buying Rob Dooley's café. He didn't love her when she whispered in his ear that they should leave Talmedge behind before he wasted both their lives in a dead end town in the middle of nowhere.

Too much had changed between them from the night of their senior prom, when he thought she was the most beautiful creature God had ever created, to the moment she threw all her stuff in the back of her car and stormed out of their house for the last time.

He couldn't admit any of it to anyone, nor did he spend much time examining it himself. Guilt wouldn't allow it. Rather than try to figure out how he had driven her away, he concentrated on ways to improve the café and keep the locals and tourists coming back. He attended a few community meetings whenever some scuttlebutt came along that directly affected his business. He gave little thought to members of the fairer sex.

One trip down that road had been enough for him.

He'd gone out of his way to avoid any contact with Darcy during her stay at the Ravenswood. In spite of his determination not to get within a country mile of her, he found himself looking for her little foreign job in the driveway when he got home from work and dreading the day it was no longer there. He never asked Leanne how long she planned to stay. He didn't ask how her book research was coming along or even what the book was about. That would look like he cared. He couldn't stand the thought of Leanne's face brightening at the prospect that he was once again attracted to a woman when he wasn't.

He wasn't attracted to Darcy Carter, at least not in any way that mattered. Of course she was attractive. He had always been a legman and it was obvious hers went on forever. He liked the way her mouth crinkled when she smiled at one of Leanne's offbeat observations and the sound of her throaty laugh. Before witnessing her nearly hysterical reaction to Maude, she hadn't seemed like any of the girls he'd ever known. Until today, he imagined her as totally self-reliant and full of herself, everything his good ole boy mentality found so unappealing in a pretty woman.

He smiled in the darkness as he remembered climbing out of the truck and hearing the ear-splitting scream from the back of the house. He had no idea what or whom to expect when he ran around the house and onto the deck. He had taken the three steps in one bound and landed on the deck right behind Darcy. When he saw Maude lying across the threshold of the back door he'd almost collapsed with relief. It had taken all he had not to laugh at this tall city girl nearly in tears at the sight of a harmless black snake, albeit an eight-foot long one. One look at her face and his desire to laugh was replaced by an urge to take her in his arms and sooth away the fear in her eyes. She wasn't as self-assured as she seemed. That was evident on her face when he set her down off the deck railing. There was still a place inside her that needed to be taken care of, a place whose existence she probably denied, but the truth was in her eyes.

His face reddened in the darkness at his bumbling attempt to flirt with her. Fortunately he had nipped that in the bud before he made a complete fool of himself. She had looked almost disappointed when he'd stopped. He couldn't worry about that. He didn't flirt. It wasn't in his plans to woo somebody.

The last thing he needed in his life was a woman. The only thing he knew about them was that his life was a lot less complicated without one.

Amber had made him think she needed him, too. For the first few years when he was young and stupid, he believed her. Finally it dawned on him; she did whatever was necessary to get what she wanted out of him. Even after he knew what she was doing, he fell for it every time. A sideways glance, a crook of her finger, a shy smile from under lowered lashes, and he'd be right back in her web. But over time he developed a thicker skin. He became immune to her tears and her tantrums—sometimes.

The night she left, he was sure it was another of her games. She would be gone for a few days, and then call begging for him to come and get her. This time he wasn't going after her. He was through chasing her. If she wanted out of their small town and their stifling marriage, he wouldn't try to make her stay. He couldn't force her to love him. He'd given up on that. He didn't even care anymore.

After he listened to her tires spinning out of the driveway, he popped the top on his last can of beer and reclined back in his easy chair. Nope, he wouldn't go after her this time. She wanted out of his life; she could stay out for all he cared.

And she had—out for good...

Hank met him at the hospital. He found out later that after he'd arrived on the scene in his semi-drunken state, the deputy who had called him about the accident immediately called Hank. Hank almost called Leanne, but then decided it would be best if Vince not see anyone else until the news had a chance to digest.

Sobered by the evening's events, Vince was glad Hank was there when the doctor came through the emergency room doors to tell him Amber was gone. He already knew, but the doctor's words were like a blow to the chest. He had stumbled backward and fell into a vinyl, waiting room sofa, disbelieving. He and Hank sat and stared at each other in shock until Hank finally got up and went to call Leanne.

Even after Vince saw Amber's mother the next day at the funeral home where they met to make arrangements for her burial, he didn't cry. He was too angry to grieve. He couldn't admit as much to anyone, but he was furious with her. He sat dry eyed through the funeral service, a wall between him and anyone who dared approach. Amber couldn't be gone. Not like this. It wasn't fair that she leave him in the middle of an argument. He needed her to come back so they could finish it, make up, and get on with their lives.

How he hated her for doing this to him.

It was a week before the anger wore off enough to realize she hadn't done this to him. He had done it to her. His guilt intensified when the insurance company called. The next call was from a buyer for their house. Within weeks he had enough money in his hands to buy Rob Dooley's café and make any necessary improvements.

Every morning, when he turned on the lights and fired up the new grill he had installed, the satisfaction of owning his own business competed with the self-loathing that none of it would have been possible had Amber not been killed.

Amber; petite, blonde, pouting lips, apple cheeks, and

exuding confidence in her femininity; she would have screamed over finding Maude on the deck too, but only to get his attention or the attention of whomever was handy.

Vince went back to bed and threw the covers over his body. He glared at the red numerals on the clock. The alarm would go off at four a.m. whether he got a good night's sleep or not. He needed to stop thinking about Amber, Darcy, and all other women on the planet. He had his café and his life here with Leanne. It wasn't exactly how he imagined things turning out, but it wasn't a bad situation either.

Occasionally he toyed with the idea of running for village council. He loved Talmedge and knew of a few things that would benefit it. He would like to see the Fourth of July celebration that had petered out in the late '80's brought back. Tourists came through the area nearly year round, but found little to do that required they open their wallets. At the same time, he didn't want to see his quaint community become a tourist trap. He had ideas that would incorporate the best of both worlds. He also realized that most potential voters were turned off by his less than sunny disposition. Only Leanne, Hank, and possibly June, would trust that he had only best intentions for the community, even though he lacked a warm personality; not exactly enough to get a fellow elected to office.

With no realistic chances of participating in local politics and no desire to become someone's husband, he was left with the café. He didn't know if it would be enough to satisfy him in his old age, but he seldom thought that far down the road. The world already spent too much time worrying about things like peace and contentment. The way he looked at it, it was all a matter of choice. He chose to ignore it.

· · · · 9

Another week went by with no guests checking into the Inn. Darcy secretly fretted over how the Ravenswood could possibly stay in business. Leanne seemed unperturbed by the inactivity. Between cloudbursts and good old-fashioned gulley washers, she spent much of the week outside working the soil in her flower gardens or on a ladder cleaning out rain gutters. She never ran out of things to do or the enthusiasm with which to do them. Darcy got tired just watching her.

Saturday night Vince stayed home with leftover beans and cornbread from the café while Leanne drove Darcy to the Chinese restaurant in Sylva in the next county. Darcy's palate was glad for the change in fair. She had eaten all the grits, cured ham, and biscuits she could stand for a day or two.

"How's the book coming along?" Leanne asked after they placed their order.

Darcy gazed around the restaurant at the muted Asian décor before answering. She wasn't anxious to admit the book was little more than an idea in her head. She had been in upscale Chinese restaurants where one could almost imagine themselves in Beijing as well as simple neighborhood ones where only the aroma of the food and nationality of the staff differentiated it from any other restaurant in town. This one leaned more toward the latter.

She slowly turned her attention back to Leanne. "I think another week should take care of my research. There's a place in

South Carolina near a town called Camden I want to visit next week. I'll be spending the night away from the Inn, but I'll let you know ahead of time."

"Let me guess—Granny Bean's."

"You know it," Darcy exclaimed disbelievingly.

"Everybody the least bit associated with travelers and lovers of southern barbeque knows Granny Bean's," Leanne said with a smile. "It's a long piece from here though. I don't guess you'd like some company?"

"Are you offering? I figured the Inn keeps you too tied down to consider a spur of the moment road trip."

"Ordinarily it does, and when I have a free moment Vince finds something for me to do at the café. I can't make any written in stone plans, but if no one calls for a reservation next week, maybe I can get away." Her eyes grew brighter the longer she talked. "It would be a blast. I've never been on a research trip before."

"Well then, for both our sakes, I hope no one calls to make a reservation."

The waitress appeared at that moment with their orders. Steam rose from the various plates she set in front of them.

Darcy inhaled deeply and smiled across the table. "Everything looks delicious," she said after the waitress backed away.

"It is. I eat here as often as possible."

Leanne bowed her head and Darcy followed suit. She listened while Leanne blessed the food and then they dug in.

"After your research is finished next week, will you be going back home?" Leanne asked a few moments later over a crab egg roll.

"I won't need to hang around much longer," Darcy said without enthusiasm.

"I gotta admit you sure made the winter pass quicker. It's usually so quiet around the inn with only Vince for company."

Darcy brightened. "It's been a fun two weeks for me, too. To tell you the truth, I'm not too eager to go home."

Leanne toyed with her chopsticks a moment. Finally she said, "Can I ask why? I mean it's fine with me if you stay here forever, but I sort of got the impression that something's bothering you about this book. It's none of my business, but I'm here if you need to talk."

Darcy hadn't realized she was so transparent. She was a typical solitary writer; she never talked about what she was working on until it was finished, even with her family. No one knew if there were problems with a project until after it was finished, and she never saw a point in talking about it then.

But her current problems weren't exactly with her latest Ultimate Guide. They were with her, her future at her publishing house, and her entire identity as a writer. Did she want to try and explain her doubts to Leanne when she couldn't even identify them herself?

She gestured for the waitress to refill her water before answering. "I don't know what's wrong. I've got more than enough material to start this book, but it's not going anywhere. Every time I sit down to write I freeze up. It's like I'm suddenly disinterested in writing. Actually I'm disinterested in my whole life."

Leanne's silence encouraged Darcy to continue. "I could go home and get to work tomorrow if I wanted to, but I almost dread it."

"Which one? Getting to work or going home?"

"Both, I guess. I don't know why." Darcy gave a slight shake of her head and ate a few bites of her dinner. "I realize the world won't end if I don't finish this book, or any other one for that matter. I am totally at liberty to do whatever I want. I could change careers. I could move to an island in the South Pacific and become a recluse. I could throw all my notes away and start something totally different. I told you what my editor wants me to write."

Leanne arched her eyebrows. "The Mr. Right book."

Darcy nodded. "I sort of jumped into this project without giving it much thought to get Carla off my back about Mr. Right. Now I have to finish it or she'll know what I did. I still believe in this project, I just can't seem to get a running start."

"Darcy, can I ask you something and you not get offended?"

Darcy nodded around a mouthful of sweet and sour pork.

"I don't understand why you're so concerned about what this Carla person thinks. I admit I don't know anything about the writing business, but so what if you don't want to write the book she wants you to? And who cares if you don't finish it? The worse thing that will happen is you won't make as much money as you did last year."

"That's a pretty bad thing."

Leanne grinned. "Yeah, I realize that. But I'm serious, haven't you been writing your whole life?"

"It's all I've ever done."

"Well, it doesn't sound to me like your problem is writing. I think you're being too hard on yourself. You've put all this pressure on yourself to produce and now the stress is catching up with you."

"Believe it or not, that's what Carla said. I told her before I came here I needed a vacation. I was going to use this trip for a little down time and a chance to clear my head."

"It's only been two weeks, Darcy. That's a pretty short vacation," Leanne reminded her.

"I know, but the longer I'm here the more confused I get. Sometimes I think it'd be nice if I didn't have to go home. I could hide out here, tell everybody I'm still doing research, and never go back to my real life."

Leanne set her chopsticks on the edge of her plate. "What exactly is your real life? Besides writing, I mean."

Darcy dabbed the corner of her mouth with her napkin. She took a sip of water and sat back in her chair. "I've been asking myself that ever since I sent in my last manuscript. I don't really know. Writing is all I've ever done. When I was in college, I couldn't think of anything else. My parents tried to get me to stay in school and study some different things before I settled on a career, but I wasn't interested. I still don't think college would have done me much good. But now that I'm not writing, I don't know what to do with myself."

Leanne leaned back in her chair. "I can't offer much advice there. I didn't even go to college. My father passed away during my last year in high school and my mother needed me at home." Darcy started to speak, but Leanne waved her away. "I don't want to make it sound like I'm feeling sorry for myself, but my life has always been the result of circumstances beyond my control. I never thought of running a bed-and-breakfast when I was a kid. The only running I wanted to do was away from Talmedge, but sometimes life has a way of making our decisions for us."

"And maybe my life is telling me it's time for something new."

Leanne lifted one shoulder, "Maybe. Maybe God is trying to get you to stand still long enough to get your attention."

"Why would He want to get my attention?"

"I don't know, Darcy. Only you can find out the answer to that question. That first time I invited you to church, you told me you didn't have time for God in your life like you used to. Maybe He wants you to see that all your searching and struggling to get to the top of the literary world is in vain if He isn't a part of your journey."

Darcy swirled a noodle on her plate. "I'm not exactly trying to get on top of the literary world."

"Well, whatever it is you're doing, God wants more than a lukewarm relationship. He wants fellowship. When you're out of town and you call your dad on the phone, what do you talk about?"

Darcy stared at her for a moment. "I don't know. It depends on where I am. I talk about my day, how my meetings went, any changes that might be coming along in the publishing world." It slowly dawned on her what Leanne was getting at. "I tell him that I love him, and I'm thinking of him," she ended hoarsely.

"That's fellowship, Darcy. That's all God wants from any of us."

Darcy took a sip of water. She remembered, too, the conversation she'd had with Leanne on the mountain. She also remembered sitting in her room the next day and feeling like God was trying to tell her the exact thing Leanne was saying now. Fellowship was more important than church attendance, and she would never find peace and contentment without letting Him back in her life.

"I'm not like you, Leanne. I've never sat on a mountain and had church or imagined the treetops raising holy hands. I think it's safe to say my religious upbringing was more conventional than yours. I'm not saying there's anything wrong with either one, I just don't bring God into daily conversation like you do. I wouldn't know how to begin. I've been on my own for the last ten years, and things are going pretty well. It's not that I don't want a closer relationship with God. It's just that as busy as I am, I don't see how I'm supposed to make time for even more complications in my life."

Leanne looked at her plate for a moment. Darcy could see the gears turning in her head. She was carefully weighing her words before she spoke again. "I don't think any of us were ever busier or under more stress than Jesus was during His time on earth. Yet, no matter where He was or what was going on, He always found time to get away from everyone and spend some alone time with God. The Bible says He woke up early or stayed up after everyone else had gone to sleep so He could pray. I don't think any of us can call ourselves a Christian unless we're willing to lay aside everything in our lives and put God first the way Jesus did."

"I agree with that, but I also believe heaven helps those who help themselves. Nowhere in the Bible does it say I should sit back and let God bless me and take care of me. I have to be realistic. I am responsible for earning a living and taking care of myself."

Darcy stopped talking and smiled. She didn't want to say anything that might jeopardize her friendship with Leanne, nor could she keep quiet and let someone judge her who had only known her for two weeks.

"Yes, my church attendance isn't what it should be, but I haven't willingly broken any commandments. I value the rights of others; I don't covet my neighbor's husband; I honor my parents. I admit I don't have the same fellowship with God I once did, but that doesn't mean I'm not a Christian."

Leanne picked at a bean sprout with her fork. "I'm sorry, Darcy. It's not my intention to judge you. Only you know if your relationship with God is what it should be. All I'm saying is, we all need to step back and examine ourselves every now and then. Are we doing things with the right motives? Are we waiting on God to reveal His plan for us before we jump in and take matters into our own hands?"

Darcy studied her plate. "My mother always told me to pray and wait to see which path God wants me to take in any endeavor, but I don't always have that luxury. And I still think everything's worked out pretty well. I make good money. I'm happy with what I'm doing. I don't always have time for what I used to enjoy, like my church group. But I can't help it that they schedule writers' conferences and book tours to interfere with Sunday service. God understands when we have to give up some things for work."

"Do you think you got where you are today with no help from God at all?"

"No, I'm not saying that. I know I'm blessed. But you have to admit, there are plenty of people in the world in much better situations than either of us, and they don't even pretend to follow God."

"Do you really believe they're in better shape than we are? Look at the divorce rate of these superstars you're referring to. Look at how many of their children are hooked on drugs, are in therapy, or not speaking to them. We really can't say they're in better shape simply from the size of their bank accounts."

"Not every rich, successful person is divorcing his spouse or comes from a dysfunctional family," Darcy pointed out. "Some of them have it made in every way."

"It's possible. All I know is I wouldn't want to trade places with any one of them. I have a peace and a joy in my spirit that no person or circumstance can steal from me. I don't know how anyone else handles tragedy, like when my parents or Vince's wife died. I just know, for me, I couldn't imagine going through anything like that without God to lean on."

Darcy swirled another noodle on her plate. "You're right, you're absolutely right. I guess when things started going right for me it took too much work, time, or whatever to let God into my life."

"It's easy for all of us to get that way. I find myself making decisions all the time without even stopping to pray and listen to see if God has any input first. When I wait on Him though, I always reap the rewards. He has never failed me or led me down the wrong road."

Darcy and Leanne ate in silence for a moment or two. Then Darcy spoke up. "I've been sitting here blaming my poor church attendance on work. Well, I'm on vacation so to speak, and my schedule is my own, so I think I'll get up and go to church with you in the morning—if the offer still stands."

Leanne beamed. "Of course it does." She reached across the table and patted Darcy's arm. "I tell you what, Darcy, you keep staying at the inn until you decide what you need to do with your writing. I'll set up a discounted extended stay price…"

"No, I couldn't let you…"

Leanne held up her hand to silence her. "My business is more of a ministry to me than anything. I don't want you to feel pushed into making a decision concerning the rest of your life because I'm charging you rent."

"Seriously, Leanne, I don't need you to give me more of a discounted rate than you already are. I can afford to stay at the inn for as long as it takes me to decide if my life is ready for a new direction."

Leanne lifted one shoulder. "If you're sure."

"I'm sure, but thanks for the offer. You don't know how much you've already done for me."

It was still dark as night when Leanne made her way down the back stairs and to the kitchen on Monday morning. She hadn't stopped smiling since Darcy came downstairs yesterday, dressed and ready for church. Leanne had asked Vince to go like she did every week, but was pleased that at least someone from the inn joined her for services. Everyone in her small congregation had been thrilled to meet Darcy. They grilled her about the writing business and where she was from. Darcy grinned at Leanne when she discovered Hank Haywood was a long-standing member of the congregation. On the way home, she pointed out that the most important thing about finding a Mr. Right was choosing someone who shared one's spiritual beliefs. Leanne reminded her she was the least qualified person in the world to offer relationship advice.

Whatever Darcy was or wasn't, Leanne was thankful they had crossed paths. Darcy was at some kind of crossroads in her life, a crossroads Leanne didn't fully understand, but God did. He had everything under control. Leanne praised God for using her as a tool during Darcy's crisis. She didn't know yet what the Lord might require of her, or what the outcome could be, but she prayed for wisdom and discernment in helping Darcy rediscover her need for a savior.

Twice in the last two weeks when she didn't have a list of chores that needed to be attended to during the slow season, she had gotten up early to join Darcy on her research trips to the surrounding areas. The change in her routine was refreshing. She could see how a person could get addicted to a lifestyle of coming and going as one chose; new people, new places, everyday a spontaneous adventure. Of course, most days Darcy spent strapped to her computer, forcing words into some coherent form to please the reading public. But Leanne would enjoy her role in the process as tour guide and food sampler for as long as it lasted.

Today though, she had work to do at the Inn. The Ladies' Historical Society was holding their monthly meeting in the East Room. Leanne had thus named the formal front parlor after it became a popular spot for business meetings and teas for various local groups. It didn't seem right that she charge a fee and serve refreshments in a room with no name. It had even been the sight of three weddings, one occurring when a sudden summer storm forced a considerably larger wedding party than the room could comfortably accommodate off the front lawn and inside.

She dumped the coffee grounds Vince had left in the filter down the sink and started a fresh pot. When there were no guests at the inn requiring breakfast Leanne slept in till six or even six-thirty. Vince was always gone before she made it to the kitchen. When they were kids, she was the family's early riser while Vince did what he could to squeeze in another few minutes of sack time. He learned early on how to manipulate their mother, so it was up to Leanne to make sure he was out of bed and downstairs for breakfast if she didn't want to miss the school bus because of his dawdling.

She was always the responsible one, always the one expected to keep things running smoothly. Even after Vince married Amber Freeman, Leanne was expected to watch out for her little brother.

She was less than thrilled with Vince's relationship with his high school sweetheart. She secretly hoped it would fizzle out on its own, but soon realized that wasn't going to happen. As always, she minded her own business and kept her mouth shut. Vince was free to marry whomever he pleased, and maybe the spoiled, high-handed Amber would mature into a good wife for her brother. Stranger things had happened.

Vince and Amber set up housekeeping in a rented trailer on a couple of acres of land. Vince took right to his new role of husband. Leanne prayed that she had judged Amber too harshly, and the two of them would be very happy together. Vince doted on Amber, wanting nothing more than her happiness, like any good husband should. The only problem was that as Vince matured, Amber reverted more and more into the selfish brat she had always been. She was beautiful and accustomed to getting her way with the opposite sex. Vince proved to be no challenge for the sanguine Amber. Leanne's hardheaded, hardworking brother was a pushover for a pretty face.

Russell, Vince and Leanne's dad, had already passed away by the time he and Amber married. When the marital problems started, Vince and Leanne went to great lengths to keep them from their mother. She was still adjusting to life without Russell and neither of her children wanted to burden her with the knowledge that her dear son's marriage was in trouble. Despite their efforts, she knew more than Leanne or Vince realized.

One day when Leanne leaned in to straighten the afghan around her legs, Olivia reached out and took her hand. "Watch over your brother for me, dear. He isn't strong like you are. He needs looking after."

Her words caught Leanne by surprise for two reasons. Firstly, because her mother thought she was stronger than Vince who could do no wrong in her eyes. And secondly, because she insinuated she might not be around to keep an eye on Vince herself.

"What do you mean, Mother?" Leanne had asked. "Vince is fine."

Olivia's grip on Leanne's hand tightened. The imploring look in her eyes told Leanne to pay attention. "After I'm gone," she said forcefully.

Leanne swallowed hard. "You're not going anywhere. Besides, Vince has Amber." She was beginning to tire of fixing Amber and Vince's marriage. Vince knew what he was getting into when he got married. Why should she rearrange her life to make him comfortable in the bed he'd made for himself?

"He doesn't have Amber," Olivia insisted. She let go of Leanne's hand and looked toward the window, a faraway expression in her eyes. "He'll be all alone except for you, Leanne. He needs you more than he'll ever admit."

Leanne straightened and looked down at her fragile mother. Olivia had never been a robust woman and after Russell's death, it seemed she lost most of her heart, too. Leanne didn't want to admit their mother's health wasn't improving. "You don't need to worry about Vince, Mother," she acquiesced. "I'll see that he's all right."

Olivia's eyes softened. "Thank you, dear. I know you'll be all right. You're strong. You don't need anybody—not like Vince…"

Her words drifted away as she looked back to the window.

Leanne went into the kitchen and cried as the sink filled with dishwater. What made her mother think she didn't need anyone? Just because everyone leaned on her didn't mean she had no needs of her own. Just once she wished she could hand over the burdens she'd carried since her father's death to someone else long enough to take a breath, but there was no one. Vince had enough on his plate pleasing his young wife, and Olivia wasn't strong. She would have to be the one.

When she shut off the water in the sink, she shut off her tears as well. She wasn't alone. She did have someone to shoulder her burdens. There was one in her life who promised to stick closer than a brother. The Apostle Paul had instructed that she be content in whatever situation she found herself. This was her life—the caregiver, the problem solver. Becoming an innkeeper was a natural fit; always the efficient, smiling hostess with no apparent needs of her own.

As the coffee pot began to gurgle and hiss, the calendar on the wall by the sink caught her eye. She kept a calendar next to every phone in the house for quick access since a reservation could come in at any time. So far April was unmarked. Not unusual for this early in the season, but she was always at a bit of a loss when she wasn't expecting visitors. During the first month or two of her slow season she had plenty to keep her busy, and she enjoyed the time to herself. But after a while, she was ready for something to do, someone to take care of.

As if in answer to her thoughts, the phone rang. Leanne checked the time as she reached for it. A little early in the day for making a reservation.

As she suspected, it was Vince. "Hey, Sis, I need a favor."

"Of course you do. What's up?"

"June's not coming in this morning. Her daughter-in-law is having an emergency C-section, so she needs to stay with the grandkids for a couple of days."

"Oh, dear, is everything all right?"

"No, everything's not all right. That's why I'm calling. I'm shorthanded."

"I didn't mean with you. I meant is everything all right with June's daughter-in-law and the baby?"

"Yeah, whatever, I don't know. I'm sure June would call if it wasn't. Meanwhile, you need to come in and fill in for her."

"I can't. I've got the Ladies' Historical Society coming at nine for their monthly meeting," she told him. "What about Missy?"

Vince snorted. "She can't handle it all day by herself. Besides, I need somebody who's not got lead in her shoes—or in her head."

"Vince," Leanne chided.

"Can you help me out or not?"

Send Darcy. The thought came as easily as if someone had whispered it in her ear. Darcy. She couldn't impose on her like that. She was already far enough behind on her writing. *Send Darcy.*

"What about Darcy? I'm sure she's awake by now."

Vince hesitated. "I doubt she's waited a table in her life."

"Don't be so judgmental. She's been spending the last couple weeks in diners and cafés. She's bound to have picked up a thing or two."

She heard him sigh, but they both knew he couldn't afford to be choosy. "She's probably got other things to do, and I seriously doubt she knows how to take instruction."

"Vince, you don't even know her. Do you want me to ask her or not?"

He sighed again. "I guess I don't have a choice." His appreciation was sorely lacking.

"If she can't come, I'll call you back. If you don't hear from me, she's on her way."

He hung up without saying goodbye, typical Vince. Leanne knew him too well to be insulted. When he had things on his mind, what few manners he had went out the window. She couldn't help smiling to herself as she imagined Darcy and Vince in the close quarters of the café's kitchen. She started for the stairs. God, I trust You know what You're doing here. Those two are either going to kill each other, or be the answer to the other's prayers.

At the top of the stairs she saw a light coming from under Darcy's door. She tapped lightly. She heard movement, and then the door opened. Darcy leaned out, still dressed in her bathrobe.

"Morning," Leanne said cheerily. "Have I got an opportunity for you."

Darcy didn't know how uninspired Vince was about her filling June's capable shoes until she popped in the café's back door a little before seven that morning. Before she could say a word, an apron was thrown at her from his general direction.

"Put this on and wash up at the sink." He pointed to the corner while turning back to the steaming, sizzling grill. "We've been open a half hour and the orders are backing up." He looked at the row of tickets hanging from a circular rack above his head as if she were personally responsible.

The busboy gave her a sympathetic smile on his way into the dining area to clear tables. Darcy smiled back, undaunted by Vince's greeting. She slipped the apron over her head. As Leanne had pointed out, this was the perfect opportunity to learn what kept a café running smoothly; one that she might never find out on the other side of the swinging doors. She realized Leanne painted a rosy picture because Vince was in a bind and needed her help, but she didn't mind. It would be fun.

She scrubbed her hands and then moved over to Vince. "I'm all yours, boss."

Vince sneered. He pointed at a tablet on the counter. "Write down what they want, and try not to mess things up. June'll be back in a day or two."

Darcy grabbed the tablet and stuck a pencil behind her ear. "Aye-aye, captain." She gave him a mock salute and backed out the swinging doors. Her exit was meant to be graceful, but the busboy was coming in at the same moment as she was going out, and the door stopped its outward motion midway through. The dishes in the plastic tub he carried rattled dangerously. Darcy stepped around the door and grabbed one side of the tub to help him steady it. Her face turned red. "Sorry about that."

The busboy scuttled around her without speaking. She caught a glimpse of Vince just before the door swung shut behind her. He looked as though he was in great pain.

She pushed the near mishap with the busboy out of her mind and swept into the dining area like she'd been doing it her whole life. Every stool at the counter was filled. Only three booths were still empty. Before she could greet the first customer, Vince's voice boomed out behind her. "Order up."

The young waitress whose name she couldn't remember looked up from where she was taking an order and gave Darcy a pleading look. Darcy spun around and hurried to the window. She took the two plates heaped with food. "Where's this go?"

Vince wagged his head in the general direction of the dining area and barked, "Table six, Bruce and Wendell."

Darcy turned and surveyed the crowded room. If only he could be a little more vague. She had no idea which table was number six or who Bruce and Wendell were. She supposed she'd figure it out as she went. Sure enough, before she got around the counter, a man in a flannel shirt and an Ace hardware cap lifted his coffee cup. "Here ya go, darlin'."

"Bruce, Wendell, I presume."

"You presume correctly, little lady," the man with the coffee cup said. "Don't tell me the old man's hired another waitress."

"I'm filling in for June." She set the plates on the table. The men promptly switched them. "Do you take your bill now or later?"

"June usually takes care of it for us," the other man said.

Darcy put her hand on her hip. "Even I know better than that. I'll hang onto it until you're ready to leave." She tucked the slip into the pocket of her apron.

"I must say, you working here sure won't be bad for the old man's business," the first man said.

Darcy cocked one shoulder and opened her mouth to respond. Vince's voice rang out behind her. She hurried back behind the counter. "Table two," he growled. She took the plates and started away. His voice stopped her. "Flirting with the customers is good for tips but takes too much time. Just give them the food and move on."

Darcy wanted to tell him if he knew anything about flirting, he would know that was not what she was doing. One look at the hard set of his jaw, and she knew he couldn't be reasoned with.

"After you deliver that order, check everybody's coffee," he added.

Darcy refused to be rankled. She was here to learn a thing or two and hopefully have a good time. Let him be an old grouch if he wanted. She turned away, stuck out her bottom lip, and mimed his parting order. R.T. and Jim were just walking through the front door and saw her. Jim covered his smirk with a cough. R. T. roared with laughter as he followed his brother to their usual table. Darcy grinned sheepishly and went about her work.

The breakfast rush lasted until well after eight. By the time Darcy dropped onto a stool to take a breath, her feet and calves were aching. She couldn't believe she'd only been here an hour and a half.

"You better grab something to eat while we got a minute," Missy, the other waitress, advised on her way to the kitchen. Darcy had picked up her name during the course of the morning.

"Thanks." She went to the coffee pot, poured a cup, and carried it into the kitchen. She blew on the coffee and took a cautious sip. Pretty good considering she had been the one to brew this pot and hadn't been sure how much to measure out. She smiled deliberately at Vince over the rim of the heavy cup. "Everybody's fed and happy, chief. Does this mean I can take a break?"

He stopped scraping grease off the grill long enough to glare at her. "Ask Missy. She's in charge when June's not here."

Missy came through the swinging door at that moment. "Since when?"

"Since today," he barked. "Got a problem with that?"

Missy sat down on the stool next to Darcy. "Not as long as the added duties mean a pay raise."

Vince glared at her and went back to his grill. Missy elbowed Darcy and grinned. "Even if he won't say it, you're doing great. You've either waited tables before or you pick up on things quick."

Darcy leaned in and whispered. "I'm not that quick. I waited tables in a little Italian restaurant off campus while I was in college. The work was hard, but I loved working with my friends."

Missy nodded in agreement. "Yeah, it has its moments." The bell jangled over the front door, announcing another customer. Missy and Darcy both jumped, but Missy was quicker. Darcy didn't have the energy to stop her.

It was hard enough keeping his distance from Darcy at the inn, and downright impossible inside the confines of the tiny café. She was there every time Vince looked up. Her deep throaty laugh filled the café too often. He got annoyed every time he looked up to see her talking and joking with his male customers. He wouldn't tell her again to keep moving and not stop longer than absolutely necessary to get the orders from those good old boys. Didn't she know better? The shameless flirting on their part was maddening.

Most of them were married men with jobs to get to. The bottomless cups of coffee alone were going to cost him a fortune if June stayed out all week and his morning crowd didn't clear out at their usual time, just so they could flirt with her replacement.

He refused to listen to the voice in his head that said it wasn't the thought of losing his shirt over free refills that bothered him; it was the sound of her voice, the toss of her head, and the ready smile she had for everyone.

Why'd she have to be so pretty—and funny—and charming? Just like Amber; yet nothing like her.

"Vince, what'd you do to these eggs?" Hank Haywood called out over the usual Tuesday morning crowd noise. The second morning without June and Vince sorely missed her.

He looked through the window over the grill to glare at Hank. Hank sat at his usual spot at the counter next to the cash register, with Earl Sneed to his right. He and Earl were staring at him like his eggs had suddenly sprouted feathers.

"What's the problem, Hank?" he asked with little enthusiasm. He could cook an egg any way a customer asked, but boring old predictable Hank took his the same way every morning. Two, over easy, yokes runny, edges crispy, with toast, bacon, and a side of hash browns—not exactly rocket science.

Hank made a display of picking up the saltshaker. "I know this is bad for my cholesterol and blood pressure and all, but it ain't an egg, if it ain't got a little salt on it."

Vince looked down at the grill. The row of eggs he'd just cracked had salt and pepper the way they were supposed to. He couldn't have missed salting the batch he served Hank out of.

"If I'd a wanted breakfast with no taste, I'd a stayed home and let Blanche feed me bran flakes," Mike Tadlock said from his end of the counter. Hank liberally salted his own eggs and then slid the saltshaker past six more disgruntled diners to Mike.

Vince scowled, refusing to admit he may have missed something as simple as salting eggs. "I think I can manage frying an egg without y'all's advice," he grumbled. "And some bran flakes every once in a while wouldn't hurt that gut of yours, Mike."

"Giving health tips to the customers again, boss?" Darcy

chirped on her way behind the counter with the coffee pot. Mike, Hank, and Earl laughed and smiled appreciatively.

Vince gave her a dirty look. She was getting way too comfortable in that apron.

"What's the matter, Vince," R.T. called from his table in the corner. "New waitress givin' ya trouble?"

Every patron in the place had stopped eating to watch the exchange. There were two ways to handle the situation. Let these vultures know they got under his skin so they could pick his bones clean, or join in the banter.

Vince chose the latter. "Considering the tips you cheapskates leave, I'm lucky any of 'em show up more'n two days in a row."

Laughter resounded through the café. Out of the corner of his eye, he saw Darcy laughing as she refilled Hank's coffee cup. He couldn't deny she looked pretty good standing there, unconscious of her own natural beauty and the impact she was having on his well-ordered life. If he could only stop paying attention to her and concentrate on making sure he salted every egg that sizzled on his grill.

Two hours later, every table and stool in the place was empty. Tyler, the busboy was now in third period History at the local high school. Darcy and Missy stood on either side of the butcher block island in the kitchen. "You need more flour on your rolling pin," Missy was saying. "Yeah, there ya' go. Now roll 'em out real thin. Perfect." She leaned across the island and lifted two corners of the dough Darcy had just flattened. "Then you flip it over like this and flour the other side real good."

Darcy sprinkled flour onto the fresh side of the dough under Missy's watchful eye and rubbed it over the surface with the palm of her hand.

"Great, you're doin' great."

Darcy never thought she'd have the need in her life to learn the art of making homemade noodles, much less enjoy the process. Every noodle that had ever shown its face in her kitchen was frozen and shrink-wrapped in plastic. She rolled the square of dough into a narrow tube per Missy's instructions and started slicing with a long knife. Vince left his bubbling pot of beef broth on the stove and came over to watch.

"Thinner, thinner," he ordered. "We don't want anybody choking to death on a noodle."

"They gotta be uniform," he said after a few more cuts with the knife. "That one's so narrow it'll rip when you pick it up, and that one's as wide as my finger."

Darcy swallowed her frustration at herself for not getting it right and for letting Vince's supervision unnerve her.

"There you go. That's better." He went back to the stove.

She supposed that was as much of a compliment as she was going to get.

"When she gets those done, you can show her the basics of a pie crust," he said to Missy. "I need twelve in the next hour."

"Lands, Vince, you should a told me that before I took all this time on the noodle lesson."

"Just do it, Missy."

"Just do it, Missy," Missy mimicked, winking at Darcy.

Vince ignored the insubordination. "Leanne'll be here to help out with the lunch rush."

"Hallelujah," Darcy exulted. She finished slicing the first roll of dough and turned the next one around on the chopping block. She was getting the hang of it, and things were going much faster.

"Having a hard time keeping up, city girl?" Vince asked.

Darcy wrinkled her nose at him. "Not at all," she said brightly. "I just want to know what makes you think I don't know my way around a pie crust."

"Does that mean you don't need Missy's help?"

"I know the basics. I think I can handle it."

"We'll see. This has to be better than something that'd earn you a Girl Scout badge. These are actually going to be consumed by real people."

Darcy hurtled a potholder at him. It hit his shoulder and left a flour print on his shirt. Vince grabbed the potholder off the floor and pulled his arm back to throw.

Missy jumped off her stool and held her hands up in front of her. "Okay, you two. Let's settle down before someone makes a mess that I have to clean up."

Vince froze in his stance, considering, and then lowered his arm to his side. "Okay, truce?"

"Truce."

Missy looked from Darcy to Vince. Darcy turned back to the countertop and her noodles. Missy walked into the pantry, but not before Darcy saw the hint of a smile on her lips. Darcy felt her cheeks turn pink. This wasn't the first time she'd acted like a teenager around Vince Ravenscraft. She needed to get hold of herself. She hadn't come here to make cow eyes at one of the subjects of her book. In fact, she had decided the very first day the Raven Café was not suitable for her book. The owner was too ill mannered and rude to bother with.

She looked over at the grill, which Vince was preparing for the lunch crowd that started oftentimes as early as eleven a.m. She didn't have time for romance while she was here, nor did she have the inclination. She would be going back to Middleburg Heights any day now. Had Leanne not pressed her into service in June's place, she'd already have finished her research and headed home. She needed to get back to her life, whatever that was. A man did not fit into her long term goals, especially not a fry cook from North Carolina.

10

Darcy was almost disappointed Wednesday evening when the phone rang and Leanne told her and Vince that June would be back to work the next morning. Vince mumbled something about things getting back to normal in his kitchen and stormed out of the room.

Darcy looked across the coffee table at Leanne. "I guess that means I'm out of a job."

"Looks that way. Listen, Darcy, we really appreciate you filling in the way you did. I'm not going to charge you rent for the last three days. You've been a big help, and between tips and what Vince pays, you'd still be in the red."

Darcy shook her head. "No, no, I told you I wasn't helping out for the money. The last three days have been a blast, and it'll really help the book. I got a lot more out of the situation than Vince did."

Leanne looked skeptical. "I wouldn't say that."

Darcy reddened. "What's that supposed to mean?"

Leanne shrugged and stood up. She rearranged the magazines in the magazine rack. When she finished, she straightened up and put her hands on her hips. "Just don't let Vince convince you he hated this arrangement as much as he acts."

"That's good to hear. I would have thought he'd prefer a root canal from the way he's acted with me there."

Leanne shook her head. "That's just Vince." She took the remote off the entertainment center and faced the TV. "Feel like watching some TV tonight?"

Darcy stood up. "No, I think I'll turn in. We've got an early morning tomorrow."

Leanne clasped her hands in front of her. "That's right. Camden, South Carolina," she squealed.

"Granny Bean's Barbeque," Darcy echoed her enthusiasm. "Wake up is at four a.m."

"I'll be ready." Leanne watched until Darcy left the room. She set the remote back on the entertainment center and put her hands on her hips. Darcy was such a wonderful girl. If Vince didn't watch it, she'd go back home to Ohio and neither of them would ever see her again.

Thursday morning Darcy woke up as planned to begin her excursion to South Carolina for lunch in a little café, famous across three states for its barbecued chicken. The restaurant had started out on the front porch of a sour tempered old woman who loved to cook almost as much as she loved to eat. When word leaked out—which was a testament in itself to the quality of the food since middle Carolinians were notoriously tightlipped about their barbeque—that Hephzibah Bean made the best ribs, chicken, and sweet potato pie in three counties, folks started taking the Camden Exit off Interstate 20 to buy it by the truck bed load to take back home. It wasn't long before Granny Bean, as she was known, couldn't keep up with the demand and recruited a couple of granddaughters to come in and cook. The health department and Uncle Sam got wind of the operation and came to see if they could get a piece of the pie, so to speak. To bring the place up to code, a grandson and a great nephew boxed in the front porch, added refrigeration units, larger ovens, and a sprinkler system.

Folks still came from miles around for the barbeque. Granny Bean still oversaw most of the cooking. Two great-granddaughters now worked in the kitchen and three more waited tables. The front porch had since seen three additions that gobbled up the front yard. Grandma bought the house next door from a neighbor she never did like and promptly tore it down to make room for parking.

Darcy fell in love with the story when she first stumbled across it during an Internet search, way back when the book idea was simply something to get Carla off her case.

Vince was delegated to keep an eye on the inn while Darcy and Leanne went to South Carolina. The only scheduled guests weren't due to arrive until Saturday. If anyone called before then, which wasn't likely to happen this time of year, Vince was instructed to tell them the Ravenswood was closed until noon Saturday, even though Darcy and Leanne planned to be back Friday evening.

It was Leanne's first overnight trip away from home since starting a bed-and- breakfast, and she was as excited as a new mother on her first outing after a baby. She was already in the kitchen, packing a cooler with drinks and snacks for the road when Darcy came downstairs. Her mountain frugality balked at the thought of paying a dollar and a half for a can of Coke on the Interstate when she could buy a case at Ermaline's for five dollars. Bottled water was plain sacrilege. An ample supply was readily available at home anytime she bothered to turn the handle on the faucet.

It didn't take long for her enthusiasm to rub off on Darcy, who didn't mention she regularly paid upwards of five dollars for a cup of glorified coffee. She doubted Leanne could handle that much of the real world. She couldn't keep from laughing out loud when Leanne dragged a second cooler from the mudroom.

"We're going to South Carolina, Leanne. We're not climbing Everest."

"But this is the small cooler," Leanne explained with great patience. "The big one goes in the back of the car, and we'll put this one in between the seats with us. We'll unload the big one into this one as needed."

"All right, as long as there's a method to your madness."

Leanne held up two boxes of prepackaged snacks, "Ho-Hos or Twinkies?"

"Actually I prefer salty snacks."

"Me too." She tossed the boxes on the kitchen table and opened a cabinet door. Snack sized bags of pretzels, popcorn, and corn chips landed on the table. "Grab whatever you like and put it into that grocery bag."

"You know, they sell junk food in South Carolina, too," Darcy said laughing. She went to the table and rifled through the bags anyway.

"I see Leanne's ready for her road trip," Vince said as he entered the kitchen.

Darcy held up the box of Twinkies. "Here's what you're eating while we're gone."

"I do know how to cook."

"That's what they tell me."

Leanne stopped rooting in the cabinets and turned to face her brother. "Are you sure you'll be all right here by yourself, Vince? We could rent another room and you could go with us."

"I'm thirty-two, Leanne. What could I need that I can't get for myself?"

"I don't know. You haven't been alone since…"

Her voice trailed off. Darcy looked from Leanne to Vince. Then she realized what Leanne almost said. Vince hadn't been alone since Amber died. Surely Leanne was worried for nothing and after four years he could handle one night.

The look on his face said he was thinking the same thing. He put his arm around Leanne's shoulder. "You know I love you, Sis, but you gotta quit worrying about me. I'm fine."

"If you're sure…"

He kissed her cheek and went to the coffee pot. "I'm the one with the cause for worry—the two of you alone on the open road. Just promise me you won't pull a Thelma and Louise down there in South Carolina. There's no canyons to drive into, and I don't think a ditch by the side of the road would make quite the same statement."

He was promptly pummeled with packaged snacks.

Leanne stared out the passenger window of Darcy's SUV, a satisfied look on her face. Darcy couldn't believe how green the trees had gotten in the nearly four weeks since she'd been here. Back home, they hadn't even started to bud. She imagined her flowerbeds, still brown and sleeping. The tulips would be poking their green heads through the pine mulch she had put down last fall. The daffodils and crocuses were surely up by now, and the forsythia bush at the end of the driveway would be full of bright yellow flowers in a few more weeks. Strangely, the mountains on either side of the road seemed more and more familiar to her than the sprawling Victorian she had dreamed of owning for so long.

"We're almost in South Carolina," Leanne said, breaking the silence. "There are several places in Spartanburg where we can get breakfast. It's a good-sized city, but still has a small town feel. The whole South is littered with places like the Raven Café and Granny Bean's, not just in the small, out-of-the-way towns."

Darcy shrugged. "Okay, whatever you decide. I trust your judgment."

They stopped for a late breakfast at the Pied Piper Café off Route 9 in Spartanburg. The breakfast buffet, for which the Pied Piper was famous, was known throughout the South for its clams, oysters, and deep fried apple fritters.

"Oh Darcy," Leanne moaned on her way across the parking lot an hour later. "In all good conscience, you should put a warning on the front of your book that its contents could be lethal for one's heart, cholesterol, sugar, and whatever else doctors lecture us about."

"Why do you think I've been wearing out that hiking trail behind the inn? I don't have the discipline to be a fulltime food writer. This will be my one and only book about food if I can help it."

"Have you made any progress?"

"On the book you mean? Not really. I thought working at the café this week would get my creative juices flowing, but it seems to have had the opposite effect. In the mood I'm in right now, I don't know if I'll ever write another word."

"Then why are we in South Carolina?"

"Granny Bean's Barbeque. Duh!"

Both women laughed and climbed into the SUV.

By the time they arrived home late Friday afternoon, Darcy was even less sure that she should write her book. But if she wasn't writing The Ultimate Guide to Dining on America's Back Roads, what was she still doing in North Carolina?

She and Leanne had a blast on their road trip. As soon as she admitted the trip was more for stalling and enjoying good greasy food than getting any actual work done, they relaxed and had a great time. Leanne was hysterical once she got away from the Inn. She confided in Darcy that she felt as if she had been paroled. After they checked into the motel on Thursday night, Darcy did still have to insist she not call Vince to make sure he was all right though.

The first thing Darcy needed to do upon returning to the Inn was touch base with Carla, whose emails she hadn't returned in three weeks. She needed to schedule a meeting with Brad in New York. She needed to get home and plan the vacation with her nieces she'd been putting off for too long. She needed to figure out where this project was going so she could clean up her notes, write an outline, and get started.

Instead she plopped her suitcase on the bed in her room and changed into lightweight sweats and a pullover windbreaker. She hoped the torrential rains that had fallen through the afternoon hadn't washed Maude and her kinfolk out of the hills and across either of the trails leading to the waterfall.

She walked down the back staircase to the kitchen. She could hear Leanne starting the washing machine and humming to herself as she sorted the laundry that had piled up in the twenty-four hours away from her beloved inn. Darcy smiled. She should go upstairs and empty her own suitcase so Leanne wouldn't have to ask about it later, but she didn't. She wanted to get onto the trail before the rain forced her back inside for who knew how long. She paused at the back door to make sure she was the only moving thing on the deck before stepping outside. A cool breeze, heavy with the threat of more rain grabbed the door and nearly yanked it out of her hand. She made sure it latched behind her before setting off down the hill to where the two trails began. At the last minute she decided to take the easier route to the waterfall. The sky had an ominous gray pallor that looked like it could open up any minute. She wasn't dressed for getting caught in a rainstorm. She should go back to the inn and change into a heavier jacket, or abort her hike altogether, but she had cabin fever. Her mood was too light to be stuck inside.

She took long loping strides down the hill to where the trails started. Under the think canopy of pines, it was even cooler. She plunged her hands into her jacket pockets and kept her eyes on the ground in front of her to watch for muddy puddles and also for Maude. Seeing the snake up close on the porch had made her jittery, now she jumped at every sound around her. She was in the mountains, she reminded herself; a snake could be the mildest thing she'd run across.

She reached the waterfall before she expected to. She was too used to the longer route. She watched the rushing water for a long time, thrilled by the beauty and sounds around her. It reminded her of what Leanne had told her about her father the first time they came here; that all creation was worshiping the Lord. She looked up at the sky through the trees. Could it be true? She leaned out over the railing and the rain heavy air whipped at her face. She could almost hear nature's choir singing hallelujahs to the Father.

She had been here too long.

She wiped standing raindrops off the wooden bench closest to the waterfall and sat down. She tipped her head back and looked up at the angry gray sky peering through the treetops. In another month, the sun wouldn't penetrate the foliage where she now sat.

But it won't matter, she reminded herself, I won't be here. I'm going home to write my book.

The thought of the book weighed heavily on her heart. Nothing about this book gave her peace, except coming to North Carolina in the first place. She had only been here a short time, but she felt like she had changed so much. She almost dreaded going home and back to her real life; back to writing books she no longer cared about, back to worrying about what Carla and Brad wanted out of her.

What if she didn't go back? Did she want to stay here indefinitely? Not at the Ravenswood Inn, but what if she bought a house of her own in Talmedge? What if she wrote fiction like Becky suggested? Could she do it? Would that make her happy? Was that what it would take to make her fall in love with the craft of writing again?

So many questions—maybe she should do what Leanne said and wait upon the Lord. Instead of focusing so hard on writing her book, she could sit here on this bench and wait for God to give her some insight. She turned her face upward and rested her head on the back of the bench. She stared at the sky for a moment and tried to formulate her request in her mind.

That was the problem. She didn't even know what she wanted God to do. It didn't seem likely that He would write the answer in the clouds or send a dove with an olive branch in its beak. How could she ask for something when she wasn't even sure what she needed?

She closed her eyes against the gray sky. She wrinkled her brow and concentrated. How should she begin? Didn't God know what was on her heart even when she didn't?

Heavenly Father… she began.

She opened her eyes and sat up. It was hopeless. She didn't know how to pray anymore. She didn't know what to ask for. She doubted she would recognize the answer if God revealed it to her. Tears of frustration welled up inside her.

She curled her hands into fists inside her jacket pockets and ducked her head. I don't know what You expect of me, she prayed angrily. I don't know what I'm doing here.

On the hillside above her came a crashing sound from the brush. Darcy's eyes flew open, and she sat up straight on the bench. She couldn't see anyone, but something was coming closer. It sounded like it was coming from the other trail that ran along the ridge at the top of the trees. Leanne had been in front of the washing machine sorting laundry when she left. She couldn't have gotten here this quickly by taking the longer trail. She was a faster and more skilled hiker, but it wasn't likely that anyone could make the trip in under an hour. Darcy had only been sitting on the bench a few minutes.

The sound coming toward her was definitely human. At least she was not about to become dinner for a bear just out of hibernation.

A portion of a figure appeared and then disappeared again behind the thick pines growing on the ridge. The trail was public, so it could be anyone, she reasoned. Lone hikers were rare on the mountain. Her first few trips here by herself, she had gotten spooked at the thought of coming across another hiker or a hunter. She had watched enough movies and read enough books about women alone in the woods stumbling across a crazed mountain man. Only here there was no suspenseful musical sequence to warn her of danger over the next rise or behind the next tree. Over time, the threat of danger had fallen to the back of her mind. Leanne had been hiking up here for years and never fallen into harm. Surely the mountain men were of a bygone era, if they ever existed.

She needed to stop watching so many late night movies.

Still her heart was hammering in her chest by the time Vince came into view. Without thinking, she combed her fingers through her wind-tousled hair. She was a mess. She hadn't showered or freshened up after returning home. Her hair smelled like the inside of her car.

She ran her tongue across her teeth and then checked herself. What was she doing? She was hiking a mountain trail. Her appearance should be the farthest thing from her mind. Even if what she looked like did matter on a secluded mountain trail, Vince Ravenscraft did not interest her in the least. She relaxed back onto the bench and watched his descent off the ridge.

"Yoo-hoo," she called out when he got within earshot.

He paused and looked around until he spotted her on the bench waving at him. He waved back and continued down the mountain. "Hey," he said when he reached her. Not surprisingly, he wasn't out of breath or even perspiring as far as she could tell. "I didn't know you were home."

"Just got back."

"How was South Carolina?"

"Beautiful. No rain like here."

"Was Granny Bean's Barbeque worth the trip?"

"Oh, my, was it ever. The place was packed from the time we drove into town till we left."

"I've been meaning to get down there myself. Check the place out."

"You could've come with us."

He gave her a look like she'd just suggested he unscrew his head and hand it to her. "I can't just close the café."

"And why not? The world wouldn't come to an end if R.T. and Jim had to cook their own breakfast. I bet you haven't closed that restaurant one day since you bought it."

"I didn't buy a restaurant so it could sit idle."

She shook her head at the futility of the conversation. "You know, it's good to get away from your daily grind once in a while. You should have seen Leanne. She was like a kid on the first day of summer vacation. Everybody needs a break, Vince," she elbowed his arm, "even you."

"The Ultimate Guide to Running Your Business Into the Ground."

"Taking a break doesn't necessarily lead to poverty."

He sat down beside her and stared out at the water. "But why risk it?"

She didn't have an answer, at least not one that would satisfy him, so she changed the subject instead. "I didn't know you were a hiker."

"I do lots of things I don't tell people about."

She looked closely at his profile, not sure if he was serious or not. She had looked at him often enough, but found herself noticing some things for the first time; a straight nose that tipped down and back up on the very end. Taken by itself, it was a rather strange nose, but somehow it worked just right on Vince's face, giving him an impish, little boy look. Dry skin on a perfectly formed ear, from too much time spent outside in the elements. That was something she had been wondering about, how could a man who spent his days over a grill maintain such an athletic, rugged appearance? She was a writer; things like that weren't supposed to escape her notice. She would have to pay closer attention to how he spent his free time.

On second thought, maybe that wasn't such a good idea.

A smile twitched the corners of his mouth, and he turned to look at her.

"Are you committing my face to memory?"

Darcy blushed and dropped her eyes. "Oh, uh, not really, I was just imagining all the things you do that no one knows about. Are you a super hero?"

He barked out a laugh, evidently pleased with the notion. "Unassuming fry cook by day," he said. He straightened his shoulders, set his fists on his hips, and lowered his voice an octave. "Fearless crime fighter by night."

"I could see you in a cape and tights."

Vince curled his lip in distaste at the image her words conjured up and slumped back against the bench. "Okay, so maybe I'm not a super hero, but there are some things I do that don't involve rolling homemade noodles."

Darcy was instantly intrigued. This was the first time she'd ever heard Vince Ravenscraft allude to anything of a personal nature. "Besides noodles, pecan pie, and dumpster patrol, what do you like to do?"

"Dumpster patrol? That's only to protect the good people of Talmedge and their sanitation needs from tourists."

"Oh, sorry."

"I love the outdoors," he said, after thinking for a moment. "I love quiet. The café is so noisy—all the time, dishes rattling, people shouting to be heard over the racket, somebody always wantin' something. It's nice to get outside where the only raised voices I hear belong to the birds. The wind in the trees, the water, my own footsteps on the soft ground, it's very therapeutic."

That explained the physical fitness and bronzed skin. "Then why in the world did you buy a café?"

"That's what Amber always wanted to know." He gave her a quick look. She didn't think he meant to say the words aloud.

Darcy let the silence lengthen between them before she spoke. "Leanne told me about Amber," she said in a tone that let him know she knew everything from their rocky marriage to the car accident that took her life.

Vince stared at the waterfall. "She was against the café. She wanted to move north, to Philadelphia," he added with a grimace.

"It's a lovely city," she offered.

"Can you picture me in Philadelphia?"

"Not really. Not too many quiet places."

"Exactly." He turned back to the water. "But I couldn't make Amber understand that. She hated Talmedge. She didn't see the beauty in the mountains. She knew if I bought a café, we'd never get out of here."

Darcy wondered how two mismatched people ever got together in the first place, but she didn't ask for an explanation. At least Vince's marriage had lasted four years. She never had the same boyfriend for longer than four months.

"The life you and Leanne have here isn't for everyone," she pointed out.

"Not for city girls anyway."

She scowled playfully at his grin. "Not just city girls. There's a reason why most of the guests at the inn come only for the weekend. It's a great place for getting away, but most people aren't interested in living here."

"I can understand that in people who weren't born here, but not Amber. How can someone grow up here," he swept his arms in a circle, encompassing the trees around them, "and then want to leave it?"

"I have to admit, it's growing on me."

Vince gave her another quick look, as if to check for sincerity before turning his attention back to the waterfall. "I wouldn't've thought you were the type."

"What type do you think I am?"

He put both arms on the back of the bench. Darcy was very aware of his hand nearly touching her shoulder. "An uptown, overeducated woman who came down here to mock all of us in a book. People do that a lot. Southerners are looked down on by pretty near the rest of the country, especially your bosses in New York." He stared thoughtfully at her for a moment. "I'm happy to say though, it appears I was wrong." He stretched his legs out in front of him and crossed his ankles. "You might say I'm not exactly the most tolerant person ever created."

Darcy gave him a look of mock horror. "No!"

His grinned widened. "When I saw your SUV blocking the dumpster that day I pretty much had you pegged before I even saw you, and I didn't like you."

"Before you even met me?"

"I told you I can be a little close minded."

"None of this comes as a big surprise, Vince. I already know how you feel about anyone born outside North Carolina."

"Not everybody. Folks from Georgia ain't all that bad. Though I once knew a fella from Valdosta…"

Darcy laughed.

"Don't go laughing at me. You're as bad as I am," he said. "You're just better at hiding it. You think I'm a bumpkin. You think that about everybody you met since you got here."

"I have not thought that about anyone," she protested.

"Yeah, right. I seen you the first day you walked into the café, like we were gonna feed you off a dirty plate—and the look on your face when R.T. and Jim sat down at your table, now that was just plain funny."

"I can't believe you were watching me."

"Everybody in the place was watchin' you. I expect you have folks watch you everywhere you go."

She didn't know if he was flattering her, or if she looked like the suspicious type people always kept an eye on.

"Once I figured out you were also the one blockin' the dumpster, well, I was sure then you were an uptight city girl, but looks can be deceiving."

"If you're trying to flatter me, Mr. Ravenscraft, you're not doing a very good job of it."

"I'm not trying to flatter you. I just say things the way I see 'em."

"You know, you can be quite maddening. You try to make me feel bad for having preconceived notions about people, and then you admit to doing the same thing."

"Yeah, but I don't apologize for how I am. I don't try to make people think I'm somethin' I'm not."

"Oh, and I do? Is that what you're saying?"

The calm look on his face only frustrated her more. "No, that's not what I'm sayin' at all, if you'd quiet down a minute and listen to what I'm trying to tell you. All I'm sayin' is, as soon as folks meet me they know I'm a close-minded, bigoted yokel, period. I don't apologize for it. Some folks live their lives trying to impress other folks. Not me. I know for a fact I make the best cole slaw and pecan pie east of the Mississippi River. I don't care what else you think of me, as long as you sit still long enough to try my pie."

"You sound pretty sure of yourself there, Mr. Ravenscraft."

He leaned over and touched her chin with the tip of his finger. "I made a believer outta you, didn't I?"

Darcy crossed her arms over her chest and tried to ignore the heat from where his finger touched her chin. "Your cole slaw is the best I've ever tasted, I'll give you that. But I'd be careful before I went spouting my mouth off about pecan pie. Yes, yours is exceptional, but I've eaten a lot of pecan pie in the last few weeks, and I'm not so sure yours is the best."

Vince leaned forward, rested his elbow on his knee, and stared at her. "You're going to sit there and lie to my face."

A flush crept up her cheeks. She tried to think of something cute and witty to say back, but all she could do was stare at his mouth and wonder what those lips would feel like on hers.

He leaned forward another inch. Darcy held her breath. "Well, are you?" he asked again.

This playful side of him totally disarmed her. She had grown comfortable dealing with the stern, brooding Vince; the one everyone in Talmedge called 'the old man'. She didn't know what to do with this one—well, she could think of a few things.

Darcy exhaled audibly. "Considering I'm the one writing the country dining book, who makes the best pecan pie is totally up to my judgment."

"I can see I'm going to have to do something to change your judgment before you finish that book."

She flushed again, her mind conjuring up another image of his lips on hers. That could certainly influence her judgment.

"While you're thinking of how to improve your pecan pie, why don't you tell me what made you decide to buy a café in the first place? You don't exactly look like most people's typical image of a café owner."

He leaned back on the bench and propped his right ankle on his left knee. "You mean big belly, greasy apron, and three strands of hair combed over my bald spot."

He had almost read her mind. "Something like that," she said.

"Out of all the cafés and diners you've visited in the past couple weeks, how many cooks have you come across that fit that description?"

"Not many."

He grinned. "See there, preconceived notions, and all negative."

"Okay, okay, I admit it. I'm as intolerant and close-minded as you are. Now are you going to tell me what made you want to buy a café or not?"

It took a minute for him to formulate an answer, and when he did, its simplicity surprised her. "I guess because I like to cook."

"That's it? You like to cook?"

"Ain't that enough? Why do you write books? Because you like to write, right? The whole world doesn't have to be complicated."

"Sometimes it is complicated. Do you ever wonder if you made a mistake, that you should be doing something else with your life?"

A shadow passed over Vince's face. He dropped his leg to the ground and straightened up. "No, I don't," he snapped. "What would be the point? If I made a mistake, it's too late to fix it. That café was for sale for five years before I bought it. If I woke up tomorrow and decided I wanted a career change, that'd be too bad for me. Nobody else's going to buy the place out from under me. I have to make the best of the situation whether it was a mistake or not. No use even considering the thing."

"I suppose not," she said after some thought, "but I would hate to think I have to do something I hate the rest of my life because I thought I liked to cook a lot more than I actually did."

"Hey, that's what life is. Sometimes you have to learn to like what you're doin'. That's the only way to live with our mistakes." The shadow darkened his features again. He looked out across the water. She hoped she hadn't made him mad. But when he turned back to her, the light was back in his eyes.

"Buyin' the café wasn't a mistake," he stated.

"I'm sure it wasn't. You must be doing something right, but sometimes people change. It turns out we haven't made mistakes, we're just different than when we started."

"That's what Amber used to say." His voice sounded like it was coming from a great distance. "'I'm not the girl you married, Vince. I've changed. I want something more from my life than this dirt water town can give me.'"

He faced Darcy, his face a mask of pain. She resisted the urge to reach out and touch his cheek. "I'm sorry. I didn't mean to..." Her voice trailed off. She didn't know what to say.

"No, hey, it's my fault." He made an effort to smile. "I didn't mean to take you on that little detour down memory lane." He was quiet for a moment. "I didn't buy the café until after Amber...after her accident. She didn't want it, and I didn't have the strength to go against her. Hey, there I go again. Sorry about that, water under the bridge." He stood up and moved to the railing used to keep shutterbugs from getting too close to the slippery rocks.

Darcy stood up and followed him. She raised her voice to be heard over the pounding water. "It doesn't hurt to talk about things. Sometimes it's what we need most."

He made a motion with his hand, dismissing her. "Water under the bridge," he repeated.

Maybe he didn't need to talk, but she did. "When I bought my house, I paid cash for it. I'm not saying that to brag." She looked across the water to the other side. After a few moments, she went on. "I'd been making pretty good money for several years, but I was still living at home with my parents. I never even considered getting a place of my own until I had enough money saved to buy the house I wanted." She chuckled. "You must think that's pretty pathetic."

Vince snorted. "I'm still livin' in my parents' house and lettin' my big sister wash my clothes."

Darcy smiled. She watched the water cascading over the rocks below them. Maybe she had more in common with the man than she thought.

"Why were you afraid to spend any of your money?" he asked.

She watched his face for a moment before answering. She knew why but felt uncomfortable admitting it. "I couldn't help wondering, what if I don't sell another book? What if I stop earning money? Writing is a very iffy career. There's no job security. Everything depends on me. What if I fail?"

"We all ask that question."

"But I didn't have anything to fall back on. It was just me. I guess I felt safer at home with my parents. I knew if I failed, at least I had them. They were my security blanket. I couldn't trust myself."

"What changed? What made you decide to stand on your own two feet?"

Darcy leaned against the railing and looked out across the expanse of rock to the water. "Nothing really. I got a big royalty check that was enough to buy my house. I'm not a gambler. I don't like spending money I don't have in my hand."

"If more people lived that way, they wouldn't be re-formulating the bankruptcy laws."

"I guess, but I think I took it too far. I didn't see myself as a real writer until I had enough money in the bank to buy a house. If I could earn that much money, then my first seven books weren't flukes."

"You didn't know that until then?"

"All I could think about was that the success could end tomorrow, along with the money. Then where would I be?"

"You had no faith in your skill as a writer," he said simply.

"Maybe I still don't. I haven't even started the book I came here to research."

This revelation seemed to amuse him. "I suspected as much."

"You did? Why?"

"You're too busy doing everything else. I know you have to run around with your research, but it seems to me like that's all you were doin'; workin' with me at the café, driving to South Carolina to eat ribs, not to mention everywhere else you've been runnin' off to. I haven't seen you sit still long enough to put a good sentence together, let alone start a book."

Darcy's shoulders sagged. She trudged back to the bench and sat down. She was suddenly depressed. "I'm afraid it's finally happened."

Vince sat on the edge of the bench and turned his body toward hers. "What's happened?"

"My well's dried up. I can't write anymore."

He reached out and touched her hand. "You don't believe that."

She looked down at his hand on hers. "Then what's wrong with me? Why haven't I written a word since finishing my last book? My editor's pushing me to start a new project, and I'm doing everything I can to avoid her. Why else do you think I came all the way down here?"

"I thought it was to research diners and cafés."

"Ha!" She pulled her hand out from under his. "That goes to show what you know. I'm hiding, Vince; hiding from the publishing house, from my family, from the writer inside me who wants to know when we're getting back to work."

"And when are you?"

Darcy combed her hands through her hair. "That's the problem. I don't know. I haven't enjoyed writing for years. When people ask me the secret to my success, I tell them what they want to hear, or at least what I think they want to hear. Nobody wants to hear the truth. The truth is there's no secret, just a lot of hard work, determination, sweat and tears, that's all. But nobody will pay to attend your conference if you say that. It's like losing weight. Everybody wants a magic pill, a quick fix. There isn't one. I know that better than anybody. Even after twenty books, I know there's no easy way around it. Writing is hard, it's lonely, and I may not want to do it anymore."

Vince took her hand in his. This time Darcy did not pull back. She looked into his eyes. "What do you want to do, Darcy?"

She sagged against the back of the bench. "I don't know. When I came here, I thought all I needed was a vacation. I was planning to do some research for a new book and get some rest and relaxation while I was at it. I thought if I could get away from my desk, my love for writing would come back. But that hasn't happened. The longer I'm away from home, the less I want to ever pick up a pen and paper again."

"Would that be the end of the world?"

"Yes." She sat up straight and glared at him, "Just like it would be for you if you lost your café. I'm a writer, that's all I've ever been. My parents and my brother, they're the giving ones. My mom and my brother are schoolteachers. You have to love what you do to commit yourself to that thankless job. My dad is a fire chief. Yes, he's been called a hero lately, but it's an underpaid job that other people talk about, but nobody actually wants. And then there's me, Darcy, the one who fell headfirst into money. I'm paid well, I travel wherever and whenever I want. I've met all kinds of famous and interesting people, not always one in the same, I might add. My family gives of themselves everyday. I don't. I take. People stand in line to buy my books. They tell me I've changed their lives. They make me think I'm something special, but I'm not. My parents are the special ones. My brother and sister-in-law raising three kids on teachers' salaries, they're special. Not me. I'm lazy and a little bit lucky. What would I do if I didn't have writing? I sure wouldn't be special."

Vince dropped her hand and leaned away from her. "All right, are you finished?" Before she could answer, he went on. "Because I've listened to about all I want to hear. Are you waiting for me to tell you how special you are, even if you never write another book? Do you want me to say how you're just as good as your family even though they sacrifice everyday? Cause I'm not going to do it. I'm not into flattery, remember? I'm into reality. I'm sorry you lost your faith in yourself. I'm sorry you don't want to write anymore." He stood up and thrust his hands into the pockets of his jeans. "People get up every morning and wish they didn't have to go to their thankless, menial jobs. They don't want to work at the mill, clean truck stop toilet stalls, or baby-sit some CEO's bratty kids, but they do it. Not because they're fulfilled, but because they have to. They have no choice. You're lucky, lady—or blessed, or whatever you want to call it. You have a choice. You have a great family who supported your sorry backside while you were huddled over a computer screen convincing yourself you were a good writer. You've had everything handed to you on a silver platter, and now you're whining because you don't know if you want to write anymore."

He looked up into the hills around them and took a deep breath. "Don't write anymore if you don't want; you can afford it. Live here at the Ravenswood for the rest of your life while you try to figure out what you want to do. Jet around the world. Whatever. Or, get back to writing. It's all about discipline anyway. Just quit your whining about it. Cause face it, lady, there's people in the world with real problems."

Darcy felt as if she'd had the wind knocked out of her. She had thought he would offer a sympathetic ear, but all he heard was that she was lazy and whiny. She jumped up and faced him. "I wasn't insinuating the rest of the world has no problems bigger than mine. I was just telling you how I felt."

"And I'm telling you what your problem is."

"Well, you sure are a good one to be telling me what's wrong with me when you've been on some kind of guilt trip ever since your wife died."

Vince's jaw clenched. "You don't know what you're talking about. My wife is dead, and all you're having is a midlife crisis."

"Midlife crisis?" she shrieked. "I'm twenty-nine."

"You want to talk about money? I spent my wife's life insurance money on the café she died trying to talk me out of."

Darcy suddenly didn't feel like arguing with him anymore.

"Yeah, that's right. Amber was leaving me. She couldn't stand the sight of me or this town. She packed up her stuff and was on her way as far away from me as she could get. If she hadn't died, the two of us would be living in Philly or someplace right now where she'd be happy. I could be one of those sorry bums who goes to a job he hates everyday, but at least my wife would be alive."

"Vince..." She reached for his arm.

He jerked away. "Don't. You don't know how I'm feelin', so don't pretend you do."

"I do know how you're feeling, because I've been living most of my life the same way—wracked with guilt. I'm guilty for having it so easy when others have to work so hard, and you, you're guilty of what you see as a crime against Amber. You have to stop punishing yourself and stop punishing Leanne."

He glared at her. "I'm not punishing Leanne."

"Yes, you are. Your sister doesn't have a life of her own because she's too busy taking care of you. She is so worried about you, she feels guilty when she goes away from the inn for a night. She could even have a future with the man she loves if she didn't think you'd fall apart without her."

"What are you talkin' about?"

"I'm talking about Hank Haywood."

"I've never done anything to keep Leanne and Hank apart."

"Except make her think you need her so desperately."

"You know, I think it'd be a good idea for you to learn to mind your own business. Leanne needs to be needed. That's the way she likes things. She's fine."

"No, she's not. She's lonely. She wants children. And that doesn't include her overgrown baby brother. Leave her alone, Vince. Let her get married. Let her have a life."

"I've never tried to keep Leanne from havin' a life. She's free to do whatever she pleases."

"She doesn't know that. She's too busy molly coddling you. If you looked up from that grill of yours long enough to take a look around you, you might see it. But she'll never do anything about what she wants because she's too good of a person to put her own needs before those of her grieving brother."

Vince glared at her for a long moment. Darcy clenched her fists and stood her ground. She was absolutely right, and it was about time someone pointed it out to him. Just when she thought he had something more to say, he turned on his heel and stomped back up the ridge to where the longer trail headed home. Darcy looked up at the threatening clouds in the sky and wondered if he'd get home before he got soaked in a rainstorm. She rested her elbows on the railing and stared unseeingly into the crystal clear water. Everything she said was true. So why did she feel so bad for having said it?

Maybe she didn't have the right to tell a person how long they should grieve over their spouse, but she thoroughly believed Vince was taking advantage of Leanne's giving nature. He pretended to be put out by her over protectiveness of him, but he clearly did nothing to stop it. Still, she had said too much. Leanne and Vince's relationship was no concern of hers. It worked for them; she needed to take a lesson from him and mind her own business.

A drop of water splashed onto her hand, then another. She stared at her hand for a moment thinking it was overspray from the waterfall before she realized it had begun to rain. She plunged her fists into her pockets and headed toward the shorter trail. She walked slowly at first, but picked up her speed as fatter and fatter raindrops pelted the leaves at her feet. Vince was going to get soaked. On the lower trail, the canopy of trees would offer some protection. Up on the ridge, he was completely exposed to the elements.

She hunched her shoulders, ducked her head, and walked faster, keeping her eyes on the ground at her feet. She'd be back to the inn in fifteen minutes if she hurried.

Maybe she was being a baby. There were plenty of people in the world worse off than she was. Her little problems about whether she wanted to write or not paled in comparison to the soldiers who lost their lives in Iraq or victims of natural disasters all over the world. But she had opened up to Vince out of what she thought was friendship. She wanted to understand him better. She wanted to care for him as another individual. Why did he have to make everything so difficult?

It was raining steadily by the time she arrived back at the Inn. She went straight upstairs to jump into the shower. Through the window in her room, she saw Vince immerge from the trees. He must have taken a shortcut through the woods to arrive home so quickly.

She watched for a moment as he hurried toward the house before turning away from the window. Since her brief stint as a waitress at the Raven Café, she had thought something was developing between them. Vince was different from every other man she'd ever known. He was definitely the most stubborn, hardheaded, difficult man she'd ever encountered. At the same time, he was strong, funny, passionate, and brutally honest. From the day she'd wandered into his office by mistake, she'd known he was much more than the hard exterior he projected to the world. He had been hurt by his first wife and still bore the scars. After talking with him today, she better understood where his guilt came from and how it had shaped him into the man he was today.

A qualified counselor possessing infinite patience and about fifty years of free time to dig around in his psyche may be able to determine how deep the scars from his relationship with Amber went, and whether he was redeemable or not. Darcy however, was not a counselor by any stretch of the imagination, and Vince wasn't likely to ever seek one.

With a clean change of clothes over one arm, she headed to the bathroom. Since she was the only person currently residing on the second floor, she wouldn't have to worry about hurrying in the shower. In a few days, she'd be back at her own house where sharing a bathroom would never again be an issue.

Nor would she have to contend with a brooding, frustrating man who had no room in his heart for anything but a diner in a dried up little town.

She turned on the tap in the shower to let the water get hot while she undressed. Instead of relief that her month of research was nearly behind her, all she felt was emptiness.

At least that was better than the lump of disappointment rising in her throat.

11

$\mathcal{D}$ · $\mathcal{D}$ · $\mathcal{D}$ · $\mathcal{D}$

$\mathcal{D}$arcy crossed the Ohio River at Marietta the following Tuesday. Home—she still had five hours of driving ahead of her, but it was great to be back in Ohio. She stopped only when she had to. She was determined to be home in time for dinner. She called her mother Sunday night to let her know when to expect her, and again from south of Canton when she was two hours out.

Mom insisted she come to dinner. Darcy acquiesced with little persuasion. The rest of the family would be there as well—Mom was probably making phone calls and planning a menu as soon as she hung up from Darcy—and she couldn't wait to see them. Now that she was home, she realized how much she had missed everybody.

Darcy stopped at her house first and deposited her suitcases in front of the washing machine. She sorted out a load of whites while the washer filled, dumped them into the machine, and stepped over the remaining bags to go upstairs for a shower in her own bathroom. She luxuriated under the running water for a full thirty minutes despite the low water pressure from the washing machine downstairs. No matter how wonderful and homey the Ravenswood Inn had been, there was nothing that compared with being home.

She pulled on an old pair of jeans, dug through her closet for her favorite pullover, and chose a pair of loafers she had left behind when she went to North Carolina. It took an extra tug to get the jeans over her hips and fastened around her waist. Apparently she hadn't climbed that mountain often enough. She pulled her shirt down over her stomach and gave herself a hard look in the mirror. Tomorrow, missy, you're going on a diet. But tonight it was Mom's meatloaf.

She went back downstairs to throw her clothes in the dryer and start another load. She sorted through the pile of mail on the entryway table her father had left for her. She could tell he had been the one to bring most of the mail inside while she was gone because nothing had been thrown away. Her mother always discarded store circulars and credit card applications, but Ben didn't feel comfortable sorting through what came into her house. She smiled as the wastebasket inside the living room door filled at her feet. She watered the plants that looked like they couldn't wait another minute, cracked the kitchen window to let in the scent of lilac from the backyard, and headed to her parents' house.

Little Zachary met her at the front door. "Aunt Darcy, you're here."

"So are you, big guy." She swept him into the air and kissed his neck. Either he had lost weight or she was stronger from her daily hike through the mountains behind the Ravenswood Inn. "How have you been?"

Zachary returned her kiss. "Fine. Can we go to Disney World now?"

Becky appeared in the living room doorway. "Sorry about that, Darcy. It's all the girls have been talking about for the past month, and they got him worked up."

Darcy set Zachary on the floor and aimed a kiss at the top of his head, but he was gone as soon as his feet hit the floor. So much for missing her! "That's all right, Becky." She stepped forward and hugged her sister-in-law. "It's my own fault for promising them something and not delivering. I guess that means you'll just have to go with us to keep the reins on him."

Becky raised her shoulders and shivered. "I suppose I could sacrifice for my children's happiness."

"It would be more fun if we made it a family trip anyway. I wonder if I can talk Mom and Dad into going."

"Talk us into what?"

Darcy stepped into her mother's embrace. "Mom! I smell garlic. I thought this was meatloaf night."

"I made lasagna. I know how you love it." She stepped back. "You're looking good, sweetheart. I'm glad you didn't starve yourself on the road like you usually do."

"That does it. I'm definitely going on a diet. I'm afraid I brought more of me home than I left with. Writing a book about down home diners and cafés isn't the best way to watch one's waistline."

Sharon put her arm around Darcy's waist. "Well, I think you look fabulous. You've always been too bony. Now you've actually got a figure."

Darcy shuddered. If her Mom thought she was curvaceous, that meant she was getting chunky. Her diet would start first thing in the morning, after a healthy serving of her mother's lasagna.

Sharon kept her arm around Darcy's waist as she steered her toward the family room. "Dad and Keith are watching the news," she said. "I think the girls are online. They'll be thrilled to see you. Now what were you wanting to talk your Dad and me into?"

Darcy's reply was cut off by squeals from her nieces as they ran down the hall to meet her. "They never react that way when I come home from somewhere," Becky observed wryly from behind her.

Darcy opened her arms and hugged both girls at once. "Girls, you look beautiful. You would have loved North Carolina. The inn where I stayed was gorgeous."

"Did you get pictures?"

"Were there any hot guys?"

"Are you home for good this time?"

"Yes, I took loads of pictures. There are hot guys everywhere, and I plan on sitting at my computer and not getting up until this book is finished." She didn't bother to mention she might be sitting there for quite some time.

Dinner was a boisterous affair. Exercising great restraint, the kids didn't mention Disney World until it was time to clear the table. Samantha was the first to bring the topic up. "Aunt Darcy, you look pretty beat from your trip."

Darcy resisted a smile and put her hand against her cheek. It was obvious to everyone she never looked healthier. "I do?" she said.

"Yes, I think it would be a good idea to get away from your notes for a few days before you start your book. What you need is to start this project with a clear head."

The adults exchanged glances. "Hmm, that's a thought."

"Yes," Bethany said helpfully, "you said yourself once you get started, you can't get up from your computer until you finish. I think the best idea is to do something totally fun and spontaneous before getting down to work."

She looked across the table at Samantha who nodded slightly.

Darcy struggled to keep the smile from her face. "And what do you think would be fun and spontaneous?"

The sisters exchanged glances again before chiming together, "Disney World."

Darcy pursed her lips in thought. Keith put his hand over Bethany's who sat next to him. "Girls, you've got another month and a half of school."

Their faces fell, but Darcy couldn't hide her enthusiasm anymore. "Well, actually, Becky and I were talking when I first came in. Maybe this is the best time to get away."

Bethany and Samantha squealed with delight.

Becky looked up in surprise. "I didn't know you were talking about right now. We can't all get away this time of year. Testing is about to start."

Darcy went on. "Oh, think about it. It would be fun. We could leave after school on Thursday and come back Monday. That would only be two days of school missed. I know you all have personal days available. No one would even know we were gone."

Becky and Keith studied each other. Becky was weakening, but Keith looked doubtful. "I hate to miss class this late in the year," he said weakly.

"Oh, come on, Keith. Think spur of the moment. You've been at that school for years, and you've never done anything like this."

"Yeah, come on, Dad," the girls echoed.

Becky and Keith turned to Sharon and Ben. "We'll do it if you do it," Keith said to Sharon.

Sharon put her hand to her throat. "No, no, this is something for you kids. We couldn't—"

"No, Mom, we have to go together!" Darcy exclaimed. "That's the whole point. We haven't been on a family vacation since the girls were babies. What do you say? Disney World—my treat."

Zachary, who had gone into the family room to play with his toys, came running back. "You mean it? You mean it, Aunt Darcy? Even me?"

She scooped him into her arms. "Even you, Zach." She looked at her parents. "What do you say? Two days away from school. It wouldn't be the same if we didn't all go together."

Mom scanned the circle of expectant faces. "Are you talking about this Thursday? I don't see how we can possibly make flight arrangements and reservations on such short notice."

"It'll cost a fortune," Dad said from the head of the table.

"Dad, please, I want to do this. I've been promising the girls this trip for years. Before long, they won't want to go anywhere with us. Come on, it'll be a blast."

"Yeah, Grandpa," Bethany put in, "we can all help with packing. It won't be so bad, and me and Sam will work super hard at school this week to make up for missing Friday and Monday."

"It's easy to make travel plans on the Internet," Samantha added, "and fast too."

"Well, I guess I'm out of arguments. It's just so much money... seven of us. I'll never be able to live with myself."

Darcy let Zachary slide out of her arms. She went over to her father and put her arms around his neck. "Come on, Dad. I want all of us to go somewhere together before the girls get too old. Don't think about the money. Think of the memories we'll make. You can't put a price on that."

She could see he was warming to the idea. "What about gluing yourself to your office chair until you get your book done?" he asked in a last ditch effort to distract her.

Darcy shrugged. Secretly, she'd do almost anything to avoid that. "A long weekend, that's all it is. The book can wait for a weekend."

He sighed, shrugged, and hugged her back. "Okay, I'm in."

Fresh squeals around the room. This time even Sharon, Becky, and Darcy joined in. Bethany and Samantha crowded Darcy out of the way so they could hug their grandfather. "I guess we've got some shopping and packing to do, Mom," he said to Sharon.

"I guess so." Sharon turned to Becky and Darcy. "But before that, we've got to book some flights. I don't care what you say about money, Darcy; I'm shopping for the cheapest seats I can find."

Darcy smiled. She expected as much.

"Darcy, where are you? I know you're home because the people at your Inn said you left yesterday. Either you were abducted from a cornfield by aliens, or you aren't answering your phone. Believe me you need to return this call immediately. Call me. Oh, yes, and welcome home. Bye."

Darcy smiled at the urgency in Carla's voice. Everything was a matter of life and death with her. She stepped out of her shoes and carried them up the stairs. She'd get ready for bed, fix herself a cup of hot cocoa, and then return Carla's call. Carla stayed up for the eleven o'clock news most nights so another hour wouldn't make any difference. The phone rang before she made it to the top of the stairs. She hurried to her bedroom and picked up the extension.

"Yes?" she said, out of breath.

Carla started right in. "Darcy! When were you going to return my call? I thought I made it clear how important this was."

"Nice to hear your voice too, Carla."

"Ha-ha, very funny. I'm serious this time."

"I'm sorry, Hon," Darcy said sincerely. "I had dinner with my family, and we stayed late planning a family trip. I've been promising my nieces—"

"Yes, I'm sure you have," Carla interjected, "but I think this takes precedence over family obligations."

Darcy's heart filled with dread. Was she being fired? Had Brad finally had it with her staying just out of reach of his caustic intrusions on her life? Would he make Carla do it long distance so she couldn't plead for her job? "What takes precedence?"

"John and Sherri Live, that's what."

"Pardon me?"

"The daytime talk show; don't pretend you don't watch it. Everybody does, even Brad the Barracuda. Which, I might add, is the only thing saving your hide! He was within two seconds of cleansing the publishing house of your bad example."

Darcy ignored the reference to her future at the publisher's. She wasn't in the mood to fret about that right now. "Carla, please slow down. I don't know what you're talking about. What does Brad have to do with John and Sherri Live?"

Carla took a deep breath. Darcy could imagine her inhaling deeply on a menthol cigarette to calm her nerves. "I'm talking about the best opportunity your career has ever seen. As you know, John and Sherri Live has the best time slot on daytime TV and the biggest audience. Their advertising budget alone makes Oprah look like local access. Anyway, they want you, sweetheart. John Rivers himself called George and asked for you by name. It seems the release of *The Ultimate Guide to Online Trading* has finally given you the attention you deserve. I guess it proves how diverse your topics can be. Regardless of what got their attention, you've got it, sister. They want you in New York on Monday."

Carla stopped talking long enough to let out an ear-piercing squeal. Darcy grimaced and moved the phone away from her ear. When she brought it back, Carla was talking again.

"What do you think, Darcy? You did it, girl. You made the big boys sit up and take notice. You should see Brad. He's strutting around the office like he's the one about to go on nationwide TV. Can you imagine what this is going to do to your book sales?"

Darcy's first thought was Vince and Leanne. She couldn't wait to tell them. Then she remembered they were five hundred miles away, not exactly her family anymore. It seemed strange to have good news and not share it with them.

She dropped onto the bed in shock. "I can't believe it, Carla. This is so exciting. Oh, no, I can't do it. They'll make me sit in those ridiculously high chairs next to that twig Sherri. And I have gained a ton of weight. Oh, Carla, maybe after a couple weeks at the gym—"

"You get over yourself right now, young lady. You are going on that show, and you'll be even more beautiful than Sherri Rivers. Don't you know what those makeup artists are capable of? Those people are magicians."

"Gee thanks. That makes me feel so much better."

"Oh, I'm kidding. You're already gorgeous, Darcy. You're the only person on the planet who doesn't know it. With your long legs, you'll look fabulous on those chairs. Sherri will be the one in her dressing room complaining."

Darcy was beginning to get into the spirit of things. "How much air time do you think I'll get? This will be my first national broadcast. And to think it only took twenty books. What am I going to talk about? I'm sure they don't want to discuss online investing."

"I'm sure they are amazed you've written so many books on such a wide variety of topics. They'll probably want to talk about you and how you've become an expert on nearly everything."

"But that's the thing. I'm not an expert. I just research and—"

"Darcy, calm down. You'll be brilliant. Now about flight arrangements, you need to be in town Monday. You go on the air Tuesday. The John and Sherri people should have their itinerary in our office by the end of the week so we can go over everything before you go to the studio."

Darcy groaned and put the heel of her hand to her forehead. "Monday—oh no, I forgot."

"What? You forgot what?"

"The family trip; I forgot about it already. I'm taking everybody to Disney World. We've got it all planned. We're leaving in two days and won't be back until late Monday. Mom's making the reservations online as we speak. I've been promising them this trip for years. I finally made it definite. You should have seen how excited the kids were tonight. We're all excited. I can't let everybody down."

It was clear Carla couldn't see a problem. "Excuse me, Darcy, yes you can. You tell them you're going to be on national TV on the show all writers aspire to. They'll be thrilled for you. They'll send you a postcard."

"Carla, I don't want a postcard. I want to go with them. Even Mom and Dad are going. It'll be the first family trip we've ever taken. Everyone's cleared schedules and everything."

"Listen here, Darcy, I'm sorry you have to disappoint your family, but they'll understand. Chances like this come once in a lifetime. Disney World isn't going anywhere, and you only have to stay in New York for two days, tops—although, I can't for the life of me imagine why someone would rather fly Space Mountain when they could be in the most exciting city in the world."

Darcy closed her eyes and pictured the three disappointed faces of her nieces and nephew when she told them the trip would have to be postponed. But she also knew everyone would be thrilled to hear she was going on John and Sherri Live. Carla was right; everybody watched that show, and it was every writer's ticket to all the major bestsellers lists.

"So, I guess I'll see you in New York on Monday."

"Yes! You're a sport, Darcy. I'll fax your travel arrangements in a few minutes. Your ticket will be waiting at the airport. This is fantastic. I hope you realize how lucky you are."

"Not lucky, Carla, blessed," she corrected, smiling.

"All right, if you insist. I'll see you Monday."

Even though she had to call her mother immediately and tell her about the change of plans, she couldn't keep from smiling as she dialed the phone. John and Sherri Live. The nervousness and anxiety would sink in later. What if she talked with her hands too much and knocked John off his chair? What if the camera really did add fifteen pounds to her frame? Right now, she was on cloud nine. Tonight was Tuesday. She had five days to decompress from her month away from home and get things in order for another trip.

A live Broadcast on national television!

Never in her wildest dreams had she imagined such a thing.

$\mathcal{D}$ · $\mathcal{D}$ · $\mathcal{D}$ · $\mathcal{D}$ # 12

$\mathcal{D}$arcy had been to New York more times than she could count in the past ten years, but this was the first time her sweaty palms kept losing their grip on her carry-on bag. Her nerves had caught wind of what was going on and were working overtime to make her miserable. She told herself over and over it was like every other time she'd been on television. John and Sherri Rivers was just another married couple who happened to have their own national television show. It was no big deal. She would go into the studio, deal with hair, makeup, and wardrobe, go out on stage, smile disarmingly to the live studio audience like she'd done a hundred times before, and talk about herself and her books. They would ask the typical questions about what convinced her to quit college and write a book, how her family felt about her decision, and what qualified her as an expert on so many subjects. She could do it in her sleep. She swallowed hard and waited her turn to disembark.

"Enjoy your stay in New York," the smiling flight attendant said.

She resisted the urge to tell him she was going to be on John and Sherri Live tomorrow morning. He would be so impressed. She wondered if he'd recognize her if he happened to watch the show. She reminded herself that he saw more impressive people than her every day, and an appearance on a daytime talk show probably wasn't that big of a deal in his book.

Instead of gushing, she returned his smile. "Thank you, I will."

She hooked the strap of her carry-on over her shoulder and headed down the runway. When she reached the boarding area, she saw a smartly dressed female chauffer holding a sign with her name on it. Wow, a limo. She could get used to the star treatment.

She stopped in front of the limo driver and held out her hand. "Hello, I'm Darcy Carter."

"Ms. Carter," the driver said, pumping her hand. "I'm Tiffany Fryman. I'll be your driver today. Do you have any luggage?"

"No, this is all I brought."

"Great. Well, then, I'll drive you to the hotel. You have a few hours before you need to be at the studio."

Darcy and Tiffany started working their way through the crush of people. "Would it be a problem to take me to my publisher's instead? I need to meet with my editor."

"No problem at all," Tiffany assured her, "as long as we are at the studio at two o'clock."

"Perfect." Darcy let Tiffany walk a half step in front of her, following her to the car. A limo, an appearance on a top-rated national television show—she couldn't get over it. As Tiffany accelerated into traffic, Darcy gave her the address of the publishing house and settled back into the plush interior to watch the city move past her.

"I'll wait here for you," Tiffany said when she let Darcy out of the car thirty minutes later.

Darcy looked up at the impressive building before her. "Oh, that's all right. If you have something else to do, I can get a cab to the studio after I see my editor. She might want to grab lunch or something."

"No, no, just leave your bag in the car. I'm not going anywhere," Tiffany said with a wide smile. "By all means, let me know about lunch, and I'll take you wherever you need to go."

"Okay, sounds great." Darcy felt like a backwoods hick who didn't know anything about dealing with a driver. Oh, well, maybe she was.

She stopped worrying about what Tiffany thought of her and turned toward the building. A doorman appeared in front of her. He was an inch or so shorter than Darcy with a graying mustache and sideburns that hadn't changed in length since she'd known him. His shoulders were slightly stooped from years on his feet, but he still carried himself with grace and dignity. "Ms. Carter, you're looking well. How was North Carolina?"

"Beautiful, Ray," Darcy said, surprised the doorman knew where she'd been. She could almost bet Brad wouldn't have any idea where she'd spent the last month without asking Carla first. If it didn't happen in the city, he wasn't interested.

"How are Patty and the grandkids?" she asked on the way to the elevator.

"Wonderful. I have pictures of the new baby." Ray pressed the button for the fifteenth floor and then reached inside his jacket. "She's six months old now." He held out a picture for Darcy to see. "Growing like a weed."

Darcy took the picture from him for a closer look. "Oh, she's a darling. Give her mom my best."

The elevator doors slid open and Darcy stepped inside. "I will, Ms. Carter," he said. "You have a nice day."

Darcy wished him the same as the doors slid shut between them. Ray had been escorting her to the elevator for as long as she'd been coming to New York. She once thought of his as the only friendly face in the entire city. Now she knew better, but Ray was still one of her favorite people. His daughter had been in college back then. Now she had three daughters of her own. An image of Vince crashed down on Darcy. She wondered if he would ever want to see her again after the things she'd said at the waterfall. Why did she even care? He had been as hurtful toward her. The sooner she got him out of her head, the better.

She stepped out of the vintage elevator on the fifteenth floor. Pearl, who manned the reception area, jumped to her feet and hurried around her desk. "Darcy, honey, it's so good to see you."

Pearl was nearing sixty and retirement. She was small and plump; the classic image of everyone's grandmother, and that was how she treated everyone associated with the publishing house. Darcy leaned forward so Pearl could plant a kiss on her cheek. "It's good to see you too, Pearl. How have you been?"

"Oh, I'm getting along fine, all things considered. When you get to be my age, you can't expect miracles."

Darcy planted a kiss on her warm, full cheek. "Don't go

discounting miracles, Pearl," she admonished. "You never know when one might be just around the corner."

A frown creased the older woman's forehead before she smiled. Darcy wasn't sure herself where the comment had come from. Too much time around Leanne, she supposed. She was rubbing off on her.

"Carla told me to expect you," Pearl said. "How's the new book coming?"

Darcy smiled noncommittally. "Oh, it's coming along as expected." Just as she expected anyway, which meant it wasn't coming at all. After a month of research and fifty cholesterol points, she still didn't know where the book was headed.

If Pearl caught the skepticism in her voice, she didn't let on. She moved back to the other side of her desk. "You go on back. I'll let Carla know you're here."

"Thanks, Pearl." Darcy wiggled her fingers good-bye and moved off down the hall. Nearly everyone she passed greeted her or asked about North Carolina. She knew most everyone at the company, but there were always new faces hanging about. Proofreaders and editors were always moving to other houses or getting promoted or demoted to other imprints within the company. And one never knew what well-known writer one might run into in the ladies' room in a house as large as this one.

Carla's door was open when Darcy rounded the corner. Her assistant, Dustin, smiled and opened his mouth to speak, but Carla burst out of the office shrieking Darcy's name. Few people got to finish their sentences, much less their thoughts when Carla was around.

"Darcy, sweetheart!" She threw her arms around her. "Girl, I can't tell you how good it is to see you." She put her arm around Darcy's shoulder and steered her toward her office.

"Hello, Dustin," Darcy said, turning her head as Carla pushed her past his desk. "She isn't working you too much, is she?" He could only smile in response before Carla shepherded her into the office and closed the door.

Carla lowered her voice conspiratorially. "You don't realize how perfect the timing was on all this, Darcy. The Barracuda was getting very impatient with you and this Country Cooking book."

Darcy rolled her eyes where Carla couldn't see. Brad's impatience was of little concern to her. She was about two seconds from telling them all as much. She had done plenty to make the publisher money; she had no reason to apologize for not producing the book they wanted in the time allotted. Didn't creativity matter anymore in this business, or was it all about the money, even if it meant sacrificing the writer's soul?

She sank into one of the leather chairs facing Carla's desk and dropped her tote bag on the floor in front of her. "Carla, about all these Ultimate Guide books..."

"Are you thirsty?" Carla asked, going to the small refrigerator under the bookshelves. "What'll you have?"

"Bottled water's fine," Darcy said. "I wonder if I could lose ten pounds by tomorrow."

Carla took two waters from the fridge and tossed one to Darcy. "Don't be silly, girl. You look great. Now, we need to talk battle plans." She shuffled through the papers on her desk. If not for an efficient assistant, Carla would never know what she was doing next. "Where are my notes? Oh, I can never find anything." She stopped shuffling papers and looked at Darcy. "When's your meeting with the John and Sherri Live people?"

"Two o'clock."

"Two o'clock." She glanced at her watch and gasped. "Oh, no, that barely leaves us enough time for lunch and the trip across town. I thought you were going to come here straight from the airport."

"I did," Darcy replied calmly. "I have a limo downstairs. That will speed things along."

"A limo. Aren't you the celebrity? Well, we may as well go. Brad's out of town. He had to go to London yesterday. He should get back first thing in the morning before you go on the air."

Darcy had hoped to get her meeting with Carla and Brad out of the way so she could relax and enjoy the rest of her trip, but she wasn't too disappointed that she could talk to Carla alone first. "I was hoping to meet with both of you while I'm in New York."

"And we will. Brad hates it that he got sent out of town before your big debut, but we'll definitely plan a meeting."

"Thanks, Carla, because there are some things we should discuss."

"I agree." Carla stood up and twisted the cap back on her water. "Let's go. We can talk on the way to lunch. You say you have a car? The big boys really know how to treat their guests."

Darcy grabbed her tote bag and followed Carla to the door. Carla smiled and chatted with everyone she passed on her way to the elevators. Darcy felt like a little sister trying to keep up. She hoped once they got in the car, Carla would wind down for two minutes so they could talk.

The studio's limo was waiting outside the building.

Tiffany stood at the back of the car, waiting. "Carla, this is Tiffany, from the studio," Darcy said as Tiffany opened the door. "Tiffany, this is my editor and good friend, Carla Daniels."

"Nice to meet you, Tiffany."

"You too, Ms. Daniels." Tiffany closed the door behind them and hurried around the car.

"This is the life, Darcy," Carla said, sinking into the limousine's plush interior. She leaned over and opened the door to the mini bar. "It's empty," she croaked.

"I know," Darcy answered sheepishly. "I already checked it out."

"Why, Darcy, you sneaky thing, I thought you were a teetotaler."

"I am, but I've never had my very own limo before, either. I wanted to know how the rich and famous live."

"Now you know," Carla said, closing the door and settling back into her seat. "They bring their own."

"Where to, ladies?" Tiffany asked through the lowered window.

"The Plaza."

"Carla, no," Darcy gasped. "Brad'll have a fit."

"I thought you wanted to know how the other five percent lives. Besides, he's been in such a good mood since he heard from the John and Sherri people he wants to spoil you, let you see how much you mean to the company."

Darcy snorted.

Carla looked at her. "Come on, Darcy. I know Brad can be a nightmare at times, but he has done a lot for your career, and so have I. Whether you want to admit it or not, this appearance on TV had a lot to do with your affiliation with a major publisher. But you mean more to us than just money."

Darcy bit her tongue. She had worked with Carla for ten years. She considered her a friend, but she hoped it was strong enough to weather her leaving the company if that's where her career was leading.

"I didn't mean to sound like I don't appreciate everything you have done for me. I know my books are better for having you involved, but at this point in time I don't know where my writing is headed. Lately I've been wondering if I have any more Ultimate Guides in me. I might be ready for something new."

Carla sighed. "Okay, I understand. Just don't say anything to Brad about that yet. He still wants a Finding Mr. Right book. Personally, I think it would be a mistake to end this part of your career before doing it. But, hey, it's your life. You do what you need to do."

Darcy let her fingers trail across the leather on the interior of the door while Carla talked. She had never touched anything so soft. She already dreaded tomorrow afternoon when Tiffany would drop her off at the airport, and she'd have to leave the car and the star treatment in New York.

"Carla…" she began cautiously. She would feel much better when she got her concerns over her career out in the open. She hadn't been able to tell her parents her doubts, and she didn't know if she had it in her to tell Carla. She looked up to see Carla watching her intently.

"Yes, little sister, what's the problem?"

"No problem really, just that I may have found something out in North Carolina that could change where my career is headed."

"I knew it," Carla cried, elated. "I knew the diner and café idea was a bust. You should have concentrated on the Finding Mr. Right book and not have worried about anything else."

"No, no, no, that's not what I meant." Darcy scratched her fingernail across the stitching of the leather armrest. She looked down at her hand and forced herself to stop. She doubted Brad would pick up the tab if she tore a hole in the expensive leather. She took a deep breath. "The fact is…" It was like pulling off a band-aid, one good yank and it was over with. "I haven't even started the southern eating book."

Carla's jaw dropped a fraction. She couldn't believe what she was hearing. Darcy Carter was a writing machine. Once she chose a topic, she pretty much had the first draft done within a month of beginning her writing. Another couple of weeks, and it was ready for the bookstore shelves.

Darcy rushed on, feeling the need to explain herself. "While I was in North Carolina, I kept wondering why I was writing. I feel like I haven't even started living yet. All I do is write books telling other people everything they need to know to get their own lives in order, while mine is falling apart."

Carla leaned across the space dividing their seats and put her hand on Darcy's arm. "Darcy, what are you talking about? You don't know what falling apart is. You should walk in my shoes for five minutes. Your life is more together than anyone I know."

"You're only saying that to make me feel better because I'm going on live TV tomorrow, and you don't want my skin to break out."

Carla grinned in agreement.

"The truth is, Carla, I don't know if I want to write anymore. My last book was a struggle, but I managed to get through it."

"It was a great book, Darcy," Carla assured her.

Darcy held up her hand. "I know, I know, it turned out fine, but I didn't enjoy writing it. Until recently, I have loved everything I've written. Maybe not during the hashing out of the details, but by the time I put the finishing touches on a book I am in love with it; but not the last one—or even the one before that. I feel like I cheated my readers. Not because it isn't a good book, but because my heart wasn't in it. And this book…" Darcy looked out the window and sadly shook her head. "I can't even get started. I took tons of notes and interviewed all the right people during my research, but I'm sorry, Carla, my heart isn't in writing anymore."

Carla looked stricken. She sank into the seat and brought her bag to her lap. She rummaged inside for a pack of cigarettes.

"You can't smoke in here, Carla," Darcy reminded her.

Carla looked like she wanted to smack somebody. "Stupid city ordinances!" She stuffed the cigarettes back into her bag and closed the zipper with a violent tearing sound. "They got nonsmokers ruling the world. Whatever happened to the good old days when even grade school teachers smoked? During class!"

The limousine slowed and turned the corner to the restaurant. Tiffany maneuvered the car smoothly to the curb and came to a stop. Within moments she was opening the door for Carla and Darcy. "I'll be waiting when you finish," she said.

"Thank you, Tiffany."

When she went back around the car, Darcy whispered to Carla, "Am I supposed to tip her?"

Carla rolled her eyes. "You need to get out more, sweetheart. She's paid by the studio to chauffer you wherever you want to go. She's well taken care of."

Carla and Darcy followed the maitre d' to their table. They declined the wine list and turned their attention to the menus. After they gave their orders to the waiter, Carla spoke in a hushed voice.

"Do you think you're just burned out, honey? Goodness knows you've been pumping out books at a furious pace for a long time. Everybody needs a break. When was the last time you went on a vacation?"

"I was going to take a vacation this weekend until I got a frantic phone call summoning me to New York."

"Oh, yes, right. Well, I meant a real vacation. And I don't mean North Carolina. When was the last time you went someplace exotic and focused on nothing writing related? I can answer that for you—never. You don't want to give up writing, Darcy. I know you don't. It's who you are."

"Maybe I don't like who I am anymore, Carla. Maybe I'm not having fun. I would like to see what it's like to live life rather than tell other people how to do it."

Carla folded her hands on top the table and nodded maternally. "Darcy, we all get like that sometimes. It's okay to need time away from what you've been doing for so long. The only problem, honey, is your timing. Brad really wants this Finding Mr. Right book.

In fact, that's kind of why we're having this lunch." She glanced down at her hands and twisted the mother's ring on her finger her daughter had given her two years ago. "Brad thinks…well, actually, we all think it would be a good idea for you to mention the Finding Mr. Right book on John and Sherri Live tomorrow morning."

Darcy jerked her head back. "What? How can I do that? The book doesn't have an outline. *I've* never agreed to write it."

Carla motioned for her to calm down. "I know, I know. But this is national exposure. Sure, your books have been great. You've got good numbers, but Mr. Right books are what national audiences want to hear about. Online Trading and Opening a Home-Based Daycare don't keep people tuned in. Now if you got on stage and brought up the fact you were writing *The Ultimate Guide to Finding Mr. Right*, well, you would have people glued to their sets. They wouldn't be so likely to flip over to see what Dr. Phil's talking about."

Darcy was stunned. "Carla, I'm sitting here watching your lips move but if I didn't know better, I would think it was Brad's voice coming out of your mouth."

Carla fiddled with her place setting. She was having a hard time maintaining eye contact. "Darcy, I'm just thinking about you."

Darcy leaned forward over the linen tablecloth. "No, you're not, Carla," she hissed. "You're thinking about money, and viewers, and I don't know what all, but not about me. I told you from the get-go I didn't want to write that book. You've got a hundred qualified writers on staff. Surely one of them could do the subject justice."

"None of them have your talent for this type book, Darcy." With an effort, Carla straightened her fork and folded her hands in her lap. "You've got the credentials and the style that would guarantee a best seller. You're the Ultimate Guide girl."

It was all Darcy could do not to get up and walk out of the restaurant. "No, I'm not, not anymore. In case you haven't noticed, I'm not a girl anymore. And I have no intention of writing that type of book. You've been trying to strong arm me into doing this from the beginning. You make it sound like it's all Brad's idea, but it isn't, it's you. I thought you were my friend."

"Darcy..." Carla began.

"Here we go," the waiter said appearing at their table. He set a Caesar salad in front of each of them. He unfolded Carla's napkin and reached for Darcy's.

Darcy waved him away and stood up, her chair rocking behind her on the carpeted floor. "No, thank you. I'm not hungry."

Carla stood up. "Darcy, wait." But Darcy was storming out of the restaurant. Carla smiled apologetically at the waiter and reached into her bag for her company credit card. She pulled it out along with a crumpled pack of cigarettes. He raised his eyebrows at the cigarettes. She wanted to tell him to go jump off a bridge.

Tiffany had just entered the lobby when Darcy stormed past her. She reached out and caught her arm. "Ms. Carter, is everything all right?"

It took Darcy a moment to regain her composure enough to respond. "Oh, um, yes. I'm not very hungry after all. I'll wait in the car for Ms. Daniels."

"Okay, wait here, and I'll have it brought around." Tiffany had been at this job too long to be surprised by a sudden change in plans.

Darcy had just settled herself into the back seat of the limo when the door opened and Carla stepped in, reeking of cigarette smoke. She had apparently lit up outside the restaurant to calm her nerves before coming to the limo. She sat in the rear facing seat, averting her eyes from Darcy's face. Darcy stared out the opposite window at the traffic whizzing by on the street. She didn't know if she was ready to speak. Her initial anger was gone. Carla was only doing her job. Money had to be made if she and all the other people at the publishing house expected to remain working, but Darcy had always considered Carla a friend first and an editor second. Shouldn't she have gone to bat for her with Brad? Shouldn't she have told him at the first mention of the Mr. Right book that Darcy had no interest in writing it? She never should have let him threaten Darcy's job to sell a few books.

An unobtrusive whir of static and then Tiffany's voice asked softly. "Ms. Carter, do you have any other stops before we go to the studio?"

Darcy snapped out of her retrospect. "No, Tiffany, I'm ready."

"Yes, ma'am."

Silence filled the back of the car as it merged into traffic.

Carla was the first to speak. "I'm sorry, Darcy. I do understand how you feel. It's just that when we heard from the John and Sherri people, we got a little crazy."

Darcy couldn't stay angry with her if she tried. Turning her eyes from the street, she looked at Carla. "I know. I'm sorry, too. You're right. The viewing audience would rather hear about a book on snagging a man than summer camp for seniors." She paused and took a deep breath as tears pushed against the back of her eyelids. She stared intently at Carla. "But I haven't written a book on snagging a man, nor do I intend to. The John and Sherri people know that, and they asked for me anyway."

Carla reached across the space between them and took Darcy's hand. "You're right, you're absolutely right. I shouldn't have tried to force you to say something you didn't want to say. You forgive me?"

"Absolutely." She leaned forward and hugged Carla. When she pulled back there were tears in the eyes of both of them. "I could never stay mad at you, Carla. I know you only have my career's best interest in mind."

Carla nodded and fumbled in her bag for a tissue. "I do, Darcy." She dabbed the end of her nose with the tissue and then smiled wickedly. "But I'd love to sell a million or so copies of your books from this TV appearance."

Darcy smiled back and wiggled her eyebrows. "Me, too. Carla, I do want you to know how much I appreciate everything you and the company have done for me. I'm just feeling pressured from every side to keep up this persona of the Ultimate Guide Girl when I don't feel like that's who I am anymore. It isn't only pressure from you, I'm pressuring myself. This is the first time I haven't been able to start a book once I settled on a subject, and it's got me a little freaked out."

"I'll say."

"I think I'm through with Ultimate Guides. I promise not to say that on national TV, but I wouldn't go counting on anymore books from your Ultimate Guide Girl if I were you."

"I can't say I'm not disappointed," Carla admitted. "But it's not my place to tell you what you should do with your career. I will say, you definitely know how to go out with a bang."

Any hard feelings between them were completely banished by the time Tiffany delivered them in front of the network building. Carla and Darcy squeezed hands like nervous schoolgirls before exiting the limo.

A young man exited the building and took the car keys from Tiffany. She slung Darcy's bag over her shoulder and escorted them into the unassuming looking building. The instant they stepped through the doors, it was like entering a different world. The building was abuzz with activity. The farther they ventured into the building, the more frenetic the pace.

Darcy had expected to meet either John or Sherri today, but she was told neither was in the building. They began their workday at five a.m. and were usually gone by noon. *Five a.m.*, she thought, *they don't go on the air until ten.* So much work before the cameras even started to roll.

She and Carla met with several important higher-ups from the studio. They explained their vision for the broadcast and what to expect from John and Sherri. "You have seen the show," a tall, intimidating woman asked.

"Oh, yes."

"Then you understand our format."

Darcy was shown the green room where she would wait until she was called. "It should be around ten-twenty, but there are several factors to consider." Darcy knew what that meant. If the guest in front of her ran long, her segment could be cut altogether. She tried not to think of that possibility.

Darcy's test runs took three hours. By the time they had finished their mock segments, timing each one, until they eventually ran to ten minutes in length, Darcy was exhausted and ready to get to her hotel room. She was also sorry for skipping lunch. When Carla mentioned they hadn't eaten, they were escorted to a buffet table.

Even though she was ravenous, Darcy couldn't eat much. All she could imagine was the way the extra ten pounds she'd picked up in North Carolina were going to look on camera, especially next to the svelte Sherri Rivers. She groaned audibly and dropped the dill pickle she was about to bite into the trash.

13

Darcy stepped out of the shower and went straight to the telephone. Her mother had insisted she call before she left for the studio no matter how early the hour. Sharon was nearly as excited as Darcy. Bethany and Samantha couldn't wait to see her on television; they were even taping it and had instructed all their friends to do the same. Darcy imagined her nieces had all of Middleburg Heights watching this morning.

"What are you going to wear, sweetheart?" Sharon asked after saying hello. "They put you on those awful stools that point your knees straight at the camera."

"I know, Mom."

"And I don't want you showing your business to the whole country."

"I won't, Mom. I'm wearing slacks."

Sharon exhaled. "Oh, thank goodness. Your black pinstripes, I hope. Those are your most flattering."

"I'm taking them with me, along with a few other choices. It depends on what wardrobe thinks."

"Just don't let them dress you up like I see all of those actresses. The dresses they put those women in leave nothing to the imagination."

"Don't worry, Mom, I intend to maintain my modesty."

"Well, that's a relief. Are you nervous?"

Darcy looked at herself in the mirror. The woman staring

back at her looked scared to death. No sense in worrying Mom though. "No, I'm fine. I've been on television before."

"Not this big of a production! Oops, I'm sorry. I didn't mean to remind you. You're right, of course. You're an old hand at this. Smile, have fun, and keep your knees together."

"Thanks, Mom. Love ya."

She and Carla arrived at the studio at seven-thirty. Darcy wished she didn't have to get there so early, knowing it would give her stomach that much more time to tie itself into knots. Food was everywhere. Apparently Carla had no trouble with her nerves keeping her from eating. The building was nonsmoking, but several executives had ignored the order, so Carla was in seventh heaven. Darcy was ushered from one room to the next, first wardrobe, then hair and makeup. She had to admit the final result was a surprise. She worried less about how she would appear on camera and more about how she would sound. The studio had no voice department to make her sound cultured and articulate whenever her voice cracked from nerves.

While she sat in her chair and chatted amiably with all the hovering makeup people, she wondered if Vince would be watching this morning. She had called Leanne over the weekend to tell her the good news, and Leanne had been as excited as everyone else. She assured Darcy nothing would keep her from watching. But not Vince, Darcy was certain. He'd be at the café, up to his elbows in grits, bacon, and sausage gravy. Her stomach rumbled. How had she developed a taste for things so bad for her? She ate a few melon balls and tried not to worry about Vince. She imagined Leanne glued to the set in her family room and tried to relax.

The time went by quicker than she anticipated and before she was mentally prepared, she was summoned backstage. A commercial break separated her from the celebrity who had just exited the stage. She saw him from the back as he strode confidently to his dressing room. She had seen him in movies for years and couldn't believe she was so close to him. She doubted they would meet after her segment. He would probably be on a plane to Hollywood by the time she got off the air. She made a mental note to tell Bethany and Samantha all about her almost encounter anyway.

"You'll do fine, honey," Sean, the makeup assistant responsible for transforming her into a minor celebrity said. He patted her on the back. She smiled gratefully in return.

Carla appeared and gave her an air kiss near her left cheek. "Break a leg," she said, laughing. Then she whispered conspiratorially, "And make tons of money."

Knowing it was coming, her heart still leaped in her throat when she heard her name announced and the audience erupt into applause. She took a deep breath, swallowed hard, cleared her throat, and started out of the wings. She cast one more desperate glance in Carla's direction. Carla put a finger to each cheek to indicate a big smile. Darcy stepped out of the shadows and into camera range. She waved at the audience and focused on the three chairs center stage, one of which was left vacant for her.

John and Sherri, whom she hadn't seen in person until this very minute, hopped down from their stools as she crossed the stage. The cheek kissing and elbow squeezing was a blur amid the audience noise and heat from the lights. No wonder the temperature inside the building was set so low, couldn't have their stars glistening on the air. Darcy took her cues from John and Sherri. When they broke away from her and backed up to their stools, she did the same.

"Darcy Carter, ladies and gentlemen," John shouted above the applause, raising an arm in her direction. The applause escalated.

Darcy smiled graciously and waved just as expansively. She hopped onto her stool at the same time John and Sherri did, imitating the professional way Sherri did it so nothing improper was revealed. She thanked God for giving her long legs so the climb wasn't a big deal. She thought of her mother holding her breath back home and glanced down to make sure her knees were together.

Behind a wide smile that made her face ache, she took another deep breath and willed herself to calm down. This was going to be fun, just three people chatting about her books—a piece of cake.

As she had been told to expect, John spoke first. The show belonged to him and his wife, but everyone knew, he was the star and Sherri, the silly and lovable sidekick. "Darcy, we're glad you're finally able to be here. We hear you've been writing for quite some time. My question is; why haven't you been here sooner?"

"I don't know, John, my number's in the book," Darcy answered glibly. She gave herself a mental pat on the back when the audience roared with laughter.

He looked into the camera and smirked. "Goes to show the caliber of investigative reporters we have working here." The audience laughed again. "Seriously, Darcy, you've written quite a few books, your last one being *The Ultimate Guide to Online Trading*." He held up a copy. "But you haven't received the recognition you deserve. How long have you been writing?"

Darcy's initial panic began to recede. The interview was going the way she preferred, light and fun. "For about ten years. I wrote my first book, *The Ultimate Guide to Writing a College Thesis*, when I was nineteen. The online trading book is the nineteenth one since then."

"Wow!" Sherri exclaimed, leaning forward on her stool on the other side of John. "You don't look old enough to have written nineteen books. Don't you have a social life?"

Darcy's heart sank. The last thing she wanted to discuss on national television was her social life, or lack thereof. An image of Vince crossed her mind, but she pushed it aside. She couldn't allow herself to get distracted by him right now.

Before she could worry about formulating an answer, John curled his lip and said to Sherri. "It isn't unheard of to write nineteen books in ten years."

"Oh, please," she retorted. "You haven't *read* nineteen books in ten years."

The audience roared with laughter. Darcy smiled; delighted they were barbing each other instead of grilling her. John glared playfully at the audience before turning back to Darcy. "What gave you the idea to write a book about writing a college thesis? I assume it's safe to say you hadn't actually written one at that point."

Darcy breathed a sigh of relief. It looked like the topic of her social life had been forgotten. "You're right, John, I hadn't. I was a sophomore in college when I got the idea for writing the book. I was researching subjects for my own college thesis and realized writing about a college thesis was more interesting than the actual thesis."

"You were way ahead of me," John said, mugging for the crowd. "I didn't start researching my thesis until three years after I earned my degree."

The crowd erupted into laughter. Darcy waited a moment and then went back to her explanation. "After the idea for the book took root in my head, I quit college, moved back home with Mom and Dad, and wrote nonstop until it was done."

"Good old Mom and Dad," Sherri sang out.

"Exactly. I don't think it would have worked out as well had it not been for them."

"So you believe college isn't for everyone?"

Darcy shrugged carefully so not to rustle the wires holding her mike in place. "I just know how it was for me. The whole time I was there, all I could think of was how I wanted to get on with my life. It took two years to find a publisher and get *Writing a College Thesis* into book form. During that time, I wrote three more books. After that, I was off and running."

"Were those also Ultimate Guide books?"

"Yes. I think they were," she ticked the titles off on her fingers, "*Caring for your Aging Parent, Planning the Wedding of Your Dreams,* and *Total Body Fitness.*"

"Those are some pretty diverse subjects," John observed. "Is that how you earned your title, 'The Ultimate Guide Girl'?"

Darcy winced inwardly, but smiled for the camera. "Some reviewer stuck that on me after my fourth or fifth book. It's been with me ever since."

"Well, I think it's high time we updated it for you," Sherri said sympathetically. "How about, the 'Ultimate Guide Queen'?"

Darcy shook her head, preferring to walk away from her Ultimate Guide persona altogether. Unfortunately it didn't sound like the audience intended to let her do that. They were cheering and clapping again.

"It's settled," John said, as if he were the last word on the matter. He reached out and tapped her on each shoulder with the *Online Trading* book. She tensed hoping he wouldn't mess up her hair. "I now crown you the Ultimate Guide Queen."

"So be it!" Sherri exclaimed.

Darcy wanted to smack both of them. Instead, she smiled like an idiot and waved the way she'd seen the royal family do on TV. The audience roared their approval.

When the applause died away, John quickly reverted to the sober interviewer. "Have you had any experience with your topics in your personal life?"

A question Darcy was asked during every interview, and the one she dreaded most. "Not really."

"In other words, you're not an expert on anything."

Sherri cut in. "She just plays one on TV."

The audience erupted into laughter. Darcy cringed but laughed with the crowd.

Sherri wiggled in her chair like an excited child. "Let's get back to what we're all most interested in; Darcy's social life. Writing nineteen books since you were nineteen has to take up most of your time. How do you balance a love life? Are you married or in a serious relationship?"

This was live TV. No time to think of glib, witty answers. Darcy wondered how she could answer and still get the conversation back around to her books. "No, I'm not married, and as far as the serious relationship..."

"It isn't a difficult question, Darcy." John wiggled his eyebrows and rolled his eyes at the audience, like she wasn't the sharpest tool in the shed.

"A girl after my own heart," Sherri squealed. "One who doesn't kiss-and-tell."

"Hey," John cried, looking properly offended, "what's that supposed to mean?"

"No, I didn't mean that," Darcy interjected.

Sherri ignored the stricken look on her face. She reached past John and patted her arm. "Don't worry, Darcy, you don't have to tell him anything you don't want to." Then she held her hand in front of her mouth as if to speak privately, knowing full well that John, audience and crew, along with the hundreds of thousands of viewers in TV land could hear every word. "Girl, we'll talk later."

The audience clapped and cheered while John shot mockingly threatening looks from Sherri to Darcy. Finally it was quiet enough for him to ask his next question.

"What's the topic of your next book, Darcy?"

She envisioned Brad leaning forward in his leather desk chair and holding his breath, willing her to say *Finding Mr. Right.* "I just got back from the Ravenswood Inn in Talmedge, North Carolina," she said instead, "where I was researching a book about southern cafés and diners; those out of the way places that are getting lost in the landscape of a million McDonald's and Outback Steakhouses."

"And what did the people of Talmedge, North Carolina think about a writer in their midst dissecting everything they ate?"

"I like to think we all had a great time. I know I gained ten pounds."

"Darcy, you sound like a busy young woman, so I'm going to help you out and give you the perfect topic for your next book."

Darcy gripped the arms of her chair and braced herself. *Please don't say The Ultimate Guide to Finding Mr. Right,* she silently begged.

John looked out at the audience, paused for effect, and announced, *"The Ultimate Guide to Darcy Carter."*

The audience erupted into applause. The applause sign blinked furiously, not that anyone needed encouragement.

Darcy held her hand up in front of her and shook her head furiously.

Sherri gestured with her hands to keep the crowd clapping. "Come on, folks, what do you think?"

"Your public has spoken, Darcy," John said, indicating the audience. "We want the real story of Darcy Carter."

Darcy felt heat on her face. She wished they would get back to her last book or teasing her about her age, anything but this newest idea for a book. She would almost prefer the Mr. Right book. Maybe it wasn't too late to mention it. At least Brad would be happy with the interview.

When the applause and laughter died down, John motioned to Darcy. "Darcy Carter, ladies and gentlemen." He held up his copy of *Online Trading* and smiled until the audience was once again reasonably quiet. "Under each of your seats, you'll find a copy of one of Darcy's books." There was general shuffling as three hundred people rummaged underneath their seats. "Thank you so much for being here," he said to Darcy. He slid off his stool. Darcy and Sherri did the same. "The best of luck with your writing."

Sherri stepped around John to take Darcy's arm. "Call us as soon as *The Ultimate Guide to Darcy Carter* is finished, and you can come back and tell us all about it, right, everybody?"

She grinned at the audience as they applauded again. Darcy had no choice but to smile, wave, and return their kisses. A woman with a clipboard appeared to her left outside the camera's range to escort her offstage. She smiled one last time at John and Sherri who had already gone back to their stools and a commercial announcement.

The first person she saw off-stage was Carla. She pulled her into a hug and then grabbed her elbow and steered her toward the green room. Everyone they passed gave her a thumbs up or pat on the arm. "Good job!" "Way to go." "You did great." Darcy smiled back, too stunned for any type of reply.

"Darcy, you were fantastic," Carla squealed as soon as she shut the door behind them. "I can't believe it. You said everything right. That *Ultimate Guide to Darcy Carter* was genius. Brad's going to go crazy."

As if on cue, the phone rang. "See, there he is now."

Darcy's shoulders slumped. "Carla, it was terrible. The thought of a Mr. Right book was bad enough, and now everywhere I go, I'm going to hear, 'When's the *Ultimate Guide to Darcy Carter* coming out?' And that Ultimate Guide Queen business—I wanted to strangle both of them."

"Relax, sweetie. The audience ate it up. That's all that matters." She hit the button on the ringing phone. "Yes, she's right here." She covered the mouthpiece and held it out to Darcy. "I told you! Brad wants to congratulate you."

Darcy took the phone, still sick to her stomach over the interview. "Hi, Brad. Yeah, I think it went pretty good, too," she said, her voice lacking conviction. "Well, great, thanks. Okay. Yes, that sounds good. Okay, we'll see you as soon as we get out of here." She clicked the phone off and turned to face Carla. "He wants to meet us for lunch…" The phone chirped in her hand again. For the next fifteen minutes, everyone she had met since arriving in New York yesterday wanted to congratulate her. If she hadn't turned the cell phone in her bag off before entering the building, everyone in Middleburg Heights would be calling, too. "Here, you take this," she said after the tenth call, handing the cordless phone to Carla. "I've got to call home." *And North Carolina,* she added to herself.

She went to her bag and dug out her cell. Eighteen messages and she'd only been off-stage twenty minutes. Without listening to any of them, she hit the memory button for her parents' home. A din of background noise greeted her ears before her mother came on the line. "Darcy, honey, is that you? Oh, baby, you were wonderful…what? Well, hold on. Honey, the girls want to say something."

She heard some confusion and then Samantha's voice, "Aunt Darcy, who did your hair? It's awesome. You should wear it like that all the time. Boy, your face sure went red when they asked about a boyfriend—huh. Wait! No!"

Bethany had obviously wrenched the phone from her sister's hand. Her voice was the next one Darcy heard. "You looked amazing. I almost didn't recognize you." Groans and raised voices traveled through the phone lines. "No, I meant that in a good way," she hurriedly explained.

"That's okay, honey. I'm glad you liked the show."

"Oh, we did. We all stayed home to watch you. It's so cool. We told all our friends about it. They are so jealous. They hate us. Did you get to meet Austin—" Her question about the actor who opened the show was cut off by someone in the background. "I'm talking here. Oh, all right, fine. Aunt Darcy, Mom wants to say hi. We love you. Bring us somebody famous' autograph."

"I'll try," Darcy answered before realizing she was talking to dead air.

Then she heard her sister-in-law's voice. "Sorry about that, Darcy. As you can hear, it's total mayhem here, but you did great. We're all so proud of you. You look beautiful and you answered everything they threw at you with grace."

"Thanks," Darcy replied. "I felt like a jerk most of the time."

"Nonsense, you were fabulous. The audience loved you, too.

Did you hear how wild they went when they found your books under their chairs?"

"There was a huge flashing applause sign telling them to go wild."

"Oh. Well, I'm sure they'll love the books anyway."

"Thanks," she said again. "Can you put Mom or Dad back on?"

"Okay, sure. Bye, honey, we love you."

She could hear more squabbling and Becky's voice. "No, girls, she wants to talk to Mom."

Finally Sharon was on the other end. "I should be in tomorrow afternoon at twelve-thirty," Darcy told her. "I'll have to check my ticket for the gate number. Anyway, I'm glad you all liked the show."

"We loved it, honey, and we love you. The girls have been carrying on all morning. Now they want to go back to school so they can rub it in to all their friends."

Darcy laughed.

"I sort of liked John Rivers' idea of a book about you."

"Mom, he was kidding."

"Well, I think it would make a great book. You're a very interesting person, Darcy. You should at least think about it."

"I seriously doubt anyone would pay good money to read a book about me, except you and Dad. I don't know if they'll want to read anything of mine after today. I felt like an idiot the whole time I was onstage."

"Oh, sweetie, you don't give yourself enough credit. You looked like a good sport who could laugh at herself. Believe me, people will remember you, and that's all that matters."

"That's what Carla said—any publicity is good publicity."

"See, that's what I mean. This will be great for your career. Now why not consider writing your autobiography as a fiction work? You said you were ready for a change. All you'd have to do is change some details. It would be very good."

Her mother had a one-track mind. "I'll think about it," she lied. "Listen, I have to go. I have a bunch of calls to return, and Brad wants to meet Carla and me for lunch. Give everybody my love."

After some air kisses, she folded the cell phone in half and dropped into the nearest chair. She dropped her chin into her hand.

Carla covered the mouthpiece of her phone with her hand and snapped, "Don't do that. You'll ruin your beautiful paint job."

Darcy dropped her hand and went to the mirror to see if she'd done any damage by touching her face. Carla and her nieces were right. She looked great even if she did wish the earth would open up and swallow her.

After the Darcy's segment ended and a commercial filled the screen, Vince reached up and turned off the television Hank had brought from home. A collective groan went up among everyone gathered in the Raven Café to watch the John and Sherri Live broadcast.

"Time to get back to work," Vince barked in response.

"Whaddya think a that, Vince?" R.T. Cavanaugh called out above the din. "She done good, huh?"

Vince glanced at R.T. over his shoulder on his way into the kitchen. His refusal to answer was enough to get everyone going again. They had cheered wildly when Darcy mentioned Talmedge and the Ravenswood Inn, making it impossible to hear what she said next. He wished they would all go back to work, or wherever they needed to be at ten-thirty on a weekday morning. The café had been bouncing all morning with people squeezing in to watch the program and grill him about what he thought Darcy would say. *How would I know*, he had demanded, but it didn't stop the speculation or the insinuation that he knew more than he was letting on. He didn't know where everybody got the idea he was the sudden authority on Darcy Carter.

Before the door separating the kitchen from the restaurant could swing closed, June stepped into the doorway and held it open with her hip. "What'd Darcy mean about a serious relationship?"

Behind June came sounds of agreement.

Vince glared at her and the sixty pairs of eyes behind her.

"From what I remember, she didn't say anything. Now, unless somebody's got an order, I suggest you find something to clean."

June didn't bat an eye. "That's my point. She didn't say anything, which leads me to believe she wanted to keep something secret."

"Well, it leads me to believe she didn't say anything 'cause there was nothing to say." He picked up a spatula and faced the grill. "If you got any questions for Darcy, Leanne can give you her number."

June slapped the door with her open hand. She grunted in disgust and turned back to the eating area. "Where's Leanne? Leanne, that brother of yours ain't talking. Let's see if we can get Darcy on the phone."

The door swung closed behind her. The window was still open, leaving Vince in plain sight of the whole café, but he had gotten adept at thinking of himself as invisible behind the grill. He glared out onto the crowd wishing for the hundredth time this morning they would all go home. The excitement was over. He needed to get ready for the lunch rush. The crowds started arriving as soon as he unlocked the doors this morning. When Hank carried in his nineteen-inch set and put it on a shelf behind the counter, everyone made it clear they were staying to watch the broadcast. More and more people crowded into the tiny restaurant, standing in every conceivable bit of floor space. He hoped the fire marshal wouldn't show up today since the building was well over capacity.

Then he remembered Darcy on television, and the hard set of his jaw softened. She looked beautiful. It had only been a week since he last saw her, but the sight of her on Hank's little TV had taken his breath away. He was thankful everybody's eyes were glued to the screen and no one was paying any attention to him.

She looked uncomfortable at first, but quickly warmed up to her interviewers. He had never seen the John and Sherri Live show before and instantly disliked the hosts. They were just looking for reasons to get the crowd going against Darcy. Vince wished he had been there so he could take the heat off her. He didn't know exactly what he could have done, but he didn't appreciate the way they threw their questions at her without giving her time to respond.

Leanne's face appeared in the window separating the grill from the space behind the counter. "We should call her and congratulate her," she said.

Vince shrugged one shoulder. "I'm not stopping you."

"No, I meant you should call her for all of us."

"I'm busy right now." He gave the knob on the grill an angry twist.

"Nobody's ordering anything, Vince. They all want to hear from Darcy."

"Well, if they're not ordering, then they're loitering."

Leanne exhaled. "Why don't you lighten up?" She turned and stalked away before he could answer. He watched through the window as Leanne pulled the phone out from under the counter. She set it on the counter and motioned for everyone to be quiet. Vince shook his head and turned away. The call would never get through this soon. Darcy was probably hobnobbing with all those New York City hotshots at her publishing house, without a thought in her head about Talmedge, North Carolina.

He didn't know why she even mentioned them on TV. It was probably a publicity ploy to connect with viewers. It wasn't like anybody in Talmedge meant anything to her. She was a celebrity. She earned more money in a year than the café made in three. What could possibly make her think she would ever fit in here?

This place was light years apart from what she was used to. What would she do when she got snowed in for days at a time because the city plows were broken down? How would she handle the small town school with its out of date books? What would she think of a town government that spent four monthly meetings in a row arguing over the polite way to get Henrietta Abernathy to move the old boat parts out of her front yard?

Darcy would have no patience for any of it. She would have no patience for him. Wasn't she the one who told him Talmedge was a great place to get away, but not to live?

Even if he had entertained a thought or two about a future with her in these mountains, he wasn't naïve enough to think it would work. She would end up hating Talmedge and hating him, just like Amber. She might stick it out a few years, but as soon as the shine wore off, she'd high-tail it back up north where she belonged.

He snorted derisively. What was he thinking? He wasn't asking her to stay. She wasn't even here. She was back at home in her own world, her research finished, where none of them would probably ever see her again. Leanne would miss her. R.T. and Jim and the rest of his regulars had grown quite fond of her. It would be hard on them, thinking they meant something to her, only to discover she had used them in order to research her latest book, and as soon as she was through with them, she'd never give them a second thought.

Not him, though. She didn't belong here, and she never would, no matter how badly a part of him wanted to believe differently. He looked around his kitchen for something to do. With everybody, including his waitresses, glued to the telephone, nobody was interested in eating. It was just as well. It'd give him time to go out back and make sure nobody was blocking the dumpster.

To his credit, Brad didn't bring up the Finding Mr. Right book. He was too thrilled with the attention his office was getting over Darcy's appearance on John and Sherri Live. Their phones kept ringing during lunch until they finally agreed to turn them off lest they not enjoy their meal at one of the most exclusive restaurants in the city. After lunch, Brad and Carla were dropped off at the office and Darcy went back to her hotel. Tiffany parked the limousine in the hotel's garage, and spent the rest of the afternoon ushering her on foot from one shopping venue to the next. Darcy bought souvenirs for her nieces and nephews and perfume for her mother and Becky. After several hours of running up her credit card balances and girl talk with Tiffany, they walked back to the hotel.

"If there's anything else you want to do while you're in the city," Tiffany reminded her, "you've got my number. I'll be available until ten."

"Thanks anyway, Tiff, but I'm beat."

"All right, then. I'll pick you up at nine-thirty in the morning to take you to the airport."

Now, Darcy sat alone in her twenty-sixth floor Manhattan hotel room, looking out over the city—wishing that more than somewhere to go, she had someone to go with. Her mother was right; she had lived an interesting life. Penning twenty books in almost eleven years had its perks. She wouldn't be staring at the

New York City skyline if she hadn't. She had appeared on national television; a stint that was sure to have major impact on her next royalty check. She'd seen fascinating places and met wonderful people. It might actually make an interesting book.

All her fascinating experiences had come with a price. The only person she knew in New York free to shop away the afternoon with her was her limo driver. That was one small step up from pitiful.

Things hadn't always been this way. It wasn't that long ago when a girlfriend or shopping chum was simply a phone call away. In high school she was voted Best All Around. She was Homecoming Queen, senior class vice-president, and everyone's best friend. Her freshman year of college was more of the same. Then as she began to pour more and more of herself into her writing, she pulled away from everything else. By the time she knew she was going to quit school, the only person she was talking to was her English Lit professor.

During those early years while waiting for her first book to be published and then letting the world know she had written a book, she remained active in her church. When she was feeling down, overwhelmed, or frustrated she had several close friends she could call to vent, cry, or even pray with. It was only after the publication of her fourth or fifth book and she became a sought after writer and conference speaker that she stopped calling. Over time, her church attendance fell away. Her career had succeeded in keeping her too busy for pursuing things like friendship.

Now she had nobody. Thanks to John and Sherri Live, all of America knew she had no personal life. No friends. No relationships. She was no more qualified to write *The Ultimate Guide to Darcy Carter* than she was the Mr. Right book, or any of the other books she'd penned. She didn't even know who Darcy Carter was. She certainly wasn't the Ultimate Guide Queen like John and Sherri's audience thought. She'd opened her big mouth on national television about the café and diners books, and she hadn't even written the first word.

So she wasn't a writer. She had no education or skills that qualified her to do anything else.

She was an expert at nothing.

"*She just plays one on TV.*" Sherri's words rang in her ears.

She made a few circles around the spacious suite. Finally she sat down on the edge of her bed. She opened the drawer of the nightstand. Like she knew she would, she found a white Bible, placed there by the Gideons. She'd been in enough hotel rooms to know what to expect when she opened a drawer.

She pulled out the Bible and flipped it open.

"*You've had everything handed to you on a silver platter, and now you're whining because you don't know if you want to write anymore.*"

Vince was right. She had been handed everything on a silver platter, and all she cared about was her writing career. It had consumed her for years. If something didn't affect her directly, she didn't give it a moment's thought. She hadn't worried about her friends' needs; what they might deserve in return for listening to her fret over the possibility that she may have made a mistake by quitting school. It never occurred to her that they might need something from her.

Nor did it occur to her that God might require something of her.

Back when she was afraid to quit school to write a book, she had prayed diligently. When she thought the book would never sell, she wasn't above dropping to her knees in abject humility. In those early days, God had been the one she turned to more than anyone else. She needed His presence in her life. She needed to know regardless of what lay ahead, He was beside her on the journey.

Help me find the right publisher.

Let someone like my work.

Open doors.

You gave me this talent, Lord. Show me how to use it.

Don't let me be a failure.

On and on her petitions went. From morning till night, she prayed, asked, and sought. Her prayers were answered—beyond her wildest dreams.

And then she did precisely what Scripture warned her not to

do. She forgot the One who showered her with blessings. As soon as her needs were met, she turned away from the Lord. She went lusting after other gods. Her gods weren't money, fame, drugs, or relationships with men she didn't know, but they were gods all the same. Her gods were her writing, her reputation. She was so afraid of becoming a failure in the eyes of her family, so afraid of disappointing them that she put all her energy into her career. Nothing mattered besides proving to them she hadn't made a mistake. While her profession wasn't self-sacrificing like theirs, she would succeed at it. She would use her writing to make the world a better place.

Darcy got off the bed. With the Bible clutched in one hand, she went to the window and looked out over the darkening skyline. The city was more alive and vibrant than it had been four hours ago. Millions of people were out there just like her; chasing a dream and offering up prayers for fame, fortune, love, and fulfillment to whatever god they worshiped. Would they, like her, turn away as soon as their petitions were answered?

She put the Bible down on a side table and picked up her cell phone.

Leanne picked up on the second ring.

"Hey, stranger, it's Darcy."

"Darcy! We've been trying to get through to you all day. We couldn't even leave a message."

"Yeah, my voice mail's full."

"Wow, I guess you feel like a real celebrity. Everybody down here is talking about your show. Hank set his portable television up in the café. Practically the whole town came in to watch. You were great! We all loved it."

Darcy smiled, imagining R.T., Jim and all the café's regulars laughing and slapping one another on the back. She pictured Vince leaning against the counter with his arms over his chest, looking remote and detached, but hanging on her every word.

"I hope no one minded me mentioning Talmedge on the show. It kind of slipped out."

"Are you kidding? That was the highlight of the show. Everyone whooped and hollered when they heard it."

"That's good. I didn't mean to offend anyone."

"There's no way you could have," Leanne said.

"It was a lot of fun," she confided. "I just wish people would forget about the Ultimate Guide Girl. I always hated that title."

"You're the Queen now, don't you remember?"

Darcy groaned. "I could have killed John Rivers, crowning me like that with my own book."

Leanne laughed. "Oh, Darcy, it was funny. That's what those shows are all about; make the audience laugh. That's what keeps them tuning in and supporting the sponsors."

"I know, I know. I just hope by tomorrow everyone will forget all about me."

"You don't mean that. You want them to go out and buy all your books. I think I'll get on Amazon and see what your ranking is now."

"Don't do that. That always seems so desperate."

"Then I won't tell you the results. Listen, Darcy, don't sweat it. You did great. You looked like a million bucks. Think of it as a great experience and a lot of fun. Have they been spoiling you since you got to town?"

"And how!" Darcy described the limousine, Tiffany, and the lunches the company had paid for. She told her how impressed Brad was, and how he was acting more civil to her than he had in all the days they'd worked together. When she hung up the phone she felt much better, only sorry Leanne hadn't brought up Vince. She had been too chicken to ask if he agreed that she looked like a million bucks.

Later that night, she left her room to go downstairs for a cold drink and a quick walk through the expansive five-story lobby. She didn't notice when three German tourists snapped her picture on the way to the elevator.

Darcy lay in bed and stared at the city lights coming in through the curtains long after she went to bed. Passages she remembered from her Bible study days kept running through her mind. Passages about the foolish man who put his faith in riches, the man who buried his talent in the ground, and the command to lay up treasures in heaven where thief could not steal and rust and moth could not destroy. Then there was the reminder that God was a jealous God and would not tolerate second place in a follower's heart. She couldn't remember the exact words, but the message was clear. Finally she drifted off to sleep.

Her flight wasn't until eleven the next morning so she had planned to sleep in. The ringing of the telephone startled her out of a deep sleep. She squinted at the phone, five-fifteen. Who in the world would call her this early? Most everyone she knew would still in bed, everyone but Vince. She cleared her throat and propped herself up on her elbow. She smoothed a tangle of hair away from her face and reached for the phone.

"Hello," she said as dignified as one could be at five-fifteen.

"Is this Darcy Carter, the Ultimate Guide Queen?"

Her heart sank with disappointment. It wasn't Vince. Why hadn't he called? She knew he was awake right now, firing up the grill at the café, turning on lights, and getting ready for business.

"Yes, it is. Who's this?"

In lieu of an answer, the male caller cleared his throat and began to sing an old Frank Sinatra love song, or was it Perry Como?

Darcy clamped her lips together to keep from laughing. She set the phone back in its cradle and fell back against the pillows—her first serenade. Then realization set in. She sat up and clutched the sheet to her chest. How did this guy get her number? How did he find out the name of her hotel? Maybe he worked at the studio and found her number in her files, or maybe he was some sort of computer hacker. What if he was a nut? Of course he was a nut! Only a nut called someone he'd never met to sing her a love song.

She shivered in the darkness. This wasn't funny. She looked at the phone and thought about calling her dad. He would know what to do. No, actually, he would get totally freaked out and tell her she never should have gone to New York unescorted. He and Mom wouldn't rest until she was safe at home, then they'd never want her to leave Middleburg Heights again. She wouldn't bother them with this. Besides, she wasn't a child. She'd been on her own before. She just wished she had someone to call who would laugh with her, tell her the world was full of harmless kooks, and that she was making a big deal out of nothing.

The phone trilled again. Darcy jumped out of bed and ran into the bathroom. She locked the door, sat down on the toilet, and wrapped her arms around herself. This was ridiculous. There was a phone in here, too. She picked up the phone and set it back down immediately. Then she called the front desk and asked them to turn off her ringer. A serenade wasn't nearly as flattering as she imagined it would be.

She went back to bed but was too keyed up to sleep. Finally she threw the covers back and got up. She went to the window and watched the sun creep up over the skyline. Even though she wasn't hungry, she ordered coffee, juice, and a plain bagel from room service since her flight wouldn't serve lunch. She ran a tub full of water while she waited for her breakfast, something she never made the time for at home. After a bath that helped her forget about the phone calls, she dressed and finished packing.

She resisted the urge to check her voice mail to see if Vince had called. She didn't want to be disappointed if he hadn't.

The hotel rang her room at nine-thirty to let her know Tiffany was waiting for her. Two teenagers were getting off the elevator as Darcy boarded. They giggled and elbowed each other as the doors slid shut. She did a quick check of her buttons and zippers. Everything seemed in order. She reminded herself that teenagers didn't need a reason to laugh at someone they considered ancient.

The doorman came forward to take her bag while she checked out. She could see the studio's limo out front. When she got outside, she waved to Tiffany before moving to the newsstand to get some reading material for the trip home. She browsed a few versions of the daily news and decided on a home decorating magazine instead. Now that she was through with her research, she could get started on some of the projects she fell in love with at the Ravenswood Inn.

She realized she should be thinking about getting back to writing and not redecorating. This was the longest period since her departure from college that she had gone without working on a book in some capacity. She believed writers needed to write; not just talk about it, think about it, or research their brains out without ever actually sitting down and doing it. Writers wrote something. She wrote—everyday, but suddenly…

Her last four or five books had practically written themselves. She researched for a few weeks and then sketched out a hundred-page draft; the nuts and bolts. Then she went back and added her personal touches, the touches that sold copies. Her readers thought she was funny. People signed up for her workshops at conferences because she was personable and witty, just like her writing. But somewhere along the way she had stopped enjoying herself.

She idly scanned the morning headlines while the man added up her total. If she wasn't writing anymore, what did she want to do with her life? She couldn't think of a single thing. She was a writer. She shuddered at the thought of sitting behind a desk in a cubicle. She doubted she could sell anything; her people skills had gotten a little rusty from sitting alone behind a desk for the past ten years. Somehow she didn't see herself talking someone into buying a house, a car, or a timeshare in Aruba.

Aruba! That was it. She could become a travel agent. Now that was something she could sink her teeth into—or running an inn. She thought of Leanne and the beautiful Ravenswood Inn. That would be the life. During the off-season, she could work on a new novel. She could become a professional hiker or an expert on hiking; *The Ultimate Guide to the Trails of Western North Carolina.*

Out of the question! Her Ultimate Guide days were over.

"Four-fifty," the man said.

Darcy reached into her wallet and handed him a ten. He kept his eyes on her face a moment longer than necessary before reaching into the pouch around his waist to count out her change. He grinned broadly. Darcy looked away, uncomfortably. What was everybody staring at this morning? She brushed her finger and thumb across her mouth in case she was wearing any leftover crumbs from her bagel. Her eyes fell on the tabloids near his elbow.

That woman looks like me, she thought. Then she recognized her linen suit and the professional hairstyle her nieces had been so enamored with.

She gasped and snatched up the newspaper. She stared at the grainy picture. It was her! The newsstand owner watched, his smile growing wider and more pleased. In the picture, she was looking at the show's host, John Rivers. Her mouth was half open as if defending herself. John wore a sanctimonious smile, and Sherri, sitting on his other side, appeared to be having the time of her life. The headline read; *Ultimate Guide Queen Unqualified to Guide.*

Horrified, Darcy read the caption. *Ultimate Guide Queen, Darcy Carter, author of nineteen ultimate guidebooks, confesses on John and Sherri Live she has never done any of the things she writes about in her books.*

"I can't believe this," Darcy cried aloud. She bit her lip and smiled sheepishly. The newsstand owner was still grinning at her, revealing several stained or missing teeth.

She cleared her throat. "I'll take this, too," she mumbled, handing him back the five he had given her. She ducked her head and hurried out of the newsstand, not bothering to wait for the change this time. She stumbled to the limo, barely giving Tiffany time to open the door for her.

"Darcy, are you all right?" Tiffany asked, leaning into the car. "You look like you've seen a ghost."

She held up the paper. "Look at this."

Tiffany held onto a corner of the paper to steady it against the trembling of Darcy's hand. "Wow, the front page. Your hair looks great."

"No." Darcy jabbed at the headline with her finger. "This!"

"Oh, that. That's nothing," Tiffany assured her. "What matters is you got your picture in a national paper with John and Sherri Rivers. This is huge, Darcy. You'll sell millions of books. I bet your editor is dancing for joy all over her office right now."

Darcy looked back down at the paper while Tiffany closed the door and went around to the driver's side. She had to admit it was a good picture. The makeup artist was an artist in every sense of the word, and her long, dark tresses had never looked better.

She leaned back into the rich leather seat as the big car pulled into traffic. Sure the headline was negative, but that would only serve to get her more press space in other papers. Everyone knew there was no such thing as bad press. At least they hadn't called her the Ultimate Guide Girl, although Queen wasn't much better in her book.

"You really think this is no big deal?" she asked Tiffany.

Tiffany threw up a dismissive hand. "It'll blow over too quickly. Enjoy the publicity while you got it."

Darcy nodded thoughtfully. She should call Carla to ask if she'd seen the paper yet. Tiffany was right, Carla and Brad would be thrilled that she made the front of the tabloids. Just as her fingers found her phone inside her tote it beeped.

Yes, somebody had seen it and was calling to congratulate her. In horror, she realized she had over two hundred stored messages.

"Hello?"

"Darcy, I know you don't know me, but my name's Thaddeus. I saw you on TV yesterday. It broke my heart when you said you didn't have anyone to share your life with. I know I could make you very happy."

Darcy didn't remember saying that. "Uh…Thaddeus, is it?"

"I can be that person, Darcy," he continued. "All I want is to make you happy. I'm a writer too, but I'm not working right now, so you can meet me anytime at…"

Darcy hit the end button and closed her fist around the phone. How in the world did this person get her number? It didn't sound like the same man who had called this morning. She pressed the play button and listened to her most recent message.

"Hello, Darcy, my name's Aleah," said a woman who sounded anywhere from twenty to forty. "I was so touched by your interview yesterday on John and Sherri Live. I feel like we clicked right away. It's so wonderful to find a kindred spirit. I live in Brooklyn and would love to meet you for lunch today."

Darcy deleted the call and went to the next one.

Another young man recited a phone number and begged her to call him back so they could begin making wedding plans.

After another profession of love by someone who didn't identify himself, but whose raspy voice sent shivers down her spine, Darcy scanned through the messages and deleted all of the numbers she didn't recognize. She was halfway through the list when she heard Tiffany's voice.

"Darcy? Are you all right?"

"Um, what? I'm sorry."

"Are you okay?" Tiffany's face in the rearview mirror was a mask of concern. "I asked you if you needed to stop anywhere else before we left the city. When I saw your face, you looked like something had upset you."

She highlighted a block of calls and hit the delete button again. She held the phone up. "Two hundred calls since my appearance yesterday on John and Sherri Live."

Tiffany's concern intensified. "Nothing freaky, I hope."

Darcy shrugged and tried to smile convincingly. "I guess not; some marriage proposals, but that's kind of to be expected—isn't it?"

Tiffany smiled. "I wouldn't know. I can't catch a guy with a club and a net."

Darcy appreciated her attempt to lighten the mood. "How do you suppose so many people got my cell phone number?"

"You can find out anything if you want to badly enough. Do you utilize any of those security features on your phone plan or anything?"

"Kind of," Darcy replied. "I never really thought about it before. I always thought it was kind of paranoid. I don't advertise my number or address, but I guess I don't keep a lot of secrets either."

"Maybe you need to start. But, hey, I'm sure all this notoriety is harmless. It'll die down, and all those men out there salivating over you will move on to the next John and Sherri Live guest."

"Gee, thanks."

"Just change your phone number when you get home. I'm sure none of this will amount to anything, but a little paranoia can be a good thing now and then."

Darcy nodded. She couldn't agree more.

She bid Tiffany good-bye at the airport and went in search of her gate. After replacing her shoes at the security checkpoint, she hurried through the airport. She was about to sit down to wait for her flight when the woman behind the counter got her attention and motioned her over.

"I'm sorry to bother you today, but are you Darcy Carter?" she asked. When Darcy nodded, she went on. "I want to make you aware that several messages have been left here for you. We do not usually relay personal messages for passengers unless it's an emergency, but we feel we should make you aware we've received about fifty email and phone messages. There have also been eleven bouquets of flowers delivered."

Darcy managed to keep her face neutral. Not only had people found her phone number, they also knew her flight arrangements. Wasn't there any such thing as airport security anymore, or was it simply another way of inconveniencing ordinary law abiding people who only wanted to mind their own business? She was starting to get a little freaked out. "What did you do with the flowers?" she asked.

"Ordinarily when it's discovered a celebrity is coming through and flowers or gifts are delivered, we examine them, and then donate them to an area hospital."

Darcy didn't consider herself a celebrity, but she was relieved the airport had already handled the situation for her.

"Great. Thank you."

Darcy returned to her seat and tucked her carry on between the chair and her legs. She noticed a few long looks from other passengers waiting for the same flight, but no one approached her. She was relieved to see so much security. She didn't want to be proposed to by a total stranger or have a misguided soul unburden all her problems, thinking she and Darcy were kindred spirits.

Within a few minutes she realized the stares she was getting were due to the furtive glances she was casting around the waiting area. She uncrossed her arms and willed her shoulders to relax. Almost immediately, it seemed like everyone went back to ignoring her the way they always did. She would stop thinking about all of the things that had been going on since she woke up this morning. She loved to fly. It was a clear and beautiful day to be in the air, and she planned to enjoy it.

"Excuse me. Didn't I see you on John and Sherri Live yesterday?"

Darcy looked away from the blue cloudless sky outside her window and to the lady standing over her.

Darcy smiled woodenly. "Yes, you did."

"I thought so," the woman said triumphantly. "I told my husband, Herb," she jabbed her thumb in the direction of the seat she'd just vacated where a portly man around fifty sat dozing, "I recognized you from TV, but he didn't believe me. I'm Florence Sanders. We're going to Cleveland to visit our daughter."

Before she could respond, Florence dropped into the empty first class seat beside her. Darcy groaned inwardly. She had hoped to enjoy her flight in peace. Now she probably wouldn't get rid of the woman until they started their descent.

"You were great," Florence was saying. "I can't wait to get to a bookstore to look for some of your books."

Darcy was beginning to see the upside to her newfound popularity. "Why, thank you. I'm glad you enjoyed the show."

"Oh, I did. Is that Sherri Rivers as funny in person as she is on TV? I love her." Without waiting for a reply, she whipped out a copy of a national news magazine and brandished it under Darcy's nose. "Will you sign this for me?"

The paper was so close to Darcy's nose she couldn't make out what it was. She took it out of Florence's hands and held it away from her face. It was a different newspaper with yet another picture of her, this time a close-up, with a caption that read *Ultimate Guide Girl Knows Nothing about Romance.* Darcy's mouth dropped open. How many papers were carrying the story? Was this a slow news week or something?

Florence did not notice her reaction. "I can't believe I'm sitting with a TV personality. This is so exciting..."

While Florence chattered on, Darcy scanned the article. Basically, she was branded as a woman who claimed to know everything about any given topic, but she was an absolute failure at her own love life. No wonder she'd received so many marriage proposals this morning.

What must her family be thinking? What about Brad? Surely any publicity wasn't good publicity when it reported she was unqualified to write Ultimate Guide books? Who would take her seriously again? Of course, it hadn't stopped Florence from coming over to meet her, and then promising to buy her books as soon as she found a bookstore.

She tuned back in to what her newest fan was saying. "My daughter is a lawyer in one of the biggest firms in Ohio. She really wants to make partner someday. You know, you should write a book about that. There are more people graduating law school these days than ever before. I think it's because of that John Grisham fellow and the books he writes. Have you ever met him? I hear he coaches his son's little league team. Wouldn't it be something to have a famous person coaching your kid in little league? Anyway, you could write a book about how to make partner in a competitive law firm. It's very cutthroat, according to my daughter."

Darcy took the pen Florence handed her and signed her name across the newspaper headline. She was happy to see another headline reporting Oprah and Dr. Phil had secretly married in Palm Springs over the weekend. Apparently the people who bought these newspapers weren't interested in the truth. "I don't know," she answered, like she always did when someone she didn't know offered her a book idea. "I really don't know much about becoming a law partner."

"That never stopped you before." Florence brayed with laughter and sent her bony elbow into Darcy's arm.

Darcy flinched in pain and handed the paper back to Florence. She pushed her seat into a reclining position. "It was nice meeting you, Florence," she said, hoping the woman would take the hint. "I hope you have a nice visit in Cleveland."

"Thanks, well, you too." Disappointed that Darcy didn't want to chat, she stood up and moved back to her seat.

Darcy turned her head toward the window and closed her eyes to discourage any further interruptions. She thought about calling her mother and asking if she'd seen any of the tabloids. Probably not, since her mother never bothered reading the headlines of papers sold in supermarket checkout lanes. She could call Carla.

Carla would have plenty to say about the publicity—whether it was a good thing or bad. She would put Darcy's mind at ease, or give her more of a reason to worry.

Once again, she realized how completely alone she'd become. When she really wanted to talk to someone, she was alone. She opened her eyes and stared out at the clear blue sky. It was a beautiful day to be in the air.

Are you there, God? she asked silently. *Remember me?*

Before she even realized she was crying, she felt hot tears coursing down her cheeks. She wasn't worthy of approaching God's throne. She only used Him when no one else was available, when no one else could help. Why would He listen to her cries now? He had probably tuned her out years ago. He knew she was only turning to Him out of desperation. As soon as things looked up, she would be gone again like the fair weather friend she was.

The tears flowed faster. She tried to breathe deeply to keep from sobbing out loud. It wasn't easy.

I'm sorry, I'm sorry, she repeated over and over again as the plane flew over eastern New York State. There was nothing else to say.

15

Vince whirled around at the sound of the back door opening. The café had been a zoo all morning. Unfamiliar cars were sitting in the parking lot when he unlocked the door at six. There were always delivery truck drivers or crew trucks from the local tree trimming company or Power Company when a storm had them working all night, but he never had ordinary customers before six. Where had everyone come from? He got his answer as soon as the first one came through the door.

"We've been driving all night," a nasal sounding woman in a cashmere wrapper offered even though he hadn't asked. "We're looking for the Ravenswood Inn. Do you know it?"

"Yeah, I know it," he'd answered testily. "Down at the end of Elm Lane. It's the second street on the left once you cross the railroad tracks. If you aren't watching, you'll miss it."

"Thank you, young man," the husband of the cashmere draped woman said. "We heard of the place on the John and Sherri Live show yesterday morning. A young writer woman was talking about it. We're retired and free to come and go as we please, so we decided to drive down and have a look. We're from Michigan."

He stuck out his hand. Vince was obliged to shake it. "I'm from North Carolina," he said dryly.

The woman stared at him, open-mouthed. After a moment, the man laughed. "Oh, North Carolina, I get it."

They were then forced to step out of the way when another

couple came in, followed by Larry Meeks who was on his way to work at the Pepsi warehouse in Winchester, and Howard Rice, the third shift dispatcher at the sheriff's office. Vince had taken the opportunity to flee to the kitchen. Let June and Missy handle the questions from the tourists. They were a month early in his opinion and their intrusion unwelcome.

The breakfast crowd hadn't dispersed by eight thirty, and when Tyler left for school at seven-forty-five, June and Missy had gone into revolt. "You're gonna have to do something, Vince," June said with her hand on her hip. "We're swamped out there. The last thing we got time for is bussing tables and washing dishes."

"What d'ya suggest, June," he demanded. "I wave my magic wand and make another busboy appear with maybe a waitress or two in his hip pocket."

"Only if you can guarantee he looks like Harrison Ford. Seriously, call Leanne."

"I can't call Leanne. She's the reason all these people are here. As soon as they eat, they head over to the inn."

"Then what are we gonna do?"

Vince had glared out at his crowded café. It was all Darcy's fault. The extra revenue would be a boon for the community, but what was he to do in the meantime.

"What are you coming in that way for?" he asked Hank Haywood when he recognized who had just broken his 'never use the back door' policy.

"Nice to see you, too, brother," Hank called out cheerfully. "Leanne called and said it's a madhouse here. I guess the inn is swamped, too, but you know her—all she's worried about is her little brother. She sent me to help out."

Vince couldn't help but be relieved, even though he was haunted by Darcy's words that Leanne didn't have a life of her own because she was too busy taking care of him.

He set down the spatula and stepped back from the grill. "Wash up and take over, would ya? I'll go out and help June and Missy."

Hank looked doubtful. "You sure you want to do that." He knew Vince didn't exactly mesh with the general public.

"I ran this place single handedly the first six months I was open," Vince snarled.

"That's 'cause you couldn't find anybody willing to work for you."

Vince glared at him. "Don't burn the eggs," he said on his way out the door.

Two hours later there was a break in the crowd. June and Missy plopped down on stools for the first time that morning.

"I never dreamed Darcy mentioning the Ravenswood on that show yesterday would have an immediate impact on business," Hank said.

Vince went to the butcher block island to start working on the green salad for lunch. "She shoulda kept her mouth shut."

"What's got into your craw?" Hank demanded. "Leanne is beside herself. In case you haven't noticed, both you and your sister rely directly on the financial stability of this town."

"You think I don't know that."

"Then what's got you all busted up?" Hank disappeared inside the walk in cooler and came out again with an armload of condiments. He set each item on the counter within Vince's reach. "Unless, it ain't what she said that's got under your skin, but the girl herself."

Vince snorted. "You don't know what you're talking about."

Hank grinned. "Yup, I think that's it exactly. She's gone back to New York and her big city world, leaving you here where nothing ever changes but the calendar on the wall."

"She's free to come and go as she pleases."

"Yeah, that's right. You ain't got any kind of hold on her."

Vince curled his lip in distaste. "I never said I wanted one. She's about the most aggravatin' woman ever born. Won't be no skin off my nose if she never comes back."

Hank chuckled. "Seems to me a body wouldn't be so worked up over another body if one didn't mean something to the other."

Vince wrinkled his nose. "Sometimes you don't make an ounce of sense when you talk, Hank."

"Aunt Darcy, you're famous!" Samantha squealed as soon as Darcy stepped out of her SUV. "Everybody at school has been talking about seeing you on TV. My history teacher even let the kids watch the show during class."

"People have been calling us and Grandma since yesterday," Bethany offered. "They even delivered flowers."

Darcy pasted a smile on her face for the benefit of her exuberant nieces as she opened her arms to greet them. Inwardly she cringed. If people had her number and her mother's number and her flight arrangements, what would keep them from showing up on her doorstep? She wanted nothing more than her newfound celebrity to blow over.

By the time the plane touched down in Cleveland, her cell phone had recorded another fifty-six messages. Ten more bouquets of flowers were waiting for her at the airport. She couldn't help but feel sorry for some of her new fans who truly sounded lonely and imagined they could connect with her and build a lasting relationship because she seemed friendly and nice on the screen.

She planted kisses on her nieces' cheeks and let them take her carryon and her tote bag out of her hands. "I'm glad everybody enjoyed the show," she said following them up the walk.

The carryon bounced uncomfortably against Bethany's legs as she moved sideways up the sidewalk so she could keep her eyes on Darcy while she talked. "Everyone at school is suddenly our friend. Today Hayley Norman asked me to have lunch with her group. I've *never* been asked to sit with them."

Not to be outdone, Samantha added her own good news. "Conner Shrupp talked to me today in Biology. He said it must be so cool to have an aunt who's on TV."

Apparently the opinions of Hayley Norman and Conner Shrupp were held in high regard in Samantha and Bethany's world. Darcy wouldn't go back to those days for love or money.

The front door opened and Sharon ushered them inside. "Hi, baby," she said, kissing Darcy's cheek. "Your father and I could have picked you up at the airport."

She always said that, and Darcy always told her it wasn't necessary.

"Are you hungry? The girls are about to order pizza. I'm sorry, but I didn't have time to cook after school."

"That's okay. I need to shed a few pounds. I'll just nibble on some fresh vegetables."

"You can eat that at home," Sharon said.

Bethany and Samantha dumped Darcy's bags inside the front door. "Suit yourself," Bethany said. "I'm calling in the order now." She took off toward the kitchen at a sprint.

Samantha ran after her. "No, you're not. You always order mushrooms. I hate mushrooms."

"Girls, no arguing." Sharon lifted her shoulders in defeat at Darcy and followed her granddaughters to the kitchen before they could harm one another.

So much for her homecoming and celebrity status. Darcy was relieved that life could so quickly revert back to normal.

It had been three weeks since Darcy Carter's appearance on the John and Sherri Live show, and things still hadn't quieted down at the Ravenswood Inn. Leanne hadn't had a weekend yet without all her rooms getting booked. Most weekdays were the same. People were calling from as far away as Oregon. She even had to turn away Sandy and Dwayne Hudson when they called for an impromptu visit last weekend—no room at the inn.

Tonight was Thursday, one of the three nights she served dinner in the formal dining room whenever she had guests. Usually this didn't become a weekly practice until much later in the season. She wasn't complaining; she loved this part of hosting an inn. She loved pampering the people she welcomed into her home and tried to make them feel like old friends.

She sat the platter down next to a retired ophthalmologist from Lexington, Kentucky. As he chose the ribs he wanted, she smiled at Vince at the other end of the table. She received a slight twitch of his mouth in response. He looked stiff and uncomfortable in a polo shirt and chinos. He wasn't thrilled with dinner guests, especially those whose presence required he wear something other than his usual faded jeans and tee shirt. For her benefit and the benefit of their first time guests, he had put on his happy face for what seemed like the hundredth time since Darcy had mentioned the Ravenswood Inn on John and Sherri Live.

Hank Haywood sat halfway down the table between a web designer from Durham and a veterinarian from Atlanta. As usual, Hank was enjoying himself immensely. He fancied himself a computer geek and loved animals so he conversed easily with both parties.

Leanne smiled and thought of how much better suited he was at hosting an inn than Vince; a handyman who was handy with guests. The platter clattered in her hand as she gripped it and moved down the table. What was she thinking? Regardless of how much Darcy said to the contrary, Hank was only a friend of the family. He would never see her as anything more than the same.

Vince watched Leanne circle the table with her barbequed ribs. She had cooked them every weekend now for three weeks straight. Not that he minded; he could eat Leanne's ribs every day of the week, but it was the idea that she had to fix ribs when guests were scheduled that rankled him. It was what people expected to eat when they came south. *Northerners,* he sniffed. *Don't they know we eat meat loaf like regular people?*

Leanne didn't seem to tire of cooking the same things for different groups of people every weekend. She was pleased as punch to wash sheets and hang them outside as often as the weather permitted because people had a notion that they slept better on sheets hung on the line. She didn't mind giving directions to all the tourist attractions and answering the same questions a thousand times about Indian folklore and rock formations. He had to hand it to her—she was as perfectly suited to hosting an inn as a duck was to water. He would have tossed somebody off a mountain by now.

He picked up a rib with his hands and bit into it because it was expected that one eat ribs with one's hands at a dinner table in the South. At least that was one misconception he was happy to oblige. Leanne stopped at Hank's right shoulder and offered the platter. Vince stopped chewing and watched the exchange. He had known for a long time that Hank had a thing for Leanne; he picked up on it when he was still working for Hank, and Hank would make any excuse to stop at the house after they got done working for the day.

Right now, Hank was smiling up at Leanne like some kind of love struck schoolboy. He had just said something to her that Vince didn't catch since he wasn't paying attention to their prattle. Leanne elbowed him on the shoulder as she laughed. The website designer on Hank's right laughed along with them, and the veterinarian leaned forward in her chair to add her comment to the conversation.

Now, there's somebody you can go after, Hank, Vince thought, eyeing the vet appreciatively. She looked about Leanne's age. She was petite and pretty with dark hair and blue-black eyes.

But when he looked at Hank, he knew the poor lug only had eyes for Leanne. He turned his attention back to his sister. Had Darcy been right? Had Leanne ignored her own feelings because she thought Vince couldn't get along without her?

Vince hated to think that for the last four years he had been taking advantage of the person he loved most in the world, and was too blind to see it until some hotheaded writer from Cleveland came down here and pointed it out. Nor did he want to think about how that same hotheaded writer had shaken up his cozy little world.

Whether he wanted to admit it or not, he'd been miserable since Darcy left— downright pathetic was more like it. On three separate occasions when he drove down the lane after work, he spotted a red SUV in the driveway and his heart had leapt in his chest. Then he'd realize it was the wrong make and model or there'd be a car seat in the back, and he'd be disappointed the rest of the night. He found himself listening for her deep throaty laugh after Leanne told one of her silly anecdotes, or waiting for her to emerge from one of the hiking trails, dressed in her less than flattering sweats with her wild mahogany mane spilling out of her jacket hood.

He had to get Darcy Carter out of his head. Thinking about her, imagining her car in the driveway, or smiling at the memory of the way she stuck her tongue out of the corner of her mouth when she shaped a pie crust wasn't doing him any good. She was gone. She didn't belong in his world and he had no place in hers. The sooner he got it through his thick skull, the better.

But he had learned something from her. He had taken advantage of Leanne's giving nature for too long. He knew how his sister's brain worked. If she thought he needed her, she would forsake her own happiness to take care of him. She wasn't happy unless she was taking care of somebody. The poor thing was always that way. When they were kids it was any old stray animal that wandered onto the property. Then it was Mom and Dad. Now it was him and the Ravenswood's guests.

Vince had to make amends. He had to make Leanne see the only person she needed to take care of was herself. She deserved a family of her own. She deserved to fall in love if she wanted to. Her baby brother was a big boy who could take care of himself. It was time he started acting like it.

16

$\mathcal{D}$arcy sat back on her haunches and surveyed the neat clusters of perennials she had just weeded around. Her flowerbeds had been a terrible sight when she got home from Florida yesterday. Everything had been such a whirlwind since spring she hadn't had a chance to maintain even a semblance of the gardens' usual early summer glory. If not for the standing appointment at the beginning of summer and winter, her gardens would have been totally unsalvageable. First thing this morning she headed outdoors with grim determination to straighten up this mess, even if it took the rest of the week. She wiped the back of her hand across her forehead and pushed a strand of hair away from her face with a dirty finger. She could see progress, but she still had a long way to go.

There was nothing she hated more than coming home from a trip to a less than immaculate house; laundry in the hamper, dishes in the dishwasher, and weeds in the garden. The interior of the house had passed muster when she walked in, but the gardens were deplorable. Next time she jetted off to Disney World the first week of June like a tourist who didn't know any better, she would make an appointment with a gardener before she left.

Still, for all its trouble, the work was good for her. She hadn't been outside with her hands in the dirt in a long time. She was always too busy—busy working on her house, busy making up for lost time with her family, busy avoiding *The Ultimate Guide to Dining-Out on America's Back Roads*, busy not thinking about Vince Ravenscraft.

It had been six weeks since her appearance on the John and Sherri Live show. Apparently her marriage proposals had been rescinded. She hadn't received a bouquet of flowers from an unknown admirer in over a month. Her cell phone traffic had gone back to almost nothing. America had forgotten her. All except for readers who were still buying her books in record numbers. She had four conferences booked for the fall and two for the beginning of the following year. Carla was working on a ten city, four state book tour slated for September.

She had found another message from Carla on her machine when she got home yesterday asking how the café book was coming along. Brad, Carla reported, wanted to know when she was going to start Finding Mr. Right. Darcy had smiled and deleted the message. The café book had stalled in the starting gate, and she had no intention of bothering with Mr. Right; not now, not ever.

She decimated a dirt clod with her trowel and covered the spot over with mulch. Six weeks since her television appearance and seven weeks and three days since her blowup with Vince at the waterfall. Sometimes she wished she could relive the day over again. In retrospect she could see she had been whining. Like he said, there were people in the world with far bigger problems than hers. But she had been right to point out to him that he was holding his sister hostage with his grief over Amber's death.

Still, hers was no longer a life of regret. God had forgiven her for the years of denying Him. She had gone to church with her parents the week after returning from New York and publicly rededicated her life to her Savior. Since then, she had put her own problems and concerns behind her and started looking for others she could bless. The last three weeks had been wonderful.

She closed her eyes and turned her face upward. She smiled gently as the sun touched her skin and a slight breeze ruffled her hair. It had been too long since she'd been aware of God's beautiful world. Like Leanne's father used to say; Creation was always having church if she'd be still long enough to hear it.

The phone rang. She opened her eyes, brushed her hands off on her pants, leaned over several zinnia clumps, and picked it up.

"Darcy, how are you? It's me, Leanne."

Darcy pushed a strand of hair that had escaped her headband away from her face. "Leanne! Hi. I'm good, how's everything with you?"

"Awesome," she declared breathlessly. Darcy could picture her back in North Carolina wearing a typically toothy smile, and running her hand through her shoulder length blonde hair. "This has been my craziest summer ever."

Darcy laughed. "Honey, summer's just begun."

Leanne's delighted laugh reminded Darcy of the tinkling bell over the café's front door. "Tell me about it. Oh, Darcy, you should see how things are jumping down here. Ever since you mentioned the inn on TV, my phone's been ringing off the hook. I've been booked solid every night. I am so busy, I had to hire June's niece to come in a couple of hours a day to help me clean and bake for the next day's guests."

"You're kidding! That's great."

"Yeah, it's great. I think I've even got Vince to agree we should build two more rooms and add another bath. But you know him, he's cautious to the core. I have a wedding already booked for next spring, if you can believe that, and a bell choir from Sylva is using the inn for their Christmas concert."

"Leanne, that's wonderful," Darcy exclaimed, happy that everything was going so well for her friend. "Well, I can believe it. You deserve it more than anyone. And I'm sure all the attention is bringing business into the rest of Talmedge, too."

"No kidding. The café is packed all the time. Vince had to hire his summer help last month. Ermaline from the general store is beside herself with happiness. In fact, it was all her idea. Everybody else jumped on the bandwagon as soon as she brought it up at the town meeting last night, but she deserves the credit. But I knew it wouldn't work till I cleared it with you. I know you're busy and everything, but we're all really hoping you'll say yes."

Darcy put her free hand on the ground to help herself up. Her knees popped painfully from being cramped in the same position for too long. "Leanne, slow down. What exactly are we talking about here?"

"Oh, I'm sorry. I got a little ahead of myself, didn't I? Ermaline had this great idea last night for the Fourth of July. When I was a kid, Talmedge used to have a huge celebration for the Fourth. All the businesses stayed open late and had sidewalk sales and giveaways. They all pitched in to sponsor a fireworks display. But the money ran out so now everybody goes to Winchester or Sylva to see the fireworks. Anyway, Ermaline suggested we have a festival like the old days with a parade and everything, since there are so many tourists in the area now because of your appearance on TV. They're not only staying in Talmedge. The whole county's filled up. The state parks are getting crowds in record numbers. Well, we thought it would be a great idea. Alma Faye Williams is making phone calls today to book some bands for entertainment. Alma Faye's cousin is related to one of the wives of a country music duo in Nashville, so she's going to get hold of her and see if they can work something out. Of course we don't have much money and it is short notice, but you never know. Even if the duo can't make it, they probably know some young up-and-comer who'd be willing to come and perform for gas money and exposure. But let me get back to why I'm calling." She took a deep breath. "Someone nominated you to be the Grand Marshall of the parade. You could make the opening speech of the festival on Thursday evening. Everyone agrees none of this would be happening if you hadn't mentioned Talmedge on TV, so we want to honor you."

Darcy waited a moment to make sure Leanne was finished with her explanation before responding. "I appreciate the offer, Leanne, but it's really not necessary. I wouldn't feel comfortable being Grand Marshall of a parade. That should be a resident who's done a lot for the community. Someone like you."

"Oh, no—not me."

"Why not? That's what a Grand Marshall is. The opening ceremony speech should be given by the mayor."

"The mayor's the one who suggested you do it."

"A politician who doesn't jump at the chance to give a speech? I've never heard of such a thing."

"Well, technically, he digs septic systems and drives a school bus. The mayor thing is a side job."

Darcy did like the idea of seeing Vince again, even if she

wasn't sure how he felt about seeing her. "There's only one problem. I just got home yesterday from a five day trip to Orlando with the family. We had a blast, but my house is a mess, I'm a mess, and the Fourth is only three weeks away. I haven't spent any time inside my house in three months."

"Oh, please, Darcy. Everyone will be so disappointed if I tell them you can't make it. Did I mention we'll throw in the plane ticket? You can use my car or Vince's truck anytime you need to go anywhere, and I'm keeping a room free for you here at the inn."

Darcy was shaking her head in protest even though she knew Leanne couldn't see her. "Don't do that. You need to be renting that room. I have to admit, the whole thing sounds like fun. But if I come, I'll drive myself. It's not totally outside my capabilities. And I want you to promise you'll rent that room you're saving, I could bunk on your sofa or on a cot in the sewing room."

"I guess I could do that," Leanne said after a pause, "but I'd feel terrible not giving you a proper bed to sleep in."

"Well, that's the only way I'll come, and ask the mayor to be Grand Marshall."

"Okay, okay. Until I met you, I thought my brother had the hardest head on the planet."

"Hey, don't compare me to that man."

Leanne laughed. "If you say so, but if you ask me, you are two of a kind. I'm so glad you're coming. You've just made a whole town full of people very happy. By the way, how's the book coming?"

"It isn't," she answered flatly.

"Are you okay with that?"

"Surprisingly, yes," Darcy said sincerely. "I kept saying I needed a break from writing. I guess God's giving me one."

"God, huh?"

"Yes, God. He and I have been spending a lot of time together the last six weeks or so."

"Oh, Darcy, you don't know how happy I am to hear that," Leanne said, her voice cracking.

"I think I do, a little."

Darcy hung up smiling, glad she'd said yes. She was tired of traveling but eager to see her friends again. She had missed

Talmedge, North Carolina a lot more than she realized. She brushed off the knees of her jeans and carried the phone to the house. She couldn't keep from smiling at the thought of seeing a certain café owner she'd missed, too.

Vince was more than a little surprised to hear Darcy was coming to North Carolina for the Fourth of July festival. When she left for home a few days after their argument at the waterfall, he didn't expect to see her again. That, coupled with the success of her appearance on John and Sherri Live—when no one was looking, he searched the Internet and found her book sales had skyrocketed since the TV exposure—made him think returning to Talmedge for a silly town festival would be way down on her to-do list.

Part of him couldn't wait to see her, while his rational side wished he'd get over this dangerous infatuation.

He was only kidding himself to think someone like her who was probably swimming in money and prestige would want anything to do with a backwoods fry cook, especially after their fight at the waterfall. She had accused him of taking advantage of Leanne and milking her for sympathy over Amber's death. In turn, he told her to stop feeling sorry for herself.

How much of what she said and wished she hadn't, he didn't know. He, on the other hand, meant every word. She had a perfect life; she was a spoiled princess and had no right to complain because her life wasn't exactly what she thought it should be. Whose was?

For the past six weeks, he couldn't get her out of his head. He thought of their argument occasionally, but usually when she crossed his mind—which was all too often for any sensible man—he thought of losing his hands in her wild tangle of mahogany hair, gazing into her chocolate brown eyes, listening to her throaty laugh, and basking in the impetuous smile that lit up her features.

In his mind, he kept seeing her emerge from the woods after one of her hikes to the waterfall, all sweaty and disheveled. He thought of the day she fell into his arms after he swept Maude off the porch. He imagined her waiting tables at the café and yelling orders back at him like she'd been doing it her whole life. He frowned when he thought of her ready opinions and quick tongue. He frowned even further when he remembered the curve of her mouth and the touch of her hand on his arm.

He hadn't been himself in the last few weeks. He forgot simple things he did every day without thinking, like salting eggs or ordering paper napkins and doggie bags. He was testy and short-tempered, even more so than usual. He knew the root of the problem. The last thing he was going to let himself do was fall in love with a writer from Cleveland who could never see the charm in his way of life.

Loving Amber had been the hardest thing he'd ever done. He had given her his whole heart, only to have it handed back to him piece by bitter piece. The price had been too high. He swore to himself he would never let that happen again. Emotions were totally within his control, and he watched his closely. He wouldn't be turned again by a pretty face.

During the Fourth of July celebration he would steer clear of Darcy Carter. Just because his heart raced at the thought of seeing her again didn't mean he had to act upon it. This infatuation would pass if he didn't humor it. Like a cough, a headache, or a barking dog; if ignored, it would eventually go away.

"Hello, anybody home?"

Vince's heart jumped at the familiar voice. He had been so deep in thought he hadn't even heard Darcy's car drive up. He should stay in the back of the house and let her figure out for herself Leanne wasn't home. She could sit out on the porch in the sunshine to wait, go for a walk to the waterfall, or get back in her fancy SUV and do a little sightseeing until Leanne got home. Instead he switched off the TV and headed toward the front of the house.

Darcy was standing in the parlor near the guest register. She had on a sleeveless blouse that hung loose around her waist. She wore khaki crop pants and a pair of worn huaraches. Her long, thick hair was held back on the sides with two clips, and she wore no makeup. She looked tired and sweaty from driving. He could have stood there and stared at her all day. She must have become aware of his gaze. She stopped rummaging in the oversized tote bag she carried everywhere and looked up. A big smile covered her face.

"Vince."

He nearly flinched at the sound of his name on her lips. He considered for a moment taking her in his arms and telling her he didn't want her to ever leave again; that Talmedge wasn't the same without her; the air didn't smell as sweet, the sky wasn't as blue, and the water on the rocks no longer soothed his tired soul.

Oh, for crying out loud, what was wrong with him?

"Leanne's not here," he growled.

"Well, I sort of gathered that."

He cleared his throat and tugged at the collar of his shirt. "She's grocery shopping in Winchester. That's all she gets done now that the inn's always booked. I told her to have June's niece do it for her, but she says she'll forget something she really needs and then she'll have to make the trip anyway."

Darcy's grin widened. "That sounds like Leanne."

"Everyone in town is anxious to see you," he said to fill the silence. "You wouldn't believe how that one little spot on TV impacted tourism, especially here."

"That's what Leanne said. During the interview I felt like a bug under a microscope, but it's good to know something good came of it."

"I imagine you sold a lot of books," he said, already knowing that she had.

She shrugged. "I suppose."

He arched his eyebrows. "A writer who doesn't care about selling books?"

Darcy turned to him and smiled. "I've learned there are more important things in life than selling books."

He smiled back. "Now you sound like Leanne."

"Thank you."

He wanted to ask her what had changed her attitude, but from the peaceful look on her face, he was afraid she'd tell him of some road to Damascus conversion. Then she would sound exactly like his sister.

"Hey, Vince, listen…"

"Yeah?"

"I'm sorry about the things I said at the waterfall before I went home. I was way out of line."

"You weren't the only one."

"I know, but that's no excuse. I've been thinking a lot about it since I got home."

He wanted to tell her he'd been thinking a lot, too. Only not about what she was thinking. "You have?" he said simply.

She set her tote bag on the floor and straightened up. He couldn't help but notice her long legs and narrow waist. He again resisted the urge to go to her and pull her into his arms.

"Yes, I have," she was saying. "I'm sorry I was so insensitive."

He shrugged. "I'm not always the easiest person in the world to talk to."

"I noticed."

A companionable silence lengthened between them. "I never thought this trip would change so many things for me," she confided.

"You mean this trip?" He indicated the bags at her feet.

"No. I meant coming here in the first place. I've been hundreds of places for conferences, retreats, and research trips. They were never anything more to me than business and I never expected anything more from this one."

Vince studied her for a moment, his hazel eyes contemplating. "What do you suppose made this one different?"

She lifted one shoulder. "Leanne, the inn, everybody at the Raven, or maybe it was me. I'm different, so the trip was different."

"What's different about you then?"

"Could we go sit somewhere to talk, maybe the back deck? I don't suppose Maude is out there sunbathing or anything is she?"

"No chance. It's too hot this time of year. You've got a couple of months before she comes back down from the mountains."

Will you still be here then? he wanted to ask.

Darcy exhaled in exaggerated relief. Vince stepped forward. "Let me put your bags away first."

"I'm not sure where Leanne is going to put me. I told her not to save a room for me, so I might have to bunk on the sofa."

He bent over and took her tote and overnight bag. "Well, then, we'll just stow this stuff behind the couch until Leanne gets here."

He headed toward the back of the house with Darcy on his heels. It felt good to have her back, even though he knew she hadn't come for him.

Darcy tried to quiet the butterflies in her stomach as she followed Vince into the family room. She had dreaded seeing him, while at the same time anticipating it more than she had a right to. Vince Ravenscraft had never shown any interest in her. His world was his café, and nearly everything else was an unwelcome intrusion. He had softened up somewhat in the weeks she spent at the inn, but she suspected he merely tolerated her for Leanne's sake.

He dropped her bags behind the couch in the family room and then motioned her toward the kitchen. "Want something to drink? I'm sure the fridge's stocked."

"Sure."

She walked into the kitchen ahead of him and went straight to the refrigerator. After six weeks away, she still felt as comfortable here as she did in her own house. While she dug inside for something to drink, Vince took two glasses out of the cabinet and filled them with ice. She backed out of the refrigerator and held up a plastic bag of lemons. "Shall we make some lemonade?" He shrugged and went to the drawer for Leanne's lemon squeeze.

Twice they brushed hands during the process of making the lemonade. Darcy couldn't ignore the electricity that went through her every time they made contact. Nor could she ignore the realization that her big house in Middleburg Heights no longer seemed like home after spending time again in Leanne's kitchen.

Not that it mattered. This wasn't her home, no matter how comfortable and familiar everything was—and everyone.

The back deck was draped in the cool shade of late afternoon. A slight breeze moved through the pines, blanketing Darcy and Vince in a tangy fragrance. They lowered themselves into two padded Adirondack chairs and gazed out at the mountains. Darcy sipped her lemonade, extremely aware of Vince beside her. She wanted the moment to last forever. At the same time, she knew sitting here next to him would never be enough to satisfy her.

Vince was the first to break the silence. "I think I'm the one who was insensitive that day at the waterfall."

Darcy turned her head to look at him.

"You were right. I haven't gotten over my guilt about Amber's death. I feel like I somehow profited from the accident. We were always fighting. She wanted out of Talmedge, and buying the café was out of the question. Then suddenly she was gone. I got a big insurance check, the house sold, and I had everything I wanted." He stopped talking and took a long drink of lemonade. He carefully set his glass down on the deck. He gazed out at the mountains.

Darcy watched his profile for a moment and then followed his gaze to the thick trees that blanketed the hills across from where they sat. She wanted to tell him she understood, but knew he wasn't through talking yet.

Finally he began again. "She was leaving me that night." He turned to look at her. "Did you know that? I never even told Hank or Leanne. They've never said anything to me, but they must have figured it out. I can't stop thinking that if I hadn't driven her away that night, she'd still be alive. We'd probably still be miserable, but at least she'd be alive."

Darcy reached across the space separating their chairs and covered his hand with hers. "You couldn't have kept her from leaving if she really wanted to go."

He turned his hand over and curled his fingers around hers. She tried not to think too much about the feel of his fingers encompassing hers. It was the first intimate gesture they had ever shared. Vince stared down at their clasped hands as if he realized it too, and then looked up at her face.

"Maybe not. Maybe she would have ended up leaving eventually, but if I had tried to make her stay that night she wouldn't have got in that accident. I didn't make any effort to stop her. I didn't say a word. I wanted her to leave." He looked back down at his fingers wrapped around Darcy's and squeezed gently. "I remember looking at her that night and thinking I didn't even know who she was. All I wanted was her out of my house and out of my life."

Darcy squeezed back. "Oh, Vince, you had no way of knowing what was going to happen."

Abruptly, he dropped her hand and stood up. He strode to the end of the deck and leaned against the railing close to the spot where she had climbed up to get away from the snake. "No, but I got what I wanted, didn't I?" He turned and glared at her for a moment before turning back to the mountains.

"You had nothing to do with her accident."

He didn't turn around. "The day after her accident, her mom met me at the funeral home. We made all the arrangements together. She was all busted up over it. You can imagine. She kept losing track of what she was saying, and the funeral director had to keep repeating stuff. She held my hand and cried. Every time she'd look at me, she'd say, 'Oh, Vince, I'm so sorry.' Then she'd start crying all over again. I kept holding her hand watching her cry and thinking, 'Why are you sorry for me? You're the one who lost her. I lost her a long time ago.' I couldn't even cry."

He turned around and leaned his hips against the railing. He crossed his arms over his chest and stared at a spot on the deck at his feet. "I felt bad for her mom, dad, her sisters, and all the relatives who came in, but I didn't really miss her. At first I was too mad. Then I didn't feel anything. It wasn't until the checks came in that I started feeling like a rotten jerk. That's when I knew it was my fault. Everybody else lost someone they loved. They lost their sister, their daughter, or their friend. I didn't lose anything. I gained my café—and my freedom."

Darcy got out of her chair and went over to him. She leaned against the railing close enough that she could feel the heat radiating off his body.

"It was all circumstances, Vince. It wasn't anything you did."

"Then why can't I get past it? Why am I incapable of appreciating what's right in front of me?"

She wondered what things he was referring to, but didn't have the nerve to ask. "Only you know the answer to that question," she said gently.

"I've never been any good at examining how I feel about things."

"Maybe it's time you start."

"Maybe I'm better off not knowing. Besides, I thought we came out here to talk about you."

"We can talk about whatever you want."

He leaned toward her and rested his elbow on the deck railing. "Then I'd rather talk about you."

Darcy froze at the intense look in his eyes. She could never tell when he was being playful and when he was being serious until after she put her foot in her mouth. "I think you've already figured out everything you need to know about me," she said.

"On the contrary, you're probably about the hardest person to figure out I've ever come across."

Again, she couldn't tell if he was paying her some sort of vague compliment or if he meant she was too frustrating to waste his time on.

"You're not exactly an open book."

"You know we could go on like this all day."

"I don't have anywhere else to be."

He chuckled and shook his head. "Let's finish our lemonade before the ice melts and you can tell me what's different about you.

Darcy followed him back to the Adirondack chairs and sat down. "There's really not that much to tell." She settled into her chair and picked up her glass. "A while back, someone pointed out to me that I was totally wrapped up in myself and my own concerns. I had this notion the world revolved around me. I realized my entire identity had become my writing. Without it, I had nothing, or no one."

The intensity in Vince's eyes was almost unnerving. She fastened her gaze on the glass in his hands and continued. "All the success in the world couldn't replace the relationship I was missing with God. I considered myself a Christian and prayed whenever I wanted something, but that was the extent of my relationship with

God. Over the years, I stopped needing things so I stopped talking to Him at all."

She looked back at Vince. "Is this making any sense?"

"Yes, perfect sense."

His expression had changed. She couldn't tell what he was thinking. "I know now I'm more than the books I write," she went on. "I'm still a writer and I'll probably get back to it someday, but there's more to me than that. Right now, I'm focusing on my fellowship with my Savior. Everything else will take care of itself."

Vince was staring at the trees again. Darcy didn't know anything about his relationship with God. According to Leanne, he had even sung in church before his problems with Amber. Had he, like her, reached the point in his life where he thought he was capable of handling his own problems without any input from God? She wanted to tell him God was right here waiting for him, with no strings attached, but she didn't know how to say it. She wished Leanne were here. Leanne would know exactly what to say.

"I think coming here the first time is what showed me how empty my life was," she said. "No, that's not true. I knew it before then. I knew it when my editor tried to get me to write Finding Mr..."

"Finding who?"

Darcy shook her head dismissively. "Oh, nothing. It was just a book I didn't want to write so I sort of came down here to get her off my back, but then I couldn't write the book I came here to write. You were right about what you said at the waterfall. I still haven't written either one of those books, and the world hasn't come to an end." She smiled broadly. "God showed me He still loves me. Even though I'd ignored Him for years, He was right there when I called on Him again. He's so merciful, Vince. I don't know what I'd do if He had given up on me the way I gave up on Him."

She stopped talking and relaxed back into her chair. A warm peace washed over her. She wasn't sure if it was the usual euphoria she always felt when she thought about her Savior's infinite mercy, or if her words had somehow ministered to him. Either way, she was thankful for the liberty to speak so freely and boldly, even without Leanne here for support.

Vince watched Darcy close her eyes against the summer sun and rest her head against the back of the chair. She was right, she was different; still hardheaded and quick-tongued, but confident in God instead of herself. When she first started talking about having nothing in her life besides her writing, he thought she was going to say that meeting him had made her realize how empty her life was. He could have related to that.

Before Darcy Carter waltzed into his diner last March, he never suspected anything was missing from his life. He had everything he wanted, or he thought he did. Now he knew he needed her, while she seemed perfectly content with only her newfound faith to fill the void in her life.

$$17$$

🍃 · 🍃 · 🍃 · 🍃

"So what's botherin' ya tonight?" Hank demanded with a wry smile.

Vince steadied the two-by-twelve board before Hank made the cut. The whir of the circular saw screamed against the grain of the board. Vince handed Hank the cut board and let the other half fall to the ground. "Nothing."

"Sounds like somethin' to me." Hank set the board in place against the risers. "Figured you'd be happy as a clam since you-know-who got back to town."

Vince made six quick shots with the nail gun, fastening the board into place. "Don't know who you-know-who is."

Hank chuckled as he unplugged the circular saw. "I think ya do."

Vince unstrapped the tool belt from around his waist and stood up. He stepped back and surveyed the completed job. Two of the steps on the back deck had worked themselves loose during the hard spring rains. Now that Leanne had guests arriving nearly every day and the big Fourth of July weekend coming up, she was insistent that a new set of steps be built.

She had several more chores around the inn for him before the weekend, and he was in no mood for Hank's games. "I guess you're talking about Darcy, since you got that cat-that-ate-the-canary grin on your ugly mug. But no, her bein' back in town has no bearing on any mood I may be in."

Hank's grin widened. "Okay, buddy, if you say so."

Vince had heard enough. Darcy had only been back in Talmedge one day and he was already getting those annoying looks in the café every time her name came up in conversation. He didn't know what gave everybody the notion he cared one whit about her coming to town to help with the festival.

He put the saw in the case and snapped it closed a little harder than necessary. He whirled around to face the older man. "Ya know, Hank, if ya got something to say, why don't ya just say it?"

Hank held his hands up in front of him, "Easy now. I was just havin' a little fun with ya; didn't mean to get ya all riled up."

"I think you did. You're insinuatin' something so you may as well speak your piece and be done with it."

Hank picked up a hammer and dropped it into the toolbox. Then he began to dismantle the workbench the two men had set up on the ground. Finally he turned to face Vince whose eyes were still shooting daggers at him. "Okay, if you wanna hear what I'm thinkin', I'll tell you. Ever since she showed up yesterday, you've been walkin' around here growlin' like an ole bear at anybody who looks crossways at ya. Only one thing gets a man worked up that way. The way I see it you got two options—either shut up about it and leave the rest of us alone or get in there," he wagged his head in the direction of the house, " and tell 'er what ya want."

"Who says I *want* anything?"

Hank sighed and went back to folding up the portable workbench. "You asked me what I thought, and I told ya. If you're gonna keep bein' hardheaded about it, I can't do no more for ya."

Vince snatched the workbench out of Hank's hands and leaned it against his own legs. "You know, you're real good at tellin' other guys how to deal with women. You couldn't even keep the one you had at home. She took off the first chance she got and never looked back. You couldn't be a man and stand up to her, and now, pfft, you've been tiptoein' around my sister for the past ten years."

Hank Haywood was a mild mannered, laid back fellow by nature. It took a lot to get him mad. Vince realized right away he had done what few others could.

Hank curled his large, calloused hands into fists and took an imperceptible step forward. When he spoke his voice was low and menacing, "Ain't no cause to bring Leanne into this."

Vince had never backed down from a confrontation in his life. Even though Hank was strong as an ox and Vince had spent the last three years of his life lifting not much more than a spatula, he looked forward to what was coming. "Why not? Everybody in town knows how you feel about her, 'cept maybe Leanne, and we all know you ain't got it in ya to do anything about it."

Hank took another step forward so that he was within an arm's reach of Vince. Vince braced himself. He was mad, and a good fistfight with his oldest friend might be just what the doctor ordered. To his surprise and dismay, Hank grabbed the workbench from in front of him. He scooped up the toolbox with his free hand and headed for the truck. Vince heard the toolboxes on the back of the truck slam open and closed, a little more clattering around, and the truck door opened and closed. The engine turned over and groaned as Hank searched for the right gear.

The tension went out of Vince's shoulders. It wasn't really fair to take his frustration out on Hank. If he was mad at anyone, it was himself. Darcy made it clear when they talked yesterday she was perfectly content with the way her life was going now. She didn't need to be writing. She didn't need to know how many copies of her books had sold since her television appearance. She didn't need him.

She was a totally different creature than the one who had jumped down his throat with both feet that day at the waterfall. He couldn't help but wonder if the peace she had found was available to him as well.

Leanne set a tray of cookies on the folding table she had set up in the front parlor. Janice Triplett, the treasurer of the Ladies' Auxiliary, took a cookie and eyed it speculatively. "I bet these aren't sugar free," she hissed to her sister-in-law Doris Unger, who didn't believe for a minute Janice had problems with her sugar or anything else. She'd been slipping away from one tragic ailment or another ever since she married Doris's brother, Harold Ray in 1961.

Leanne heard Janice's comment about the cookies as easily as everyone else in the room. "I have sugar-free cookies in the kitchen," she announced to the room at large. "I'll bring them right out."

"Don't bother," Janice grumbled. "I'll eat these. I guess a few won't kill me."

Doris rolled her eyes. Leanne smiled and filled the delicate china cups with coffee.

The Ladies' Auxiliary president, Alma Faye Williams stood up and cleared her throat. "Let me call this meeting to order by saying how much we appreciate Darcy Carter coming all this way to help make our Fourth of July celebration the best it's ever been."

Alma Faye faced Darcy and clapped her hands. The other three Ladies' Auxiliary office holders clapped enthusiastically.

Darcy smiled graciously, secretly wishing they would stop making such a big deal out of everything she said or did. Since she got into town, everyone in Talmedge had treated her like royalty. She would be glad when they all forgot about her six-minute segment on national TV. Apparently the rest of America already had.

"Now," Alma Faye said after the applause died away, "let's bring our esteemed guest up to speed on what we have planned for this weekend. The Boy Scouts are organizing the parade. Marv Hastings, the den leader, called me last night…"

"Alma Faye, shouldn't I read the minutes from our last meeting before we get into all that?" the secretary, Evelyn Rigsby, Marv Hasting's mother-in-law wanted to know.

"That isn't really necessary, Evelyn. This isn't a real meeting. It's just us officers getting together with Darcy…"

"But you called the meeting to order," Evelyn pointed out. "That makes it a real meeting, and if we're going to have a real meeting, we should do it properly."

"Oh, for pete's sake," Doris said. "We don't want to be here all night, Evelyn. None of the other members are here, so it isn't a real meeting."

Evelyn started rummaging in her briefcase for her parliamentary procedure handbook. "Minutes are to be read at the start of each meeting," she mumbled, her head buried in her briefcase.

"Let her read the minutes," Janice said, "or we'll never get out of here."

"We don't have time," Alma Faye said. She smiled at Darcy. "Miss Carter has taken the time to be here tonight, and I think we should be considerate of her schedule."

Evelyn stopped leafing through her handbook. Janice stopped scraping the sprinkles off a cookie. All eyes in the room turned to Darcy. Darcy looked helplessly at Leanne. Leanne promptly turned and went into the kitchen.

"However you usually run your meetings is fine with me," she said, not wanting to ruffle any feathers.

"So we should read the minutes," Evelyn said triumphantly.

"This isn't a real meeting," Doris repeated.

Janice took a huge bite of her cookie and reached for another.

Hank couldn't remember the last time he'd been so mad at anyone. He'd had a problem with his temper in his younger days, but that was before God came into his life and made him a new creature. The old Hank wouldn't have resisted smashing his fist into Vince Ravenscraft's smug little face. As it was now, it took every ounce of resolve he had not to do just that. The only thing that kept him from it was the fear of Leanne's reaction. She loved her brother, and even though she gave him as hard a time as anyone, she would never forgive Hank for losing his cool and punching his lights out.

The last time he'd been angry enough to raise his fist to someone was when Sue Ellen left him. To say he was surprised by her departure was the understatement of the decade. He truly had not seen it coming. In his mind the two of them had the perfect marriage. He left for work every morning before sunup. His contracting business was growing at such a rate he had to turn down work. Sue Ellen had recently earned her real estate license and was working in Winchester. She loved the job. The month before, she had sold her first house and Hank took her to Asheville to celebrate at one of those posh restaurants she liked but they could seldom afford.

No, Hank never saw it coming.

After nine years of marriage, she announced she didn't know who he was anymore. He was stifling her. For her own sanity, she had to get away. Hank argued, cried, cajoled, and suggested counseling. Sue Ellen wanted no part of it. She got an apartment in Winchester where she could reevaluate where her life was headed. Since Sue Ellen wasn't forthcoming with details such as the location of the apartment, Hank did a little detective work. A buddy who worked at the post office found out the apartment where she was living was leased to a Mr. Steven Grooms. A little more investigating involving a few more buddies revealed Mr. Steven Grooms had not sub-let the apartment to Sue Ellen as Hank had hoped, but was living there with her. So much for alone time to reevaluate her life!

By the time Hank realized his loving wife was now his not-so-loving ex, Sue Ellen had become Mrs. Steven Grooms and moved to Marietta, Georgia where the two of them bought a real estate agency. He hadn't heard from Sue Ellen in years, but he'd heard through the grapevine that she was the mother of two girls, and that she and Steven Grooms had a lock on the north Georgia real estate market.

He eyed himself with disgust in the rearview mirror as he backed out of the Ravenswood Inn's driveway. Vince was right; he was the last person in the world who needed to be giving anybody relationship advice. He'd lost Sue Ellen and was terrified of Leanne.

He vaguely remembered Leanne as a tall, gangly girl with a gap-toothed grin who often came to the house to play with his sister, Iris. Neither girl served no greater purpose as far as he could tell than to make prank phone calls, giggle at jokes only they found amusing, and generally disrupt the general peace of his home. Then he woke up one morning to find he was ten years older, his marriage had just blown up in his face, Iris had earned a B.A. from the University of North Carolina Charlotte, and Leanne's lopsided grin had gone from annoying to endearing.

She was taking care of her mother by this time. Hank hired Vince to work for him, hanging drywall, roofing, and general sub-contract work. Much of those early years after Sue Ellen's departure were spent at the Ravenscraft home. Leanne always had dinner waiting when he dropped Vince off for the day, and she would invite him in to eat with the family. He didn't realize until much later how much those nights in her kitchen helped heal his broken heart. He didn't know how he could have stood going home alone night after night to his lonely trailer, the only thing he could afford after Sue Ellen cleaned him out.

His business continued to grow while Mrs. Ravenscraft's health declined. Vince married Amber, and Hank had a standing invitation at the Ravenscraft home for dinner every night. He seldom took Leanne up on it, but the nights he did, he helped with the dishes after Mrs. Ravenscraft retired to her room. Before long she was gone, leaving Leanne at the house alone. Hank wanted to say something then; something to let her know how important she was to him; how much she had helped him through the darkest time of his life, and he was here for her if she needed someone.

He still was unclear on how he saw his relationship with Leanne when Amber was killed. Vince moved back home and Leanne once again became someone's caregiver. Hank couldn't very well waltz in and make demands when her own brother needed her so badly.

Before he knew it, several more years went by. He stayed in close contact with the family and still had dinner at the house at least once a week. He worked with Vince every day until Vince bought the café. Leanne renovated the house, giving Hank plenty of opportunities to see her. But she was busy, and seemingly satisfied with the way things were working out. No time for herself and certainly no time to cozy up to the handyman who kept the pipes from backing up and re-roofed the house last summer.

He took what he could and expected nothing more. He thrilled at the sound of her honest laugh whenever he or Vince cut up about something. He secretly admired the way she walked across a room. He respected her commitment to her Heavenly Father and making the inn a success, in that order.

Well, enough was enough. He wasn't getting any younger and neither was Leanne. He was through tiptoeing. He was through finding satisfaction in taking what he could get in small doses and expecting nothing more. He wanted more of a relationship than a phone call whenever something went wrong at the inn and Vince couldn't get to it in a reasonable amount of time.

He had just turned the wheel and slipped the clutch out of reverse when he slammed on the brakes, throwing his thermos into the floorboard and rattling the toolboxes on the back of the truck. If everybody in town except Leanne Ravenscraft knew how he felt about her, he may as well fill her in, too. If she didn't want him, well, that was her prerogative. She could turn him down; he wasn't a stranger to rejection, but he wouldn't let himself be taken by surprise anymore. It was time he started acting like a man and stopped letting circumstances dictate his life.

He stomped the gas pedal to the floor and slung an arc of gravel behind him as he pulled back into the driveway. He braked a mere two inches from the rear bumper of Evelyn Rigsby's Dodge Caravan. He jumped out of the truck and hurried up the walk he helped Vince lay three years ago. He bounded onto the porch and threw open the front door.

Darcy Carter and the four queens of the Ladies' Auxiliary, as most everyone in Talmedge referred to them behind their backs, looked up in alarm.

Alma Faye Williams put her hand over her heart. "Lands sake, Hank Haywood, you like to've scared us all to death. We're trying to have a meeting."

Leanne entered the parlor, carrying a tray of unappetizing looking cookies. She followed everyone's gaze to where Hank was standing in the doorway between the foyer and the parlor. "What's the matter, Hank? Did you forget something?"

He remembered he was still wearing his cap and snatched it off his head. "Yes, yes I did." He swallowed hard. Alma Faye looked annoyed at the interruption. Evelyn Rigsby held her coffee cup halfway to her mouth. Janice Triplett and Doris Unger, the sisters-in-law who openly supported and adored each other, but gossiped mercilessly to anyone who would listen about the other every chance they got, stared at him from their places at the table. Darcy's face was the only one that showed a modicum of patience, and something resembling amusement.

Leanne set the tray of cookies on the table. Her brow furrowed in concern. Hank could imagine how he looked standing there in his muddy clothes on her clean East Room rug, twisting his cap and staring anxiously at her.

"Hank..."

"I forgot..."

"Yes?"

"I..."

"Well for heaven's sake, Hank, spit it out," Alma Faye said. "Can't you see we've got things to take care of here?"

Hank kept his eyes fastened on Leanne. "I forgot to tell you— I..." His feet finally came unglued from their spot near the doorway. He advanced another step into the parlor. Out of the corner of his eye, he saw Vince coming down the hall toward them.

"What is it, Hank?" he asked tersely.

His words spurred Hank to action. He practically lunged across the room and pulled Leanne into his arms.

Leanne gasped as his clumsy embrace knocked the wind out of her. Hank didn't stop to consider her stunned expression or the six other pairs of eyes in the room watching his every move. "Leanne Ravenscraft," he said with a forcefulness he didn't know he had, "I've been meanin' to tell you..."

Leanne leaned back from his embrace so she could see his face. The shock and concern in her almost made him lose his nerve. She probably thought he had come to deliver some kind of bad news. She would be blown away by his proclamation. He considered the range of emotions that would register on her pretty face; shock, confusion, maybe even disappointment. What if she refused him in front of Vince and Darcy and the Ladies' Auxiliary? What if she laughed in his face? Was he ready for that kind of public humiliation? Then he remembered his vow to himself in the truck. Circumstances weren't dictating his life anymore. Besides, he'd come too far. He had to say something. Leanne's eyes were searching his face for an explanation for his strange behavior. She probably thought he'd lost his mind. Well, he had—and his heart, too.

"Leanne, I love you. I always have," he said in a rush.

"Well, it's about time," Alma Faye exclaimed behind him. "I never thought he'd get around to it."

"Shhh," Janice hissed, leaning forward in her chair to see around Doris.

Leanne put her hands on his shoulders, "Hank, I…"

Hank realized he was grinning like an idiot. At the same time he felt tears stinging his eyelids. Whether she rejected him or not was neither here nor there; he wasn't leaving this room without going for broke. "Marry me, Leanne. Make me the happiest man in the world."

Leanne's expression turned from amazement to joy in the span of a heartbeat. "Oh, Hank, I had no idea…" She glanced over his shoulder at Vince standing in the doorway. She became aware of Darcy, Alma Faye, Janice, Doris, and Evelyn sitting and standing around the parlor, holding their breath and waiting for her answer.

Hank tightened his arms around her. "I know I've been a fool. I wouldn't blame you if you told me it's too late, but I hope you won't. I hope you'll say yes. Leanne, I love you."

"Oh, Hank." She melted into him, and her tears dampened his cheek. "I love you, too, you big lug." She tightened her arms around his neck. Hank put his hands on either side of her face.

"Does that mean you'll marry me?"

Leanne nodded through her tears, her answer caught in her throat. Hank brought her face to his and kissed her as if his life depended on it, which it almost did.

"Woohoo!" Vince yelled from the doorway. The Ladies' Auxiliary burst into applause.

Leanne broke away from Hank, her eyes moist and cheeks flushed. She put a hand on her cheek. She turned away from Hank to face the others. "Oh, my, I don't know what to say."

Doris was the first to recover. She was already making a list in her head of all the people she needed to call the instant she got home. *That old stick in the mud, Hank Haywood finally got up the nerve to propose to Leanne Ravenscraft.*

She jumped out of her chair. "You don't need to say anything, Leanne, honey." She pulled Leanne away from Hank and into her own arms. "Congratulations, I'm so happy for you." She turned to Hank and slapped him on the arm. "About time. Where's the ring?"

Hank ducked his head, embarrassed. He hadn't even thought of a ring. So much for the romantic proposal every girl dreamed of. He hoped Leanne wouldn't hold it against him.

Darcy, Alma Faye, Janice and Evelyn came forward, everyone kissing and congratulating at once. Finally the crowd parted, and Vince wrapped his arms around Leanne and lifted her off her feet. He set her down and turned to Hank. The two men stared at each other. Vince extended his hand. Hank looked at it for a moment before reaching out to take it. Vince grabbed Hank's hand and pulled him into a one-arm hug. He mumbled into his ear, "If I'd known that's all it'd take, I would a chewed you out years ago."

"And if this had a turned out any other way, you'd still have a stompin' coming."

The two men separated. The women in the room had no indication of the tension that had been between them outside.

For the next few minutes, the reading of the minutes and festival preparations were forgotten as the Ladies' Auxiliary pressed Leanne and Hank for details of their romance, and now, upcoming wedding.

Darcy and Vince wisely kept out of the melee. Tears sprang to Darcy's eyes at the happiness she saw on Leanne's face. *No one deserves it more*, she thought. Her gaze fell on Vince, standing on the other side of Hank and Leanne. He felt her eyes on him and looked up. Darcy couldn't read his expression although she was sure he wanted to say something. Reluctantly she looked away. She loved him; she knew that now, but it hurt too much to know that he could never forgive himself for his first wife's death and would never love her back.

Hank and Leanne retired to the family room for their first conversation as lovers.

Darcy and the Ladies' Auxiliary tried to get back to the business of putting the finishing touches on the Fourth of July parade and festivities. No one had much luck concentrating. They couldn't stop speculating over what had finally spurred Hank to action after all these years.

Vince kept his part in the matchmaking to himself. A firm believer that people were better off figuring out their own affairs without the interference of a bunch of busybodies, he never would have said anything to Hank tonight had Hank not gotten under his skin about what he was or wasn't thinking about Darcy.

He fixed himself a sandwich and carried it and a bottle of water to the little TV room that had become his hideaway from the inn's guests. He was happy for Leanne. He was even happy for Hank. They both deserved to grow old together. They'd wasted too much time already.

He flicked the remote and settled into his recliner as the theme music for SportsCenter filled the tiny room. A running ticker of sports scores for college baseball games ran across the bottom of the screen, but his distracted brain couldn't decipher the abbreviated school names before they disappeared from view. What was happening to him? He took a bite of his sandwich and realized it was almost gone without him even tasting it. He set the remainder of the sandwich on the plate and put the plate on the coffee table.

He was truly happy for his sister. She deserved happiness, and he had no doubt that Hank Haywood would provide it. So why did his heart feel like there was a huge gaping hole in the middle of it?

A union between Hank and Leanne would mean freedom for him. He would no longer be the man in Leanne's life. She wouldn't wake him up in the middle of a spring flash flood to tell him the sump pump was overflowing into the back yard. She wouldn't bother him with renovation ideas and projects that could easily fill every spare moment of his day if he allowed it. Every little thing concerning the Ravenswood Inn would become Hank Haywood's problem. Yes, Leanne would have it made in the shade. And Hank, who loved nothing more than being at her beck and call, would be in hog heaven.

Of course Vince would have to move out. He couldn't keep living with a couple of newlyweds. Knowing his sister, she would want children somewhere down the line. Hank was forty-six and unconcerned with such matters, but Leanne was probably already picking out baby names and decorating a nursery in her head. He smiled at the thought of Leanne with a baby in her arms. He could picture the smile on her face as she bent down to kiss a soft downy head; he'd be an uncle. He never thought he'd live to see that happen. The Ravenswood Inn would be filled with the laughter of children again. It had been too long.

The café earned him a good enough living that he could afford to buy a modest home. He wouldn't go far. He wanted to be within a mile or so of the café, and he couldn't imagine moving so far away from the inn that he couldn't pop in and see his nieces and nephews whenever the mood struck him. Things would change in the next few months, of that he was sure, but everything for the better.

So why did he feel so rotten?

The warm smile from thinking of Leanne and her babies faded from his lips. He threw the room into silence by clicking the TV remote, stood up, and went to the window. Feminine laughter came from the front of the house. How much longer was that Ladies' meeting going to last? Those old biddies could discuss the yellow off of cheese. He should go in there and rescue Darcy. She was probably worn out from all the talk of cake walks, three legged races, chili cook-offs, and whatever else they'd come up with to fill the seventy-two hours of the upcoming holiday weekend.

Darcy—just thinking of her made his heart swell in his chest. He'd been attracted to her from the very first time he saw her and threatened her with legal action for blocking the dumpster behind the café with her little SUV.

He held her at arm's length as long as he could. He refused to notice her wit and sense of humor or the budding friendship between her and Leanne. He didn't acknowledge the unreasonable jealousy that rose up in him every time one of his male customers flirted with her, or the way her laughter could make him smile when he was so irritated he wished she'd just go back to where she came from.

Darcy Carter didn't belong here. She was an outsider. It was hard enough for women born to the mountains to love them enough to stay. Amber was a local girl, as was Hank's Sue Ellen. Neither of them could bear the thought of rocking away their old age on a front porch overlooking the haze-cloaked mountains. Like them, Darcy would grow to resent the man who stuck her here in this valley where the houses were shoved up against the hillsides and rockslides changed the geography of the land every few years. She would miss her social calendar. She would miss art openings and poetry readings and whatever else women from her circle did for entertainment. They were from two different parts of the globe. They had nothing in common besides a mild attraction for the other. Most of all, she would blame him that she had gone from appearing on national television to washing the grease out of his clothes every night. After the life she'd lived, how could she possibly find fulfillment in the arms of a yokel fry cook?

The Ladies' Auxiliary meeting finally broke up around nine. It was another hour before Hank left the Ravenswood. No matter how worn out she was from the ladies' meeting, Darcy couldn't wait to talk to Leanne. Both of them had things to do in the morning and planned to get up early, but couldn't help chatting and laughing until well after midnight.

Darcy was so happy for Leanne. She was the sweetest, most kind-hearted person she had ever met and deserved the love and adoration of a man like Hank. Darcy lay in bed that night and stared at the ceiling, replaying the scene in the East Room in her mind. She smiled at the memory of Hank's panicked face when he came into the room. None of them had a clue what he was up to, least of all, Leanne.

Sleep wasn't coming so she switched on the lamp by the bed and reached for her Bible. She had read more Scripture in the past two months than in her entire adult life. God had been so gracious and patient with her. The last ten years had been exciting and productive; everything she put her hand to had proven successful. She hadn't even noticed God's blessings showering down around her. If her life had not gone the way she wanted, she would have blamed God. But since everything came up roses again and again, she attributed it to talent and good fortune. The Bible warned that no man earned a place in heaven based on good works lest he glory in himself. Darcy realized now she had been doing exactly that. Instead of seeing her writing as a God-given gift to glorify Him, she had gloried in her skills and timing.

She turned out the light and lay back against the pillows. She was truly blessed. She was a child of the maker of heaven and earth. She had a home waiting for her in glory. Her family loved her. Her career brought her fulfillment, a touch of fame, and a good living.

She thought of Leanne downstairs probably staring at her own ceiling, too excited to sleep. After all these years, she knew Hank loved her; she would live out the rest of her life with him.

What about me, Lord? Darcy prayed before she could stop herself. It wasn't right that she ask for more when she already had so much. She closed her eyes and willed herself to sleep. She wouldn't ask God to make Vince love her back. She wouldn't wait for some grand romantic gesture. That fell under the category of free will. If Vince loved her and wanted to do something about it, he would have to move without any prompting on her part or that of the Almighty.

18

The first person through the café door when June switched the sign from _Closed_ to _Open_ was Larry Meeks. Larry drove the Pepsi truck, and personally exchanged the café's empty containers for full ones every three days. Even on the mornings the café wasn't part of his route, he stopped for breakfast on his way to the Pepsi warehouse in Winchester.

"So when's the nuptials, Old Man?" he called out to Vince as he swung one leg over a stool and settled himself at the counter.

June and Missy snapped their heads around to see Vince. "You're getting married?" Missy squealed.

Vince glared at the three of them, doing nothing to conceal his irritation. This town was too blamed small. "No," he snapped, "Leanne and Hank. How'd you find out?" he asked Larry.

Larry chuckled. "Are you kidding? The whole town knows about it. My phone started ringing a little after nine last night. Tammy's sister, Lavita belongs to the Ladies' Auxiliary. She called Tammy and said Doris Unger called her and told her that Hank Haywood barged into your house last night during their meeting and proposed."

Missy squealed again. "How romantic!"

"Congratulations, Vince." June wiped tears from her eyes with the corner of her apron.

"Oh, for pity's sake," Vince grumbled. "Leanne ain't the first person to get married."

"The phone rang three more times after Lavita hung up in the space of a half hour," Larry continued. "I finally made Tammy turn off the ringer so I could get to sleep. Lavita's fit to be tied because she wasn't at the meeting. She called Alma Faye Williams and complained that it wasn't right to be having a meeting without all the members present. Well, Alma Faye said it wasn't really a meeting, and Lavita knew about it and coulda been there if she wanted, but Lavita's still miffed. I told Tammy she was just mad 'cause she missed seeing Hank Haywood on one knee proposing to Leanne."

"He wasn't on one knee," Vince interrupted. "He was standing on two feet like any sensible man would. Now are you gonna order anything or not?"

The front door jangled as two more men entered. "Way to go, Vince," Howard Rice from the sheriff's department, called out. "Ya finally married off your big sister."

"I never thought Hank'd have the nerve to do it," the other man said.

"Nerve, nothing" Larry said from his stool. "The boy's done lost his mind. Had it made, he did, and now he's done blew it. No offense, Vince," he said quickly. "Your sister's a good woman, but every woman becomes a ball and chain the minute you put a ring on her finger."

"Watch what you say, Larry," June exclaimed. "I'm the one's going to be bringing you your food here in a few minutes."

Larry held a hand up as a peace offering. "Well, of course, I wasn't talking about you or Missy."

Neither woman looked mollified.

Vince shook his head and tuned out their conversation. Talmedge would be buzzing with this news until the wedding. He hoped for his sake, it would be soon. The last thing he wanted to do was field questions and congratulations intended for the happy couple.

"Pull your group over there behind the fire trucks," Dale Wagoner said into his megaphone and motioned wildly with his free hand. No one was listening to him. He'd been here all day, and if people didn't start doing what he said, the parade wouldn't be ready to start until Labor Day.

It was Saturday afternoon, the Fourth of July. The parade would start behind the abandoned feed and grain and make its way through town where it would end on the football field behind the high school. The fireworks display was already set up there for after dark. This was the first parade in Talmedge in over twenty years.

The town and surrounding county were crawling with tourists. Every business in the area was ecstatic over the extra business. The churches had set up booths at the festival to sell baked goods and hand out free water. The festival had been a huge success, and would culminate tonight with the fireworks display. Dale was as excited as anybody for the boon Talmedge was experiencing, but he vowed he would never again let the mayor, Herb Forsythe, rope him into directing the parade, even if he was his brother-in-law.

"Dale. Yo, Dale."

Dale groaned and turned around. Vince Ravenscraft was weaving his way through a Brownie troop, his hand firmly holding onto that of a tall, gorgeous brunette. Darcy Carter, Dale hoped. He was one of the few residents of Talmedge who hadn't seen Darcy's appearance on the John and Sherri Live show or run into her anywhere in town.

"'Bout time," Dale growled at Vince over the heads of two dozen or so Brownies. "The Ravenswood's float is up that way behind the Grand Marshall," he said, pointing. "You can't miss the sun glinting off Herb's bald head." Herb, the Grand Marshall, was sitting in a brand new, air conditioned Caddy that had been sent over from the GM dealer in Winchester while Dale was out here in the blazing sun making sure his parade went off without a hitch. The car dealer had also graciously sent a brand new pickup truck to pull the wagon that held the queen and her court—none too graciously to Dale's way of thinking since the newly crowned queen was the car dealer's own daughter.

Vince came to a stop in front of him. Darcy Carter looked winded and sweaty from the hike across the hot field. "I couldn't close the café till after one," Vince said. "Don't blame me that our esteemed mayor and the Ladies' Auxiliary decided to have this thing during the most profitable weekend the café's ever seen. The tourists wouldn't leave."

"I imagine nobody wanted to go out into this heat. At least we finally got some cloud cover headed this way. Hopefully, it'll lower the temperature. By the way, y'all did a fine job with that float."

"Thanks. Hank and me have been working on it all week. I thought Leanne was crazy when she suggested we set the swing and arbor from the back yard on the wagon, but—"

"Dale Wagoner!" a woman shrieked. Dale, Vince, and Darcy turned in the direction of the voice.

Dale groaned audibly.

"Do you have any idea what you've done?" the redhead demanded. "You can't put the children from the dance studio behind those fire trucks. They're going to be performing some of their routines and they won't be able to hear the music over the sound of those sirens. I can't imagine why a sensible person would want fire trucks in a parade in the first place. Who cares about them?"

"A lot of folks want to see what their tax dollars are paying for."

"Well, they can't be near my dancers," she repeated. "The best place for us would be in the front."

Dale wiped a weary hand across his sweaty brow. "The boy scouts are in the front. They're the ones who organized this thing. You can switch places with the bank. Their nice quiet little float will be between your dancers and the fire trucks. How's that grab you?"

"You don't have to get snotty, Dale. If your brother-in-law wasn't the mayor, you never would have got this job in the first place." She turned and flounced away.

Dale shook his head at her retreating back, and then faced Vince. "Like any sane person would want to do this. Well, anyway, what are you still doing here, Vince? Go get on your float. This parade can't start without Miss Carter." He nodded politely at Darcy.

Then he slapped his forehead. "Lookee there, who's the genius putting the marching band behind those horses? Have they ever heard the word 'stampede'?" He raised the megaphone to his lips. "What are you doin' over there?" He took off running across the field toward a group of mounted horsemen.

Vince smiled at Darcy. "Poor ole Dale, I wouldn't want to be in his shoes for nothing today."

Darcy smiled back. The whole week had been fun for her. She had never been so closely associated with a festival and parade before. She'd learned a lot, while at the same time, had a good time watching everyone involved get on everyone else's nerves. The whole world might love a parade, but she hoped this was as close as she ever got to another one.

What she enjoyed most about the week was being at the inn with Leanne and Hank—and Vince. Ever since Hank's proposal Monday night Vince had been more open and animated than she'd ever seen him. She could tell he was annoyed by all the attention he got everywhere he went, answering the most inane questions from curious townspeople, but at home behind closed doors, he let his hair down and had fun. He teased Hank and Leanne about babies and sending him out into the cold dark night without a roof over his head. Leanne had assured him the Ravenswood was his home, and he never should feel like he had to move. Vince had laughed and insisted he had no desire to live under the same roof as a couple of newlyweds with ten years to make up for. Leanne had blushed down to her toes and hadn't brought the subject up again.

This morning Leanne sent Darcy into town early to make sure Vince closed up the café in time to meet their float on the parade grounds. The café had been packed when she arrived, and like Vince told Dale, no one made a move for the door when Vince turned the sign to *Closed* at one o'clock. Only after they refused service and practically begged people to get up out of their comfortable—and cool—booths did the place begin to clear out. It took another hour to clean up. By then, Vince and Darcy were good and late. They didn't even know where their float was.

"It can't be that hard to spot," Vince had said as they walked through the back lots from the café to the parade grounds. When they arrived, they were amazed to see how many people were already there. Every high school in the county had sent a marching band. Two banks, one grocery store, the public library, the Boy Scout and Girl Scout troops, and eleven 4-H clubs were represented. The county newspaper had a float and a few reporters were on foot circulating through the crowd interviewing people. Two sheriff's cruisers were ready to roll with lights flashing. Howard Rice was riding shotgun in the first cruiser, ready to throw candy to the children assembled for the parade. A dog groomer was lining up with three volunteers and eight dogs that apparently hadn't spent much time on the end of a leash. Ten members of an equestrian club were shuffling around in full regalia in the middle of the crowd. The Veterans of Foreign Wars looked like they were wilting on their float in the middle of the field.

"Someone should get those old men and all those dogs into the shade," Darcy observed as she and Vince hurried in the direction of the Ravenswood's float. "It's so hot out here."

"Don't worry, Dale's right. Look at those clouds over there. It'll probably rain on all of us anyway."

"Don't say that. That will be terrible."

Vince glanced at his watch. "It's almost three. We need to find Leanne. Come on." He grabbed her hand and pulled her through the crowd.

Despite the heat and humidity, a chill traveled down Darcy's spine.

Thirty hot, grueling minutes later, Tyler, the busboy from the café, turned the key in the ignition of Vince's truck that would pull the Inn's float. "I hope that boy doesn't strip the gears," Vince grumbled from his spot behind the swing.

"Don't worry," Hank said from where he sat next to Leanne on the swing. "He's an old farm boy. He's probably been driving since he was eight."

Vince glared at the back of Tyler's head through the glass. Tyler turned in the seat and gave all of them a thumb's up.

"Y'all should've let me drive. He's not even watching where he's going."

"You're part of the Ravenswood, Vince," Leanne reminded him. "Your place is on the float with me. Now, relax and smile like I showed you last night. We're only going two miles an hour."

"Yeah, so was the Titanic."

The parade slowly inched its way off the field and onto Talmedge's main street. It looked like most of the county, along with a record number of tourists had turned out. Darcy was thrilled for the Boy Scouts and the Ladies' Auxiliary that everything had turned out so well. She gazed anxiously at the ominous clouds behind her and hoped the rain would hold off until after the fireworks display.

The Ravenswood's float had been designed to look like a country garden. Potted plants were placed around the garden swing and arbor where Leanne and Hank sat. A four-foot long garden path of creek rocks led to the bench. Darcy and Vince stood behind the lovebirds, smiling and waving. Well, Darcy was smiling and waving. Vince seldom took his eyes off the back of Tyler's head. All along the parade route, well wishers called up their congratulations to Leanne and Hank. Poor Hank got all kinds of advice from husbands. His face was as red as a beet by the time they turned the first corner on their way to the grandstands.

A crack of thunder sounded in the distance. Leanne flinched and looked over her shoulder at Vince. "Oh, dear, you don't think it'll rain yet, do you?"

Vince stopped glowering at Tyler long enough to study the darkening sky. "It's moving pretty fast."

Hank squeezed Leanne's hand. "I'm sure it'll hold off till we're through."

Leanne smiled gratefully at her future husband.

Vince rolled his eyes.

Tanner Tackett had the most important job in the parade. He knew because his grandpa had told him so. Wearing the black tuxedo his brother Colin had worn for a wedding when Tanner was only three, he carried a short handled shovel Grandpa had cut down for him and pulled his little red wagon. Ahead of him was the equestrian club of which Grandpa was president. The horses were so tall and their hooves made such a loud noise on the pavement, any other boy in the first grade would have been scared of them. But Tanner wasn't scared. Grandpa had been putting him and Colin on horses since they were tiny babies. Tanner loved the horses, and he loved Grandpa. When Grandpa told him what he wanted Tanner to do in the parade, Colin had laughed, but Tanner hadn't. He was proud Grandpa had asked him and not Colin. That proved he wasn't a baby anymore. Now that he was seven years old, Grandpa knew he could handle the job. The first mess happened while they were still on the parade grounds. Grandpa had a wheelbarrow waiting because he didn't want to fill up Tanner's wagon before the parade even started. He showed Tanner a quick, easy way to scoop up as much of what the horse left behind as possible and keep on going.

"The parade's not going to stop for you, Tanner," Grandpa had warned. "It's scoop, dump, and go. Got it?"

"Got it," Tanner announced proudly.

Mom took a picture of him in his tuxedo with his shovel and wagon, and the parade began. A half a block later, Tanner still hadn't scooped up anything. People smiled and waved and took his picture as he walked along. Some big kids laughed at him. He didn't care, his job was important. He pulled his wagon and kept his eyes on the back ends of the horses for any telltale signs.

Up the street, the grandstand came into view. A man and a lady sat there and introduced the floats and groups to the crowd as they marched by. There was also a television camera. The parade was being televised into all the homes in the county on the closed circuit channel Tanner never watched. Grandma had set the VCR before they left the house and when Tanner got home after the fireworks, he was going to watch the parade on TV, especially himself in his tuxedo. He hoped at least one of the horses would cooperate so Colin and Grandpa could see how hard he worked while everyone else was enjoying the parade.

He didn't hear the thunder over the sound of the marching bands. He didn't notice the adults gazing anxiously at the sky. Who cared about a little thunderstorm? He loved playing in the rain. When Mom was at work and the babysitter wasn't paying attention, he and Colin always sneaked outside when it rained. They were always good and drenched before the babysitter caught them and made them come back in the house and change their clothes.

Through the forest of horses' legs, Tanner saw a horse at the front of the group make a mess. "Don't walk through the horses, Tanner," he remembered Grandpa saying. "Wait until they're out of the way before you clean it up."

So Tanner kept following until all the horses were clear, then he let go of his wagon and ran forward to scoop up the pile. Another horse lifted its tail. Tanner grabbed the wagon's handle and hurried along. He heard the engine of the antique car behind him. He knew the owner of that fancy black car didn't want to drive through a horse's mess.

Just as he reached out with his shovel to scoop up the second mess, a crash of thunder shook the ground beneath his feet. One of the horses in the middle of the equestrian group whinnied. Another reared up. Its rider shouted a command. The other horses shuffled out of the way. More shouts went up from among the horses' riders.

A handful of heavy raindrops hit the street in front of him. Tanner heard Grandpa call out. He looked up. Two of the horses at the back of the group were backing toward him. Their riders were squeezing their legs around the horses' bodies and telling them to calm down. Lightning zigzagged across the sky. A shout went up in the crowd. Just when the riders had their horses quieted down, thunder crashed and the rain came down in a deluge.

None of the horses were moving forward now. The people on the side of street were shouting to each other. Some of them opened umbrellas but most of them were unprotected from the rain. Two teenage girls broke from the crowd and ran into the street on their way to the awning of the beauty shop across the street where Grandma got her hair done. Tanner watched in disbelief as they ran straight through the equestrian group. You weren't supposed to walk through the horses. Hadn't their grandpas taught them that?

The horses didn't like it either. When one of the girls ran directly in front of a horse, it whinnied and backed up, bumping into another horse. That horse backed up further and hit the horse behind it. Most of the people watching the parade didn't see what was going on with the horses. The rain was coming down in buckets now and everyone was shouting and running for cover, even the people with umbrellas. Tanner thought he heard Grandpa's voice over the rain and the crowd but couldn't be sure. He looked up and saw two horses backing up fast, headed straight for him. Tanner froze in his tracks. He didn't know what to do. Those horses would trample all over his wagon. It was the only wagon he had. When the first horse was only a half pace away, he felt two large hands lift him off his feet and start running. Tanner craned his neck but couldn't see his rescuer until he was thrown into the antique car behind him.

Then Grandpa was at the driver's door. "Hey, buddy, you all right?" he shouted to be heard over the rain beating on the car's roof.

Tanner nodded. "I didn't run through the horses, Grandpa."

"You sure didn't, buddy. You did good."

The man who drove the antique car handed Tanner through the open window into Grandpa's arms. It wasn't until much later when Tanner watched the footage of the parade on TV before the camera had been shut off and Mommy and Grandma cried that he saw how close he had come to being trampled by those horses.

Fortunately they missed his wagon.

Ahead of the equestrian group and unaware of a little boy's troubles, Hank, Leanne, Vince, and Darcy watched the darkening sky. There was no way they were going to make it to the football field and the end of the parade before the rain hit. Nothing to do except watch and wait to get wet.

"Our beautiful float," Leanne lamented through smiling lips as she continued to wave to the crowd.

"It never occurred to me to bring an umbrella," Hank said.

"Maybe I could jump off and run to the café," Vince said.

Darcy grabbed his arm. "And leave the rest of out us here to get soaked? Think again, cowboy."

Vince lowered his voice and leaned toward her. "We could

make a break for it. The two of them would never know we're gone."

It was at that moment they felt the first raindrops. Hank put a protective arm around Leanne. "Take her up to the truck," Vince told him. The truck was moving forward at a snail's pace so Hank and Leanne got off the bench and started moving carefully forward to the tongue of the wagon.

Vince put his hand on Darcy's shoulder. "You go with them."

"There isn't enough room."

"We'll make Tyler get out."

"He's just a kid. I don't mind getting wet."

The rain cut loose, and the parade came to a standstill. Leanne and Hank leapt off the front of the wagon and dove for the shelter of the truck cab. "You still don't want me to make Tyler get out of the truck?" Vince shouted over the sound of the rain.

Darcy threw her hands over her head as if she could hold off the water. "Too late, we're already soaked."

Vince grabbed her hand. "Come on, it's lightning."

He stepped to the edge of the wagon and jumped off. He reached his arms up and Darcy leaned over the side and into his arms. He took her hand and pulled her across the street. They were only a half a block from the café. The crowd was thinning fast, but it was still slow moving through the streets. When they got to the café parking lot, Vince reached in his front pocket for his keys. They stopped under the eaves trough of the building as he kept rummaging.

Then he looked at Darcy and slapped his forehead with the heel of his hand. "I can't believe this. My key ring is hanging from the ignition of my truck."

Darcy burst out laughing. She pushed her hands through her thick hair and a river of water fell to the sidewalk. "What'll we do now?"

Vince paused for a moment. "Come on." He grabbed her hand again and dragged her around the side of the café. At the back door was an overhang big enough for the two of them to crowd under. "Wait here," he said. He ducked back into the rain and stooped down behind the metal bin where he poured used grease. Darcy watched as he slid back a piece of metal that looked like it was attached to the bottom of the grease trap. He wiggled his index finger into the narrow slot. She grinned at the look on his face as he fumbled for whatever he was trying to get. Water was running into his eyes making it impossible to see. His shirt was plastered to his skin, showing off every muscle on his back. She realized her clothes were just as wet. She wrapped her arms around her body.

"Ah-ha," Vince declared and straightened up. He held a key up for her to see as he crowded under the overhang. After unlocking the door, he stepped back for her to go through the door into the dry kitchen.

"You had a key hidden outside?" Darcy said incredulously.

"I locked myself out one morning when I first bought the place. I had already hung my coat up and stepped outside for a minute. I had to walk all the way back to the inn for my extra key in six inches of fresh snow with no coat or boots. After that, I hid a spare key under the grease trap. You're the only living person who knows my secret." He wiggled his eyebrows at her. "I guess I'll have to kill you."

"Could you get me a dry shirt first?"

"Oh, sure. Sorry." he went to his locker in the back room off the kitchen and took down a flannel shirt that had been hanging there for months. He sniffed it to make sure it was relatively clean and then took it back to her.

"Thanks." She slipped her arms into the sleeves and pulled it up over her shoulders. The fabric caught on the wet shirt underneath. Vince reached around her and pulled the shirt up over her shoulders. Both of them reached for her hair at the same time to bring it out of the shirt. Their hands touched. They froze and stared into each other's eyes. Darcy lowered her arms back to her sides. With his arms encircling her, Vince pulled her long thick hair out of the shirt. Then he pulled a strand of hair that had stuck to her cheek away from her face. He stared at the strand of hair and caressed it between his finger and thumb. With his other hand he gently smoothed the shorter, flyaway hair away from her forehead.

Darcy stopped shivering. She looked from the lock of hair in Vince's hand to his face, mere inches from hers. She studied his mouth, his jaw, and the ear she had committed to memory that day at the waterfall. He leaned toward her, slowly closing the gap between them until his lips were against her ear. She held her breath, no longer cold inside her wet clothes and barely able to think.

"You don't belong here," he whispered plaintively.

"In your kitchen or in your arms?" she whispered against his cheek.

He took her hand and placed it against his chest. She could feel his heart beating through the wet fabric of his shirt. "Here."

She whispered again against his cheek, barely able to hear her own voice over the pounding of the rain on the old metal roof. "Isn't that my decision to make?"

Vince pulled back so he could look into her eyes. He continued to hold her hand in place over his heart. "I don't want to hurt you."

"I'd never let that happen. We city girls aren't as helpless as we look."

He smiled and a tiny dimple appeared on his left cheek. "That's what worries me."

He moved toward her so slowly she was almost unaware he was getting closer until she felt his wet shirt against her. She ignored the cold and leaned into him, relishing the touch of his lips against hers.

After the kiss, Vince stepped back and looked down at the wet print he had left on the dry shirt she wore. "Sorry."

Darcy smiled at the sound of his slow, southern drawl and imagined she'd like nothing better than to listen to it the rest of her days. She grabbed the collar of his shirt and pulled his face back to hers.

Epilogue
–Nine months later

$\mathcal{D}$arcy stepped away from the door and faced Leanne. "Would you listen to that commotion out there? I think half the town's shown up for this wedding."

Leanne looked beautiful in her chiffon dress. "Of course, they did, silly. They've been looking forward to it since the Fourth of July."

"I guess a lot of them never expected it to take place."

"I guess not, but tongues sure are wagging now."

"You certainly are calm," Darcy observed.

"Why shouldn't I be? I've known most of them my whole life."

Darcy stepped forward and wrapped her arms around her friend's shoulders. "I want to thank you for everything you've done for me, Leanne. I never dreamed when I came here last year how important this place would become to me."

Leanne hugged her back. "You've become important to us, too, Darcy. Sometimes I wonder if things would have worked out between me and Hank if you hadn't come down here and given me a little kick in the pants."

Darcy straightened a wisp of Leanne's chignon and then moved to the mirror to check her own appearance. "I just stated the obvious. Vince was the one who got Hank to make his move."

Leanne laughed. "Poor Hank. When he came in the inn the night he proposed, he looked like he'd been hit by a truck. I had no idea what he was going to say until he said it. I have to admit he bowled me over."

Darcy looked at her through the mirror's reflection. "It's so romantic; the two of you."

A knock sounded at the door. Leanne and Darcy exchanged glances. Leanne moved to the door. She opened it a crack and peered out. Then she opened it wide enough to let Sharon through.

"Leanne, you look beautiful." Her eyes scanned the room until she saw Darcy sitting in front of the vanity mirror. Tears sprang to her eyes. "Oh, honey."

Darcy started to get up, but Sharon motioned her back down. She smoothed a wrinkle out of the skirt of Darcy's white taffeta dress and leaned in to hug her. She touched Darcy's face. "My baby's wedding day."

Darcy's own eyes filled with tears. "Mom, don't. You'll get me crying again."

"I can't help it. I'm so happy for you. Vince is out in the vestibule with his best man, greeting the guests. He's a nervous wreck." Sharon straightened up and looked at Leanne. "Speaking of Hank," she put her hand on Leanne's rounded belly, "is he ready to become a father?"

Leanne covered Sharon's hand with her own. She beamed through fresh tears. At four months along, she was a bundle of emotions. "He confided in me a few weeks ago that he never thought he'd be a father at forty-seven. But he's beside himself with joy. We both are."

Sharon pulled Leanne into an embrace. "You'll never know this side of heaven how much of a blessing you were to our Darcy. You deserve all the happiness in the world."

"Thank you, Sharon."

"Are my other bridesmaids ready?" Darcy asked.

"Almost—Bethany's having a little problem with her hair, but Samantha acts like she's done this a hundred times. Don't worry, Becky is pulling everything together. Wait until you see little Zachary in his tux."

Darcy's eyes misted over again. "I can't wait."

Sharon dabbed her cheek with a tissue. "Don't cry, baby. You don't want to go out there all red and puffy." She glanced at her watch. "Twenty minutes and counting. Are you ready?"

Darcy smiled her response. "More ready than I ever thought I'd be."

Sharon leaned over and cupped Darcy's chin with her hand. "Be a good wife, Darcy. Don't nag, and put something in the oven once in awhile."

"I will, Mom."

"Listen to his problems, and pay attention when he talks about playoffs and RBI's. Men seem to think they're important."

"Yes, Mom."

"And make him pay attention to you." She squeezed Darcy's chin for emphasis. "He won't know how to do it on his own. He has to be taught."

"I'll remember."

Sharon kissed her cheek and stood up. "I know you will. You're a good daughter." She went to the door. "I'll see you two out there." She left to wait for Hank to escort her to her seat at the appointed time.

Leanne arranged the short veil around Darcy's shoulders. "Have you ever thought that if Marjorie Reed hadn't been overbooked at the Danbury Inn that first weekend, we might never have met?"

Darcy finished her thought. "And Vince never would have yelled at me for blocking the dumpster behind the café."

"My brother always did have a way with the ladies."

Darcy laughed and then grew serious. "I remember wondering if it was more than a coincidence that I happened to start my research trip on a university weekend when all the hotels in the area were booked. Hey, I never did get my two free nights at the Danbury Inn Marjorie promised me."

"I like to think God had His hand in the design all along."

She and Darcy exchanged smiles in the mirror. "That trip changed my life; not only by my falling in love with Vince, but everything is different now. I never thought I'd do anything besides writing."

Leanne laughed. "I bet you never imagined you'd be renting a house from Dale Wagoner and waiting tables in one of the cafés you came here to research."

"And loving every minute of it."

"I'll tell you what I love—my baby brother singing in the church choir again. If only Mother and Daddy could be here to see the two of you."

"Now Leanne, don't. I don't want to cry anymore today."

"All right, I'll stop." Leanne sniffed and dabbed at her own nose. "Do you ever miss that big old house back in Ohio you'd dreamed of owning since you were a kid?"

"Not really. I loved that house, but it wasn't really a home. Now Keith and Becky are getting more use out of it than I ever did."

Another knock sounded at the door, but it burst open before Darcy or Leanne could react.

"Darcy!" Carla Daniels squealed.

It was too much trouble for Darcy to get up in her full skirt, so she remained seated in front of the mirror and held out her arms. Carla rushed into them. "You made it," Darcy cried.

"I wouldn't have missed it, sweetheart. I even got Jacob and Hilary to come down with me. They actually love it."

Darcy smiled. It wasn't often Carla dragged herself away from the city, let alone with her teenage children in tow. "Too bad you couldn't have made it sooner. I'm leaving tonight and won't get to spend any time with you."

Carla winked. "Don't worry about me, Darcy. You'll have your hands full with that new husband of yours."

Darcy blushed.

"Besides," Carla went on, "I need to get a little work done if I plan on writing this trip off as business."

Darcy made a face. "Not business. Not now."

"Just a little." She took Darcy's elbow and pulled her close. "'Fess up, love. I know you haven't been living here for six months amidst these gorgeous mountains and colorful characters without some kind of book idea whirring around in that head of yours. The world's starving for the next Darcy Carter book. When can I tell Brad to expect it?"

Darcy grinned at Leanne over her shoulder and then at Carla. "Well, I have been thinking…"

Carla clapped her hands together. "I knew it."

"I always wanted to try my hand at fiction," Darcy said, the prospect of a new project lighting her features. "Romance, to be exact."

Carla snapped her head back in mock horror. "Romance? Not my Darcy!"

Darcy grinned even wider. "I even have the perfect title—*The Ultimate Guide to Finding Mr. Right.*"

She could almost see the dollar signs reflecting in Carla's eyes.

"Killer idea, Darcy, a guaranteed best seller. I almost wish I'd thought of it."

The End

Learn more about the author and her books on her website:
www.TeresaSlack.com

Teresa always enjoys hearing from her readers.
You may contact her at: teresa@teresaslack.com